THE NIGHT LIES BLEEDING

Also by M.D. Lachlan from Gollancz

Wolfsangel
Fenrir
Lord of Slaughter
Valkyrie's Song

THE NIGHT LIES BLEEDING

M.D. LACHLAN

GOLLANCZ

LONDON

First published in Great Britain in 2018 by Gollancz
An imprint of the Orion Publishing Group Ltd
Carmelite House, 50 Victoria Embankment
London EC4Y 0DZ

An Hachette UK Company

1 3 5 7 9 10 8 6 4 2

A CIP catalogue record for this book
is available from the British Library

ISBN 978 0 575 12968 9

Typeset by Deltatype Ltd, Birkenhead, Merseyside

Printed in Great Britain by Clays Ltd, St Ives plc

www.gollancz.co.uk

*To the memory of Heather Heyer and all
those who have fallen fighting Fascism*

Monsters exist, but they are too few in number to be truly dangerous. More dangerous are the common men, the functionaries ready to believe and to act without asking questions.

PRIMO LEVI

Philomathes And are not our war-woolfes one sorte of these spirits also, that hauntes and troubles some houses or dwelling places?
Epistemon ... if anie such thing hath bene, I take it to have proceeded but of a naturall super-abundance of Melancholie ...

JAMES I OF ENGLAND — DAEMONOLOGIE, 1597

1 The Wolf and the Moon

The full moon had always brought him peace before. But as Endamon Craw looked out from his rooftop over lightless London, he thought it more like some grisly lantern searching out the corners and nooks of the city so that Death might see clearly to take his pick.

In the distance a low voice seemed to murmur beyond the clouds, as if some mumbling giant was trying to say its names in words more familiar to Craw than the English he had been speaking for two centuries: Heinkel, Dornier, Junkers. Death was coming in on motors and wings, under the bomber's moon.

Craw had watched London's light change for decades, from the weak glow of the first gas lamps, to the burning incandescence of the arc light, to the softer silver that had lain over the city in the years before the war. Now the city was flat black, under an old dark, with the moon shimmering off the rooftops as if off the surface of a lake. He felt an ache in his guts. Humanity at its old game – destruction. He held up his hand.

'Stop,' he said. 'Turn back. Be brave for love, not hate.'

But he was not a magician and the rumble of engines grew louder.

'Will there be anything else, sir?'

At his shoulder was an old man in tails, holding a tray upon which was balanced a shaking bottle. Although Craw strived to keep a modern home, he still couldn't imagine life without the help. He was still a feudalist at heart.

'More whisky,' he said.

The old man took Craw's glass, placed it on the tray, and

poured it out with an unsteady hand. It wasn't age that caused him to tremble, but fear.

'I would go to my wife, sir,' said the man. 'She's in the shelter and ...'

Craw started, like someone remembering that they'd left their umbrella on the train.

'My dear Jacques, I'm so sorry,' he said. 'I forget ... Go to her, and take the rest of the whisky. A man needs to get his courage from somewhere on a night like tonight.'

'It's the last of it, sir,' said the butler.

Craw waved his hand, his familiar gesture of dismissal, and smiled.

'We all must suffer at times like these.'

The old man withdrew and left Craw looking out down Crooms Hill towards the Thames, thinking of his own love, Adisla, so long gone. Was she being reborn tonight, on the other side of the world, or was she about to die beneath the bombs, calling for him an inch out of earshot? He remembered her, by the fjord on a hillside, the sun making a halo of her hair. And then? Just a jumble of images down the centuries, without order or sense, whose meaning flashed fleetingly in his mind before falling away to nothing. He loved her, felt that love as powerful as a tidal rip pulling him towards her down the centuries. But the meaning of that love, the detail, came to him only in fugitive glimpses.

A thousand years of transformations, of the wolf rising and falling inside him. His mind was like a sword, broken to pieces, melted down and recast. Still a sword, yes, but the same one that had been broken? He recalled a long time underground, a prison of darkness where the wolf had set him free, the reek of the prisoners, the fear of those who had tried to oppose him. Why he had been there, what he had been doing, was a mystery to him. He knew languages he had no memory of ever speaking, recalled a line of verse or conversation from five hundred years ago but could not say who had spoken it, or to whom he had been speaking. Tiny details from a millennium before came back to him – the moon through the roof of a shattered church, the turf saddle of a Viking horse. But the plot of his life was lost. Only she remained – Adisla – his need of her a lighthouse to his thoughts. If ever that went, he thought, then he would be no more than a beast – purposeless, watching the sun rise and fall, kingdoms come and go, without feeling or comprehension.

Death had followed him, he recalled that – the terrified faces, the flailing arms, the spears jabbing uselessly at him, the swords bouncing from his skin. How many had he killed looking for her? He swallowed another gulp of the whisky, taking the drinker's gamble – heads it makes me forget, tails it makes me remember.

The sirens sang out their lament and searchlights lit the night, hunting the enemy, little moons circling their parent. In minutes came the flares. The pathfinding aircraft were on their mark. Huge burning candles dropped over London on parachutes, beautiful in their way, like angels descending, whiting out the parts of the city that the moon had missed. They turned the river into a shining avenue to guide the bombers home.

The anti-aircraft fire began, the Bofors guns' dull hammering like an insistent visitor who wouldn't go away, the flak bursting in the sky. Incendiaries rained down, phosphorous white blooming into lilies of flame as they settled around the river.

Then came the main body of the raid, the dark mass of bombers becoming visible in the silver light, crossing the moon as witches do in children's tales.

The first bombs proper fell, a few cowardly crews dropping early over Shooters Hill and Thamesmead and Erith, before they hit the thickest of the ack-ack defending the docks. The distant *crump*, *crump*, *crump* was like a giant treading over snow, plumes of fire dogging his steps as he approached.

On the whole, though, the Germans held their nerve until they reached their target. Craw knew them for brave men, warriors from a long line of warriors. Down the centuries he had fought alongside them and fought against them. They had always impressed him.

The city under flame was a beautiful thing, greens, reds, oranges and blues blooming from the soil of the dark like a summer garden. Craw's finger drew out a shape in the air, like the head of an arrow, an absent-minded gesture, sketching out the *Kenaz* rune, the Viking sign of rebirth by fire that he'd learned at the court of King Forkbeard of the Rygir, whose ward he had been over a thousand years before. He shivered. Change was on the wind.

Now the enemy was above him. He felt strange pressures in his nose and ears as the bombs pushed hot walls of air towards him and artificial vortexes rushed into the vacuums of the fires.

Craw spoke to Death.

'Come on,' he said, in the old language, 'here I am. Can't you hear me? Can't you see me? It's me, your servant.'

But Death didn't want him. He wanted the Davis family sheltering under the stairs at Number 16: Dr Davis, who had just looked in to check on his family, Mrs Davis, all the children, and Pluto the dog. He wanted the newly wed Mrs Andrews at Number 4 with her funny stories and engaging smile, and he wanted old Mr Parsons at Number 23, the one who'd killed the girl and said she'd run away, the one who deserved it most, next to Endamon Craw himself.

'Help them,' he said, though he didn't know who to. The old Gods of his fathers would delight to see such destruction. Christ? Surely a god of compassion could not look down on this and do nothing. Those who say the gods are creatures of love have a lot of evidence to ignore, he thought.

He watched the last drops of his whisky evaporate in the burning night and, on an impulse, dropped his glass over the edge of the roof. It caught the firelight as it fell towards the earth, a little Lucifer ejected from his heaven.

He felt giddy as he watched it fall and smash. Despite the

heat of the flames he was cold; prickles ran down the back of his neck. His transformations had never been easy on him. He could recall very little of them but he remembered their beginnings at least, that restless, almost adolescent mental itch where he simply did not know what to do with himself. He didn't want to stand up, he didn't want to sit down; he didn't want stay in, but he didn't want to go out; he was hungry, but for nothing that the larder could provide.

From what he remembered of the previous times, things had begun slowly – a subtle shift in his perception, flavours and smells becoming more intense, concentration more difficult. On this occasion there had been a definite starting point.

It had been midnight and he had been in his study. The tranquil light of the Anglepoise lamp, the sparkling amber of the brandy decanter, a handmade Egyptian cigarette by Lewis of St James's and a copy of St Thomas Aquinas' *Quaestiones disputatae de malo* were his only company.

And then he had felt it – the cut. It ripped into him as if it would split him in two. It was a familiar agony, that of a sword blow. Craw had been wounded before, but always he had seen his opponent. Here, it was as if some invisible attacker had struck him as he sat in his armchair, jolting his book and his brandy to the floor, leaving him bent double and gasping for breath. The pain shot straight to the centre of his chest and he would have feared it was a heart attack, had he thought himself susceptible to such things.

Twenty minutes later, he pulled himself to his feet, all discomfort gone. He had become aware of a noise, an odd rhythmless drumming from downstairs and he had gone to investigate. A light had been left on in the scullery and a moth was beating itself against the Bakelite lampshade. Craw had sat down on a bench and pondered the implications of that. He had heard it from three floors away.

The wolf, he thought, was rising in him. It could be in a year, it could be in ten years, but it was coming, as sure as the tears of Mr Andrews as he tried to dig his wife from the wreckage of their home, as sure as Mr Andrews himself would one day die.

Craw had known the feeling many times before – the fates wanted their wolf. He looked out into the night, beyond the flames, beyond the city, into the encircling dark. Somewhere out there, he sensed, was the reason why.

2 The Gone

Daylight, and Craw sensed visitors. From Crooms Hill, London lay out before him in the sun like a continent. Even after twenty lifetimes, the sheer size of the city could still take his breath away.

Out of the window of his top floor study he could see the damage of the night before, the houses opened up into ramshackle theatre sets. Some fires were still burning, the smoke rising in the cold October air and giving the impression of something just minted, rather than destroyed.

The trams had survived the attack and were gliding through the streets like buildings on skates, as if looking for gaps to fill. There were enough of those and yet, no matter how battered and broken, life went on.

Every time you looked out after a raid it seemed things should be more destroyed than they were. But the trams moved, the shops were open. Normality was robust, it appeared, and yet you knew things were changing beyond retrieving. The grocer's was next to the bank, which was next to a hole, which was next to the butcher's, which was next to another hole. Each raid would leave more holes, but how many holes were needed before it would no longer be a street but just one big hole? How many bites can a moth take from a coat before it ceases to be a coat?

In a way Craw found the damage exhilarating.

The bombs imposed their own order on the city, cutting their own avenues and squares according to their type and number. A stick of incendiaries might unite Number 59 Eton Avenue with Number 68 Fellows Road, down to Number 38 Wadham Gardens and Number 3 Elsworthy Road, burning a path through the city which to Craw almost seemed polite. 'You preferred the road running this way, but have you considered what it would look like going north?' said the firebombs, marking the new path with the charred stumps of timbers running through the houses like a dragon's back.

Then there were the butterfly bombs that shredded your flesh if they caught you in the open but did little damage to buildings, just breaking windows and blasting away plaster, as if the shops and houses had come down with chickenpox. The landmines were less subtle, floating down sweetly on their parachutes before tearing out a chunk of nine or ten homes and leaving a gap like a palazzo in Hell. After every raid the morning light changed as, shorn of a tower here, a gasometer there, spaces where there had been walls, the city awoke to new horizons. But the cost, the human cost. So many precious things burnt and shredded, loves, desires gone, the music of the soul stilled.

The morning confirmed his fears. The wolf was awake inside him, for certain. The world seemed brighter to the wolf, its colours more intense like in a film. Not exactly Technicolor, more like the first Kinemacolor films he'd seen, when the reds and greens had danced around their subjects in peculiar auras, as if God was a child who had selected the brightest colours but not quite got the hang of keeping them inside the borders of the shapes they were meant to fill.

Then there were the smells: aromas, scents, stinks and fumes rising up from the streets in a palette of odours both grisly and enticing. The wider sensations of his wolf mind swept over him like the feeling of relief like when you suddenly remember that name that was on the tip of your tongue. It was as if a piece of lost knowledge had returned to him, and as if he was more fundamentally himself than he had been without it. There was rain coming from the west, from beyond the blue sky. Then there was cordite, the mould of building dust, a hundred shades of burning, from curtains, to skin and hair, to the morning toast of the still-surviving houses. There was a burst sewer that any human would have found repulsive, but which the werewolf found pungent and intriguing. He was coming alive to a city of smears and secretions: his own sweat on the glass top of his desk; the sour mothballs and cheap tobacco that trailed after his butler; the pigeon droppings on the balcony; vinegar on the window panes; mould in the wood of the windows; road grime and dust. The world seemed gloriously stained.

He could not allow himself to enjoy the sensations too much and he lit a cigarette, banishing the overwhelming biology of the streets from his nostrils.

Smell is the sense that is most linked to memory. Even the dull nostrils of humans are gateways to the past, to kisses we had forgotten, angers we had thought quenched. Wet newspaper can recall the delivery job held as a child, a bonbon can put us outside a shop, reaching up to our mother.

Under the city's odorous assault the werewolf's memories seemed to engulf him in a way he found frustrating and disturbing. Yes, the cordite recalled the Great War, yes, the building dust took him back to Constantinople's walls as they crumbled under the cannons, but there were other connections that were more troubling. Why did that smell of burning recall his childhood, a blonde girl on a hillside? Why did it make him think of her, and of love?

It is not just the physical creature that is torn and rearranged when a werewolf changes. The mind warps too, like a piece of metal bent in the hand that you can never quite put straight again. The smells were roads that led to the past but, for Endamon Craw, some were impassable, overgrown, ruptured and cratered. He could look down them but could not see them to their ends. Parts of himself, he knew, had been torn away by what lived inside him. At this distance of years, did he remember? Or did he remember what he had remembered, that memory itself a memory of a memory of a memory of a memory – his past coming down to him in a series of Chinese whispers whose final message might or might not reflect the original one spoken.

A wolf smells nothing as keenly as fear. London seemed to hang in an acid fog of terror left over from the night before. The sweat lying on corpses, the spilled guts, the vomit and the piss were not blown away by the relief of morning. The cortisol and adrenaline hormones that had pumped from the glands of the population under the bombs smelled sweet and appetising. He drew the sharp smoke of his cigarette onto the back of his throat. Cigarette smoke, Craw thought, was unique in the world of smells, in that it sent the mind to the future – the next cigarette – rather than into the past, that garden of snares.

The bell rang downstairs. A Detective Constable Briggs and a Detective Inspector Balby were coming to see him on urgent and confidential business. He'd received their telegram the day before. Telegram was the only way to communicate with Craw. He had put a telephone into his home just as soon as they were available. It had, however, represented the most enormous threat to his repose, ringing at all sorts of unexpected moments. The final straw had been when it had gone off during dinner. His commitment to the modern age was insistent, but there were limits as to what a gentleman could bear. He had sent it back before it could cause any more chaos.

Two men were led in, one small and powerfully built, around fifty, with a thick neck and shaved head. He had the demeanour of a man who could be smacked over the head with a spade without it disturbing his breakfast. This was Inspector Balby. The other was tall and slim, with a look to him more like an academic than a policeman. This was Constable Briggs, thirty-five years old – the thug. On him, Craw could smell blood.

The butler made the introductions and the men shook hands. Craw could never quite overcome his distaste for this – the encroaching meritocracy, greeting these men as equals. In a sane world they would bow, not touch him. One of the appeals of the house on Crooms Hill was that its Victorian plumbing provided different water mains for the servants and the masters. To him, drinking water from the same source as the help was the thin end of the wedge. Still, he knew that his distaste would pass as all his opinions passed or, rather, came in and out like the tide. He willed himself to like the informality and forget who he had been. Welcoming the future – delighting in it, even – was a condition of his sanity. Everyone, he reminded himself, is constructed. It's up to you if you have a hand in the building.

'You look well, sir,' said Briggs. It was not a compliment. Any man of Craw's age should have been sporting the swollen face of a firefighter after the previous night.

Craw smiled. 'Thank you, Constable.'

Even if Craw had wanted to fight the fires, he was forbidden to. His job, which he had not wanted but had been given, was as master curator for the London museums and antiquities. He was chosen not for his knowledge of the past but for his eye to the future. He decided what could be moved to safety – where it was moved to and how it was stored – and what would have to wait a while under the bombs. His was the task of deciding what was history and what was ashes. The government deemed him too important to lose, and so he was mandated to spend his evenings in a Whitehall shelter, something he contrived to avoid.

He wouldn't have gone on fire-watch even if he'd been free to do so. It would have been as demeaning to him to man a hose as to cower in a hole. Craw did not like war but, when he did participate, he preferred to do so directly. His family motto, given to him by King Charles I of Sicily in 1274, expressed it neatly: *Iugulum* – The Throat. It had inspired Craw's modern name.

Craw's study would have led a casual observer to deduce that the room belonged to some interior designer or avant-garde artist. Balby, however, was perhaps the least casual observer Craw had encountered in five centuries. Watchful by inclination, the inspector had trained any remaining sniff of lackadaisical attention from himself in thirty years of diligent police work. His title was Inspector, but it could have also described his personality.

He had been in many rooms in the course of his career, but he had never been in one like this. It was very large for a living space, and had clearly had several walls removed to make it that way. There was so little in it, too. Balby had expected strange native heads, weapons, photographs of expeditions, and all manner of native tat from an anthropologist. This place was virtually bare and everything that was in it was as new as in a showroom.

Balby had never seen such a room of chrome and leather. There was a desk with a glass top which struck him as dangerous, a cube of an armchair that looked very uncomfortable, and bookcases that seemed very ill-designed for holding books. They were no more than strips of pale wood. There were no curves or comforts, or even carpet on the polished wooden floor, just a plain-as-porridge rug.

He thought of his own wife, Lily, who had been taken in the 1919 influenza. 'Frill it up, Jack!' she would have said. And he would have done, because he liked to please her.

He also noted, because not much missed him, that there was only one representation of a living human being in the room – a stark black and white photograph of Craw himself looking out from a sleek silver frame on top of the desk. Beyond that there was not so much as a snap of a wife, a lover, a favourite nephew or a pet.

Besides what Balby considered the hugely egocentric photograph, the room's only other adornments were three large pictures. The one above the brushed steel fireplace was no more than a collection of smudges and lines that he thought a child could have done. The other was a large reproduced advertisement, of all things, for the record-breaking Coronation Scot steam train which ran between London and Glasgow. Why anyone would want an advert on their wall was beyond Balby; there were enough of them outside, weren't there?

Only one painting struck a jarring note. It was on the wall with the tall window in it. It was an old thing for such a modern room, a collection of three boards with a background of Byzantine gold. The painting itself was done in some sort of powdery oils. Balby knew nothing about art, but he looked on the strange, flattened but not flat, faces, the ornate halos, the rich golds and reds, and he had a feeling that the painting must be both very old and also foreign. On the centre board a young woman with blonde plaits sat holding a child at a strange angle, a small figure of a man at each shoulder. Two boards served as wings, each with two larger figures of men. The woman's face, he thought, was extraordinary – evaluating, cold almost, but expressing a yearning and a restlessness that made you think that any second she might get up and run away.

'Taddeo Gaddi, *Madonna and Child Enthroned with Angels and Saints*,' said Craw.

There she was – Adisla, looking down at him from the wall. He'd found her through the visions of an Arab hermit in the Rub al Khali desert, the Empty Quarter. The man was a descendant, it was said, of the mystical tribe of Ad, hated by God, they of the lost city of Iram of the Pillars. Forty years of meditation in the sands, under the heat of the sun and the cold of the stars, living off scorpions, rats and the bitter desert flowers, sucking the water from the rocks of fugitive springs, had retuned the hermit's mind to the frequency his ancestors had known. He recognised Craw for what he was – one of the cursed. That meant he could connect with him. The man had touched him and said 'sleep'. Craw had awoken in the morning knowing exactly where he had to go to find his love.

He'd raced from the towering sands, down the camel trail that the frankincense merchants had abandoned a thousand years before when the dunes had turned from hills into mountains, through Persia and Turkey where, at Antalya, he had taken a Venetian glass galley to Italy, buying his place with a seat at the oars, then on over the Apennines, running with

13

the wolf packs through the forests, and down into Florence itself, to the church of Santo Stefano that he had seen in the visions the hermit had lent him. And there she was, staring out at him from the altarpiece, a hundred and fifty years dead. He had taken it with him, encountering some difficulty with the priests. There had been blood.

'The lady is extraordinary, don't you think?' said Craw.

He remembered so little of her; only snatches of conversations – those, and the dull ache of his bond of love. How many times had she been reborn? How many times had he failed to find her over how many human lives?

Balby snorted. To a man of his persuasion, saints and Madonnas were idols, plain and simple.

The painting aside, the spare and tidy space of Craw's rooms appeared to the policeman like something from a silly story in the newspaper – life as it will be lived in the year 2000 – and it all looked as if it had been put up ten minutes before they walked in.

It would normally have made Balby suspect Craw of being a poseur or a dandy, or even a homosexual. Craw, however, looked like a serious man. He was on the short side of average, dark and pale and sharply suited, more like an architect than an academic. Balby had noted the signet ring when they shook hands. He found its wolf's head motif a little, well, suspicious.

'A very interesting room, sir,' said Briggs, as if 'interesting' was a quality of dubious legality.

The policeman perched himself uncertainly on the sofa. It seemed too deep for him to sit on it properly.

'Yes, officer,' said Craw, 'it's the Bauhaus style – do you know it?'

'Sounds German to me,' said Briggs.

'How insightful of you, it is German. From the design school at Dessau.' The policemen exchanged a look. 'If you're interested I could put you in contact with a dealer.'

'I shan't be wanting any Nazi furniture, sir,' said Briggs. He too had seen the ring.

'Well then, this would be ideal for you. The Nazis shut the school down. Degenerate art, you see.'

'I thought you said it was German,' said Briggs.

'Not all Germans are Nazis,' said Craw.

'And not all Englishmen aren't,' said Briggs, who tended to view conversations as a sort of toned-down fight.

Craw smiled. 'Shall we get to business, gentlemen? Please, Inspector Balby, sit down. This is 1940 and manners are no longer the thing.' His eyes flicked towards the seated Briggs.

Craw was mildly annoyed at the implication he was a Nazi. Nothing so low born, he. The upstart Hitler had been a corporal, a dirty, sweating, toiling corporal. How could the proud princes of the Rhine, who traced their right back beyond Charlemagne, allow themselves to be ruled by such a creature? At least Britain was led by a man of the blood.

'Professor Craw,' began Balby, 'we have reason to believe . . .'

(My God, Craw thought, they really say 'we have reason to believe'.)

'. . . you may be able to help us. You are an anfro— An anthara—'

Balby was an intelligent man but not a learned one. His brain ran to practical pursuits. He left the long words to the coroners and the judges. Craw did not try to help him with the word.

'Antharapologist,' he finished.

Craw lowered his eyelids in assent.

'Specialising in . . .' Balby paused over the next words too, not because they were unfamiliar, but because he disapproved of the ideas that they raised.

'Systems of belief,' said Craw. 'When I'm allowed the time to get on with my proper work.'

'Heathen systems of belief,' said Balby.

'All systems.'

'I hope not Christianity, sir.' There was one subject capable of cracking Balby's professional demeanour – that of the living Christ.

'That too,' said Craw.

Balby rocked his shaved head from side to side, like the boxer he had once been loosening up for a bout.

'Christianity is not a system of belief, sir, it is the word of God.'

Craw had no wish to enter a debate with a believer because, as he had found down the centuries, you cannot debate with a believer. Believers believe, they don't question. If you want a debate you had to pick a debater, people of very different mindsets. A change of subject might be appropriate, he thought.

'Perhaps, Inspector, you and the constable would like a drink after your long journey. Shall I ring for my man? I'm afraid all we have is advocaat. The last of the whisky went last night, and it may be a day or two before we can get any more.'

'My church doesn't allow alcohol, sir,' said Balby.

'I find nothing against it in the Bible,' said Craw.

'I don't know which Bible you're reading,' said Briggs, with a short laugh. He had never read it himself, though he tried – unsuccessfully – to kid his boss that he had.

'Well, I prefer it in the French, the vulgate. The language sings, don't you find? So much more so than the *vetus Latina*.'

He instantly regretted his flippancy. When you've lived so long you learn many different ways of being. You can try them on like clothes and discard them like last season's fashion. This is not to fight boredom, it is to remain sane. If you simply are what you are then you get left behind, become a relic.

The aloofness of the English upper classes of the 1920s and 1930s, their refusal to treat anything seriously, the lightness of the *jeunesse dorée*, had appealed to Craw, but sometimes he became carried away. He didn't want to belittle people; to him they were already little. Mortals exuded a strange sort of sadness, even in the fullness of their youth. Like cut flowers, he thought, they were beautiful and must die. He had no wish to add to their woes in the brief moment of their lives.

'Alcohol is the drink of the devil, sir,' said Balby.

Craw smiled. 'In the case of advocaat we are in agreement, Inspector. It's not a drink, it's an assault on a perfectly good brandy. You should prosecute.'

'I don't prosecute, sir, I just arrest.'

Craw stopped himself from saying that he was impressed by the man's literalism. Balby showed an admirable exactness. It was refreshing to be with someone to whom words actually meant something.

Balby, a professional student of people, scrutinised the academic. He could tell that the levity was a veneer, that something else was under the urbanity, the polish, the charm. What, he couldn't say. Still, Balby liked charm, not for its own merits but because of its weakness. Men asked to explain why they were loitering at midnight were charming, murderers were charming, con men ... Well, some of them. Those in control had no need to be charming, only those seeking to control. Kings weren't charming, only courtiers, he thought.

Charm wasn't a weapon at his disposal. In fact he had to guard against its reverse, a sort of clodhopping earnestness that he could neither like nor prevent in himself.

He didn't regret raising God, but he regretted having to raise God. He would have been happier to know he was dealing with a pious man. Not that Balby often dealt with pious men; the impious were his bread and butter. It was just that he expected better from a man of learning than he did a criminal. Still, as Craw had been unintentionally flippant, he had been unintentionally too serious and was keen to return to business. He didn't want to antagonise the professor – he needed him.

'We need your help, sir,' he said.

'Yes?' said Craw. 'How can I enlighten you, gentlemen?'

Briggs bristled. This man, he decided, gave himself airs. He was wrong there. Someone else had given them to him. If Craw had to guess, he would have said he took on such views after the mind-warping effects of a transformation, some time in the age of chivalry. He wished he had not done so, but what is, is.

'Take a look at this,' said Briggs.

He removed a large flat photographic box from his briefcase. He opened it and passed the first photograph over to Craw. Briggs watched Craw's eyes as he examined the print. He'd hoped to see him start, to watch the smoothness fall away before the picture of the first corpse. Ann in the canteen had nearly fainted when he'd given her a glimpse. Was it asking too much to see this upper-class ponce do the same? It was.

One of the fallacies the lower orders maintain about their betters, Craw had noted many times, was that those on top were in some way delicate creatures, cut off from life. Briggs and his like mistook them for the bourgeoisie. Craw had been brought up to the hunt and the battlefield. He had seen worse than that photograph before he was six years old.

'There are some strange marks upon him,' said Craw, squinting closer.

Balby took a large magnifying glass from his pocket and passed it to him.

'Oh, you really carry those, how delightful.'

'Only when required, sir, they're not part of the uniform.'

'Pity,' said Craw, suddenly feeling rather foolish for his enthusiasm. The police wanted his help and all he could think of was the excitement of looking like Basil Rathbone as Sherlock Holmes. He'd never read the books until he'd seen the films, and hadn't been able to believe what he'd been missing.

'The young man was kept somewhere before he was killed?' said Craw, studying the photograph like a vintner assessing the colour of a wine.

'How do you know that?' said Briggs, as if Craw had just given himself away as a spy.

He didn't like this fellow's cool. It had taken Briggs himself years in the CID before he could look at things like that unflinchingly. He was proud of his professionally armoured personality. Craw, he felt, had not earned his calm in the face of horrors. And 'the young man'. Craw himself was no more than thirty-three, and yet was taking on as if he was in some wholly other category to the boy before him, some wise head to shine the light for the lumbering dolts of the police.

'I don't know, I was simply asking a question. He has bruises on his wrists which might indicate manacles and, though I am no expert on the fashions of the young, I would be surprised if these other marks are among them. Presumably someone did this to him? How long do you think it would take to raise the flesh like that?'

'We think at least four months,' said Balby. 'Have you seen anything like it before?'

Craw had seen most things before and, yes, he had seen something like it. And yet he had never seen anything exactly similar.

The photograph showed what looked like the body of a youth, naked and lying in a freshly excavated grave.

The entire surface of his flesh was marked with what might have been mistaken for pimples, had it not been for the regularity of the pattern. Viewed in one way they might be swirls, in another, regular lines. Craw had seen the technique before, in Africa. The skin was cut and had substances rubbed into it until it formed permanent calluses. It was a form of tattooing, though more painful, lengthy and intricate. Never, though, had he seen it quite so extensive. The marks, some new with scabs, others quite established, covered every inch of the boy's flesh, with one notable area of exception.

'And who,' said Craw, 'do you think removed his face?'

'Well, that, sir, is what we're trying to find out,' said Balby.

'Quite,' said Craw, with a neat smile. 'I can say nothing without indulging in speculation, which may obscure as much as it illuminates. I'm afraid you may have wasted your time here. Do you have a hotel or are you returning directly?'

'Half time, sunshine,' said Briggs.

Craw raised his eyebrows. He was more fascinated than insulted. Was this the modern age, butting its way into his

19

drawing room? Did people really talk like that nowadays, with such brutality, such lack of respect? It almost made one pine for the age of the rapier and the small sword. There were downsides to each gentleman carrying his own weapon, but the general effect on manners was not one of them. Not that Briggs was of high enough social status to be challenged to a duel. But even giving such a man a beating was against the law today. The world has grown soft, he thought, the world has grown soft.

Balby put his hand into the air, embarrassed at the constable's manner but unwilling to criticise him in front of Craw.

'There are others like this,' he said. 'Other murders. We would like you to come and examine the bodies personally. I have permission from the War Office to take you up to the Midlands.'

'Are they ordering me to go?'

'No, but they have no objection if you do.'

'Unfortunately, gentlemen, it is quite out of the question. My work here is valuable.'

'More valuable than the people who are being killed?' said Balby.

Again, Craw raised the eyebrow, what the Romans had called the *supercilium*, from where we get 'supercilious'. Balby did not know the word, nor its derivation, but he had no doubt of the meaning of the gesture.

Craw shrugged and said, '*Qu'importent les victimes, si le geste est beau?*'

For a second he had forgotten the company – honest, simple, working men, not the slightly too-sophisticated aristocrats he chose for friends. Quoting the opium-addicted anarchist poet Tailhade at policemen was unlikely to endear them to him, even – or especially – if they were familiar with the man's work.

'Hark at Charles de Gaulle,' said Briggs.

'I'm afraid neither of us have the benefit of your education, sir,' said Balby.

'Something about the enduring power of beauty. I'm needed here. Do you know what I do, I . . .'

Now it was Balby's turn to raise his eyebrows. Craw felt mildly ashamed of his condescension and stopped mid sentence. Why did he feel the need to justify himself to this man? It was as if Balby's quality of attention was so strong that it pulled you in like a current, forcing you to join his examination of yourself. Craw's words sounded pat and unconvincing, even to him.

'We'd like you to look at something else,' said Balby.

Briggs reached into his suit pocket and took out a bulging envelope. Craw noted that the smell of blood became stronger, but this wasn't the smell that drifted through the windows, stuck to the furniture and tapped at his palate – the blood of fear. This had a different note, different secretions and sediments. Craw read it exactly: excitement.

Briggs slid the envelope across the table. Craw opened it. Whatever was inside had spent some time immersed in blood. If Briggs had been disappointed at the academic's reaction to the photographs, he was astounded now. All the colour seemed to drain from Craw's face as he looked at the item in front of him.

Craw felt terribly light-headed, but he didn't know why. It was as if his memories were submerged in a filthy lake, trying to make the surface, but as much as he tried to reach down and pull them out, they slid from his grasp. Something inside him was searching to connect, an electric charge in his head building and looking for a point to which it might leap to fuse a gap to form a bridge of memory.

Craw swallowed to compose himself. He examined the envelope's contents. It was a pebble, small and triangular. The policemen were surprised to see him pick it up and sniff at it. He detected the residue of that eager blood he had smelled earlier and something else – new leather, wet leaves, sandalwood, even.

He looked at the pebble and had a feeling as if he had

encountered someone he had known for years but whose name he could no longer remember. How can you forget the most important moments of your life? Easily. Can you remember your birth? What of Craw, who had been born a man, become a wolf, been reborn a man and reborn a wolf, and reborn a man again? What had the trauma of his formation and reformation done to his memories? You cannot recall your nursery but, standing in it at age twenty, might you not find it strangely familiar?

On the pebble was scratched a motif, or rather the remains of a motif. Someone had spent some time scratching out the majority of the design. All that was discernible was the representation of a hand, though that too bore several scores across it, as if someone had been interrupted while trying to erase it. Craw was intrigued. In just a few lines the artist had managed to catch something in the shape and position of the fingers. The hand seemed to him to reflect tension, or a fight against tension – the fingers were curling over into a fist, the thumb seemed at an unnatural angle.

'It was associated with one of the bodies,' said Balby. 'It seems to be some sort of primitive art.'

Craw heard his own voice speaking, although his mind was racing, trying without success to work out where he had seen something like this before.

'Neo-primitive. The execution is impressive. This is the work of someone with a good eye.'

'But it's primitive? Caveman stuff?' Briggs asked.

'Neo-primitivism is an art movement of this century,' said Craw, with a dimssive wave of the hand. 'This is not old, definitely not old. The rendering is too ...' he searched for the right word, 'knowing. I'd say it was created within the last thirty years.'

'So how does it relate to the marks?' Balby asked.

'Who is to say that it does? Was it found near one of the bodies?'

'Yardley, one of the victims, had it in his hand,' said Balby.

'Rigor mortis had set in and they had to break his fingers to get it out.' Briggs seemed to relish the details.

Craw stroked the pebble. He was intrigued. He looked up at the mortals. Craw never knew if there were others like him but, when he'd seen the work of Van Gogh, he had wondered if the artist, too, had borne his condition. There was something in that competition of colours, those swirls and smears that seemed to show how a werewolf saw the world – or rather experienced it, in sights, smells and tastes. To him the policemen's flesh was alive with sweat, soot, residues of meals and drinks, grease from hair. Their hands were hanging in the smells of trams, trains, tobacconists and newsagents, the soap of washrooms, the bay rum they had splashed under the arms, the talcum powder they had applied to their feet. Their skin gleamed and teemed as the world clung microscopically to them as they passed through it. If he could have painted, he thought, he would have wanted to paint like those bristling self-portraits the Dutchman had produced in the years of his greatest genius.

His senses were becoming acute, but that signified little. The cells of the palate and nose renew themselves most readily – once a fortnight in even ordinary humans. It is there that, as far as he could recall, his encroaching transition first showed itself. How long before the change? Months, perhaps; years, even.

He tapped the pebble and looked at that strange, resonant hand. He felt almost as if he might grasp it and, in so doing, touch something that had been lost to him for a long time. He looked up at the face of the Madonna that seemed to scrutinise him from the wall.

'For how long do you gentlemen think you might need me?' he asked.

3 An Accidental Magician

'This is the life, eh, Gertie?' said Dr Max Voller to his wife as he reclined in the back of the staff car.

The deep black Mercedes had picked them up in Paderborn and was conveying them the thirty kilometres to Wewelsburg Castle, where Max would begin his new appointment. It was six months before Balby had knocked on Craw's door, summer, and the German countryside was blooming. The road ran through fields deep with poppies and cornflowers, which Max imagined as the flags of a tiny nation cheering him in to his new life.

He was glad to avoid the train. They had travelled up that way and, the nearer he had come to Paderborn, the more SS had joined the carriage. In his regular army uniform he'd felt conspicuous among the sharp black tunics and jagged rune insignia of the *Schutzstaffel* – Hitler's special guard who seemed to be penetrating every aspect of German life – and the arrogant bastards did nothing to make him feel easier.

One, part of a gang of grinning troopers, had even made a pass at Gertie, asking her where she was going and if she was busy that evening. She'd shown him her wedding ring and he'd said it was 'a pity that such a credit to our race should be with a regular army man'. He'd sat back in his seat and stroked at his collar, drawing attention to the grinning death's head insignia that marked him out as a concentration camp guard.

Gertie was a credit to the race, for sure, a real stone cold Nordic beauty. Max had been going to say something to the trooper, but she had put the goon in his place.

'You don't really know how to approach women, do you?

Perhaps you have very little experience of them, given your age.'

The trooper had gone red to his boots, far more embarrassed than he really had any need to be, and Max had suddenly realised how young the SS man was. No more than eighteen, at a push. The sinister uniform had blinded him to the fact that his tormentor was only a boy. Not so Gertie. She was not an unkind woman but, when crossed, she could always put her finger on a weak spot. She had a sensitivity to her; everyone who knew her saw it.

Still, he didn't need to worry about train louts. It was he who was taking the staff car, swastika pennants fluttering in the breeze, and they who were stuck on the filthy nineteenth-century locomotive that took them up to Wewelsburg.

Gertie smiled at him, a tight and nervous movement of the lips, no more. Part of him felt proud and flattered that he had been able to get the posting, but he knew his wife disapproved of him working with the SS. Still, he told himself he hadn't actually applied for a job so, in that way, his conscience was clear. He was there essentially because of a bet.

Dr Voller's old job had been as a doctor at an army clinic in Salzgitter – treating the clap in the artillery garrison defending the steelworks, largely. He worked alongside his friend Dr Arno Rabe and, to lift the boredom on slack days, they would test their debating skills on one another.

The subjects could be frivolous. 'How did we end up in this shithole?' was one of them. Arno had argued that the state was stacked against people like them – bright lower-middle-class boys. Max had argued that they were personally responsible, for arsing around too much at medical school.

'Cheese: An impediment or a help to the National Socialist state?' was another hot topic. They'd gone on about that for days. Maybe the argument wasn't so useless after all, because many of the things he'd said against cheese weren't too far off what the Nazis said about swing music or modern art, two cultural forms Max personally very much enjoyed.

'Cheese is by nature decayed milk. It represents the corruption of a pure natural *German* product. Cows are all German, by the way. Note the Friesians.'

'Cheese is improved and perfected milk. It is *Übermilch*!' said Arno, saluting with his outstretched right arm. He'd pulled out his ration book – it was still a novelty then and the allocations were generous.

'Look,' he'd said, 'if you want proof, here it is: "Reich Cheese, Reich Milk, Reich Eggs, available on these, the Egg Coupons of the Reich!" Salute the coupons!' He'd brought his heels together and shot out his arm. Max had laughed. The Nazis really used those names.

Then had come the debate that had changed his life. 'It is more important for an argument to be consistent than it is for it to be right.'

Max had reasoned that it is immaterial if an argument is right or wrong. If it is believed, it is right. If it is disbelieved, it is wrong. So an argument that was right in the nineteenth century – the earth went round the sun– was utterly wrong in the seventeenth.

'Galileo was wrong,' he'd said. 'You're never more wrong than when you're locked up by the Inquisition.'

Arno, who Max knew well was no Nazi – though, like Max, he was a member of the party because things were a lot easier that way – had said that right and wrong are eternal values.

'The willingness to endure can change reality,' he'd said. 'What if Galileo had given in?'

'He did give in,' said Max. 'He recanted. It made sod all difference in the long run what he did.'

This argument had continued for days and it had begun to occupy a large part of Max's thoughts, largely because there was nothing else to occupy them. Then he'd read, in an advertisement in a medical publication, that the Ancestral Heritage and Research Teaching Society – the *Ahnenerbe* –

were inviting papers on possible fruitful areas of medical research for military purposes. There was a small prize for the best three papers and, if any submission was of high enough quality, it would receive a research grant.

'Here we go, Arno,' Max had said. 'It is time for our argument to move out of the theoretical and into the experimental. I am about to demonstrate the power of bullshit!'

And so he'd drawn up his paper. As a younger man, before he'd qualified as a doctor, he'd been interested in psychic phenomena – the latent powers of the human brain. One medical degree and a little cold thinking later, he'd come to the conclusion that there were no such powers. Never mind. He had plenty of raw material to draw on.

Years before, when he was sixteen, he had been courting Gertie at her parents' house. They'd been laughing and joking on the sofa when she had suddenly cried out 'Bruno!' Bruno was her dog, a fat black mongrel, shiny as a beetle and, to Max, half as charming. Max liked dogs but this one was a leg-shagger and a threat to his trousers.

'What about Bruno?' Max asked.

'Farmer Volz has shot him! Down in the lane by the sheep pens.'

'No, he was in the garden when I came in.'

'I saw it, as clear as I see you, he's been shot!' she said. She was red-faced, blotchy and almost hyper-ventilating. It was the hottest day of a hot summer and Max had suspected heatstroke. But Gertie had been dreadfully upset and he'd agreed to go and look.

Sure enough, the dog was missing. He'd followed the lane down to the pens and there he'd found the animal with a gunshot wound in the front left hand side of its skull. The dog had obviously been half hit by a shotgun blast. It wasn't dead, but it was as good as. The brain was clearly visible. It was breathing but the motor faculties had gone, and there was no hint of recognition in its eyes when he approached.

Max didn't know what to do. Gertie certainly couldn't be

allowed to see her pet in such a state and, for all he knew, it could take the dog days to die.

He looked around. The farmer had caused this mess and, as far as he was concerned, the farmer could clear it up again. But Volz had legged it. Brave enough to shoot a dog, not brave enough to see its owner's tears, he thought.

In the end, he'd gone back, broken the bad news to Gertie, consoled her, held her, kissed and comforted her. Her mother had refused to let her go and see the dog – it would be too upsetting, she said. Then he'd borrowed her father's overalls and gone back with a spade. He had hesitated to kill the dog but he didn't really see what other course of action was open to him. It had taken all his resolve, but he had finally given Bruno a whack with a spade on the site of the wound. The dog, mercifully, had died almost straight away. Then Max bagged him and buried him in the back garden. Max was a sentimental sort and, though he disliked the dog, he felt sorry for his beautiful young girlfriend. He made her a little cross for the grave and drew a bone on it. She felt his sympathy, as solid as a touch, and the bond had grown between them.

How had Gertie known the dog had been shot? The incident had intrigued the young Max, and he'd started to collect stories of premonitions and sudden realisations that someone was dead. Clocks occasionally stopped at exactly the second a son fell out of the sky in a test aircraft; dogs suddenly howled at the moment their owners had been hit by a tram. Even after his belief in the paranormal had faded he'd continued to collect the stories out of habit. He'd also never quite got round to cancelling his subscription to *New Metaphysical Round-Up*.

And hadn't he made a note of it when a woman in Salzgitter told him how she'd had a vision of her husband catching a girder in the head at the moment a careless crane operator had killed him? And weren't the visions of shamans and magicians all induced by stress and pain – the Red Men lying tethered waterless in the sun for days to see their gods, the Aztec temples dripping with the blood of sacrifice, even the

Christian saints communing with the divine in their moments of agony? For his paper, his 'master-bullshit-work,' as he'd described it to Arno, he went back to his old file.

Almost all the incidents of sudden realisation of death involved either a severe head injury or very quick denial of oxygen, such as drowning. Well, that was if you looked at it with a certain prejudice – that is, looking for evidence that psychic powers existed, rather than keeping a more open mind. The technical term for this sort of thinking is teleology – coming up with a hypothesis and setting out to find the evidence to prove it, rather than deducing your result from the evidence. He'd buried his doctor's scepticism and contacted that part of him that still wanted to believe in wonders. He began to ask what mechanism might be at play here that, as the conscious faculties are destroyed, something else for a second finds its voice and can speak over miles of ocean, over intervening mountains or vast deserts. Could this power, he'd thought, be used, trained and harnessed? No, of course not. But you might argue that it could.

What if we could understand what was going on when the everyday brain was destroyed, study the mechanism, and then replicate it in our soldiers without the need for trauma? We'd be able to ditch every radio set in the Reich, have a secure and instantaneous communication network.

Max had laughed even while he was writing this stuff but, then again, he had enjoyed himself and really got into the flow of it. He was in that spot that he sometimes found himself in when playing tennis well – as if it wasn't really him playing, but as if he was the expression of some external force that wanted the ball to return over the net. The work came easily; the ideas followed one from the other with little direction from himself. It was more as if he was reading the paper than writing it.

When he read it back then, for a second, he even believed it could be true. He'd been very pleased with his efforts and sent them off to the *Ahnenerbe*.

He'd been expecting, at best, to win enough to take Gertie to dinner. What he hadn't expected was a job offer.

He'd been invited to take up a research post at Wewelsburg, seconded to the SS and under their orders but not actually part of the organisation. If things went well, the letter said, perhaps membership might be considered at a later date. Professor August Haussmann himself, regional head of the *Ahnenerbe*, would meet him there to explain his new duties.

Max replied immediately, accepting. The chance to get out from under the shadow of the stinking steelworks had been too good to miss. 'Yes,' he'd said.

He hadn't stopped to think what Gertie might think.

She'd just shaken her head when he'd told her.

'The SS, Max?'

Gertie's objection to the Nazis was not so much political as instinctive. She'd been only sixteen when they came to power and, though she had her views at that age, they had not coalesced into anything you could call a coherent ideology. Debate had been stifled by oppression and fear, so she had little chance to find the like-minded people who might have given her dislike of the Nazis a focus, even a name.

There is, though, a sensitivity particularly – though not exclusively – found among women, that sits close to a psychic power: the ability to sense not so much another person's personality as their tone, to hear them like music. It was the presence of the Nazis, and the SS in particular, that she hated. They seemed to emit a sensation she could almost feel on her skin, like the buzz of a fat fly too close to the ear, like the smell of Bakelite burning.

'Working alongside them, not as part of them. We'd probably hardly see them. It's got to be nicer than Salzgitter.'

Gertie hadn't said anything, just looked at Max with her deep blue eyes, a look that seemed to reach into his soul and remind him who he was, what was right and what was wrong.

He'd recognised her posture – one foot in front of the other, hands on her hips as if braced against someone who was seeking to push her over.

'Mule stance!' he'd said.

She'd smiled and laughed, but he'd known she wasn't going to move on this one.

'I'll write and tell them "no",' he'd said, with a laugh

Luckily, there had been a way out. His own commanding officer, 'Fatty' Meer, had refused him permission to accept. Max was relieved because it got him out of a tight spot with Gertie, and he had written to Haussmann to tell him he was forbidden to take the job. By return he had received an authorisation to quit his post signed by none other than fish-face himself – Heinrich Himmler, the SS top dog. No getting out of that, then. He'd told Gertie that she didn't have to come with him, that she could stay at her parents'. She would have none of it.

'For better or worse,' she'd said. That was one of the hundreds of reasons Max loved her. Other wives might have sought recriminations. She, seeing that there was no way out, had kissed him and told him she'd stand by him.

Arno had been incredulous that he was going.

'But it's bullshit. 'You've sold them utter bullshit.'

'Well,' said Max, in a low voice, 'we've been buying it from the fuckers for long enough.'

Arno had nodded and laughed. 'You watch yourself.'

'I'm pretty good at that. Who knows, if I do well maybe they'll make me an SS man.'

'Lucky old you.'

'I don't know, I think I'd look pretty good in black.'

'It'd go with your heart. Heil Hitler!' Arno had clicked his heels and said the greeting with such overbearing seriousness that neither man could really keep from laughing.

'Heil Hitler,' Max had said, pursing his lips in mockery of 'Fatty' Meer's comic stern expression.

Anyone looking at them would have had difficulty being certain they were taking the piss. Anyone who knew Max, though, would have known that he was. Taking the piss was pretty much his base state; it was something that came as naturally to him as earnestness did to his wife.

The car rounded a bend and the castle came into view.

'Wow!' said Gertie.

'Do you like it, darling?' said Max. 'If it's not to your taste I can always buy you another.'

'I have to say, it does look lovely.' Gertie would have liked anything better than the tin hut that had been her quarters for the past two years.

The castle was enormous, rising out of the forest around it like a huge locomotive from billows of green smoke, Max thought. There was a large round crenellated tower like a chimney, linked by a long sloping roof to a smaller domed tower that could have been the driver's cab. The day was bright and sunny but the place possessed its own haze. It seemed to steam in the sunlight, its many windows flashing light out over the valley.

'Welcome to the centre of the world!' said the driver, 'Wewelsburg – the black Vatican!'

'Yes,' said Max. 'Very soon I hope to be part of it!'

Gertie squeezed his hand and smiled. Things, he thought, were finally on the up.

4 Survivals

The facts Craw deduced from the police statements were these:

David Arindon went to bed, drunk, at around 11 p.m. on 14 March 1940, in his home at 23 Somerset Road, Earlsdon, Coventry. It was an unseasonably warm night and, the drink boiling his blood, he had left the window open.

His wife, who had nowhere else to sleep, joined him at around 11.15 when she was quite sure he was out for the count. She too had been drinking, though not as heavily as he. At 4 a.m. Mrs Arindon woke and got up to fetch a glass of water. She was quite sure her husband was in the bed when she left. Once downstairs she smoked a cigarette and contemplated murdering him, leaving him or putting up with him, the option she found the most attractive being the one she was least temperamentally inclined to see through.

At 4.15 she returned to the room and her husband was gone. None of his clothes were missing, and neither were his shoes. When he had not returned four days later, Mrs Arindon called the police.

'You'll find the criminal record attached,' said Balby to Craw as the train pulled out of Watford station.

Craw looked at a pink sheet.

'A wife-beater and a spiv and a racketeer and a mugger?' he said. 'Oh, and a former burglar. And a con artist!'

'Man of many talents,' said Briggs.

Watford receded and, the prospect of home turf in their minds, the policemen felt freer in Craw's company. They'd only just got on to the morning train. It was packed to bursting, but the guard had allowed them to sit in the mail van as they were on police business. The war had meant that fewer trains ran, and the bombing meant that more people than ever were going to stay with half-known relatives at the other end of the country. Nerves, brought on by an uncertain future and the threat of German attack, saw cigarettes smoked at competitive levels. Craw, a committed and enthusiastic smoker, thought it more likely the passengers would be asphyxiated than fall victim to a Stuka.

In the guard's van it was as if you were standing next to a bonfire. In the straining corridors and carriages the human heat was enormous and the smoke choking, so it felt more like you were in one. Craw had seen one man smoking so close to his wife that it looked like she was trying to puff away on the lighted end. Still, the smoke did something to stifle the competing smells of animal humanity – salty skin, fatty lipstick, greasy breakfasts and hair oil, of money on the hands and bread and dripping on the breath.

So the mail van was the most comfortable place on the train. Craw's man had placed a towel over some sacks and Craw sat back to make himself comfortable. He fitted a cigarette to its holder, put it to his lips and waited for Jacques to light it for him. A strange look from Balby made him wonder if this was quite the modern thing to do. His friends wouldn't find it unusual, but they were all of a certain class. The future, he knew, belonged to men like the policemen: clerks, shopkeepers, salesmen and businessmen. One should look to them for clues on how to survive. Perhaps he would not allow his butler to light his cigarettes any more, barbaric as that would be. He took the lighter from the butler.

Craw was a puzzle to Briggs. He was desperate to know what it was he did for the government. Something to do with paintings, he thought he'd said. Why had that made the War Office so confidently recommend him, after a request from the Home Office, after a request from his chief inspector – an idiot who knew nothing about policing, why did they insist on giving retired army brigadiers that job? – after a request from Balby? And why had the War Office become involved?

Hadn't they enough to worry about with Hitler?

Antharopologiser was just another name for a bookworm. 'Craw will know' the telegram had said. But Craw didn't know.

'I collate and order antiquities,' said Craw.

'You read my mind,' said Briggs.

'I read your face. You've been glancing at me on and off for the past hour. I deduced on my odyssey to the lavatory that I have nothing stuck to my teeth, so I assumed you were curious about me. Since the modern age is increasingly pre-occupied with what one does, rather than who one is, then it was clear you were wondering about my job for the government. Any good, Constable? I fancy myself as something of an amateur Holmes.'

Actually, Craw did sometimes find himself trying to ape Holmes' dry nature. Over the centuries you can wear identities out or even, given enough trauma, forget who you are. When a new and engaging personality comes along, courtesy of the pen of Mr Conan Doyle, it's tempting to try it for size.

'Holmes was an amateur, sir,' said Balby.

'A freelancer. Surely, Inspector, that's distinct from amateurism.' Craw shifted on his mailbag.

'In law enforcement there are two sorts of people – proper policemen and amateurs,' said Briggs. 'Holmes was not a proper policeman.'

Craw raised his brows as Holmes might have done and sat back on his sack. There was a slight criticism implied about his involvement, even though the police had come to see him, asked his help, which he had graciously granted them at no little cost to his own work.

Craw didn't really know why he was there.

He did have some fun referring to Jacques as 'Watson' along the railway journey, but he was slightly regretful that he had been called away with so little time to pack.

He had no idea what sort of society he might be in once he arrived in Coventry, so he'd erred on the side of caution and had Jacques take the full range of what a gentleman might require, from tweeds to evening dress. Craw was meticulous in his appearance as it showed that he still cared for the opinion of humanity. To let himself become slovenly wasn't just bad form; it was a gateway to something he refused to contemplate on a sunny day in late autumn. He adjusted his cuff link. To move among men untroubled he needed to retain his respect for them.

The stone, though. That hand. Not just the hand – the tension in the hand. It might, of course, have had no meaning at all. Whoever had killed the person the stone was found with may have placed it there as a red herring. He had endured an Agatha Christie once and knew about red herrings. Or perhaps it was just a comfort to the dead man, some token of his youth. Strange comfort. And why the scratching and scoring, the attempt to erase the design? It was clearly that. The lines of the hand were fine, the scoring done with a much less exact instrument. A screwdriver, perhaps?

He returned his attention to the file.

The earliest disappearance, in 1939, involved the death of a man no one could mourn. John Hamstry had killed four children for the pleasure of watching them die. The case was too gruesome for the papers to do more than even hint at the details. Because he was insane he could not be hanged, and had been committed to life in an asylum.

Later that year he had escaped from a prison van while being transferred from solitary confinement in Birmingham to Broadmoor. How this had occurred was unclear, but it was thought that the driver and guards had been overcome by some fumes from the engine and the vehicle had crashed, allowing the lunatic his freedom. In late 1939 his body had been found by a tramp searching a rubbish tip. It was identifiable by a single fingerprint – one of four square inches of skin left on him. At first it was thought that animals had stripped his flesh, but the coroner had disagreed.

He had concluded, in a report never made public, that the

flesh had been removed by something that controlled the depth of cut – something like a wood plane. Whether the stripping had begun when Hamstry was alive or dead, he couldn't determine. However, he leant towards alive. The finger that had identified him had not been found on his hand, but in his gullet. The coroner thought it most likely he had bitten it off himself in an attempt to suppress the pain of his flaying.

'Death by sarcasm,' said Craw as Balby ran him through the file summary.

'I'm sorry?'

'Sarcasm, officer, from the Greek *sarkasmos*, a ripping of the flesh.'

'A man is dead,' said Balby, dropping the fact like a stone on Craw's levity.

'Just the beginning of Hamstry's agonies, if you're right.'

'You're too clever for me again, sir.'

'I should imagine there are few better candidates for Hell than he.'

'That's God's judgement, not yours,' said Balby.

'Thankfully,' said Craw.

There were four other cases, three who could broadly be termed members of the underworld – two spivs and the safebreaker, the young man Yardley, on whom the pebble had been found. The pebble meant nothing to his associates, it seemed, although one had suggested he might have found it on a job and used it as good luck charm. Yardley, too, had been found brutally murdered, his face flayed. He had been identified through a tattoo he bore on his leg. He had last been seen when he had gone out 'to take the air' late at night. The policemen were sure he had been looting in bomb sites, particularly since he had been arrested on suspicion of such not a week before.

The file went on to describe another disappearance – that of an old man who, it seemed, had no enemies, no real friends and had offended no one. He wasn't long for the world anyway, having just been diagnosed with lung cancer. What linked them was that, with the exception of the excoriated Hamstry, their bodies had been found showing similar signs of torture – the raised flesh, the torn faces.

The spiv David Arindon was more perplexing. Like the old man, he had been to bed at night and, in the morning, he had been missing. This wouldn't have bothered Balby in the least under normal circumstances. In fact, he would have been pleased that such a pest had vanished.

But Arindon's wife, a woman for whom he had a measure of sympathy on account of the beatings she took at her husband's hands, had been convinced something had happened to him, something associated with the company he kept. So Balby had enquired and discovered that the man had neither run off – he had five pounds' worth of winnings left uncollected at the bookmaker's and all his clothes left in his wardrobe – nor, apparently, been done away with by any of his associates. In fact, Arindon was wanted because the city's criminal fraternity had taken possession of a good deal of ironmongery – frying pans and pots and the like diverted from war effort scrap collection – and were looking to shift it door to door.

Murder wasn't in the Coventry gangs' style. Arindon had never even received so much as a stripe from a razor in punishment from his bosses. Why kill him out of the blue with no warning, particularly with all the attention it would bring down upon them? Also, most of the lads from whom the gangs drew their muscle were being called up. Criminal was not a reserved occupation, though you could be forgiven for thinking it so. It was only old lags like Arindon who were left running the moneylending and selling stolen goods. The young hotheads, the sort who might lose their temper and do away with Arindon, were all in the army. His wife might have killed him. Balby half-wished she had, but she wasn't that sort of woman. He didn't think it added up.

In fact, the person who had come closest to killing Arindon in recent years was Briggs. The police often used his regular visits to the cells to let him know what they thought of a man who treated a woman that way, in what Briggs termed 'the only language his sort understand'– the Morse code of fists tapped out on faces.

What linked the disappearance to the murders was only that there had been the sound of a car moving away, heard by neighbours in the night. It was thin evidence of a connection – cars were not that common late at night but they weren't unheard of either – so Balby had merely appended the case to the file.

Briggs had disagreed. Arindon, he thought, had crossed the wrong people and made a beeline for another town, he said.

'Naked?' said Balby.

'Perhaps he had hidden clothes somewhere else.'

'In order to create a mystery and have the police looking for him? If he'd wanted to disappear then he'd have told his wife he was leaving and gone.'

Briggs had been quiet after that.

'You are agreed, though, Professor Craw, that this has the signs of devilry?' said Balby.

'Yes,' said Craw, 'it would bear that interpretation.'

Balby nodded. 'Have you any idea what the marks mean?'

'No,' said Craw.

Briggs gave a roll of his eyes, as if to say *Fat lot of good you turned out to be.*

Balby seemed to digest the 'no' for a couple of seconds, like someone trying to place the taste of some strange food.

'But you have seen things like it?'

'Yes.'

There was another pause.

'Oh, go on,' said Briggs, 'let us in on the secret.'

Craw sensed his dislike and was pleased. That was generally the level on which he preferred to deal with humans, to watch them to their graves without too much in the way of regret.

'In Africa the natives cut themselves with stones or glass

and rub certain plants into the wound to stop it healing normally. This raises the skin in bumps. They can make some rather fetching patterns, believe me.'

'Are these patterns like the ones on our victim?' Balby asked.

'Not that I've seen, and I have to say the work I've witnessed in Africa has been more expertly done than the designs in those photographs. The native patterns can be quite beautiful.'

'Savages,' said Briggs, shaking his head.

'Well, that's the interesting thing about the cuts,' said Craw. 'The tribesmen would regard you as a savage because you don't have them. They are the mark of humanity, separating it from the kingdom of beasts.'

'And do these tribes mutilate people?'

'They don't cut off each other's faces, if that's what you're driving at.'

'So what do the marks *mean*?' Briggs asked.

'I'm afraid I'm rather stumped on that one, officer. Anything I said would be a guess.'

'Guess then,' said Briggs.

'Now hold on,' said Balby. 'Let's not cloud the issue just yet. If it wasn't some savage practice, what other interpretation would it bear?'

'That is the end of my specialism, officer. As a layman I'd say madness, plain and simple – madness.'

'It's an odd madman who can take a man from his house in the middle of the night without disturbing his wife sitting downstairs,' said Balby.

'Arindon, Mr Underwood and Dawson were the only ones who are thought to have gone in the night, sir,' said Briggs. 'Yardley and Falk simply went out and didn't come back. Well, not in one piece, anyway.'

Craw couldn't be bothered to listen to the policemen argue. He closed his eyes and lost himself in the comforting rhythms of the train.

He still had a sense of the wonder he'd felt when he'd seen his first steam train, his first journey with the country racing by. He often asked himself where it would all end, this procession of marvels that had started, he thought, at the fall of Constantinople. The effectiveness of the Turks' new cannon, it had to be said, had taken him by surprise.

Although Craw had forgotten so much, he had not forgotten that – Adrianople teeming, that endless plain, dervishes wheeling their death dance just like the berserkers of his youth. Had he known what would follow he would have surrendered to the Turks, who could be merciful in such situations.

Back then Craw, though he had not taken that name, had not known the exact nature of his curse. He had taken his wolf form four times – as far as he could recall – and he had lived longer than any man alive, but he hadn't met death face to face. They had written a poem for him, he'd discovered when he eventually returned to that city. Craw spoke it to himself as the flat Midlands countryside rolled past his window.

> *How the waters of the blood moon bubbled*
> *on the stone steps three cliff-lengths*
> *above the sea.*
>   *He stood before the Gate*
> *impregnable in his loneliness.*
>
> *His crooked teeth*
> *whitened strangely.*
>   *'Noon out of night – all life a radiance!'*
> *he shouted and rushed into the horde.*

The Constantinian Christians were bloody awful poets, he thought. There had been some stuff about his return, too, about virgin maidens, black ships sucked into a great whirlpool, and myrtle uprooted from the bottom of the sea.

He'd vowed, when he came back to serve the Turkish

Sultan and saw how the city had suffered, that he would never do anything that would end up in an epic poem again. They don't do happy stories, on the whole, he'd concluded.

Some time in the 1920s one of his friends had put him into a limerick when he'd acquired a talking bird after the old lady who lived downstairs had died. It appeared she had rather a foul mouth in private because the bird's language was ripe:

> There was a young man called Craw
> Who inherited a handsome macaw
> Though the bird's goose was cooked
> When he told Maisie 'get fucked'
> And Maisie removed Craw's hot paw.

That was the extent of his ambitions as far as appearing in verse went. He liked his new, flippant, distant, *English* way of being. Seriousness can begin to feel like a heavy burden after ten centuries.

The colours were really all he remembered about death. Colours that seemed to suck in the light. Life really did seem a radiance by comparison. Perhaps the Constantinians weren't such bad poets after all.

Suddenly Craw came back to consciousness. He'd been dozing where he sat. He got up, stretched his legs, and peered through the tiny window of the guard's van.

There was Coventry approaching; the city of the Three Spires, though Craw could only see two of them. It was a pleasant-looking place and he would enjoy the sightseeing at least. The medieval heart of the town would appeal to him, he thought. He'd spent much of the Middle Ages in Germany and found the architecture of some English towns similar. He didn't know why the Germans insisted on fighting the English. They were the same people, he thought. The English were slowly learning the valuable quality of humility, but there was nothing so fundamental it couldn't be decided by talking.

Craw's mental map of Europe would have differed from that seen by the War Office. To him, Yorkshire and those lands that had fallen within the Danelaw, was a separate country from the Norman south. The Normans, of course, were Norsemen by heritage but had largely lost contact with their cultural past by the time they invaded. The English were a mixture of the various Norse bloods of the conquerors and the Saxon of the conquered. The Germans were virtually the same. Britain, of course, still contained a good many of the real slaves – the Celts. Craw, with his dark looks, had always suspected he may have been one of them. A word, an insult, flashed in his mind from long ago: 'Thrall'. Had that been directed at him? Still, he thought, ties of race have never counted for too much when it really comes down to it, no matter what Hitler would have us believe.

Briggs got up to visit the lavatory. Balby moved over to Craw, speaking in a low voice to avoid the butler's hearing.

'If you're going to offer any speculation it would be better if you did it now.'

Craw shrugged. 'As speculation, and pure speculation, I'd say they were designed to fend off evil.'

'Why?'

'The report speculates that they might be in a spiral form. I take that to be a labyrinth. This is to confuse bad spirits and render them powerless. Presumably the victims feared some supernatural influence, or whoever raised the mark on them did. I should guess they're marks of protection.'

Balby blew out heavily and shook his head.

'Well, if you're right they don't seem to have done a very good job, do they?

'You have a point, Inspector, you have a point. There is, of course, the other explanation – that they are marks of sacrifice. The stripping of the flesh recalls certain African witch doctor practices, where human flesh is held to be a powerful ingredient in medicines. There the victim is usually kept alive in order that their screams add potency to the magic. Human sacrifice is considered a powerful means of communication with the spirit world.'

'You think that's happened here?' Balby asked, hoping his job was going to be made vastly easier by narrowing the field of suspects to African blacks.

'No. There is no component of marking in Muti murders. The possibility of ritual self-sacrifice suggests itself, however weakly.'

Balby put up his hand. 'Why would someone want to sacrifice themselves? It seems rather a short-term strategy.'

Craw was expressionless. 'Isn't that what Jesus did, officer?'

Balby swallowed down his anger.

'If Arindon has died, then it's for his own sins and no one else's,' he said. 'He had no reason to sacrifice himself. For what?'

'Hundreds of our boys sacrifice themselves every day, and do we ask why they do it?'

'Queen and country.'

Craw nodded. 'And because they're told to. The facts of the case seem to indicate this happened to these people against their will. I merely raise the spectre of self-sacrifice so you have the full range of possibilities in front of you. In such cases there is often a belief in some sort of spiritual reward. Martyrdom. The assassins of Hassan-i Sabbah would fling themselves from the towers of his castles if he ordered them to. The possibility is remote, however. These men, after all, were abducted. That would seem to militate against that end of the hypothesis.'

'As do the characters involved. Self-sacrifice isn't Hamstry and Arindon's style.'

'A fair point again, Inspector. My instinct says the marks are for protection. It would take a period of formal study to establish conclusively that that was the case but that, I should imagine, would be the most fruitful line of investigation.'

'Are you sure that's what they are?'

'I have just spent the last five minutes explaining that I am not,' said Craw, as Briggs returned into the carriage.

The train pulled in to the station and the men disembarked. On the platform was a young, uniformed policeman. He was in an un-policeman-like state of excitement as he waved to Balby and came half running across the platform.

'Yes?' said Balby.

'It's Arindon, sir, we've found him.'

'In what state?'

'He's covered in those marks.'

Balby didn't even glance at Briggs. It didn't seem to matter to him that he'd been proved right that Arindon was connected to the other disappearances, though Briggs looked away. It seemed to matter to him that he'd been proved wrong.

'Where's the body, in situ, I hope?' Balby asked.

'There's no body, sir,' said the policeman. 'He's alive.'

5 At Wewelsburg

'I am under the instruction of my superiors to welcome you to Wewelsburg. "Welcome to Wewelsburg." Please note that I have carried out my orders and follow me.'

It was another SS mannequin, twenty-four, blond, blue-eyed like they were supposed to be. This one, like many of them since the war had begun, wore a tailored uniform of mouse grey, still with the skull and cross bones at the collar.

'Thank you,' said Max. 'You have a great career in hospitality ahead of you when the war is over.'

'I shall remain in the SS,' said the guard.

'Well, perhaps best,' said Max under his breath to Gertie as the youth led the way. She pinched him and mouthed 'Don't!' at him. One of the things he loved about her was her sense of propriety, how easy it was to pull blushes from her with his silly comments.

Max lit a Salem, sat down on his luggage, and looked around him. This was a lot better than Salzgitter, it had to be said – clean mountain air, a pleasant village abutting the castle and in the same pale limestone, deep green hedgerows and a feeling of peace. The gardens were neat and bright with summer flowers. It was one of those days when you can almost smell the heat, where the scent of grass and honeysuckle infuse the senses with inner calm.

'I hope we're in the village,' said Max, 'it's like a fairy tale!'

Gertie looked about her. 'Which fairy tale? They don't all end well, do they?' she said, and then regretted it.

Max had only done his best and it was ludicrous to keep expressing her doubts so clearly. She would try harder to put on a brave face. But Gertie didn't notice the honeysuckle and the flowers. All she heard was the sound of the flies, buzzing through the summer heat.

Max had expected to be taken to the main doors of the castle, but the youth had walked them around the building. It was shaped like a large triangle, two domed towers at one end and the large crenellated tower making the point. There was scaffolding all down one side, though no sign of workers. They went beneath the scaffold and into a door that had been cut into the wall.

The door opened directly into a large oak-floored room, bare but for a few oak benches, an oak table and a blackboard, also in oak.

There was one other door in the room. The guard opened it and they followed him out to the other side, where Max guessed the courtyard might have been. It was, however, screened off by tarpaulins to construct a narrow run down the side of the building. From behind the screen he could hear the sounds of heavy labour.

'Home from home,' he said to Gertie.

'Does this noise go on long?' Gertie asked. Virtually the only thing she had been looking forward to in the posting to the castle was some country quiet.

The SS man said nothing, but led them along the tarpaulin, past doors that bore signs such as 'Workforce', 'Design', 'Supplies' and 'Records'. He knocked at a green door. The door's sign read 'Ancestral Research'.

'Come,' said a voice.

The guard opened the door to reveal a jolly-looking, slightly fat man of about fifty, balding, and with pink cheeks the colours of rare steak. His office bore several large maps on its walls – Max couldn't exactly see where they were of; certainly not of Germany. The place was scrupulously tidy, a blotter, a single sheet of paper and a telephone the only things on the modern desk – again in oak – and with impeccably clean grey filing cabinets to one side.

'Heil Hitler! Announcing Doctor and Mrs Voller, Heil Hitler,' said the SS man.

'Yes, Heil Hitler, Heil Hitler,' said the man. 'You may wait outside. Come in, come in, make yourself at home! I am Professor August Haussmann, I will be your *Ahnenerbe* contact here.'

'Thank you,' said Max, relieved to meet an SS man who didn't appear to be an automaton.

'Sorry about our friend,' said Haussmann. 'The lower ranks tend to lay on the official style a bit thick. It's for the benefit of outsiders, but you're not to be an outsider for long. I understand you're soon to be one of us.'

'I ... well,' Max had not expected this so soon.

'Don't worry, you'll get used to it. This is the SS world. Things move at a different pace here,' he said, eyeing Gertie.

'Good,' said Max, whose pace, even when rushed, never really moved above that of a man reaching for his pipe while listening to the wireless.

'And this must be Mrs Voller,' said Haussmann. 'Delighted, madam. I am overcome by your beauty. You are perfect.'

'Oh, really, I have my faults,' said Gertie. Max blushed a little at the slight edge to his wife's voice.

'No,' said Haussmann, looking at her slightly sideways as if he'd like to examine her teeth, 'I am still on the board of racial classification and I tell you, you are perfect. One hundred per cent Nordic. Perfect. You are a lucky man, Voller.'

'I know,' said Max.

'Very lucky. It's a good job you're largely Aryan too, or some of our younger bucks might be tempted to arrange an accident for you. We'll have to sign you up quick. A woman like this must produce heirs for the SS, no question. It would be unthinkable for her to breed with a regular army man.'

Gertie let out a heavy sigh. Max laughed, though Haussmann didn't. No matter, Max thought. The SS like to be disconcerting, in fact they're told to be like that by their senior officers. If that's what floats their boat, let them get on with it.

Haussmann smiled. 'Come on, I'll show you to your rooms and then we'll leave Mrs Voller to settle in while we talk business. I have your report. Remarkable stuff, remarkable stuff. Himmler himself read it. Went nuts for it, apparently, that's why you've been given a lab here.'

'A lab?' Max thought, exchanging a *fancy that* glance with Gertie. What did one do in a lab, he wondered? He hadn't been in one since his undergraduate chemistry classes.

'Just find the key,' said Haussmann, much to himself.

He patted his uniform, smiled an embarrassed little smile at the Vollers, and then looked in his desk drawer. Max was surprised to note that it was overflowing with crap – balls of string, scissors, coins, some light bulbs, jars of pills, papers, envelopes, even the remains of a sandwich, and about six packets of cigarettes, some of which were spilling out. Haussmann caught him looking at the drawer. His face stiffened, as if angry. Then he relaxed.

'The cleaner sticks everything in here, even though I tell him not to,' he said. 'Bible Students. Inattentive bastards. Ahh ...' He smacked his hand down on a meaty bluebottle that had landed on the desk. 'We do suffer with flies in the summer here, and ...' He seemed to lose his train of thought.

'Bible Students?' said Max. He'd never heard the name before.

'Jehovah's Witnesses,' said Haussmann, turning a key in another drawer. This was equally messy, and bore the remains of several newspapers and some old well-used handkerchiefs. 'You'll see enough of them here. There are Jews too, of course, but we don't get so many of them as the other camps and those we do don't tend to last long. Less reliable, less compliant. We've started a camp for the Bible Students down the road and they're rebuilding the castle. Aha! Here it is! In my pocket all along.'

'Do we take Jehovah's Witnesses into the work camps?'

Max had never paid much attention to the news before the Nazis came to power, and paid even less now that it never seemed to contain anything he found particularly agreeable. Against Gertie's advice, he'd joined the party, though. Well, you had to if you wanted to get on but, as he had told her, he was more of a 'Can't we all just get along-i?' than a Nazi.

'First in, 1933,' said Haussmann. 'Last out, as well, I bet. The buggers are fine survivors, I tell you, and the best barbers. You should get one to shave you. Much better than the commies or the Yids.'

'Why's that?' Max was beginning to prefer the first SS man's chill to Haussmann's warmth.

'The Reds and the Yids tend to be a bit heavy-handed with the razor,' said Haussmann, drawing his finger across his throat with a broad smile. 'Thou shalt not kill! The commandments had to be good for something, don't you think? Right, let's run along! Christ, I've forgotten the key for your rooms now. Hang on.'

He went back to rummaging in his junkyard of a desk, while Max mouthed '*Rooms*, that's *two* at least,' at Gertie.

Gertie wasn't really looking at him, though; she was looking at Haussmann. He still wore the black uniform the SS had favoured before the war and, to Gertie, he seemed just like the fattest fly of that summer day.

Eventually, after several oaths, apologies to Gertie for the oaths, and then more oaths, the key was located. Haussmann came out of his office, realised he had forgotten his own key but just waved at the door, in a *can't be bothered* gesture.

'I have so many keys it gets ridiculous, and why, what's to steal?'

He led them down the screen and then across another arm of the castle's triangle until, Max guessed, they were standing roughly opposite where they had come into the castle. They were in front of an impressive set of double doors, again in oak. Everything seemed to be in oak.

'Right,' said Haussmann. 'Mrs Voller, to get to your rooms we must go briefly through the main hall of the castle. There may be some ... hmmm, some scenes you are not used to yet.

I suggest you keep your eyes on the back of my neck and that you remind yourself that no enemy of the Reich receives a punishment he does not deserve.'

He gave a smile that reminded Max of a shark he'd seen at a fishmonger's once. Gertie looked back at the SS man blankly.

Max took her hand. 'It'll be OK,' he whispered.

They had seen rough stuff before, of course – *Kristallnacht*, when the Jewish shops had been attacked; the police attacks on the trade unionists at the steel works – and they had survived it, buried their disgust. This was just a matter of doing the same thing at closer quarters.

Haussmann led the Vollers into a large hall, with a staircase directly opposite him and a balcony overlooking the room on all sides. The interior was under heavy reconstruction and open scaffolding ran up to the ceiling. There was the noise of intense labour and everywhere, it appeared, were people in pyjamas. These were the prisoners.

Max nodded in appreciation. He thought that the SS liked to be flattered, as do most people, so he – a natural people pleaser – set out to flatter them. 'Good work, good work,' he seemed to say. Haussmann returned a conspiratorial smile.

Halfway through Max's nodding, though, his eye was taken by what appeared to be a gang of drunken tramps trying to fix some ducting to a wall in front of him. They were working with almost comic inefficiency. It was like a party of clowns; one man was trying to pass another a hammer but, if the one holding the hammer managed to keep it still, then the one trying to take it couldn't get his hand in the right place. If the one trying to take it kept his arm still, then the one proffering the hammer swayed away.

'Are they drunk?' said Max, as they moved through the hall.

'Exhausted. No food, no rest. Such is the plight of the unskilled prisoner. Perhaps the example will make others think before refusing to acknowledge the supreme authority of the Führer.'

Max looked around. As far as he could see there was no one there to witness the example – SS men who didn't need it, other prisoners for whom it was too late. He'd known the labour camps were no picnic but he hadn't been prepared for this sort of spectacle. A good half of the people working looked to be at death's door due to starvation. Why wouldn't they acknowledge Hitler and be out of there? You don't have to mean it, you just have to do it, he thought.

'Surely this sort of treatment isn't good for their long-term health,' he said. 'I mean, in terms of keeping the workforce productive.'

Haussmann giggled out through his nose, like someone interrupted by a joke halfway through a cup of coffee. He gestured to a door.

'Not very good at all. I like you, Voller, you're funny. Here, I'll give you a laugh, show you the most effective element of our productivity incentives.'

He unclipped the flap of his pistol holster but caught the look of horror on Gertie's face. 'Perhaps on the way back. Just a joke, Mrs Voller.'

As Gertie went ahead, he whispered in Max's ear, 'When we have settled Mrs Voller into your quarters, I'll show you. You can have a lot of fun with these people. It alleviates the boredom of garrison life anyway.'

Max said nothing because, for once, he could think of nothing to say.

The Vollers followed him through the room and down a corridor where prisoners were working.

'Stand to attention for the lady!' said one of the prisoners, fatter than the others and slightly differently dressed. His uniform was cleaner and it bore a red triangle on the breast, rather than the pale purple triangles of the stumbling workers.

The workers pulled their attention round to the group in front of them.

'Faster, you bunch of ...' The fat prisoner was clearly unused to bullying in the presence of important ladies, and mentally leafed through a library of choice expressions to find one that was mild enough to use. 'Bible-bashers!'

The prisoner bowed his head, and Haussmann patted him on the back affectionately as he passed.

Max looked at Gertie. As Haussmann had advised her, she had her eyes firmly clamped on the back of the SS man's neck.

They passed through the hall, up some stairs, down corridors and up more stairs. Everywhere the workers were mending, fixing and reconstructing. Finally they ascended a spiral staircase.

'You are in the south-east tower,' said Haussmann. 'Quite a privilege, although the climb's a bit of a difficulty. There are SS men who would very much envy your place here.'

'Where do most of the SS live?' Max asked.

'Officers in the castle or the village, other ranks in the new labour camp. It's quite pleasant there, they have very well-appointed dwellings, gardens front and back, but they don't enjoy this sort of view.'

He opened the door. For the second time in a day, a 'wow' escaped Gertie.

The room was huge and high-ceilinged, with large windows giving a breathtaking view of the forest below.

Gertie went into the room and looked out through the windows. She ran her hands down the curtains. She had always loved fine things, though she had seen little enough of them in her life. Max could see that she didn't know what to think. The sight of the prisoners had clearly shocked her, but she didn't want to appear ungrateful in front of him.

In fact Gertie, with her fine understanding of history, was making a calculation. They were where they were, caught in the stream of events and powerless to resist for the moment. To weep and wring your hands over the fate of the poor prisoners was nothing more than sentimentality. The point was to do something for them. Having seen what was going on at the castle, running away from it would just be cowardice. She sensed Max's nervousness, his trepidation at what she would think, his guilt at bringing her to such a place. There was no point in criticism, no point in recrimination. They were in it together, to stand or fall.

'Look at these, Max, they're pure velvet,' she said, stroking the curtains. 'And look, proper gas heating in the fireplace.' There was, as well — a fire of ceramic bricks built into the old-fashioned opening.

If anything in life made Max happy, it was to see Gertie happy. Their accommodation at Salzgitter had been like something out of the Ark, with several of the more unpleasant sort of animals still in it. These rooms were old, a little musty, but of very good quality. And surely the reconstruction of the castle would be over relatively quickly and, when it was, then the prisoners would be gone.

'There has been, I'm afraid, no refit in here, as so the style is still rather sumptuous for SS tastes,' said Haussmann.

'Yeah, it'd be nice in oak, wouldn't it?' said Max.

'Exactly,' said Haussmann.

'Max, look!' said Gertie.

'What?'

Gertie opened an already ajar door on a cupboard to reveal a gramophone.

'We have no discs,' said Max.

He'd given all his jazz to Arno several years before. It wouldn't do to be heard playing them. Arno, however, was determined that the Nazis shouldn't take every pleasure in life, and would listen to them in the mornings in his office. One of the very few benefits of working close to a steelworks was that sound didn't carry.

'I have a collection of marching songs I could lend you,' said Haussmann.

'Too kind,' said Max, only just draining the sarcasm from his voice.

'Well, we'll get some discs,' said Gertie, 'and look — come with me.'

She led him to the kitchen area. There at the sink was a very welcome sight. Two taps.

'Hot baths!' she said.

Gertie felt nervous. The state of the prisoners had sickened her, but she had lived so long in a mouldy hut that this luxury seemed almost intoxicating. She was putting on an act but it was as if the role of the excited housewife itself was like a hot bath for the soul, something she could step into and forget her troubles.

'Between six and eight, Monday, Wednesday and Fridays,' said Haussmann. 'We have a central boiler and plenty of firewood, but there is a war on.'

'It's good to see you happy, Gertie.' Max could see she was thinking of what they had seen in the main hall. She smiled, though.

'I didn't like Salzgitter, Max.'

'I know.'

He'd almost been able to feel the discontent coming off her; it virtually hummed through the concrete of the floor as she walked. Just as Gertie was sensitive to the emotions of others, her own feelings seemed to colour the air about her. If she was sad, Max could not be happy; if she was happy, he could not be sad.

'But my clever husband has taken me out of it. Well done, Max.'

She kissed him and he felt a rare electricity course throughout him. He would never tire of her kisses, and each one seemed to strike some note inside him which went resonating out into the universe.

Was she putting a brave face on it just for him? Probably, he thought. It would be a terrible disappointment to have to return to Salzgitter. However, he still had doubts about how his young wife, not to mention himself, would bear the proximity of those zombie-like prisoners.

'The lab,' said Haussmann.

'Yes.'

Really Max could have done with a rest, or at least a cup of coffee, but he got the feeling that attention to the job in hand was very much the SS way, so he made no complaint.

They went down the spiral staircase again and arrived in the corridor at the bottom.

'Now,' said Haussmann, smiling, 'let's shoot one of the Jehovah's fucking jerks for you.' His manner had changed, as if civility was an itchy shirt he'd been dying to pull off.

'What?' said Max, coming into a sweat. 'Isn't that illegal?'

Haussmann waved his hand. 'Shot while trying to escape. And anyway, there won't be any witnesses, other than the Jehovah's ones – oh, I'm no good at puns. Come on, let's go.'

'Won't killing the workers delay the building?' said Max, trailing after Haussmann. He had a feeling of tumbling downhill, helpless.

'Plenty more where they came from and, anyway, it'll give the others the hurry-up.'

'I thought you said they were difficult to train.'

'As cleaners for my office, not as general labourers. Don't worry, I won't shoot anyone useful.' He had the tone of someone urging on a slightly overcautious aunt, assuring her that another slice of apple pie wouldn't ruin her figure.

'I ... Er ... I have an ear infection at the moment,' said Max. 'I prefer not to hear any loud bangs.'

'There is more than one way of using a gun!' said Haussmann. 'A pistol makes a very effective club. Now let me ...' He opened the door to the main hall. 'Heil Hitler!'

Haussmann came to salute as if he'd had his toe plugged into the electricity mains. He'd opened the door just as a tall figure in a pale grey uniform had been about to open it the other way. Max was no expert on SS ranks, but he knew that you didn't get uniforms of that cut for working in the latrines. The four silver pips and stripe on the man's left collar patch announced him as a Senior Storm Command Leader, or so Max's rather shaky grasp of SS insignia told him, the equivalent of a regular army lieutenant-colonel. The death's head on his right collar announced him, Max was beginning to suspect, as a murderer.

Despite this, he almost had to suppress a slight laugh in himself. The man had gone for the full icy SS style straight out of the organisation's handbook. He had a pair of white gloves tucked under his epaulette, carried a swagger stick under his arm, and looked at the two doctors as if he'd just found them stuck to his shoe. In less serious circumstances Max would have liked to have taken a bet with Arno that the man had a monocle. 'If he has a monocle, Arno,' he'd have said, 'then you owe me a couple of rounds at the beer hall.'

'OK,' Arno might have replied. 'Do you want to bet on a cigarette holder too and make it a whole evening's drinks?'

'Fine – if he flies a red triplane then you owe me beer for life.'

These jokes, these echoes of a normal life, seemed to swim in his mind, just out of reach.

'Professor Haussmann,' said the man, 'and, yes, Doctor Voller, it must be.'

Max looked harder at him. Oh my God, he had sabre scars, one big one in particular running from the cheek to the chin of his waxen face. He'd received the marks in a youth of duelling, schnapps and Jew-baiting, doubtless. Max really did almost laugh. Here was virtually a parody of a senior SS man, like the bloke had woken in the morning and thought, 'I know what, I'll dress for menace.'

Haussmann said nothing and the man made no attempt to introduce himself.

'I have read your paper, Voller.'

'What did you think of it, Group Leader?' Max decided to err on the side of safety when guessing the man's rank.

'Please, not so elevated. Senior Storm Command Leader.' The attempt at flattery seemed to make him angry, though Max guessed there was quite a lot that made him angry. The man went on: 'Yes, "Conjecture on Psychic Experience Caused By Brain Injury." Appendix on an experimental model involving primates – that was it, wasn't it?'

'Yes,' said Max.

'I should congratulate you,' said the man. 'Quite the biggest heap of shit I've read in a very long time. You think you can summon the Gods with a scalpel? I know you cannot, and do you know why? They have told me so.'

'Right. I ... I ...'

Max found himself stammering, resenting his inability to even hide the fact he was intimidated.

'Don't worry, old chap, Heinrich Himmler thinks otherwise, so my opinion is quite incorrect. In fact, it is not even my opinion. It's the kind of ridiculous rubbish I would have believed were Himmler not here to guide me. You have his protection. For the moment.'

'Lucky old me,' said Max, regaining some of his habitual flippancy.

Haussmann found his voice. ' Voller's is only a side project, sir, everyone knows that you carry the weight of the Reich's hopes in this field.'

'Isn't that secret information?' said the man.

'Yes, Senior Storm Command Leader, yes. Sorry, Mr von Knobelsdorff, sir.'

Max was possessed by a strong urge to leave before things went any further.

Von Knobelsdorff smiled. 'I expect one of Dr Voller's monkeys would have told him anyway, eventually.'

Max stood shuffling his boots.

'It is not the theory that a monkey can speak,' he said, head down, addressing the same boots.

'Oh no, I know,' said von Knobelsdorff. 'Let me paraphrase. In years gone by the mentally handicapped and ill were often used as seers. Disfigurement rituals or human sacrifice were often used to shock the brain into using its latent parts, even into madness. The mad have access to parts of the brain that the sane do not. The future of the Reich lies not with supermen, but with madmen and cripples.'

Max said nothing. He momentarily gave up defending

himself, largely because he knew there was nothing to defend. His paper was an intellectual conceit that had gone wrong, been taken too seriously. He had never really thought he'd get any more than a night's free booze out of it.

Von Knobelsdorff went on, 'You feel that the conscious mind might serve as an inhibitor for the psychic powers, a sort of insulation. Remove it, or disable the parts of the brain where it resides, and you unlock the key to telepathy, spiritual experience, maybe even the Gods themselves.'

Max could see that the SS man was using his knowledge like a head-butt, slamming it into his face to cow and bully him. His instinct with bullies was to let them have their way, render them impotent by not caring about what they cared about, shifting the rules. Here, though, it felt as though he was fighting for his life and he had to compete, whether he liked it or not.

'It is an undisputed fact that the human brain uses only ten per cent of its capacity,' he said. Where had he read that? He knew it to be bullshit, but also to be commonly believed bullshit, but here he was arguing it, like one of the debates he had with Arno, but for much higher stakes. 'If you cut back to the ancient brain then it may be that older powers . . .'

Von Knobelsdorff held up his hand, laughing. 'Only ten per cent of the brain in use? Then I am fortunate indeed. Whenever I've shot a man in the head I've hit the right ten per cent every time.'

'I don't mean literally, I mean—'

Von Knobelsdorff cut him short. 'And if the reptilian brain is the site of psychic powers, why aren't crocodiles calling forth the Gods?'

Max wanted to say that the basic brain wasn't the same as the reptilian brain. We don't all have an alligator lurking inside us, he wanted to say, but instead he tried to explain, stammering and blushing like a schoolboy shamed by some bullying master.

He said, 'The Gods are metaphors, shared ways of

understanding, symbols or archetypes perhaps, that help us organise the relation between our subconscious and conscious. They may have a role in helping us access the telepathic aspects of the mind.'

'The subconscious? Is that the Jew Freud?' said von Knobelsdorff, with a twitch of his nose as if he suspected a fart.

'Jung,' said Max. 'A good German Swiss.'

Von Knobelsdorff snorted. He moved closer to Max.

'The Gods are not metaphors, they are not symbols or dreams. The Gods are real.' He hit himself hard on the breast. 'I have seen them.'

He was an inch away from the doctor's face, his breath hot and smelling of sweet glazed violets. Max found himself shaking slightly, though he faced von Knobelsdorff as best he could.

'There you have it then,' said Haussmann. 'The Gods are real – that clears it up. Shall we continue to your lab?'

'Do that,' said von Knobelsdorff, finally stepping backwards. 'I wish you every success. And Doctor, good luck in your studies. I will send you a present to help you, Herr Crocodile Man.'

Max didn't really concentrate on where he was going after that, moving through what appeared to be a huge building site staffed by half-starved zombies. The Witnesses were the majority of the prisoners – marked out by the violet triangles on their breast, though there were Jews too and others. He felt sorry for them. How does someone exist in such a way, with the likes of Haussmann and von Knobelsdorff stalking about, he thought? He concluded that they must come under the protection of kinder SS officers. From up the stairs there was another scream. One of the *Kapos* – the trustee prisoners – was stamping on what appeared to be a bag of bones, though Max knew it was not. No one, not even his fellow prisoners, seemed to pay any attention. Only Haussmann commented.

'You got to see a show after all!'

Max noticed liquid running onto his hands. At first he was convinced that he must have unwittingly walked under a burst pipe. His shirt was soaked and he could feel his legs slimy beneath his trousers. It was his own sweat.

'Don't worry about old von Knobelsdorff,' said Haussmann, who had seemed to Max pretty worried himself. 'He's one of the Knights of the *Schwarze Sonne*, and they can get a bit uppity.'

'*Schwarze Sonne?*' said Max. Black sun? Nothing in the castle seemed to make sense.

'The innermost of the innermost. What SS really stands for. Who knows what the buggers get up to? Well, I do actually, but top secret, like he says.' Haussmann tapped his nose. 'You should read my files though, make your hair go white.'

He said it almost like it was a good thing to be shocked into premature greyness. Max was convinced he had arrived in an asylum and, fine velvet curtains and hot and cold running water or not, he was going back to Salzgitter by the next train. Just moving around the building, he could tell Haussmann's attitude was not that of a lone madman. Cruelty was almost a management credo, the organising principle of the place.

He would explain that he had revised his theories, he no longer considered telepathic communication possible, and he wished to be returned to his former duties.

They wound around a tangle of staircases and found themselves opposite a door on a mezzanine floor off a staircase. A guard outside it came to attention as Haussmann approached. Haussmann waved him away with some brief instructions to fetch Dr Voller's things, and the man disappeared down the stairs.

'Your lab!' he said, opening the doors.

The room was very, very small – like an elongated broom cupboard – and it smelled strongly of damp. It was no more than three metres long and around 150 cm wide. It was brightly lit by a single powerful bulb in the centre of the ceiling, had a tiny desk and stool at one end, shelving above head height down one side, and a curious chair directly in front of the door. He'd have to virtually climb over it to get to the desk. The chair was more like a throne, really, bolted into the wall. It had a high back, a tight-fitting headrest, and was equipped with buckled straps on the arms and legs. In later weeks Max would laugh at his own naivety. He really hadn't a clue what it was for. On the desk was a roll of surgical instruments, a telephone and a folder.

'The briefing is on the desk, the lab is adequate to your needs,' said Haussmann. It didn't sound like a question. Max had noticed the *Ahnenerbe* man's attitude seemed to change by the second.

'I'll want a typewriter,' said Max. He needed something on which to write out his resignation letter.

'On its way. This is the SS, remember, efficiency is our watchword.'

'Yes. I'd like to get back to my wife.'

Where had that come from? His thoughts had suddenly come out of his mouth unbidden. Haussmann's mood seemed to change again and become truly dark.

'First things first,' he said, sitting down at the tiny desk. 'Himmler kicked your file down to me and I drew up some suggested experiments. I don't mind telling you, Voller, that I could have done without this job at this time. Still, Himmler gets what he wants, as is right, and he wants you to investigate psychic phenomena, mainly telepathy, through lobotomy. You'll find the details in the file on the desk. I'm afraid I couldn't get my hands on a powered skull saw, so you'll just have to go about it the old-fashioned way for now. A bit of elbow grease. *Eeee, eeeee, eeee, eeeee, eeeee.*' He mimed sawing. 'Don't get too comfortable in here, by the way. If, or when, you fuck it up you'll be out pretty quickly.'

'Back to Salzgitter,' said Max, like a man dying of thirst might say 'water'.

'No. You'll have failed as a doctor, and people who fail here tend not to prosper elsewhere. I should think a front-line unit might be a better idea. Perhaps you'd be better off in the back of a bomber, having a crack at those jolly boys in the Spitfires. I'm sure we could arrange for your wife to stay here, though.' There was something almost violent about the way he spoke, as if he was relishing the idea that this terrible destiny might befall Max.

'You can't do that.'

All the heat seemed to drain from the air.

'You don't get it, do you?' said Haussmann, leaning forward. 'This is the SS. We do things differently here, or hadn't you noticed? We do what we fucking like. You might be lucky not to end up in a concentration camp yourself if you don't play your cards right. Then where would your pretty wife be?'

It was clearly Max's mention of the beautiful Gertie that had incensed Haussmann. Max looked at his fellow doctor. Those veined cheeks, that fat, ball-like body, the thinning hair with the sunburnt scalp mottled like a slice of sausage. Was Mrs Haussmann a beauty too? He doubted it.

The big chair stood in front of him, grim as a spectre. They were restraints on the arms. That, he realised, was where he would have to strap the poor ape. Surely they couldn't expect him to crawl over a bloody monkey to get to his desk. And how could he operate in such a confined space?

Max's mouth was dry and he felt dizzy. This was not what he had expected at all. How many of the abuses of this SS unit were known? He couldn't believe Himmler allowed this sort of thing to go on. He'd heard the rumours about the camps, but thought they were just that – rumours designed to scare off conscientious objectors and criminals. He'd expected to see some rough stuff occasionally, but in less than an hour inside the castle he'd seen one man kicked to death, scores half-starved – more than half-starved – and brutalised, met an avuncular doctor who seemed prepared to shoot people as a welcome present, and a high-ranking aristocrat who seemed to Max to have the moral vapidity of a vampire.

'Your subject will be delivered immediately and you can

get cracking.' There was a knock at the door. 'Ah, here it is – one chimpanzee, hot from the zoo!'

Haussmann opened the door to reveal the guard, who had returned with a typewriter and, standing meekly in front of him, a bent figure in a prisoner's uniform. On his breast he bore a pink triangle.

'Bring the monkey in!' said Haussmann.

The guard pushed the prisoner roughly into the room using the typewriter. Max almost shot forward his hands to prevent him from mistreating the old man, but thought better of it. He didn't need to think things through. He instinctively knew he should learn how the place worked before making hasty interventions.

'Here is your subject,' said Haussmann. 'I must say, I wish I had the pleasure of chopping up this bastard myself.'

Max felt as if he was on a boat that had just hit an iceberg; the floor seemed to shake underneath him. He was Max Voller, wisecracking underachiever, not some torturer. He wouldn't do it.

The guard came into the room too. There were now four of them in a room where two would be uncomfortable. Neither Haussmann nor the guard seemed concerned.

'My work specified a chimpanzee. I am to experiment on animals.' Max leant back to avoid virtually kissing Haussmann.

In fact his work hadn't specified anything. It had been a concoction, a tissue of dreams. He might have mentioned experimenting on animals but he certainly hadn't asked for a chimp. He liked chimps.

'We cannot provide a real chimpanzee.'

'Why not?'

'Chimpanzees are protected by law. Subhumans are not. I am not prepared to commit a criminal act, Mr Voller, whatever the needs of science.'

So he was *Mister* Voller now, was he? Not Health Leader Voller, not Doctor Voller – Mr Voller. Haussmann was also, weirdly, completely serious. He appeared horrified by Max's suggestion he might operate on an ape.

'Sign,' said the guard to Max, pressing a clipboard on him.

Max retreated a way into the room and sat back on the stool. He really felt his knees might go at any minute. He looked at the strange chair, for the first time noticing the formidable neck collar, the screws with which the headrest could be adjusted to immobilise the neck. He heard a rattling noise and looked down. It was the paper on the clipboard. He was shaking. He steadied himself and read the form. With relief, he saw there had been a mistake. The requisition was for a young boy. This was an old man.

'Wrong prisoner,' he said, trying to show some composure. *Pray to Jesus that they can't find the right one.*

Haussmann looked at the form, looked at the number on the pyjamas, and then rolled up the sleeve for the confirmation of a tattoo on the prisoner's arm.

'No mistake,' said Haussmann. 'Michal Wejta − probably not his real name, you know what these gypsy fuckers are like − caravan traveller, criminal, homosexual − Jesus, he'd only need Jewish, cripple and communist for a full house. Anyway classified as a queer, looks queer, probably is, when I see wolf's ears I expect I'm dealing with a wolf, so to speak, probably a gypsy, might not be a gypsy but touch of the tar brush at any rate, picked up in Poland, thirteen years old at time of internment, fourteen now. What's the problem?'

'*He* is fourteen?' said Max, looking at the withered figure in front of him.

'That's what taking it up the arse from an early age does for you.'

'There has been a mistake, my paper was theoretical, not practical. I am not capable of doing this work and shall resign forthwith. I can't do this, I can't . . .' He wanted to say 'become you', but he wasn't able to finish the sentence.

'You're going to tell Heinrich Himmler "Thanks but no thanks"? Now that would be an experiment no one has tried

65

before, although I think I can predict the results. A man with that sort of bravery deserves to serve in our most courageous units. You should be first off the landing craft when we invade England. Knight's Cross, oak leaves, swords and diamonds. Posthumous.'

'I ...' Max really had no words.

'Now, if you will excuse me I have other things to attend to. All that is required from you, Doctor Voller, is solid proof of telepathy within the next three months. I'd get cutting if I were you. I hope you do well, I really do.'

Haussmann suddenly sounded genuinely pleasant. It struck a jarring note after all that nastiness but, Max realised, Haussmann had been around such vile things for so long that he had lost the capacity to differentiate between menace and charm.

'My paper was conjecture,' he said. 'It was most likely wrong.'

'No,' said Haussmann. 'Himmler has said: "If the state or party has declared that a certain view must be taken as a starting point for research, then that view is to be regarded as a scientific fact." I can get you the order reference if you like. Your experiments will work. Himmler says so.'

'Himmler wants this?'

'Yes?'

'Does Hitler know?'

'Yes. Hitler and Himmler know and, beneath them, God too, before your next question. Hitler knows everything that happens in the Reich, Max. Do you expect him to be easy on our enemies?' He gestured to the boy.

'No, I, I ... I don't know what I think,' said Max.

'Don't think then, just do.' He was suddenly pleasant again, charming, coaxing, even. 'Do the experiments, make your report. Sometimes it is necessary to be a little inhuman in the service of a greater humanity. Few people enjoy this sort of thing when they start but, in time, you get used to it. In a month you'll be doing it with your eyes closed. You might even be bored by it. It happens.'

'But I'm a general doctor, not a brain surgeon.'

'Your words do you great credit, and confirm your suitability for the job. Our Reichsführer himself has said that sometimes the layman is more qualified to carry out scientific research than the expert. Much of science is Jewish anyway – you know that, don't you? Good German common sense is all that is required. You are unencumbered by the prejudices of Semitic medicine.'

'I'm unencumbered by knowing what to fucking do!' said Max.

Haussmann tapped him on the arm and said, 'Then you have a blank slate. What excitement you must feel! All you need is the faith of the Reich's Leader. He is never wrong.'

'I—'

'Your paper was uncertain if cauterisation or straightforward cutting was the best way forward. I should stick to cutting if I were you, soldering irons are in short supply at the moment with the rewiring of the castle. I'll be back in a week. If you need cadaver removal or a fresh subject in that time, let me know, although if I read you right the boy will not die quickly. You know where I am if you need me. Stick it out and remain a decent fellow. *Bonne chance* and Heil Hitler!'

'Heil Hitler,' said Max, returning the salute rather limply.

He looked at the boy at the end of the bench. The boy looked back, his eyes unnaturally large in his hunger-shrunken face. He really did look like some zoo animal – dazed, disoriented, only half aware of his fate.

'Jesus,' he said, 'what are we going to do with you?'

Max's first priority was to get the boy something to eat. He went to the canteen and endured the stares of the SS men, the cold silence that greeted his regular army uniform. He felt like decking a couple of them, but the pragmatist in him held back.

Max took Haussmann's file with him as he walked. There were three proposed lobotomies in the first week. Max knew

very little about brain surgery, but he knew enough to recognise a fellow duffer in that department when he read one.
Haussmann kept confusing the terms for the various parts of
the brain – medulla, cerebellum, cortex. If Max – basically
a clap and constipation man – could spot the mistake, he
thought, then Haussmann's brain surgery was weak indeed.
In fact, the mistakes were so basic that it made him wonder if
Haussmann was a doctor at all. He must be, though; he was in
charge of medical research at the castle for the most efficient
organisation of the most efficient political party the world had
ever seen. Perhaps he'd just been overworked and written the
brief when he was tired. It was utter rubbish, though.

Max loaded up a tray with soup, bread and meats and
headed back to the lab and unlocked it. He had expected to
find the boy cowering but he was simply standing, in exactly
the position he had been when Max left him. Max looked at
his eyes. No fear. They were, the doctor sensed, beyond that.
Max entered the tiny space and closed the door behind him.

'Sit,' he said.

The boy did nothing. Did he speak German?

'Sit,' said Max, again, miming sitting.

The boy sat, not on the restraint chair but on Max's stool.
Max gave him the soup. He drank it at a gulp but put the
meat into his pocket, along with the bread.

'What's up, aren't you hungry? You look hungry,' said
Max. 'That'll get dirty in there. Eat. Eat!'

The boy looked back at him. Picked up in Poland?

'Do you speak German?' Max asked, slowly and clearly.
'German? Speak?'

The boy made no response. Great, Max thought, I'm meant
to prove telepathy with someone who I can't even communicate with by talking. First things first.

'Eat.' He mimed putting food into his mouth but the boy
shook his head.

'Friend,' he said, 'sick.'

'Well, if your friend's sick he should ask to go to the

infirmary.' He felt a hot rush come upon him. He guessed that option wasn't exactly available. He sat for a moment, thinking of what he'd seen in the courtyard. 'You are sick, you are very sick, very thin. You must eat.'

Still there was no sign that the boy had understood anything at all that he had said.

A drill whined from somewhere. To Max it almost seemed to emanate from inside his head, knocking his thoughts sideways and making him feel dizzy. Still, he was no fool and was quick to grasp the realities of any situation. This is where he was, so this is where he must be. He didn't have to like it, though.

Loafers, and Max was a loafer, have their talents too. Employers design systems to make things hard for the lazy. By ingenuity and guile, though, the lazy seek out the cracks and contradictions in the best-laid schemes and find ways to make things easy on themselves. It's not something you can learn, it's an attitude to life. Max had been avoiding work ever since he'd been asked to do any. He just needed to apply that slippery little skill harder here.

He looked at the boy. He was shamed by the child's bravery. Would Max risk his life for a friend? No. Did he, then, have any friends, if he wouldn't risk his life for them? He didn't know. Only Gertie could inspire him to noble action, he thought. He would die for her, he had known since the second he met her. Until he had arrived at Wewelsburg, he had laughed at himself for such melodramatic thoughts. Looking at Michal, they didn't seem so melodramatic any more.

The boy would not eat the bread and meat, but the doctor had seen enough about the castle in his short hours there to be sure the child would be in grave danger if he was discovered carrying it. He had a large bruise on the side of his shaved head, a lump that reminded Max of a misplaced skullcap.

'Here,' he said, 'I have an idea that will be good for both of us.'

He went to the first aid cabinet and withdrew a coil of bandage, along with a pad.

He took the bread roll from the boy's pocket and put it on the bench. Then he hammered it flat with the heel of his hand. He put the meat on top of it and then applied it, meat first, to the lump on the boy's head and wound the bandage around it. By the time he had finished, it was indistinguishable from a normal head wound dressing. He was pleased with his work. Even if the meat seeped a bit, it would only look like a leaky wound.

He smiled at the boy. 'Off you go, and don't worry, we'll work something out.'

He opened the door to the guard.

'This boy is to be returned to the camp and rested. I have done my preliminary work on him and require him unmolested for my experiments tomorrow. Is that clear? He needs to come back in a state that I can work on him. No beatings, no hard labour. Rested. And fed, well.'

'Yes,' said the guard.

'Yes sir, to you,' said Max.

'I am a member of the SS. Your army rank means nothing to me.'

'Well, let us hope that, when my SS commission comes through, then you will feel as confident in your insolence. Heil Hitler.'

'Heil Hitler!' said the guard.

Max returned to his lab. Step two, he thought, would be to play these bastards at their own game. He drew up a requisition notice.

'Note to Prof. Haussmann, *Ahnenerbe*. Lab facilities inadequate. Require the following:'

The list was as comprehensive and unattainable as he could make it. Silver electrodes, he thought, would be the thing to wire to the brain. Silver had a good deal of occult significance, and would be scarce and difficult to fashion. Nothing could commence without the electrodes, he decided, which – if he had anything to do with it – could take years to develop.

At the bottom of the note he added: 'Lab must be completely

redesigned. Work party will be detailed as matter of urgency.'

The matter of urgency was a good touch, he thought. There is nothing a bureaucrat likes better than pointing out the problems that the urgent demander hasn't even guessed at – supply issues, proper process, the need to go through the correct channels and gain proper permissions – particularly if it was an SS bureaucrat responding to a regular army request. Even if they had workers standing around doing nothing, then the 'matter of urgency' – along with the bristle-raising 'will' – would delay his request by weeks, he thought.

Also, wasn't most of his research on relatives? Max wrote on the form: 'Require relative of prisoner 223 456 otherwise experiment impossible.'

If the boy had relatives then they were unlikely to be at the camp, he thought. That was bound to cause some delay. He had an afterthought.

'Also require EEG machine.'

He thought it a good bet that Haussmann wouldn't have a clue what an EEG machine was. The brainwave reading device was relatively new science, and Max had only read about it by chance in a newspaper. That should set them a few problems, he thought.

He was satisfied with his work and pleased with his clever-ness. He wasn't going to be chopping anyone up for a very long time indeed. Now, he thought, time to get back to Gertie and open that bottle of wine.

6   The Corpse Shore

Craw settled into his Stratford-upon-Avon hotel. Coventry was a pleasant enough city but Craw required a level of refinement quite unavailable there. The hotel was a large brick-built seventeenth-century affair overlooking the river. Balby had gone to interview Arindon, and said he would return later to brief him.

This left Craw with time to kill, and he decided to walk along the Avon to take advantage of an unseasonable spell of late autumn sun. In his white flannels and boater he felt himself quite the gentleman at leisure, and decided to enjoy his unexpected visit to bucolic surroundings. His relaxed mood was tempered by that feeling of mild stupidity unique to an immortal in Stratford. He'd had the chance to meet Shakespeare, in that he'd been alive at the same time as the playwright. However, in the 1600s he had become tied up in Albania for a while. By the time he saw *Hamlet*, the Bard had encountered darkness as a bride and hugged it to his arms – copped it, in Briggs's language.

Craw strolled the riverbank, watching the swans. He found the dislocations of the modern age difficult to deal with. Less than twenty-four hours ago he had stood with the world burning around him, death among the people like locusts among corn. Now, the sunlight, some pretty girls, the boats upon the river. It was as if the evening before had just been a nightmare, some inconsequence now receding in memory, until it would enter that field of grey known as the forgotten.

After a short walk he sat on a bench next to the riverbank and closed his eyes to let the low sun soothe him.

A voice at his ear: 'What's the time, Mr Wolf?'

Craw sat up as if someone had put ice down his neck. No one living now knew his secret. The last one had been Isabel, in the early 1800s, and she hadn't really believed him.

Or rather, she had wanted to believe him because she loved him, but the facts of his existence were so hard to take that she felt he must be either cruel – in teasing her – or a coward, too scared to say the truth, that he didn't love her.

'I must say,' Isabel had said, 'there are more conventional ways of letting a girl down.'

He hadn't meant to tell her but his old weakness – the third glass of whisky – the moon and the scent of roses in the garden had got the better of him. The cost of ending his loneliness, of sharing his burden, was to be alone.

'What's the time, Mr Wolf?'

He looked up to see a small girl of around six facing him. She had bone-blonde hair and wore a white home-made dress in a rough cotton. The riverbank that afternoon was heavy with ghosts; she reminded him of his own daughter, Kari – a thousand years dead. Or maybe five hundred. When had he known her? It had gone, only the fact of her existence remaining, out of time and place.

'You have to say "one o'clock", "two o'clock" and then "time to eat you",' she said.

Craw regained his composure. 'I'm not sure I like being a wolf.'

'You only have to be a wolf for the game, you don't have to be a wolf forever.'

Craw felt his stomach skip. 'No, I don't think I'm interested. I used to be a wolf but the bottom fell out of the wolfing market so I became a human. And besides, no self-respecting wolf would eat a little girl. He'd find someone of his own size to pick on.'

'Wouldn't a little girl be easy to eat?'

'Well, yes, but no good to a wolf.'

This was a kind of truth. He felt a great temptation to confide in this child, not really that she might know the truth, but for the relief of telling the facts of his life out loud. His adopted people, the Norsemen, had been great storytellers, and to keep everything in, to wrap it all up inside you for years and years, was difficult. Occasionally he needed to let a glimpse of himself into the outside world.

'Not good enough for a wolf?'

'I'm afraid not,' he said. 'A wolf needs to eat big strong people to build him up.'

'When did you stop being a wolf?'

'Well, the last time was about a hundred years ago.' Was it one hundred years? Was it fifty or two hundred? Time seemed to mean less than it did when he was young, to register less on his mind, to leave less of a mark.

'That's a long time,' she said.

'Yes,' said Craw, 'but wolves haven't been welcome at the top restaurants for a very long while, so things are easier as a human.'

'Could I become a wolf?'

'I'm afraid not, applications are currently closed.'

'Be a wolf again,' she said.

'I generally try to avoid it.'

'Why?'

'Complicates the tax return,' he said. 'Income from professorship in one column, income from wolfing in the other. What counts as an expense and what doesn't? Can sheep's clothes be regarded in the same light as a mortarboard and gown? Is falling as the wolf upon the fold a business practice or a leisure pursuit? It's vastly difficult stuff, and I refuse to put that kind of dough into the hands of accountants, I really do.'

'My daddy was an accountant,' said the little girl.

Was. The soul of humanity summed up in a single word, like its signature note sounding in the music of time, Craw thought. 'Was', humming through the summer day like an angry wasp.

'He was at Dunkirk,' she said, 'and he drowned in the

74

water but it's OK because he's in Heaven looking down on me and when the wind blows in the chimney at night it's him blowing me a kiss.'

'Yes,' said Craw.

He felt it again, the pull of the mire of attachments. In the mortal world he steered a perilous course, to touch but not be touched, to connect but not to stick. The Big Was, history, milled the present and emotions – love, feelings, the touch of warmth as a father takes his daughter's hand by a riverbank – were crushed on its wheels. After so many years love of humans could have become an unbearable weight, had he let it. You can't drag the dead around with you.

This was why he'd been so drawn to the company of frivolous young men who found the world ridiculous. It was easier to marvel at the kind of person who would give a young child the exact details of her father's death and then try to sugar-coat it with tales of kisses on the wind, than to think of that man reaching out for his daughter and the air in the cold waters of the Channel.

'I should go and find your mother now, child,' he said.

The girl was suddenly frightened by Craw's change in manner. She turned and was gone, her white dress disappearing like the sun caught for a second on glass.

Balby was already in a bad mood because Craw hadn't been in the hotel as he'd said he would be. Stratford was a small town and it was a sunny day, so he would have worked out that Craw was by the river even if his butler hadn't told him so.

He saw him from a way away, almost luminous in his white flannels and boater, like someone from a different age. Unlike Craw, Balby was absolutely a man of his time; he had had no other. Accordingly he had a sense of the modern as something he lived, rather than Craw, who took it from magazines and books and sometimes, as in the case of the flannels and boater, got it wrong.

It seemed to Balby that time didn't proceed smoothly; there

were flaws and crevices in its structure. The boater had been fashionable not ten years before but now, the country at war, it looked incongruous and jarring, almost as if Craw had settled on the lawn in a tricorn hat and stockings. A rift had occurred in 1939 when the past had broken away from the present like a wedge of sand from an eroding cliff, and Balby felt it could never be reattached.

Craw stood up from his bench as he saw the detective approach. This was the sort of thing that bothered him. The noble in him wanted to remain seated but, as the lower orders could no longer be relied upon to prostrate themselves, then he would be faced with the unpleasant situation of talking to the inspector's crotch.

The two men shook hands and Balby caught sight of Craw's signet ring again, a wolf's head in silver and ruby. The inspector did not like that ring one little bit.

Craw saw his glance and spoke.

'If I were a Nazi spy I should hardly wear a ring featuring one of the many venerable symbols they have so presumptuously appropriated. It's from my family's crest.'

He'd caught some of what Balby was thinking. Craw's manner, his distancing arrogance, fitted well with how he imagined Jerries, and Jerry Nazis in particular. The policeman had finally put his finger on what was lurking beneath the pat comments and the mildly condescending wit. Craw, he thought, was as hard as stone.

'What would you do if you were a spy, then?' said Balby, glancing again at the ring.

'Become a policeman, I suppose.'

For the first time since he had met him, Craw saw Balby smile.

'No,' he said, 'bad choice. No one tells the police anything. You'd be better off as a bookmaker or a publican.'

Craw looked at his watch. 'Speaking of which, the sun's over the yardarm and— Ah, sorry, I forgot. You don't. Perhaps we should take some tea at my hotel.'

'Yes, very good,'

Balby briefed Craw as they walked.

'Arindon was found in Crackley Woods. It's to the south of the city, in quite a rural area. He was discovered by a spinster lady walking her dog. I'm afraid to say that she received quite a shock. He was quite naked and in no good state. He was incoherent.'

Craw raised a questioning brow. 'Cut?'

'No. He was covered in blood, but we have ascertained that most of it wasn't his own. He was living in a hollow under a tree that he'd dug out with his hands. He also, from an inspection of his vomit, appears to have been subsisting on earthworms and insects.'

'He vomited?'

'In the van on his way to the station,' said Balby.

'Not his own blood?' Craw asked. 'Not a lot of blood in earthworms and woodlice.'

There was a short silence. Craw sensed Balby was a man who liked to proceed at his own pace.

'Arindon has some distinguishing features on his body,' said Balby. 'Those patterns we saw on the other victims in the photographs, but not nearly as extensive. They are mainly confined to the facial area, unlike the other corpses which have had their faces removed.' His delivery, Craw thought, could be improved. The man was a droner.

'Do you have photographs of the marks?'

'They're being developed.'

'And has he said anything?'

'Nothing intelligible. I think he's lost his mind.'

'Well, with a little care and a good meal he may remember where he's put it,' said Craw.

Balby looked at him with those vacant eyes again. Craw quite liked the inspector, he decided; he was one of the few people capable of making him feel young. Under the policeman's evaluating stare he felt like a giddy youth beneath the eye of a reproving parent.

'My thoughts exactly,' said Balby, tempering the distaste in his voice. 'I intend to attempt to interview him again in the morning. I would appreciate your help to interpret anything he might say.'

'Will it need interpreting?'

'I fear it will, sir, for he's using a number of words which I take to be foreign. A man of your education will be useful to us.'

Craw shrugged an *If that's what you want* shrug.

The policeman looked hard at Craw, giving the werewolf the idea that he was in some way accusing *him* of reducing Arindon to a babbling wreck. That wasn't exactly right. Balby wasn't making an accusation – he only accused on the most solid grounds – but he was blaming Craw. Something odd was happening and leaving a trail of dead and mad men around Coventry. Craw was an expert in the odd, and therefore was to an extent tarred with the same brush as whoever was abducting and killing people. Balby recognised this thought as irrational, but it didn't make it any less powerful.

Still, he respected Craw. Most experts he had met ventured thirty opinions in the first ten minutes of you asking them for their help. Craw had yet to really say anything, which Balby liked. The man didn't leap to conclusions, nor was he so insecure in his own knowledge that he had to show it off.

Craw stood at the doorway to his hotel. The sun caught the glass of an opening door, recalling the little girl in the white dress, recalling Kari.

'Actually, Inspector, would you mind if you take your tea in the bar, I could do with a little drink as insulation from the cares of the world.'

'You should study the Bible, sir. I find that's all the insulation I need.'

The two men stood looking at each other. Craw had a keen appreciation of the human form and he noted the policeman's muscularity, the short levers of his arms. He would have been a good boxer, he thought, if he could trap his man. At a distance, though, he'd be cut to pieces. Why did this man have the talent for making Craw feel stupid, young, immature? It was a quality Craw liked. Few people got under his skin like that.

'Arindon kept mentioning a name. If you get the chance before tomorrow you might want to look into it.'

'Yes?'

'It could be where he's been kept, we're examining the possibility,' said Balby, 'but just in case, have you heard of a *nastrond*?'

The word hit Craw like a smack in the mouth. He couldn't reply to the inspector. For a second he was somewhere else – in the country of his dreams, listening to the song of a dying man scraping through his head in a choking incantation.

> *A hall I saw, far from the sun,*
> *On Nastrond it stands, and the doors face north*
> *Venom drops through the smoke-vent down,*
> *For around the walls do serpents wind.*

Nastrond was the corpse shore, the hall on the hill of dead. Craw had only seen it in visions but, cold in the heat, the colours of the bright day receding in his mind, he could feel the bonds that held him to his chosen reality loosening, a strange joy mounting in his blood.

He heard another voice in his mind.

> *The fetters shall burst and the wolf run free,*
> *Much do I know and more can see.*

He had forgotten much, but he remembered where it had all began – in the ritual of the drowning pool, where he had gone to seek the counsel of the Gods after Adisla had been abducted by berserkers. There, the wolf had put its eye upon him. There, visions and songs had streamed through his mind.

At first he had thought they were an expression of something inside him. Only later, in anger and in blood, had he known the truth — he was an expression of them, the servant and victim of a magic as old as time.

He recalled too the mountain witch, Gullveig, and her hoard of gold. That mind-blown child who had set herself in the winds of great magic, as if she was a reed to give them voice. She had set out to call him, to invoke Odin, let him look out through her eyes and to die as the god needed to die, living out his ordained death here on earth so that the fates would spare him in the realm of the Gods.

He willed himself back to the Stratford day. Balby was looking at him with concern.

'I shall have to think about that one, Inspector,' he said.

The corners of Balby's mouth turned down as he looked at the pale, sweating figure in front of him.

'Worse men than you have come to God,' he said. 'Please, turn away from the demon drink. Save yourself. Hear Jesus speaking to you.'

But it wasn't the voice of Jesus that Craw could hear echoing down the centuries.

7 Mrs Voller's Dream

Max had a desperate need to see Gertie that night. She felt like an island of sanity in a sea of madness. He'd arrived back in his rooms at eight – having spent four hours in his lab scribbling out plans by which he might avoid becoming a murderer.

Gertie sensed his distress; a tin bath was drawn and the wine was on the table. She'd actually found some ice from somewhere and the drink was pleasantly cold.

'How was it?' she asked.

'Good,' he said. 'Own lab.' He found himself laughing. It was a habit, just what he did. He didn't find much funny at Wewelsburg. 'How about you?'

'I stayed in here. I think I'll try to stick to the bits of the castle they've finished in future.'

The drilling, the hammering, was muted in their part of the castle, but it was incessant. Max, his thoughts turned morbid by what he had seen, imagined it as the scrabblings and bangings of someone who finds themselves buried alive.

'Good idea,' he said.

The horror they both felt settled on them with the clammy feeling of clothes worn too long, but they didn't need to discuss it. She knew that he would hate what he had seen and would try to leave, and she knew that, commanded by the orders of Himmler, he could not. There was nothing to be said. As so often under the Nazis, they were making the most of a bad lot. Better to keep the frustrations inside than to voice them. In some ways talking about them seemed to give them life.

'I have a chimp to operate on,' he said. 'It seems a shame to harm the poor fellow.'

'Oh dear,' said Gertie, coming to hug him, 'a great shame. Is there no way around it?'

'Seems not. I ...' Not for the first time that day, the words refused to come.

Other women would have noticed the tears in Max's eyes, the change in his manner. Gertie, who had a sensitivity for such things, saw them too but, beyond that, she felt the pull of his sorrow, a feeling like the sense of deep water as you gaze into a lake.

'Oh, Max, are you all right?'

'I'll be fine.'

But Gertie, who had known when the dog was shot and who could feel people's emotions on the air like others could feel cloth or stone, fire or water on their skin, knew he was far from all right. But he was Max. He would be all right. Being all right was what Max was good at and one of the reasons she loved him. He would laugh his way out of his sadness and be his old breezy self.

Max got out of his sweat-soaked uniform and had a bath in front of the gas fire. Gertie sat on a small three-legged stool next to him and poured water over him to wash his hair. She dried him and helped him on with his robe, lit him a cigarette. She loved to minister to him, to feel she was taking away his cares. They drank a bottle of wine, and then another. Max opened a third and the buzzing in his head seemed quieter.

'Dance?' she said.

'Oh yes! I'll be rhythm.'

'And I'll be melody,' she said, fluttering her eyelashes at him.

'What shall we play?'

'Jumpin' at the Woodside!' she said, like a little girl suggesting a midnight raid on the larder. This was a record they'd heard on the BBC on a radio they'd taken beneath the blankets one night the year before. The naughtiness of what they were doing had drawn them together, the enjoyment of this banned pleasure.

'Dum dum dum dum dum dum dum dum, ratatat tat da ratatat tat! Ratatat tat da ratatat tat!' Max sang in a whisper, as Gertie softly began the melody, 'Dedodedo! Quack quack, quack, quack, dedodedo, quack quack, quack, quack!'

They linked hands, jived and hopped, as if their lives depended on it, Max even going into the splits at one point. They gyrated and turned, whirled and leapt, all in a whisper. They were performers in their own silent film, run slightly too fast and providing their own jerks and flickers while makin' whoopee.

Eventually they were exhausted and fell together on to the bed. Gertie kissed Max and moved her hand between his legs, but he took it away.

'Not tonight,' he said.

'You're tired.'

'Yes.'

And so they lay in each other's arms. Max sank into his wife's comfort. With Gertie he truly knew what it meant to be human. With her he felt the tender bond of shared sleep, her female warmth enveloping him in the night. She engaged his every sense, from the way she looked to the flavour of her breath. He loved to wake before her in the mornings and curl into her as she slept, to kiss her and to feel his life passing and not to mind as long as he was with her. Gertie, if anything, felt an even stronger bond to him.

'Why do you like him?' her friends had asked.

He was everything she wasn't – frivolous, overflowing with words, never, ever, serious. She, to whom everything seemed important, weighty and difficult, could not have been more different. So why did she love him? Because from the second she'd met him she sensed his love for her as something she could almost touch, like the beating of the heart of a little rabbit she'd held against her breast as a child, like a hum that resonated in her soul.

Max, the alcohol drowning the horrors of the day, the castle works finally silent, fell quickly to sleep. Gertie, so sensitive she seemed to hear people's thoughts and intentions like music, taste them sour and sweet as vinegar or wine, was not so fortunate.

Places, too, sound notes that the very sensitive can hear, and Gertie was very sensitive indeed. No one was ever going to Lindy Hop to the tune that Wewelsburg Castle played when the hammering stopped. Misery and dread had seeped into its walls long before the Nazis had begun their horror show.

Gertie knew nothing of the Roman crucifixions on the site, nor of the Germanic tribes' brutal revenge on the legions, the hundreds sacrificed to the Dark Lady of the Forest so that the dead might staff her hall; nor did she know of those held in the hot holes of Wewelsburg's dungeons, accused as witches, tortured and burned within its walls; nor yet did she know that the castle was being reconstructed on the blood and the bones of the Christian martyrs, the self-appointed chosen she had seen at work on her way in, and of the Jews appointed by God and bad luck, but she felt it tight as a cancer in her throat. The walls whispered 'murder', and Gertie heard their voice.

She lay turning on her bed, too scared yet to reach over to the table and turn off the light. The shadows seemed to steal sleep from her, lapping at the edges of the lamplight like eyeless beasts groping for her from the dark.

She had eventually turned off the lamp, she remembered that, but, in the infinitesimal moment as the light disappeared and the dark poured in, she saw things – a gallery of pale and contorted faces caught as if in a photographer's flash, but the opposite of a flash, a sudden emanation of the true dark.

It was her imagination, she knew, and she scrunched up her eyes tight and willed sleep upon herself. She felt it would never come. Yet sleep did come; it must have come. What else but a dream could have accounted for where she found herself?

It was night and she was among cedars, not a wood so much as a copse, facing a large house in the English manor style.

There were only a couple of lights on but she sensed activity within, something seething and several, human but indefinably strange.

The night was warm and the scent of the trees filled her up. A high half moon shone sharp and small in the sky, though there were no stars.

'Would you see yet more?' said a voice at her shoulder.

She tried to turn to see who was speaking, but she couldn't. Either her head wouldn't turn or the man – it had been the voice of a man – had moved. She could not tell which.

'Can't speak?' said the voice.

Gertie could not speak, though she wanted to.

'Do you know I'm here?'

She forced herself to turn. In daily life the scene that greeted her then would have made her faint. In her dream state, or whatever had taken her to that place, she didn't regard what she saw as particularly disturbing.

It was two men, clearly Americans by their style of dress. Both wore wide-lapelled suits in the jazz fashion, one bright sky blue, the other a lurid pink. The first man she saw wore an eyepatch, had snowy, tidy hair and a neat white beard. One arm was around the shoulders of the second man in a pally, almost patronising manner. There was something about the second man's face, a quality that she thought she could name. It was on the tip of her tongue but the word would not come. His face didn't reveal him as a black man – that was it. It was his hands. What was it about his face?

'Hey, Jack, waddya say to the lady?' said the man with the beard. He spoke in English – which Gertie spoke poorly – but in the dream she understood him perfectly, feeling her stomach skip at the musical quality of the words.

The other man spoke, slowly and hesitantly.

Sal sá hon standa
sólu fjarri
Náströndu á,

norðr horfa dyrr;
falla eitrdropar
inn um ljóra,
sá er undinn salr
orma hryggjum.

Now that she didn't understand. Gertie tried to complain and tell him to speak German, but she found herself mute. Then, she thought, maybe she did understand. She knew what the words meant, she was sure. Again she had that tip of the tongue feeling. If only she could start speaking then the meaning would become clear.

'Lady don't want none of that jive talk,' said the man with the beard. 'Lady looking for her friend the wolf. She been lookin' for him long time. Wolf's a-comin'! Lady's missah bettah bring his axe! Lady want, uh ... Oh ... Er ...'

Gertie looked at the man with the eyepatch. His face was loose on his bones, she thought, and getting looser. It almost looked as if it might fall off. Then she realised what was odd about the man who had spoken the rhyme. Finally she could put her finger on it. He had no face at all, and his sinews and eyeballs were revealed to her like a page from an anatomy book. She was fascinated by the raw gleam of his flesh, like some strange and precious coral. She wanted to touch it.

'Well that's peculiar,' she said, finally finding her voice. 'What does all this mean?'

But then it was morning, ten o'clock; the sunlight filled the room and she reached out for Max, but Max, it seemed, was already at work.

The new day lifted Gertie's spirits. The horror of her dream had not touched her; the visions had failed to scare or disturb her. In fact, she felt peculiarly comforted by them, as if a tension inside her had discharged, and all morning she found herself humming a rhyme she must have heard from somewhere.

More fair than the sun, a hall I see,
Roofed with gold, on Gimle it stands;
There shall the righteous rulers dwell,
And happiness ever there shall they have.

Her dream had seemed, for a moment, to drain the dread from the castle's walls and, as she looked down on the courtyard shining in the sun, she thought for a second that happiness there might be possible. Yes, she thought, this could be home.

8 Mr David Arindon

The mental hospital at Phrenton Abbey sits under cedars in a natural valley just outside Stratford-upon-Avon. Arindon had been taken there after his behaviour had proved too disturbed for the police to handle in the cells at Little Park Street.

They'd eventually had to sit on him for a couple of hours until the men from the loony bin turned up, the sergeant would later tell his wife, to stop him banging his head against the wall.

'We'd only just had that painted,' he said, which is the kind of thing policemen find amusing.

Craw, Balby and Briggs drove towards the abbey through the early morning sun. Craw closed his eyes as the vehicle moved under the trees, enjoying the sensation of the flickering light on his eyelids. He hadn't slept, though he didn't feel tired, just perplexed.

He was desperate to see Arindon but fearful of what the man might have to say. A prophecy had attended Craw's last transformation and, to an extent, he was still living with the legacy of that huge upheaval, body, soul and mind ripped apart and reconstituted in an unfamiliar and deeply unsettling way.

Craw breathed in the leather smell of the back of the police car, a Rover 12 hp, large and luxurious like a living room on wheels. Normally Craw was interested in cars simply because he'd never quite got over the absence of horses and the sensation of travelling at such speed, like a god, through the countryside. Today, though, he hardly noticed he was moving.

He had not slept, that word going round and round in his head.

Nastrond. The corpse shore.

Phrenton was a mid-sized hospital. It had been established under the Mental Deficiency Act of 1913 in a country house as remote as possible in a relatively populous county like Warwickshire. The aim of the act was to separate the lunatic completely from mainstream society, and so places like Phrenton, deep in the countryside, were ideal.

This quarantine was not at all to spare the nerves of the sane majority, but to isolate the gene pool and ensure that insanity was not passed on. The government had no problem with madmen walking the streets – it just didn't want them to reproduce.

Phrenton had been the first place in England to experiment with voluntary sterilisation of the insane, although some in government recommended sterner measures. Churchill himself had written of the 'race danger' and recommended that moral degenerates should be sterilised in order to protect the superior stock. There were plenty in Britain who would have gone a step further than that.

'Is this the asylum?' said Craw, opening his eyes to see a large sandstone building with pleasant French doors overlooking a ha-ha. Clearly the hospital building had been built before the motor car had come to wide use, and the tarmac road approached from the rear.

'The doctors will be happier if you call it a mental hospital,' said Balby. 'They haven't been asylums for ten years.'

'Really?' said Craw.

'Yes, and it's "patient", not lunatic. I made that mistake myself and you'd think I'd set fire to the building.'

'The world is becoming too gentle, Inspector Balby,' said Craw, almost on autopilot. His practised manners and lightness would have to proceed by reflex for a while.

'I haven't noticed too much evidence of that, sir.'

They got out of the car and walked round to the front of the house, entering through a substantial black door and into a competition of smells, the polish and the wood of the original country house combined with the disinfectant and vomit of a working hospital.

A doctor in a white coat and stethoscope greeted them. Craw knew some medical men, and it seemed to him that the top consultants in the glamour professions of surgery and medicine were willing to walk around in tweeds. The psychiatrist, who wanted recognition as a real doctor, preferred the uniform.

Balby introduced the doctor, Craw's mind too distracted at his impending meeting with Arindon to remember his name. They were led down a parqueted corridor into the building. It reminded Craw slightly of a public school, though in his brief experience of one of those the lunatics had worn mortarboards and been called 'sir'.

Some of the inmates were wandering about in dressing gowns. One man looked as though he had nothing wrong with him at all and was sitting reading a paper, yet not ten feet from him another hugged his legs and rocked back and forth on the floor, keening in a mind-blown way. He'd seen this sort of thing in films, but it was something you assumed only occurred on the screen. The reality, you assumed, would be different, but there it was, like something out of Alfred Hitchcock.

The doctor showed them to a door under the stairs, the sort of thing that in most people's houses would have led to the cellar and the air-raid shelter. They descended and were hit by a damper, colder smell than that of the house above.

The decor here was newer too, concrete and bunker-like with metal doors leading off an electrically lit corridor. Craw thought that it would be enough to try the nerves of the sanest man alive, particularly when combined with the cries of the tormented souls in its cells.

'He's in number four,' said the doctor. 'I don't like padded cells if at all avoidable, but I'm afraid in this case it's not.' Craw realised he was being addressed.

'Is he still in the straitjacket?' asked Briggs, whose instinct for possible violent confrontation was acute.

'He was much calmer this morning so we've managed to let him out of it,' said the doctor, 'though he is still sedated. It's debatable what you'll get out of him even if he has found a little more internal equilibrium.'

'You should give me ten minutes with him,' said Briggs. 'He'd have his internal equilibrium back smartish, you can bet on that.'

Balby looked at Briggs disapprovingly. Craw couldn't completely recall the Bible's line on beating the mentally ill, but he was sure it didn't exactly smile upon it.

'That won't be necessary, officer,' said the doctor.

'You don't want to trust him,' said Briggs. 'I know this fella and I can tell you, if he's mad then there's money in it. I bet he's somehow found out about what's been happening and he's gonna try to flog us some inside line on it for a consideration.'

'Is he wanted for any crimes at the moment?' said the doctor.

'No,' said Briggs, 'but hang around and he will be.'

The doctor flicked back the viewing hatch and looked inside.

'There you are, Inspector. Quite calm.'

Balby looked in briefly and then gestured to Craw, who replaced him at the hatch.

Inside was a man staring directly at the door. His face was covered in what looked like a dense spiral of raised bumps rising up from a straggly beard. Craw was reminded of an Aborigine he'd seen at the Curiosity Circus in about 1874. Of course, it wasn't just African tribes who raised their skin. As far as he could remember, though, Aborigines did it to show social status. Why would a modern man want to do that? He could wear an expensive suit.

Arindon stared into Craw's eyes and Craw looked back.

'*Forad!*' Arindon was pointing at Craw, his finger not a foot from the hatch. '*Forad!*' Craw drew in breath. Arindon had said 'monster'. Where had David Arindon learned to speak Old Norse?

Craw didn't know what to say; he just stared at Arindon. Then Arindon seemed to come to his senses. He sat back on the floor.

'Not from me,' he said in English, 'I will not be.'

'Perhaps I should ...' said the doctor, miming closing the hatch.

Craw was about to draw back from the slide when Arindon fell into a dead faint. He hit the padded floor with a dull thud.

Craw gestured to the doctor to look at the hatch. He did.

'Hmm,' he said, 'that's the first time he's done that, though it is the sort of thing I would have expected. He looks as though he's still breathing, though. Not choking. I'm inclined to give him ten minutes and see if he's still in that position – they're not above faking, you know. It might only disturb him more if we go in right now.'

'You're scared of him,' said Briggs, to whom such things mattered.

'I'm concerned for his safety and that of my staff.' The doctor thought for a moment. 'Which is another way of saying I'm scared of him, yes. Look, he's on fifteen minute observation anyway, why don't we nip upstairs and relax for a couple of mo's. Anyone for a bit of tiffin?'

'Did you make anything of what he said?' said Balby.

'Nothing,' said Craw.

In a way he was speaking the truth. Hearing David Arindon speaking the language of his forefathers was, to Craw, as incongruous as if a cat had asked him to leave a window open because it planned on coming home late. Then there was what Arindon had said: 'Monster'. Craw was slightly shocked but still trying to reach for the least strange explanation. His problem was that he hadn't yet reached any explanation at all. Without interviewing Arindon at length he wasn't going to get any nearer the truth, but he needed to speak to him in the old language and see how much or how little he understood.

On the way up the stairs there was a brief discussion on the plan of attack for Arindon. The doctor, it was agreed, should question him, and the police and Craw simply act as observers.

'Or we could jump up and down on him until he tells us what we want to hear,' said Briggs.

'Is that legal?' said the doctor.

Briggs shrugged. 'He's a criminal,' he said, as if that ended the argument.

Craw became lost in himself again. He felt touched by a past that came to him only in fragments but he recalled lunatics and seers had recognised him before, predicted his change. The wolf was rising inside him. He felt sad for the life he would have to leave. Even under the bombs London was a cheerful place; he knew people, touched their lives and was touched in return. That alone should have told him it was time to move on.

They retired to the doctor's deep brown study and took tea served by a rather twitchy-looking serviceman.

'Dunkirk,' said the doctor after the man had left. 'He was a long time in the water.'

'And that was enough to drive him nuts?' said Briggs.

'He was a *very* long time in the water.'

'Should have gone back on the beach then, shouldn't he?'

'It's a bit difficult when your boat sinks ten miles from shore,' said the doctor, draining the last of his tea and then looking at his watch. 'Ten minutes up, shall we check our pay-shi-ent?'

They descended the stairs once more and made their way down the concrete corridor.

'A tanner says he's made a miraculous recovery,' said Briggs, producing a sixpence from his pocket.

'I'll take that bet,' said the doctor. 'I don't think a man in perfect mental health would disfigure himself like that.'

'Well, at least it's going to make him easy to spot the next time he knocks some old lady over their head for their purse.'

The doctor raised his eyebrows in a *Here we go* way and slid back the hatch. *Bang!* Arindon struck him forcefully on the nose from inside, sending the doctor spiralling into the wall behind him, with a great shout of 'Jesus!' No, no, that hadn't happened. Craw had seen no fist, so the doctor had flown back against the wall pushed by some unseen force.

Briggs sprang at the hatch and looked inside. He clearly had made the same mistake as Craw, because he put his hand on the door and looked through the slot at arm's length as if anticipating a punch. Then he too recoiled, falling back with his hands over his eyes and a kind of harsh whimper. Again, he acted as if he'd been struck, although Craw was certain nothing had hit him.

Craw and Balby glanced at each other. Balby, the professional policeman, did the obvious thing. He took hold of Briggs and asked him if he was all right. Having seen two people fly back from the door as if someone had thrown boiling water in their faces, he was in no hurry to try the experience for himself.

Craw, however, was drawn to the hatch. Briggs had slammed it shut when he'd leapt away, so Craw slid it back gingerly, approaching it at an angle.

Arindon was sitting cross-legged in the middle of the floor smiling a big smile up at him. The smile was one of the largest Craw had ever seen because, in the ten minutes they had spent drinking a cup of tea, Mr Arindon, wife-beater, black-marketeer and bar-room wit, had managed to reach out through his sedation to chew away his lips and much of his cheeks. The severing of his facial arteries had released two dancing fonts of blood that played where the sides of his face had been, little spurts of lava shooting up from a ragged hillside.

What his teeth hadn't destroyed, his filthy nails had. The only skin remaining on his face and forehead was a few pink tatters. Craw had once been in Italy and seen a woman put a plate of the spaghetti bolognese over a man's head. The effect was not dissimilar.

The sight alone would have been enough to sicken a normal

man. Craw, his senses turned up to the top of the dial by the red ends of flesh in front of him, had more to contend with. He could smell the blood – salt and iron but with a deeper note, like roasting beef – and he could taste it too, the fine particle spray settling invisibly on his lips from those two ghastly fountains at Arindon's cheeks.

He swallowed the saliva that had formed in his mouth and struggled to force his thoughts to human form. The change was perhaps closer than he had thought.

He had his defences, though. There were so many ways to be at that juncture, so many responses to choose other than answering that strange voice he heard howling inside him, an echo of an echo of something he had once been and would never want to be again. He had to say something, something human. Of course – concern for the patient.

'Get up, doctor, you're needed,' he said.

The doctor, pale and sweating with his hand on the wall, swallowed, nodded and regained his professional composure.

'Get ready to sedate him,' he said to one of the orderlies, 'and prepare yourself for a mess.'

The doctor opened the door and went in with the orderlies. The smell of the blood moved an old hunger in Craw, like the pull of bacon sizzling on the hob. His senses red, he searched for words to reconnect him to the mortal world. In his mind he was running hard as the evening fell, but his body was moving to different rhythms, not the plodding polka of his human sprint but a hammering 4/4 like the drums of Africa or some mad jazz. He could smell a summer night and hear strange cries, a sound more than sound, in registers no human has ever heard.

'It's fine,' he told himself, 'you will not let it slip,' though his eyes were drawn back inside the room, where the medic was trying to staunch the flow of blood and calling for cotton swabs.

It was as if Craw heard him underwater, as if time wouldn't quite flow as time was meant to flow. Come back to humanity,

Endamon, he told himself, think of those days on the river with the banjulele and the punt, of the laughter of the girls, of that way of being where nothing meant anything and them meats is a taste, my right say I feeds first. His thoughts were falling apart, the animal rising up in him, or rather the man sinking, his humanity thrashing out for something to cling to in order to pull it from the sucking swamp of feelings that was engulfing it.

A line from a film came into his head: 'The stubborn beast flesh creeps back'.

Who was that? Charles Laughton in *Island of Lost Souls*. Charles Laughton, that was who he needed – the icy hauteur, the unshakeable, unshockable, silky screen Englishman who can see horrors unfold in front of him and shrug. People were pushing past him, some falling away to be sick. Balby was in the room, stumbling on slime on the padded floor.

'My God, he's gone clean through the cheek,' said a voice.

There was a low noise from behind him. Craw turned and looked down at the sobbing figure of Briggs who had curled into a ball, hands over his eyes.

'I think you've lost your tanner, old man,' said Craw.

He was back.

9 An Administrative Error

The note Max received back from Haussmann was rather to the point:

'The experiments will be conducted under current conditions. We have located the boy's grandmother in the main camp at Sachsenhausen KZ and have sent for her. Preliminary results will be presented within one month.'

Great, Max thought. I'm trying to save the kid, now I end up killing him in front of his granny. Fucking terrific.

He read on. A PS was added in Haussmann's handwriting:

'Anaesthetic is for German troops, not enemies of the Reich! Will see what can do on EEG machine.'

Max's mind seemed paralysed. He simply didn't know what to do. He spent his days teaching the boy German. Michal was a quick learner, as people who rely on communication to survive tend to be.

Otherwise he sat concocting wild theories about how psychic phenomena might be obtained – none of them requiring anyone to be cut to bits. Perhaps he had been wrong, he typed. The dog had not transmitted the vision of its death to Gertie because of a brain injury, but because of stress. Other forms of human religious and psychic experience were caused by stress – induced by pain rituals, near death, drugs or starvation. Yes, it was stress! He wouldn't have to cut anyone to bits, he was sure.

The child sat in the operating chair as he worked. Max was not half a metre away on the chair of his desk. The boy was almost perched on his shoulder. They kept the door shut and it was clammy and airless, but they were unseen. More to the point, Max was unseeing. Neither he nor Gertie wished to witness the childish brutalities that the SS and the *Kapos* – the trustee prisoners – visited on the captive workforce, so they lay low. He had seen a few of the SS tricks – schoolboy pranks deformed and distorted into a grotesque attack on dignity, health and – very often – life. Max was disgusted by them. Luckily a door had been cut in the bottom of their tower and Gertie could come and go without going through the main body of the castle. She spent her days playing tennis with some of the other wives and reading in their room.

However, they were not completely immune from the cruelties of the SS.

Max was in his lab one day in late October. He had no books to help Michal with his German, so had been proceeding by example.

'My name is Max. I am from Berlin. Your name is Michal. You are from ...'

Oh God, where was the boy from? As a gypsy he didn't really have a nation. He wanted to teach him the German for Gypsy so the boy could know when people were talking about him. It might give him a better chance of survival.

'I am German. You are a gypsy,' said Max.

The boy looked blankly at him.

'You are a gypsy. Romany.'

The boy shook his head forcefully. 'No Romany.'

Ah, Max had it. He was a Sinti, the other gypsy ethnic grouping.

'Gypsy. Sinti. You,' he said.

The boy shook his head again. 'No gypsy. Gypsy shit.'

Max was shocked slightly by the strength of the boy's denial.

'You caravan.'

He drew a caravan on a piece of paper. The boy had been picked up in a horse-drawn caravan. The boy shook his head forcefully. He took the pen from Max and wrote something in Polish. Then he handed it over, tapping at the writing, then at his eyes. 'Read it', was his clear message.

'Wait there,' said Max. If Michal wasn't a gypsy, then one of the obstacles to getting him out of the camp would be gone.

Max went out of the lab and down one of the corridors in a fever of anticipation. A Jehovah's Witness was fixing some electrical ducting.

'*Polska?*' said Max.

'I am German,' said the Witness.

Max looked into his eyes. He had expected to see hatred, but the man had a kindly, almost amused expression on his face. Max began to tremble, to feel ashamed. How did this man manage to retain his faith in his awful situation? What he would give for just a glimpse of such belief, some anchor to cling to in the chaos of his life? Michal, though – his health and his survival would be that anchor.

'Do you know any Poles here?' Max asked.

The Witness smiled, softly. 'God bless you,' he said.

'I said do you know any Poles. I'm trying to save a boy's life. Do you know any fucking Poles?'

'Turn back,' said the Witness. 'Be declared righteous in the name of our Lord Jesus Christ and with the spirit of our God.'

'Oh, for fuck's sake.' Max went to go past the man, but he stood, barring the doctor's way.

'Jehovah forgave David. He forgave Manasseh. He can forgive you too.'

'Get out of my way,' said Max. The man did not move.

'"God's will is that all sorts of men should be saved and come to an accurate knowledge of truth." – 1 Timothy 2:3–4,' said the man.

'I am trying to save a child's life and I am ordering you to get out of my way.'

'We must obey God as a ruler rather than men.'

'Get out of my way!'

The weeks of living at Wewelsburg, of deceit and hiding, the screams and the brutality, the endless reconstruction that thumped in his head day and night, his concern for Michal, his worry for Gertie – it all came bursting out of Max as he shoved the shrunken, ragged man off his feet and onto the floor.

'Getting into the swing of things, Voller?' It was von Knobelsdorff, who had come up behind him.

'I—'

'Good show, maybe you'll make an SS man yet. Perhaps you're not as soft as they say. Do you want to finish the bastard off, or shall I?' He unclipped his pistol.

'He's an electrician, we need him.'

'Pity,' said von Knobelsdorff. 'I've had a shit of a morning. By the way, you'll find my present for you has been delivered to your lab. Look after it. I'll be checking on you. Heil Hitler!'

'Heil Hitler.'

Max made his way out into the main courtyard. The tarpaulins were gone and he could see the peculiar truncated shape of the yard, narrower at one end than the other. The scaffolding on the top of the building cast shadows across the paving stones. For a second, he thought, they looked as though the floor had been sunk with deep dark pits. He located a *Kapo*, who dug him out a Polish speaker.

The man, luckily a political prisoner rather than an evangelising Bible Student, read the note with a blank expression.

'My name is Michal Wejta. I am not a gypsy, I am a Pole from near Poznan. We are a middle-class family and are registered with all relevant authorities. Our family had a caravan that was used as a play hut. When the Germans invaded we took this and made for the Czech border, but we were taken prisoner by a regular army unit. We were robbed of everything we owned. I am not a homosexual. Neither am I a communist. I should be free to go. Please get my identity proof from the relevant Polish authorities.'

Max could hardly believe what he was reading. This boy had ended up at Wewelsburg by some freakish mistake. Relief came over him in a cold wave. He had to get back to his lab and get to his telephone. He had to speak to the concentration camp commander, Haas; he had to make him see that they were holding this boy unjustly, even by their own warped criteria.

He opened the door to the corridor with the electrician in it. He had gone. There was nothing there, just a bitter smell of cordite and a bloody stain about a metre up the wall. Max gulped. It was just the height a man's head would be when kneeling. He had tried to protect the man, said he was an electrician, but von Knobelsdorff, with typical attention to detail, had checked, it seemed. Then he thought: Michal. He was still in the lab. What had von Knobelsdorff sent there? Whatever it was, Max doubted it was anything he would want to see.

10   A Surprise for Mr Craw

Craw was smoking underneath a cedar as the bandaged figure of Arindon was loaded into the ambulance. The bouquet of the blood was still in his nostrils; the fine red mist that had settled on his lips continued to give up its deep and enticing taste.

It was too much, he had decided. In the presence of the blood he had only just held on to his humanity. He couldn't be sure that would happen next time. And yet, Arindon had spoken to him in the language of his forefathers. It was a connection to his lost wife, no matter how tenuous.

He'd needed to get out of the clammy air of the house and clear his head to think. He was under no doubt what his duty as a gentleman required. He should leave immediately and try to isolate himself as best he could. There were strong pulls within him, though – a vision of a young woman crying as she said goodbye, and the tantalising possibility that she had come back, as he was virtually certain she had done before and would again.

This wasn't the sort of certainty you achieve by learning, or reading a book, or even from seeing evidence with your own eyes. It was a certainty stitched together from hopes, hunches and gut feelings, but it was a certainty nevertheless. He could no more account for the enduring power of his attachment to his wife than he could be free of it, even if he had wanted to.

From the ambulance, the squat figure of Balby made its way towards him.

'How is Briggs?' said Craw.

'He'll be all right. I've told him to pull himself together. A cup of tea and he'll be back on his feet.'

The two men said nothing for a couple of minutes. Craw offered Balby a cigarette and the policeman took it. They stood shifting from foot to foot and breathing out smoke in the chilly autumn air. Wet leaves and bonfires were on the country breeze. Dark clouds brought the suggestion of dusk to the sky.

'That's a new one,' said Balby, nodding towards the ambulance.

'Yes,' said Craw, 'cannibalism normally restricts itself to other people for rather obvious reasons. A singular case, Inspector.'

'You can say that again,' said Balby, breathing out a heavy plume.

The age of explanations, of telling, of unburdening and confession was not yet upon the English. Balby had been shocked to his boots by what he had seen, so he did what his entire upbringing had conditioned him to do. He talked about something else.

'I think yesterday was the last of the sunshine.'

'Bad weather's on its way, I think,' said Craw.

'Very likely.'

Craw, who was beyond shocks, who was himself a living shock, was at a loss as to know what to do. A werewolf must always think of himself first. This is not an egocentric act but a practical one. There are few situations that can be improved by biting someone's throat out though – as Craw knew – such situations can exist.

Among the cedars, on the wind, in the still-present smell of blood from that awful cell, he could feel the change coming more strongly. It was like eyes on the back of his neck. He had no idea how long it would take. The unpredictability terrified him. Did his curse always follow the same course? Would it always take so long for him to change? What if he did indeed fall behind a sofa and come up howling for blood? He'd seen that in a trailer for a Lon Chaney film and it had given him quite a start.

The first time, with that *meat* in his hands, it had been a matter of weeks from start to finish. Had it? He thought so. An image. Awakening on a ship of corpses. He shivered. He would have to make preparations to go away, but to where?

Australia, he'd thought, sounded promising, with its miles of empty space – or America, where he'd been the last time. But America, now the USA, was contracting. There were places he could go but who was to say that some motorist – some settler – wouldn't happen by. The war, though, made travel difficult. The passage east and west was teeming with U-boats and fraught with peril. It wasn't the torpedoes he feared, but delay. Imagine if the hunger took him at sea. The results would be unimaginable.

But first he wanted to speak to Arindon. *Forad.* Monster. It was a connection to what he had been and, however tenuous, a connection to his wife.

Silence fell between the two men again. It was as if they were testing the resilience of the calm between them, seeing if it could bear the strain of what they had to discuss.

Finally Balby was ready to talk about what had happened.

'What do you make of that?'

'What?'

'*That!*' said Balby. 'That mess.'

Craw scratched at the dirt with his shoe. He would walk away, he thought, as soon as it was practical to do so without exciting too much comment. Proving himself useless might be the best way of doing that.

'Clearly something has affected his mind.'

Balby gave him a look that indicated he should aim his comments outside the range of the completely obvious.

'Why did he do it just as we arrived? He had the whole morning out of the straitjacket if that was what he wanted to do.'

Craw shook his head. 'I can't imagine anyone *wanting* to do that.'

'What if those marks weren't for protection, Professor? You said there were other possibilities.'

Craw shrugged again. 'What seems most likely?'

'You're the anthropologist,' said Balby. Clearly he'd spent some time getting the word right. 'We have several corpses and one lunatic covered in these marks, the only exception being Hamstry, who had no flesh at all. We agree the marks weren't done by the victims themselves, so they were done by someone else.'

He breathed in, reminding himself not to run too far ahead in his deductions.

'So,' he went on, 'did the person or persons who committed the murders inflict the marks? We cannot say conclusively that they did. If they did, then why would they want to protect someone they were about to kill? Is whoever inflicted the marks even the same person as who caused the murders?'

Craw nodded. The inspector's thought processes were a good deal clearer than those of some academics he could think of.

'There's no real evidence one way or another,' said Balby.

'Indeed not, we are in the realm of speculation.'

Balby breathed out, the smoke pulled past him by the rising breeze. 'Square one.'

Craw nodded. *Nastrond, Forad*. They were words he hadn't heard out loud for a very long time. *Nastrond*: the corpse shore. *Forad*: Monster.

'Tell me,' said Balby, 'what you can say for sure, and then give your guesses.'

Craw looked up into the trees, as if asking for inspiration.

'We know for sure that we are dealing with some ritual practice that is capable of causing the most extreme forms of insanity, and we know it uses what appears to be body markings that have some sort of spiritual significance. They most closely resemble marks used by African hunter-gatherer peoples as identifiers of humanity. They do not resemble any form of sacrificial markings that I have seen. That, I'm afraid, is the limit of the certain. Beyond that, I should say it seemed sure that Arindon was keen to get those markings off his face. Perhaps he believes the markings may give away significant information that might prove useful to his enemies.'

'The police are his enemies, and the marks mean nothing to me.'

'Perhaps he fears he might suffer as a result of having the markings on his face, suffer more terribly than he would suffer by inflicting those injuries on himself. That might account for why he wanted to get them off. That leads us back to the sacrifice hypothesis. But it is not sacrifice, I am sure.'

'Why not?'

'For a start, Arindon's alive,' said Craw. 'It's not generally seen as much of a success if your sacrificial victim gets up, says "Is that the time?" and bids you adieu.'

'This could have been botched.'

'Very possibly, but what went wrong here that went according to plan in the other instances?'

An idea was forming in Craw's mind, but he didn't want to share it with the inspector yet. It was his original thought of Muti magic. There was nothing to suggest an African influence on these murders, but what if the principles employed were the same? What if the victims were being used as some sort of ingredient in a ritual? But which part – the part that was removed or the part that remained? Craw, in his rather callous way, imagined the victims as like oranges. There are dishes that require the zest and there are dishes that require the flesh. Perhaps Hamstry had been one, Arindon the other.

'He must have been pretty scared of something to be able to do what he did,' said Balby.

'A terror known only to the insane,' said Craw, once again throwing up his mask of banality.

'If he was scared of us, then why didn't he do that on our previous meeting?'

'The straitjacket. Wouldn't have stopped him having a chew at his face, though.'

'Oh yes. But he was nowhere near as disturbed by us yesterday as he was today.'

'What was different about today?'

'Only you,' said Balby.

Craw let the words sink in for a second. It was too much of a coincidence. Arindon was linked to him in some way. He would stay. No, he should go.

'Why would he be scared of me?'

'Well, he wouldn't be, would he?' Balby shrugged. 'Square one.'

A heavy winter storm was coming. The light seemed to change in quality, the air darkened, and the wind moved beneath the trees. Craw shuddered. And then he remembered the uses of duty. To perform an uncomfortable but correct course of action it is not necessary to want to do so. All that is necessary is to perform it. It was beholden on him to try to leave. He spoke the words like an actor, hoping to be refused but feeling bound to speak them anyway.

'And now you have it all, Inspector. Everything I know and all I can imagine. I shall gladly speak to Arindon again, should he recover sufficiently, and please keep me abreast of any other changes in the case, but now I really must return to my other work.'

Balby shook his head. 'I would prefer you to stay. You have more to offer.'

'I really must go.'

'If I call the War Office I feel sure I could have you ordered to stay, given the nature of events.'

Craw breathed out. Balby's refusal to allow him to do what was right and walk away emboldened him. He could protest more strongly, convince himself that he had exhausted every stratagem at his disposal to tear himself free and then, denied, stay with a clear conscience. He would have tried, and so he could justify the risk he would bring down on himself and those about him. He would not let himself off so lightly, though. He had to try, and try properly, or he could no longer consider himself a gentleman.

Craw sought a way to make the man release him. Then he had it. Fifty years before, under a different name, Craw had taught at Yale University. He had loved his time there, but had had to leave before the rumours regarding his perpetual youth could build up too much of a head of steam. The plight of the immortal who does not wish to be known as an immortal is to always move on. It had been a pity. In his last years at the famous college he'd met an extraordinary youth, Ezekiel Harbard, the Delaware Dynamo, the Small Wonder himself, the man who put the 'aware' in Delaware. Some people are bright; some are even gifted; but rarely does a human burn with the intelligence that Harbard exhibited.

The boy's mind seemed to know no bounds. Physics, maths, anthropology and history all came easily to him. His work on linguistics alone, where he had worked out how Old Norse should be pronounced, marked him as a genius. When he'd spoken to Craw it was like listening to one of his kinsmen sitting at the fire by the shore. Craw would have liked to have replied, to have had a conversation in the old language, but he had not revealed to Harbard that he could speak it, more out of superstition than any genuine fear of exposure. And besides, he couldn't have borne to have had to argue with Harbard on the subject. If there were areas of disagreement then Harbard would hold to his argument like a terrier to a stick. Craw couldn't face being told that his Old Norse was lacking – and worse, to be told so very convincingly.

Ezekiel Harbard, however, had been made to leave Yale. He had what the university establishment regarded as a weakness. His fascination for ancient lore led him on to look at numerology and the occult. He'd set up his own institute in New Orleans dedicated to research into the paranormal, largely in the field of debunking fakes, but also with the aim of documenting and understanding man's real occult experience.

Craw had followed his career from afar with interest. If

there was any man alive who could interpret the message in the murders and madness, then it was Professor Harbard. Balby would have to telegraph his requests over to America, but he was sure Harbard could help. Craw regretted not being able to talk to him personally. Harbard at twenty had been the most fascinating person he had met since his wife. At seventy he would be something to behold. Still, a meeting was impossible. Harbard's heart might not be up to the shock of seeing him just as he'd been fifty years before, not to mention the implications for Craw's cherished anonymity. And, for all that Craw enjoyed Harbard's intelligence, it in no way made him consider the professor his equal. The northern European aristocracy had always felt intelligence to be a little 'trade'. Though Craw was very clever indeed, particularly by human standards, he didn't value cleverness. He didn't need to be bright. He had breeding, which was so much more important. To him, cleverness was no more valuable than an amusing trick. He appreciated intelligent company in the same way as, when he'd been a prince, he might have appreciated a fire-eater or a good cook. It was an adornment to life, not essential to it. The blood was what mattered. Always the blood.

'I would very much like you to stay,' said Balby.

'You don't need me, Inspector,' said Craw, 'this is outside my expertise. However, I know a man who will be more useful to you – a Professor Ezekiel Harbard of the Harbard Institute, New Orleans. I'll write that down for you, the Home Office should be able to get your questions sent through. I'm sure Professor Harbard will be able to help you, he's a remarkable man.'

'That's funny,' said Balby. 'He recommended you.'

11 Reptilian

'A crocodile?'

'Yes, a crocodile,' said the SS guard standing next to the small crate outside Max's lab.

'What sort of crocodile?'

'A green one.'

In other circumstances, Max might have laughed.

'What am I supposed to do with that?'

'Care instructions are enclosed,' said the guard.

'I don't want it,' said Max, 'send it back.'

'I have express orders that the crocodile is under no circumstances to be returned. It is in your care and its welfare is your responsibility.'

'Is it bollocks! I have more than enough on my plate. Send it back or I'll wring its neck.'

The guard passed Max a letter. It was in a beautiful ivory white envelope sealed with a wax stamp of a sort of multi-limbed swastika. He opened it.

'Dr Voller. For help in your experiments. This crocodile is property of the SS, requisitioned from Dortmund Zoo. As such it is to be maintained in pristine condition. If any damage occurs to SS property then the severest sanctions will be imposed against those who have caused it. My men will be in to check on the creature's progress periodically. I hope you enjoy your chats with it and look forward to hearing its telepathically garnered opinions very soon.'

It was signed by von Knobelsdorff.

'This is a fucking joke!' said Max. But when he looked up, the SS man was gone.

His voice seemed to echo in his mind. Why was he swearing

so much recently? He hated swearing really, not for any prudish reason but because it always seemed so insecure to him, such an effort to prove yourself one of the boys. It was the stress, he concluded. He wasn't himself.

He peeked into the crate. It was lined with straw and it stank, but he couldn't see anything within. So there was going to be him, an adolescent boy and a reptile in the broom cupboard now. So much of what was happening to him was so ridiculous that it was almost funny, but also so much was definitely not.

He turned the key in the lab door and, seeing Michal gazing out of the tiny space, wide-eyed, like something stuffed in a case, he remembered his purpose.

'No gypsy,' he said.

'No gypsy.' Michal grinned. It was the first time Max had seen him smile in the time that he'd known him. 'Cigarette?'

Max flicked him a Salem and picked up the phone. He rang down to the camp, asking for Haas. He was put through.

'Yup?' said Haas.

Max identified himself.

'What can we do for you, bender?' said the commandant.

'What did you say?'

'I said what can we do for you, Doctor?'

It was depressing, thought Max, that even among such daily horrors that occurred in the castle and the growing labour camp that served it, people could find time to be bored enough to speculate on what he was doing, hour after hour, in a broom cupboard with a fourteen-year-old boy who had been labelled a homosexual. The idea that he was protecting Michal simply out of decency, to save the boy's life, really didn't occur to them. In fact, it would have been more dangerous for him if it had. He felt a hot anger rising in him and he did his best to remain polite.

'I have some shattering news,' he said. 'You know the boy Michal Wejta?'

'Your little friend, the fat one who we're not meant to punish?'

Haas had a cheek calling anyone fat. Michal was still five or six kilos underweight, despite Max feeding him up. That was fat, however, by camp standards.

'I hope you're sitting down. He's not a gypsy.'

'Yeah, I know.'

'You know?'

'Yeah, we actually have some gypsies here and they told me. We stuck him in a work party with them but they didn't exactly get on. That's why we added commie to his classification, but they definitely didn't want him, and then we decided he must be a homo, so he's ended up as all three. It was making my head spin, I tell you. I was all for shooting him just to tidy up the paperwork, but then you stuck in the requisition and we thought we'd kick him up to you.'

'But in no way is he an enemy of the Reich. He should be free to go.'

'Well, he must be something or he wouldn't be here, would he?'

'It's a mistake, plain and simple, a mistake.'

'Yes and no. He's down as a gypsy, he's been given a number. He's a gypsy, as far as we're concerned. And a commie. And a homo. Not a Yid, though. Saved by the skin of his cock.'

'You need to declassify him now.'

'No chance,' said Haas. 'Have you any idea what kind of paperwork storm it would set off if I gave any of these fuckers a sign that they could wriggle out of here? We'd only have Witnesses left and, as I'm sure you know by now, they're not exactly interesting company.'

Max was nearly speechless.

'This boy shouldn't be here. It's ludicrous. It's ... It's immoral.'

There was a pause on the line.

'Don't, Doctor,' said Haas, 'I've only just changed these trousers and if you go on like that I really am going to piss myself. Have you taken a look around the place recently?'

'Let him go,' said Max.

'Say please.'

'Please.'

'That's not how you say please properly.'

'How do you say please properly?'

'Kerching!' said Haas. 'I need a little for my retirement fund, doc.'

Max was boiling with rage but he controlled himself.

'I'll see what I can do,' he said.

'Five hundred marks or an afternoon with your missus,' said Haas.

'What did you say?'

'Only pulling your plonker. Six hundred marks will do it.'

Max put down the phone. Michal looked at him.

'It's going to be OK,' said Max, and ruffled the boy's hair.

Michal smiled back and took another cigarette from the doctor's top pocket.

'Thank you,' he said in his heavy accent. 'Fire?'

The doctor lit his cigarette for him and sat back to ponder. He hadn't got six hundred marks. How could he buy the boy's freedom? Success in his experiments, he supposed. What would success mean, though? How do you provide evidence of telepathy – something that doesn't exist? The question that had dogged him since he had come to Wewelsburg leapt up in his mind. The air in the cupboard was becoming thick with smoke. He wanted to get away and think.

Max left the crocodile by the door and the boy with a packet of cigarettes in the lab, and walked down into the courtyard of the castle. The construction on the outside of the building was coming to an end; the tarpaulins had been removed and it was almost pleasant to sit in the deep shadows of the summer's end and smoke beneath the towering walls.

'Voller. Heil Hitler.'

'Storm Command Leader Haussmann. Heil Hitler.'

Haussmann's fat arse slid past Max into the inner castle. Max hardly registered him, just catching him out of the corner of his eye as a flash of uniform and bald head, grey and pink disappearing into black. A clink and a chink and he was gone.

A clink and a chink? The keys! Max suddenly saw his chance. He looked left and right and made for the *Ahnenerbe* office door. As he'd guessed, it was open. Haussmann hadn't bothered to lock it. Max stepped inside.

He glanced around the immaculate interior. Where to begin? He knew exactly what he wanted – details of what von Knobelsdorff was up to. Max was, it has been noted, a loafer. He knew well that the quickest way to do any work was to copy it.

If he reproduced the results of whatever experiments von Knobelsdorff had been conducting – if he came to the same conclusions by a different route – then von Knobelsdorff would have to give him credit. He would transform himself from a competitor into an ally. Finding the same thing that von Knobelsdorff had found but, crucially, finding it *after* he had found it, made Voller a supportive second, an able lieutenant, no threat to the Senior Storm Leader's authority. Then funding requests could be given or, better, authority obtained to tell Haas to sort his game out pronto. Boots at the door. The boots passed. He would have to work quick.

Max opened a filing cabinet. There were no files in it, just a mess of documents. He picked one up.

'Mesmeric ray for hypnotising enemy pilots,' it said in a childish script. The document was illustrated by a drawing in crayon, dots zooming up from a cannon to represent the ray. These were entries in the competition that had given Max his job at the castle.

He picked up another. 'Numerological calculation of position of warships.' A stamp on it said 'Action', but the stamp had been crossed out and other handwriting said 'Occultist. Arrest.' And yet it was stuck at the bottom of Haussmann's filing cabinet. He'd obviously just thrown all the applications he wasn't going to act on immediately into the file. He'd condemned the man who had sent in the numerological idea, but he had been too lazy to post off an arrest warrant.

On such trifles, thought Max, are lives decided. He tore off the man's address, just in case Haussmann had a sudden fit of hard work.

He closed the file and opened another. That had just an old apple core in it. Then he opened a third. This contained a relatively well-ordered series of thick divider files. These seemed to be about some expedition to India, where the *Ahnenerbe* had tried to contact ancient beings. There was no mention of von Knobelsdorff or a black sun in that, though.

Max had an idea. The most frightened he had seen Haussmann was coming into contact with von Knobelsdorff. What was the expression? You keep your friends close and your enemies closer. He went to the desk. There was the drawer he'd seen when he first arrived, stuffed with stationery and chewed pencils. To the left side was a smaller series of drawers. He started at the bottom, but found only a notebook. It appeared to be some poetry Haussmann had been trying to write to his wife.

> *Oh Little Flower, I love you so*
> *I just wanted you to know*
> *That every day when I see you*
> *I don't feel low and I don't feel blue*
> *You are my sunshine, my buttercup*
> *When I am down you pick me up.*

Max closed the book and put it back, feeling faintly ill. The next drawer up there was nothing, nor the one after that, but in the top drawer, there it was. A neat, ivory white file marked with that many-legged swastika symbol of the black sun. Max wanted to steal it, but something like that had to be missed, didn't it?

He opened the file and read.

Project Forefather. Contact with extra-terrestrial beings.

Max put his hand on his head. He was past laughter but, had that still been in him, he would have hooted. He wished Arno had been there to read this rubbish.

Project leader: Manfred von Knobelsdorff, Knight of the Black Sun.

And all-round arsehole, thought Max. He read on.

Aims: To contact Nordic forefathers.
Details of ceremony:
The twelve chosen of the Black Sun assemble in the *Over Group Leader Room* having undergone the specified period of fasting contained in Document 1002a. No food must be taken for three days nor liquids for 24 hours prior to the ceremony. Ritual A3 is performed, the cleansing of the chamber. The communicant is brought in. It is essential that he is of pure Nordic blood. Alpine or mixed characteristics are not acceptable. Ritual E2 is performed, the welcoming of the host. To reach the correct level of sensitivity it is recommended that chanting continue for at least 12 hours. The communicant must also reach the required level of receptiveness so it is desirable that he should be bound and immobilised during this period. Experiments will need to confirm if it is better to maintain a hood on the communicant or to allow him to see what is occurring. He cannot be gagged.

If any vestige of levity remained in Max's soul, then it left as he read that last sentence. Someone had been bound. Someone had been hooded. Gags were mentioned. Why? He read on.

It may become difficult for the Knights of the Black Sun to estimate time correctly. It is recommended that they arrange to have a gong struck outside the chamber when the necessary period has elapsed. The chief celebrant may decide that the chanting needs to continue longer. If this is so, he will sound the continuation bell. When the necessary sensitivities have been attained, the communicant will be led to the block and the knight who holds the office of the Opener of the Way will prepare the silver axe. In previous ceremonies the stiffness caused by so long sitting has caused the knight difficulty in achieving a clean severance. For this reason, future experiments may require this office to be undertaken by someone from outside the immediate ceremony. No non-knight who has seen the knight's ceremony can live so it may be best to use a prisoner for this role. Eliminating another member of the SS in addition to the communicant may give fuel to gossip. However, it is undesirable to have a prisoner kill an SS man. This topic will need further discussion and it may be that we are stuck with an untidy kill.

Max gulped. These murdering bastards had started on their own kind now, had they? He found that mildly shocking, though it pleased him. The fact that the SS were severing heads, which once would have been such a shock, didn't seem like a surprise any more. In fact, he was surprised they had allowed such a clean death.

The head should be severed at one blow if possible and mounted on an oak branch that is sprouting mistletoe (significance see addendum). Ceremony 2f is now initiated and the chanting continues until the head speaks or the knights' endurance fails. The knights should not move from their positions, nor cease their chanting for any reason.

Commentary: So far effects have been promising but limited. Practical limit of the ceremony is three days, at which point most celebrants require water.

'Promising but limited?' Max thought. That was SS bureaucratic code for 'complete and utter failure'. So von Knobelsdorff and the senior SS who Himmler had decided were knights sat there for three days without so much as a drink or a toilet break, stewing in their own stink, waiting to see if some fairy story they had dreamed up for themselves came true. And how many of their own pals had they killed doing it?

But if it had failed, what had von Knobelsdorff meant when he said he had seen the Gods? Hallucinations produced by starvation and discomfort?

He flicked on to the back of the report.

Successes and directions for future exploration.

SS Knight M. von Knobelsdorff has reported a vision of a forefather, pointing west with a staff. The forefather was bearded and one-eyed and corresponding to the ancient descriptions of the God Woden, Odin or Othin, the furious. SS Knight Friedman confirmed the vision and Knights Hoch and von Schwab added that ...

So that was it. The whole of the Nazi war effort on the occult, summed up by twelve idiots starving themselves for days without using the loo. No wonder von Knobelsdorff had been keen to see him fail.

'What are you doing?'

Max nearly dropped the file.

He looked up to see a prisoner in the green triangle of a common criminal prisoner looking at him. The man also bore an armband bearing, in Gothic writing, *Kapo*. He was a trustee.

'I could ask you the same,' said Max.

'I saw you through the window. You're not SS. This is Professor Haussmann's office, you should not be in here. What's that file you're reading from his desk?'

'Well, what the fuck is it to you?'

The prisoner smirked. 'Twenty-five cigarettes and a couple of tins of beef, maybe. Can you do better?'

Max rolled his eyes. 'I . . .'

The door opened again.

'What's going on?'

Max didn't think. He didn't even consider what he was saying. It just came out of his mouth.

'I just caught this bastard in here,' he said.

The prisoner's eyes widened. He seemed to be fighting to get his words out. He never managed it. Haussmann drew his pistol and blasted three shots into the man where he stood. The retort of the gun nearly shattered Max's eardrums. Just a few weeks before, the sight of a man summarily executed in front of him would have made him faint. Now? Nothing. The body hit the carpet. There was blood. A man was dead. The scene had no more meaning than that to the doctor, no resonance outside the physical facts of what had happened. Max's calm shocked him slightly. So did the nature of what remained of his outrage.

'He was a *Kapo*,' said Max. It seemed strange the man had been confident enough to threaten him. Hadn't he realised that might be the response?

'I've had a bad day,' said Haussmann. 'Haas in the camp owes me one anyway. Would you like a drink? I have some whisky in here, probably what he was after.'

'Yes, I would. Lovely stuff.'

Haussmann opened the fourth filing cabinet with a key that was under a plant pot on top of it.

'Some cabinets get extra security. No losing the key for this one!' He tapped his nose in that conspiratorial way of his.

Haussmann took out the whisky and poured Max a glass.

Max put the Black Sun file face down on a chair next to him. He wanted desperately to get it back into the desk, but that was out of the question. If he left it out, even someone of Haussmann's sloppiness was going to notice it had moved. He had to steal it; he had no choice. Haussmann prodded the corpse with his foot.

'How far away was I, do you think, when I shot him?'

'Three metres.' Max gave Haussmann an extra two and a half for flattery.

Haussmann nodded and turned down the corners of his mouth in appreciation of his work. With effort, he moved the corpse over with his foot. The holes at the man's back had been ragged but on his chest there were just three points of red, like some badge.

'Three shots. Not a bad grouping from there. Hmm. I'm pleased with that.' He raised his glass. 'To the unerring accuracy of the Luger P08. I don't like these new Walthers, do you?'

'If it ain't broke don't fix it.' Max felt far away, as if he was controlling himself from outside, wearing his limbs like an ill-fitting costume.

'Exactly.'

Max knocked back his whisky, checked his watch, said, 'Is that the time? I really must be off.' He tucked the file under his arm.

'How are things?' Haussmann asked.

'Splendid. I think I can promise you some spectacular results very soon.'

'Good-o, I had a feeling you'd say that. Psychic research – I had a feeling. Do you see the joke?'

'Yes, you are a natural comedian.'

Haussmann smiled and Max left him in his office, telephoning the cleaners to take the corpse away.

12 Fugitive

'Professor Harbard is in England?'

'Yes,' said Balby, 'he's offered his services to us. He'll be here this evening.'

'And you didn't see fit to tell me before?' said Craw.

'No, I wasn't sure he was going to be available. Two heads are better than one, surely.'

Craw stared far off through the dying light. A feeling he hadn't felt for a century or more was coming over him. He was hot, prickly, and his clothes seemed more like things that had been tied to him than things that he wore. It was the itch a snake must feel as it sheds its skin – a sensation of becoming, and of leaving behind. He needed to be human, felt it like a thirsty man needs a drink, but he sensed he would reach a tipping point and the need would go the other way. He would start to feel starved of his beast state. Large parts of his mind were ceasing to function, or rather ceasing to see the point in operating, and other parts were waking. Soon they would spring up with the urgency of someone who has overslept his alarm.

He returned to reason, forcing his mind to it like someone trying to remember where he put his keys, hoping that suddenly he would stumble into clarity. He touched his tie, then the wolf ring, then took out a comb and sleeked back his hair. He came to himself. The sensation wasn't unlike recovering the senses having stood up too quickly. His cover had been blown, he knew, with all that implied. Craw had respected Harbard but knew that he was showy in his knowledge. If he had discovered something as remarkable as Craw's existence, then could he resist passing it on – putting it in some ghastly paper, perhaps – if he got proof enough? It was possible this was some sort of coincidence, but doubted it. Harbard had to know. What was it the Skalds had said? 'All know what is known to three.' Harbard was capable of exposing him to the world.

Why did Craw not wish to be known as an immortal? He was, he knew, at the beginning of the age of fame, where simply being known could attract wealth and power. It might have put him in a position to do tremendous good.

Craw was not interested in doing good, nor was he interested in doing bad. All he wanted was a life unbothered, to quiet the buzz of over a thousand years of existence and to lose himself in the anonymous crowd. His people had valued fame above all else, but Craw had come to see it as worthless.

To be known would to be pursued, tested, questioned and examined and, eventually, to be confronted with his many crimes. The burden on his mind would be too great, and under its weight would come the fall and the pain of his wolf existence. And then there was the question of what other forces the knowledge of his existence might attract. He knew it was likely that others like him had survived, in whatever manner, and he had no desire at all to meet them. But beyond this was the feeling he had when he imagined exposure, like that when you awake to the memory of a terrible embarrassment the night before, but magnified a thousand times. No good would come of it, he knew, in a way that was beyond thought and seemed to resonate in the bones. Fame simply wasn't the done thing.

Craw lit another cigarette.

'Well, do give Professor Harbard my hotel address and ask him to meet me there at his earliest convenience,' he said, controlling the panic he was feeling.

'I didn't mean to slight your professional knowledge,' said Balby.

Craw was light again, his mask back on.

'Oh, Inspector, I've been trying to tell you. My professional knowledge is slight. Shall we return to town?'

So this is it, he thought – time to move on, to withdraw and start again. Would it bring him closer to Adisla? He didn't know. It was time to go, to be reborn, in a way. He would take some money, he would take a change of clothes, but everything else would remain. He could have no connection with his previous life at all. Death would not come to him, so he had to impose the effect of death on himself – an utter and total break with the person he had been. Endamon Craw was over. Who would he be next?

They went back towards Stratford, Balby saying something about plans, about meetings, and how the case would progress. Craw couldn't focus. In the car, the taste of blood came back to him. He felt a deep hunger. The storm had come in and rain turned the windows to blurs. The inadequate windscreen wiper beat out its rhythm, as if the car was a beast with a heartbeat. Craw put his face to the cool window, fixing his gaze at right angles to it, the world distorting. Balby disappeared beside him, the driver no longer existed in front of him. That is, the recognition that they were people, personalities, individuals, faded. The ways in which he differentiated them from the trees and the buildings were changing. The fact of their consciousness did not matter to him; it did not seem important or a quality worth noting, any more than the way one bush rattles in the wind differently from another. Only his hunger was important. He began to see the policemen as patterns of movement, not as people, but to understand them totally and in an instant. His mind consumed them and categorised them in one broad group: prey.

He shuddered. Did it always happen so quickly? He could not quite recall. Maybe, maybe not.

'Stop the car!'

'What.'

'Stop the fucking car!'

The driver pulled up. 'Are you all right?'

'The demon drink!' said Balby.

To him it looked as if Craw really was possessed by a devil. He was sweating, he had disordered his hair, and there were actually marks on the leather of the seat where the professor had gripped it. His face, though, was what really disturbed the policeman; it was a mixture of deep pain and an almost childish rage.

Craw scrabbled at the door, trying to get out, but he couldn't find the handle, or rather couldn't understand the handle, make it do what it was designed to do.

'Let me out, let me out!'

The driver exchanged looks with the Inspector and Balby gestured for him to open the door.

'In this weather?' said the driver.

'Just do it,' said Balby.

The driver came round to Craw's side and opened it. The professor burst from the car and went running into the woods.

'Do you suppose he's seen a pub?' said the driver, regaining his seat. 'And can we follow him?'

'It's not funny.'

Balby got out of the car but could not see Craw, nor which way he had gone.

Craw had made the woods, away from the company of humans. He needed to lie down, to sleep and to cool his bubbling brain. He drove his head into the soft soil and allowed the rain to soak him. The storm was a sharp one and he was soon wet through, the depression in which he was lying turning into a small pond. It was intensely uncomfortable, which is what he intended. He needed to wake the human inside himself. Craw sat upright in this mire, forcing his mind back to the everyday. He tried to recall chess moves, scales on the violin, his fascination the first time he had seen a clock. By reflex and practice he found his way back to himself. He took out his hip flask and unscrewed the top, allowing the aroma of the single malt to fill him. Then he took out a bottle with a dropper top and unscrewed that. Decades before, he'd been knocked unconscious in a bar by a 'Mickey Finn', a drink spiked with chloral hydrate. When he'd eventually killed his assailants he'd taken the bottle and had always carried some with him since. Mixed with alcohol it was the quickest way he knew to render himself unconscious and buy some time if the worst came to the worst.

Carefully, and with shaking hands, he applied three drops to his whisky. And then he drank it down. The world lost its sharpness, the storm receded, and Craw was flying back in his mind, to a time over a thousand years before, holding hands with a girl with bone-blonde hair, looking out over a view across a mountainside with a fjord sparkling in the sun below him.

He heard his own voice, but young, saying, 'What will they say of me when I am dead, Adisla? Will they write songs of my battles?'

'No, Vali, they won't. How many enemies have you killed?'

'Well, they don't stand still, they just run off.'

'They stood still for your father.'

'They tried to run. He was quicker than I am.'

'I'm only teasing. You do your part but they won't sing songs about you.'

It was a girl's voice, silent now for a millennium or more, speaking at his ear.

'Then what will they say of me?'

'They will say that you loved and were loved.'

'Is that enough?'

'It would do for me.'

And then it was quiet. The rain fell and Craw was no longer in the wood. He was himself again, ascending a perilous mountain path. Beside him was a strange, white-haired man who bore in his hand a cruel curved sword that he knew had cut him before and could cut him again.

13 Mrs Voller Visits a Medium

It was autumn and Gertie had noticed a change in Max. It wasn't that her husband was short with her, or that he no longer told her he loved her, or anything tangible, but just a feeling between them.

And then the dreams returned. It was as if her first dream was an addictive drug that had satisfied her inner mind for a while, but now it required more and more to calm her.

Time and again she found herself on a shore of glistening black sand next to a flat metal sea. As she walked along the coal-dark dunes she came to a large hall that seemed to be covered in writhing black snakes that snapped and hissed at her. Something, she knew, was behind the doors of that hall, something of vast importance, but she could neither approach it nor see inside. Then the doors opened and, just before she could see what was inside, she woke up. The experience was very unsettling for her. She was afraid it was the strain of life at the castle and the change in her husband that was causing such a horrid nightmare.

She'd explained a little of her concerns about Max to one of her new friends at the castle, Mrs Reiter, a senior administrator's wife. She left out the dreams, concerned that Mrs Reiter would think her mad.

'It's as if the feeling of the air between us has changed, I know that sounds silly, but it has.'

'He takes mistresses?'

'No!'

'That is his duty.'

'He's not in the SS, he's still a member of the regular medical corps.'

'Oh,' said Mrs Reiter, in a tone of slight social disappointment.

'He was appointed by the Reich Leader Himmler himself,' said Gertie, eager to make a good impression.

'Oh,' said Mrs Reiter. She was a woman who could work an 'oh'. Now she used it with a tone of respect, combined with intrigue.

The women could not discuss Dr Voller's work, though Mrs Reiter dearly wished they could. She wouldn't have got very much from Gertie had she asked her directly. Gertie knew her husband was researching the hidden powers of the mind and she knew that he was under a great deal of pressure, but he had spared her the details of the tortures he was to perform. Gertie's sensitive nature would not have been able to comprehend what her husband was being asked to do. He could scarcely comprehend it himself.

'I think he is afraid the Reich Leader won't be pleased with his work,' said Gertie.

'Oh,' said Mrs Reiter, now lending the vowel a sympathetic note, in a bid to elicit more information.

There were rumours among the administrative staff of the castle about what went on in the lab, but no one exactly knew. Some said he was supporting the efforts of the *Schwarze Sonne*, some that he was in competition with them, and others that he was training a crocodile to weigh the souls of criminals in order to more quickly determine guilt or innocence.

The senior administrator's wife had, however, an idea of how she was going to find out.

'Gertie,' she said, 'I have become good friends with one of the Hindu ladies. She's an absolute marvel. She cured my headaches, and you know how I suffer with those.'

'Yes,' said Gertie. Boy, did she know how Mrs Reiter suffered with her headaches. She'd had one herself by the time the woman had finished going on about them.

'Well, she also reads fortunes. Why don't you let her see

what the future holds for you? She's a fantastic listener and nothing goes further than the four walls.'

Gertie was a little afraid of fortune-tellers, but the promise of a neutral person to whom she could pour out her heart was too tempting.

So, two days later, Gertie found herself sitting in a small chamber at the top of the north tower. The room smelled unpleasantly of a thick incense and the walls were hung with tapestries depicting monstrous creatures – men with elephants' heads, a woman dancing with a severed head and wearing a necklace of skulls. On one wall lay a shrine arranged around the symbol of a large gold swastika and a photograph of the Führer. It was accompanied, though, by bizarre icons – a many-armed woman with a snake's body, a man with four heads, fat blue women, and terrifying pale men thrusting spears into writhing enemies.

Bright powders were sprinkled around the shrine and the walls were smeared with the same strange pigments. The sensation was of overwhelming colour and Gertie was not sure she liked it at all.

Opposite her was Devya Shankara, otherwise known as Miss Heidi Fischer. Miss Fischer had been drawn to eastern philosophy from an early age and, having the means to do so, had travelled to Tibet to study under the Himalayan masters. In 1938, visiting Nazi mystics had found her and persuaded her to come to Wewelsburg as a defender of the Aryan race. Her belief that the Führer was an avatar – an incarnation of the god Vishnu, who holds back the tides of chaos – was very attractive to the party leadership, and they had asked her to produce several leaflets and books on the subject.

However, that was the extent of her employment. Political manoeuvrings at the castle had left her in a position where they would neither find a use for her nor let her go. The day of Gertie's visit had been particularly bad. The mystic had meditated, practised her yoga, and read, but the overwhelming memory of her activity was looking through the tiny slot window of her room and wishing the rain would clear so she could go for a walk in the countryside. Tall, blonde and beautiful, magnificent in her silks, her turban, her earrings and nose stud, Devya only craved an audience for her knowledge.

Accordingly, she decided the time had come to make a name for herself. She already made a little spending money reading fortunes for the women of the castle, but that night she was planning something special. Mrs Reiter had assured her that her visitor's husband was practically Himmler's right-hand man, so Devya thought that she should go the extra mile in trying to impress her. As an Ayurvedic vegetarian, she had been concerned when castle gossip had revealed that Dr Voller was keeping a crocodile in his tiny lab but she was prepared to overlook her fears for the present. Dr Voller had a lab. No one else at the castle did. That made him an important man. The friendship and respect of his wife would enable her to advance the interests of both the crocodile and herself.

Each of us, Devya believed, has attendant spirits around us and within us. In this she was not too far from the psychoanalysts, with their motive and suppressing forces of the personality, only she tended to give them different names.

Others might have believed that the personality is formed of choices made and influences received at an early age, and that the choices we don't make, the paths down which we do not go, lie dormant in our brains, like undeveloped photographic negatives. These can come to consciousness in certain individuals, giving us the phenomena of split personality or possession. Still others might believe in shared symbols of identity that can be dug from the subconscious, and almost have a life of their own in the mind or minds. And then there is always the idea of gods, angels and demons. Are all these metaphors for the same thing? Devya wasn't sure, but she knew that she needed to impress this woman.

'Sit down, my dear,' said Devya. She normally sat on the floor but had discovered that the ladies of the castle preferred a more formal approach, and so had bought a low table with padded benches either side.

Gertie sat. Mrs Reiter sat beside her, somewhat uncomfortable in her fashionable skirt. She held Gertie's hand, feeling her nervousness in her tight grip.

'Don't worry, dear, it's only a bit of fun,' said Mrs Reiter.

Devya restrained herself from explaining the seriousness of the matter to the woman. The horoscope of the Vedas was, to her, a sacred rite, not something to amuse bored wives on a night away from the stove.

'I have all my details,' said Gertie, 'I was born on—'

Devya put up her hand. 'They won't be necessary tonight, Health Leader Voller's wife deserves something special.'

Gertie looked slightly panicked and Mrs Reiter squeezed her hand in comfort.

'I just want to know my fortune,' said Gertie.

'And you shall,' said Devya, 'but I am not going to be the one to tell it.' She left a pause for theatrical effect.

'Who will?' said Gertie.

'You will. I sense you have a psychic power in you.'

In this, Devya was only a little different from the knowing fakes of the astrological world, who always tell people that. She often told people such lies, based on a quiver of the lip or a sincere look in the eye which she took for evidence of extraordinary insight.

'Do you ever think of someone and then a letter arrives from them?'

'Yes, yes I do,' said Gertie, shifting on the low bench.

Devya nodded. 'And?'

'And I can feel the air between two people, almost like it's a colour or a note of music or a taste, or all three of those things together. And at night, since I've been in this castle, I have the most terrible dreams. I see snakes writhing around the place and the bones of snakes all knitted together to make a huge hall, and I know something terrible is going to happen very soon and I run down a corridor in this castle, not one

I've ever seen but one that I know is here, and I pull back this huge door because I know the terrible thing is behind it and just as I can see what it is I wake up.'

The memory of the dream brought tears to her eyes.

Devya raised her eyebrows. She was more used to women saying, 'I had a feeling my husband was coming home early and then he did.' Mrs Reiter let go of Gertie's hand.

'Yes,' said Devya. 'Well, I hope we will be able to find out a little more of what all that is about and you will be able to rest a little easier.'

'I hope so,' said Gertie.

'We are going to meditate. Do you know what that means?' said Devya.

Both her visitors shook their heads.

'It is simply a way of calming the thoughts and attuning ourselves to the vibrations of the cosmos. We talk of the practice of *jnana*. Do you know what that means?'

Again the women did not.

'It's self-knowledge. It will enable you to see what is real and what is temporary in your life. We say that it puts you at one with the universe.'

'What does that mean?' said Gertie.

This question rather stumped Devya, who had never been asked it before.

'It will harmonise you, my dear.'

This sounded good to Gertie, who thought she could have done with a bit of harmonising.

'When we are relaxed I shall call forth my *Gandharva*.'

'We don't know what that is either, before you ask,' said Mrs Reiter.

'It is a spirit of a sort, very benign and pleasant. Somewhat sexy.'

She said the 'somewhat sexy' in a self-conscious cod-Indian accent, hoping to impart a little exoticism to the two women. She had expected a polite laugh from the women but only got one from Mrs Reiter.

'Have you any questions before we begin?'

'Will my husband be successful in his experiments?' said Gertie.

Mrs Reiter looked at her in a *well, well* sort of way. So there was some doubt as to their outcome. She had no idea that experiments could fail and thought that, if they could, then they couldn't be very good ones.

'It will be revealed,' said Devya, 'although I am sure that a doctor of your husband's standing could not help but be a success. He strikes me as one of those men to whom everything is easy.'

Gertie relaxed a little when she heard this. That was the sort of thing she'd gone to a fortune-teller to hear, not this silly stuff about spirits.

Devya laid out two padded mats and invited the women to lie down upon them. They did as instructed, both women carefully inspecting the mats for dust before they did so. Gertie looked up to the ceiling where another swastika was drawn in pencil in an arty, eastern-looking way.

'You are looking up at the holy symbol of the sun,' said Devya, 'life-giver of the universe. Let that be the symbol, too, of your true self, your soul. Close your eyes if you wish but concentrate upon your breathing, your inner self. Think only of the breathing. Practise the technique of *Neti Neti* – that is, if a thought that is not the true soul comes to your mind simply say "*Neti, Neti*" or, in your language, "Not this, not this", and dismiss it. Concentrate on the breathing. Bring every thought back to the breath.'

Devya continued to intone these words of calm for a long time; how long, Gertie could not tell. The incense filled up her mind. The woman's voice seemed curiously in accord with it, as if the scent was a vibration and the voice a colour and the pigment on the walls was a sound. No one sense seemed distinct from any other.

'To facilitate the meditation process,' said Devya, who was quite determined to get some results to come to the attention of Himmler, 'I am going to anoint your lips with a special preparation of the lotus flower.'

She took out a small clay pot, within which was a slimy ichorous blue substance. She undid the stopper and dipped in a brush, intoning softly to herself as she did.

'Aum, Aum, Aum, Aum,' she said; the word was as strange as the many-headed icons and the pink and yellow powders to Gertie and Mrs Reiter. Devya spread the substance over the women's lips. Someone interrupting the proceedings would have thought they were taking part in a beauty treatment.

The lotus preparation was remarkable, in that the essence of the crushed blue lotus was just about the only hallucinogenic substance available throughout Asia that it didn't contain. The basis was cannabis and two or three nightshade varieties, along with a pot-pourri of other herbs, but the real horseshoe in the glove was a generous sprinkling of fly agaric mushroom and the merest smidgen of cobra venom. Gertie, who occasionally allowed herself to be persuaded to a dry sherry at Christmas, was in for something of a shock.

Already, under Devya's hypnotic voice, she was floating down and down in her consciousness, to a place she hadn't even been in her dreams. Had she been attached to the EEG machine her husband had ordered, it would have shown that her brain waves were descending from the fast vibrating beta level, to alpha, to the creative level of delta – where she had a sudden vision of how she would like the curtains in her room – to theta, and the slow cycles of deep sleep. There, the needle would have fallen to a zone for which there is no name, other than death. Though not quite death.

Dr Voller had thought he was at the edge of science when he'd ordered his machine. His idea of where the edge of science was might have been radically different had he actually been at that edge, but that is by the by. However, the brain levels were treated as a discovery when Professor Berger published his first EEG results. They were not.

An examination of the Hindu Aum symbol, that weird curly

three with its strange bobbing hat next to it, shows that this knowledge vastly predated the invention of the EEG machine. The symbol is made up of three curves and a dot. The big lower curve represents the waking state. The upper curve represents sleep and the unconscious, and the smaller lower curve represents the area between them – that of dreams. It attempts to symbolise how these are indivisible, and play into each other from sleep to dreams to creativity to wakefulness.

The Hindu metaphor fits roughly over that of the EEG scientists, but it contains an extra level which cannot be detected by any machine. This is symbolised by the dot separated from the main body of the symbol by a curve like a crescent.

The crescent represents the illusion of reality, and the dot symbolises the state of absolute consciousness. Devya would call this *Turiya*. The symbol shows how this level, sometimes called the sun of the soul, illuminates the others but is kept separate from them by the illusion of reality.

The Aum glyph, however, works at a much deeper level than the scientific description. It is more than the sum of its parts. It reflects the belief that the universe, and all in it, is the expression of a vibration of that one sound, Aum, reverberating in an infinity of subtle shades. And who's to say that, as Gertie's brain activity fell, it wasn't to this universal note that it descended?

Gertie, who could sense the colour of the air between people, who could hear personalities like musical notes, heard Devya's voice falling upon her soul like a silver rain. Then the potion hit her and something fell away. The Hindu occultists would call it *Maya*, the curve in front of the dot that tells us that the physical world we see is the only reality. The doctors would call it sanity.

It was jettisoned from her like ballast from a balloon. She hummed with the universe, was simply a note in a symphony, a molecule among the surging surfs of the infinite. Then, in a blink, she was herself again.

'Not this, not this,' she said.

'Just concentrate on the breathing,' said Devya, pleased to see Gertie was following her instructions.

'Not this! Not this!' said Gertie, with more animation than Devya had expected. She almost leapt off the floor. Mrs Reiter just lay still and rigid.

Gertie was standing in a grey half-light on a blackened shore. The sea was a field of crumpled lead and the beach a mound of glistening coal. Above her loomed a hall, of sorts, the one she'd seen in her dreams, but much clearer. What she'd taken for snakes writhing around it could now be seen to be pipes. The bones of snakes and the scales that had covered the roof were only tiles and coping. It was clearly a factory of some sort, because it had a large chimney and was belching smoke. The normality of the scene comforted her.

An old man was standing next to her, tall with a white beard, illuminated by a dirty grey sun. Perhaps this was the spirit of which Devya had spoken. In his hands he held a pebble, marked with an inscription. She took the pebble and looked at it. It was small and triangular, etched with a horrible design – the jaws of a great wolf clasped around a severed hand. She gave it back to the man and began to sing to herself.

> *A hall I saw, far from the sun,*
> *On the corpse shore it stands, and the doors face north,*
> *Venom drops through the smoke-vent down,*
> *For around the walls do serpents wind.*
>
> *I saw there wading through rivers wild*
> *Treacherous men and murderers too,*
> *And workers of ill with the wives of men;*
> *There the snake sucked the blood of the slain,*
> *And the wolf tore men; would you know yet more?*

'I would know more,' she said. Then the strangeness of that remark struck her. How could she ask herself for more information? The man took a pace backwards. He appeared surprised that she had spoken to him.

'She can see us,' he said.

'She can see everything,' said a voice from somewhere. The voice was wrong. She couldn't see everything. She couldn't see where it was coming from, for a start.

Gertie trembled and she spoke, and she did not know the meaning of the words she spoke.

'You need to pay, Fenrisulfr, wergild for all your murders.'

'You are the delight of evil women everywhere,' the voice replied.

The man with the stone in his hands just stood looking amazed, almost trance-stricken in that odd metalled light. Something was happening to his face too. It was peeling away, revealing the livid pink flesh beneath.

'Murderer,' said Gertie, 'kinslayer. You killed your brother who I loved, Fenrisulfr. I will have my gold!'

The man with the stone continued to gaze into it, his face a mask of blood.

'This,' he said. 'This or something like it can control the wolf. Such was revealed at Gévaudan.'

Gévaudan. That name. She recognised it. From where?

'You are the seer,' said the voice, which had descended to a low growl, 'you are the seer whose greatest power is her blindness. Your blindness stretches out over your country like a fog, sorceress. See, seer.'

And the hall burst open its doors and from within a raging tide of corpses swept down the hill, the dead running and howling and falling and clawing their way towards her in a surge: children, men, women, the old, but all tattered and grey and putrefying. At the head of this wasted, piss-stained, shit-encrusted, rotting army was something more terrible still. A great wolf, its maw the size of a man, came sputtering and snuffling and grizzling and growling at her.

'I will have my gold,' said Gertie. But the wolf was upon her.

14 Destiny in Tea Leaves

Craw awoke, human. His clothes were soaked and muddy and his head ached comfortingly. It wasn't the ache of his wolf nature trying to break free but just a cosy, familiar hangover caused by drinking half a bottle of whisky at a gulp. He guessed Balby must have tried to find him but, in the rain-soaked woods, given him up as a stupid drunk.

He was thirsty. The storm had passed, but the woods were wet and he was lying in a large puddle. It occurred to him for a second to drink from it, but he didn't. While he was a man, he would drink like a man.

He shivered and looked around. He was still in the same clothes that he'd been in in the police car, in the same place in the woods where he had fallen asleep. There had been no transformation, he was sure. When that happened he would wake years later, under unrecognisable horizons, changed and strange to himself. The transformation was still coming, but the bursting feeling he had experienced in the car was gone.

He stood up, his suit wet and heavy. He had only one aim now – to disappear. He would head back to his hotel, take his money and his house keys, send word to Jacques to put his affairs in order and where to store the Gaddi, and then he would be gone. His time in the Midlands was over, his pursuit of his wife suspended for another lifetime. What would be the point of finding her if the transformation took him?

It was early morning and, though he had no idea which way he needed to go, he decided on downhill. It was a lucky guess and in seconds he was at a road. The clothes were almost painful to wear, the sodden tweed rough against his skin.

Even on the road, he had no idea where to go. He took a

right. It seemed an unlucky guess. He walked a mile, and then another, and then a third, without seeing a soul. Then, at the bend of a road, he saw a farmhouse. The sun was up, it was a glorious morning, and the wet slates of the building's roof seemed to have their own halo of steam as he approached.

Craw needed help – a lift into town so he could change his clothes, pick up his money, and be gone. However, if you've formed your outlook on life during the heroic age, if you've been a king in such an age, then asking for help from a peasant, as he still viewed the people who worked the farm, doesn't come easy.

He descended to the farmhouse and knocked at the door. It was answered by one of that species of English women who resemble a pinafored bulldog. At first Craw almost thought she was wearing some sort of warpaint until he realised, with a suppressed laugh, that she was covered in flour.

'Yes?' she said.

Craw put on his most correct English. 'I wonder if you can help me, I find myself in a spot of bother and was rather wondering if there would be anyone here who could offer me a lift to Stratford. I can pay.'

'Yow what?' said the woman.

Craw recognised her vowels as from the Black Country of the English Midlands, a voice that seemed to have been created by heavy industry, it being incomprehensible that something so thick should have grown naturally. The vowels had been steam-hammered, the consonants electroplated. He could hardly understand a word she said.

'My what?'

'Ar yow half cut?' she said.

'I am not cut, just wet.'

'Half cut, kaylied, drunk, yow soft 'apputh. Caan' yow un-nerstan English?'

'I understand standard English but I have difficulty with some of the regional dialects. Stratford. I will pay. I have money. You will take me?'

It was meant to be a question but sounded more like an order. He had never been particularly good with the lower ranks and really did not know how to ask for things. For ten centuries he had only known how to command.

The woman's eyes widened and Craw noticed her grip on her rolling pin became tighter.

'Ooh my God!' she said. 'Ahh, yes, we'll take yow, right enough. Come in.'

Craw did so. The kitchen was warm and had the comforting smell of baking. He was glad to get inside in his wet clothes. The woman told him to sit down and then called up the stairs.

'Johnny, ge'down here now!'

There was a clumping and a bumping and a thickset boy of around seven came down the stairs. The woman whispered to him and sent him away.

'He's gone down the field to get my husband,' she said, slowly, deliberately and loudly, as if to an idiot. 'He will be back with the lorry in a minute.'

'Thank you,' said Craw.

'Do you drink tea?' she said, very deliberately.

'No, I—'

'Coffee, I expect.'

'No, tea. I prefer tea.'

'Have a cup then. Don't worry, I got plenty swapping some sausages last week.' Again she spoke very slowly, enunciating her words. Then she said in an underbreath, 'I expect you like sausages.'

'You are kind,' said Craw, wondering if he was overdoing the formal politeness. 'And I shall see to it that you are rewarded.'

'I don't want your sort of reward,' she said, gripping the rolling pin again.

Craw drifted off rather, relaxing into his hangover and breathing in the smell of the baking bread. The woman left her pastry half-rolled and sat between him and the door, saying nothing but watching him carefully, hand on the rolling pin.

'*Sie haben eine rauhe Nacht gehabt?*' said a voice.

'*Ich erinnere mich nicht viel von an ihm,*' said Craw.

'He is a Jerry!'

Craw came to his senses. There were three soldiers in front of him. One had a Thompson sub-machine gun aimed at his head. Behind them stood an officer. All wore red caps. Military police.

'I clocked him for one straight away!' said the woman. 'Look at the state of him, he must have parachuted in last night. Give me that tea back, yow squarehead bugga, I only give it you so yow wouldn't run away.'

Craw felt his heart sink. Did this woman really think to bind him with tea? Well, she sort of had, hadn't she? He had to give her that. A fat farmer and the boy came into the room, looking at him as if he were something in a freak show.

'I am an English academic helping the police with their enquiries,' he said.

'Well, you got the second half of that right, you dirty German bastard,' said the man with the sub-machine gun.

'That will be enough, Davies, there are ladies and children present,' said the officer. 'We're here to hand this man over to the correct authorities. There's no need to abuse him. That way it will come as more of a surprise when they shoot the blighter. On your feet, Fritz.'

Craw looked to the heavens. 'Call Inspector Balby at Little Park Street Police Station. He will identify me.'

'Never heard of him, you're going straight over to Military Intelligence,' said the officer. Of course they hadn't heard of Balby. They were military police, not civilian.

'Call the Home Office. I am Professor Craw.'

'MI can do all that. You're theirs now.'

'On your feet!' said a soldier.

Craw stood. Things could not be going worse. He had hoped never to see Balby again. Now he needed to contact him if he was to go free. Either that, or he had to run from the men with the guns. It had been so long since he had been in a battle that he was no longer sure if the bullets would hurt him. He had been injured by weapons before when in his human form, he was sure. How badly, he could not recall. Not so badly, maybe; he was here, wasn't he? But would the stress of being shot hurry along his transformation? It wasn't a risk he was prepared to take.

Should he run for it? While he was deciding they had manacled him. No, best go along with it, call the War Office rather than Balby, and take it from there. Running off would mean they'd search for him as a spy, diverting valuable resources from the war effort.

He was loaded into the back of a truck and, an hour later, was thrown into a cell on a military camp.

'Permission to kick the living shit out of this bastard, sir!' said a soldier.

'Permission denied, Private, that's Military Intelligence's job.'

'Very good, sir. How do I apply to join Military Intelligence?'

'Get another brain, Private.'

'Very good, sir!'

Six hours later, no food, no water, his clothes still damp on his skin, there was a scrabbling of locks. It was the military police again.

'You've got a visitor, Fritz,' said the private.

Craw was frogmarched over to some stores and taken inside. There, among piles of blankets and tins of bully beef, a table had been set up with an ashtray and a light on it. He had seen enough detective films to recognise it as an improvised interrogation room.

'I'll be outside. Escape and it'll be my great fucking pleasure to blow your fucking bollocks off,' said the private, tapping his .303. Craw nodded. He could see the man spoke from the heart.

Alone in the interview room, he sat up in his chair. It was important to him to show no fear, no discomfort – even to himself. He heard a voice.

'Very good, Private. I'll take it from here. For God's sake get him a cup of something warm and wet.'

'Piss?' said the private's voice.

'Tea. Strong, no sugar, is the way he likes it. With milk.' Craw felt dizzy. He knew the voice. He knew the voice.

'Who has tea without milk?' said the private, as if it was some unbelievable perversion. 'Jerries, I suppose. Makes you realise what we're fighting for.'

'This man isn't a German spy, I can vouch for that.'

Craw felt a dread rising up in him. It was as if the past was alive and speaking to him.

The door opened slightly, and through it he heard:

> As one who long hath fled with panting breath
> Before his foe, bleeding and near to fall,
> I turn and set my back against the wall,
> And look thee in the face, triumphant Death.

'Crawford, Crawford, how you loved your Longfellow! And how wrong you were to do so. Crawford, Crawford, it's so good to see you.'

Those booming, rather sweet American tones were like a fanfare on bassoons. It was Ezekiel Harbard, drinking companion, intellectual tormentor, friend, and theatrical enterer of rooms.

Craw sat back in his chair. He had not prepared himself for this. The world had shrunk and he hadn't even noticed it. The Atlantic was no longer a barrier, it was a road, and down it had come the past, in the laughing, smiling, life-shattering form of Ezekiel Harbard.

'Or would you prefer Endamon nowadays?'

'Professor Craw is fine,' said Craw.

Harbard laughed. 'You never did get the American taste for informality, did you?'

Craw said nothing; he just sat looking at Harbard. How lovely it would be to greet this man as a friend – even, yes, to touch him in the modern way, with a handshake and a pat on the shoulder. How gorgeous to sit and hear his conversation, listen to the buzzing and crackling of his intellect and, for a second, to be diverted. Craw looked at the professor, so showy in his emerald green cravat, his silver-topped cane and his broad-brimmed hat. So much older!

'Do you think you could get me some dry clothes?'

15   A Meeting With a Lady

'Gertie, Gertie.'

Max had been called to the mystic's chamber roughly four hours after his wife had gone into her trance.

Gertie was still flat out on the mat, her eyes focused on the swastika on the ceiling, while Devya stood nervously wringing her hands.

Mrs Reiter was still there, looking a little bleary but quite relaxed. She was concerned for her friend, but relieved that it had been revealed to her in her meditation that Dr Voller was, in fact, training a crocodile to play trombone in a bid to obviate the need for Negro musicians in dance bands. The next morning the ludicrousness of the idea would strike her but then, the hallucinogen still in her blood, it seemed a perfect explanation of what was going on in that strange lab.

A medic bent over Gertie, checking her vital signs. She had a pulse, albeit a very fast one, and her breath was very shallow.

'What's happened?' said Max, bending to his wife in concern.

'She just had a funny turn,' said Devya, who in fact had been trying to wake both women for a good three hours. Mrs Reiter had been given a relatively light brush of the hallucinogenic paste, whereas Gertie had been treated to a couple of coats of the stuff because Devya was so determined she should have a memorable experience to report to her husband. This was the last thing she'd expected or wanted.

Whenever she'd tried the paste itself it had caused the most pleasant sensations, like floating on a river. It was there she'd first seen her *Gandharva*, half man, half horse, appearing to her from behind a cloud.

'I've tried to rouse her with Vedic medicine,' she said.

'And then gave up and sent for the proper stuff,' said Max. 'Get out of my sight, you fucking stupid upper-class bitch.'

Max surprised himself. He'd never spoken like that to anyone before, never even suspected he had a temper. Even through his concern for Gertie, he was ashamed of what he'd said.

Devya was certainly struck by the violence of his language and looked around for somewhere to go. This being her own room at one o'clock in the morning, however, there was nowhere. Instead she just sat down on her sleeping roll and made a special note to impress on Junior Storm Leader Dorfmann the necessity of making sure that the crocodile's care was exemplary, the next time she saw him.

'Gertie, Gertie.' Max turned to the medic. 'Have you tried an adrenaline shot?'

'Her heart's already at 179 beats a minute,' said the medic. 'That could kill her.'

Max looked blankly at the medic. He couldn't think straight, couldn't even focus on what to do to help someone who was ill – the job he had done for over ten years. He loved her so much that the doctor in him completely disappeared, and he became like a child begging its mother not to die.

'I think, given the fact that her pulse is racing, phenobarbital may be in order,' said the medic.

'... barbital may be in order,' echoed Max, pulling helplessly at his wife's arm, as if telling her not to be so silly and to snap out of it.

The medic pushed a syringe into a bottle and loaded it up.

'Ahem,' he said, gesturing to Max.

'What?'

'Lift her skirt, please.'

Max did as he was bid, pulling his wife's knickers aside at the buttock so the needle could get in. The medic shot the sedative into her muscle and her heart rate fell.

'Gertie,' said Max, 'Gertie, come back to us. Don't go,

darling, don't go, you're too precious, you're all that keeps me sane, you are my faith, my reason, everything. Nothing means anything without you. I love you, Gertie, oh, Gertie, do come back.'

He was sobbing. Max had never had an ambition. He'd never believed in anything. Rather than living life himself, he had stood at the sidelines mocking the efforts of others. Only one thing he hadn't mocked: Gertie. She was everything good in the world and without her there was no joy, no anything. He had only love and he felt helpless as he watched his life's meaning expiring on the hard flagstones of the castle floor.

The terrible noise of the wolf's attack subsided and it was as if Gertie was falling, like the sensation you get when you doze off and suddenly awake – a little scoop in the consciousness, as if the mind has gone over a cerebral hump-backed bridge – but enduring, as if it would never end. But end it did.

Now Gertie was in a very strange place indeed. To her it looked like a small barn with rough wooden walls and a thatched roof. The hall was impossibly smoky and she was finding it difficult to breathe. The reason for the smoke was that in the centre of the barn was an open fire, just burning away in a fashion that she thought must be very dangerous. There seemed to be a hole in the ceiling, a sort of chimney, but it didn't seem to be doing a very good job of removing the smoke. This wasn't the hall she had seen when the wolf had attacked her, it was somewhere else, she thought.

Men moved through the smoke but there was something wrong with them. There were modern German soldiers, and also those in the uniform of the Great War, but there were enemies too, Tommies in their khaki and some in coats of red. She tried to look at them more closely but she couldn't see their faces in the haze.

Then she became aware of a figure by the fire. On a low three-legged stool was a beautiful woman. She was blonde and blue-eyed and dressed in great finery, a splendid red apron on top of a pale blue linen dress, bare arms heavy with gold and silver bracelets. The apron was fastened at the shoulders by two golden brooches, large and ornate, and around the woman's neck was the most enchanting necklace that Gertie had ever seen. It seemed to burn with every precious stone you could think of – diamonds, emeralds, rubies, garnets and sapphires – all the colours, she thought, of a city on fire. This was an unusual thought for her, because she had never seen a city on fire.

The lady smiled at Gertie and gestured for her to sit down on another stool next to her. There was something familiar about her, Gertie thought.

'You don't look well, dear,' said the lady, 'not well at all. You haven't been tangling with that nasty old wolf, have you?'

'I think I have.'

'Don't worry. I tangled with him once. I lived in Middle Earth, where you live, and I tried to call him. I succeeded but I didn't see who I was.'

'Who are you?'

'My name is Gullveig,' she said. 'They called me a witch and so I thought myself. But I was so much more than that. I am so much more than that. I am someone's dream,' she said. 'The dream of a god.'

'Which god?'

'Odin. He tricked me, or tricked himself, to offer his own destruction to the fates in Middle Earth to avoid it in the realm of the Gods. To forestall the end of the Gods.'

'That seems ...' Gertie didn't know quite what to say.

'Awful, dear, awful is what it seems. But now the signs are that Ragnarok – that's the end of the Gods – is coming properly. Doubtless, though, the All-father Odin will have come to Middle Earth again to try to forestall it. I'd like him to die in revenge for what he did to me. He has future plans for me, I am sure. Suffering, terror. I would be rid of him.'

'But you are safe in your hall.'

'No. It is the hall of a friend of mine. Where the great ladies dwell. And half the honoured dead. If he orders me out I will be gone in an instant. Oh, look at you, dear, you're quite the mess.'

Gertie was aware of something wet at her neck. She put her hand up to see what it was. Blood. She moved her fingers across her throat and pushed them into a deep wound. Then she looked down at her body. She was absolutely covered in blood, and large gashes covered her legs, arms and torso.

'There was a wolf,' she said.

'Quite a pest, dear, a regular bête noire,' said Gullveig, with a theatrical wave of the arm, 'but don't worry about him now, sit by the fire and I will comb your hair.'

Gertie moved through the smoke and sat on the stool. From a pouch at her side the lady took out a fabulous golden comb that burned with the light of a lava flow. She came to stand behind Gertie.

As she combed she sang a song.

> *I see one in bonds by the boiling springs;*
> *Like Loki he looks, loathsome to view:*
> *There Sigyn sits, sad by her husband,*
> *In woe by her man. Well would you know more?*

'I would know more,' said Gertie.

The combing of her hair was so restful, sending a wonderful electric tingle through her scalp and down her spine. She put her hand to her neck. The wound and the blood were gone. Her body was whole, too.

'You see,' said Gullveig, 'that wolf isn't too much harm. He's quite a puppy if you know how to deal with him.'

'I would know more. Please continue your lovely song.'

The lady went on:

> *Five hundred doors and forty more*
> *So I deem stand in that hall;*

Eight hundred champions go out at each door
When they fare to fight with the Wolf.

'Is that the wolf I saw?' said Gertie.

'Oh yes, dear, I'm afraid champions aren't as useful as a trick where he's concerned. He's quite used to champions – in fact, I believe he considers them something of a delicacy. The slaughter beast, that was his name in these parts, you know. Melodramatic, but I'd say it about summed him up. One of twins and, when the magic that formed him was made, he killed his brother and ate him. Two became one. Well, three, if you include the wolf.'

'That doesn't sound very nice.'

'He's a wolf, dear, he isn't concerned about nice.'

Gertie was certain she'd seen the lady before. Perhaps she'd been a member of the tennis club back in Salzgitter.

'Will the wolf get me again?' she asked.

'No, not you.'

'That's a relief.'

'He will kill everyone dear to you, though. He has followed you for centuries and only ever brought you pain.'

Gertie began to cry. 'I thought you said he was no harm.'

'Well, that's no harm to me, dear,' said Gullveig with a little laugh.

Gertie began to weep in earnest. She had taken the lady for a kind woman, but her joke showed her to be cruel.

Gullveig sat down next to her and took her hand.

'Let's you and I be friends, then your troubles are mine,' she said.

'Yes, let's,' said Gertie, glad for the expression of goodwill.

'My, that is a lovely ring, my dear.' She was playing with Gertie's engagement ring. It was a beautiful antique diamond that Max had got at a very good price through a friend in the party. 'As we're such pals, why don't you give it to me?'

'My husband gave it to me. I can't. It is a sign of our love.'

The woman inclined her head and put her tongue to her lips.

'Does your husband often give you jewels?'

'He is not a rich man.'

'The wolf will kill him,' said Gullveig. At this Gertie began to wail. 'Unless you would like me to help you.'

'Yes, I would like you to help me.' Gertie tried to wipe away her tears. She fought down her sobs. There was a silence and the women sat looking at each other.

'Well, you silly old sausage, what would you like me to do for you?' Gullveig asked.

'Can the wolf be killed?'

'He is here for a purpose. Once his purpose is fulfilled, then he will go.'

'What is his purpose?'

'To save the Gods. The fates have determined that Odin, the father of the Gods, must die at the teeth of the wolf. So the Gods come to earth and call the wolf to earth to take form here, offering a little death to the fates to forestall the big one to come. But the Gods have had their day. Imagine if the wolf, by some great magic, could be controlled and kept from doing his work. Then the Gods would die. And who would rule?'

'Who?'

'Why me, dear. Me. I am Gullveig, wise in magic, dream of the All-father Odin.'

'But if the god dies, then, if you are his dream ...'

'Can not a dream outlive the one who dreamt it?'

'I don't know.'

'The dream of a god can.'

Gertie didn't understand this at all. 'It would be nice if you could help me,' she said.

'I'll tell you what,' said Gullveig. 'You lend me your ring and I'll go out and see to the wolf.'

Gertie didn't know. She wasn't sure the lady would give the ring back, and then Max would be angry with her for treating his love so lightly. She needed her help, though, if he wasn't to be killed by the wolf.

'What will I do while you are gone?'

150

'You'll wait here by the fire,' said Gullveig. 'Here's a mat you can doze upon.'

A dead man in a breastplate came over and placed a lovely padded mat and a cushion on the floor. A badly burnt man in a tank commander's uniform bought her some furs, which she thought very kind.

'I would like to sleep,' said Gertie, 'I am very tired.'

Gullveig guided her to the mat. She laid her down and put furs on top of her. Gertie had never known such comfort. She hardly felt the lady slipping the ring from her finger as she began to fall into the most wonderful sleep. Just before the tiredness took her completely, she decided she knew where she had seen the lady before.

'I'm going out now, dear, but don't worry, I shall be back before long.'

'Yes,' said Gertie. 'You're me, aren't you?'

'No, dear, although we are sisters of a sort. Why, we have been together for so long!'

'Bye-bye,' said Gertie, as the lady opened the doors of the hall and went out.

In Devya's chamber Max kissed his wife's forehead and, like a princess in a fairy tale, she woke up.

16 The Grand Louvetier

Craw sat in a pair of dry overalls, his soaking clothes folded on a chair by the door. He was facing Harbard over a table. The overalls had actually been in the storeroom on the shelves next to him, as Harbard had pointed out. Not for the first time in his life, the professor had made him feel rather stupid.

Ezekiel Harbard, it had often been noted, did things differently. It was customary to offer the interviewee a cigarette, but not a cigar, and not whisky and fine pies from a Macy's hamper. Craw didn't take the cigar. He'd always seen them as a vulgar expression of the capitalist age, smoked by men who had grubbed fortunes from steel or brick, cotton or gas. He still thought it ignoble to indulge in trade and the cigar, looking for all the world like a turd in a golden band, seemed its very symbol. To suck on shit and account it a glory. How strange, he had thought, how strange.

'Do you know,' said Harbard, 'that in some medical circles the idea is forming that these can be bad for you? Hard to credit, isn't it? Still, Crawford, you wouldn't have to worry about that, would you?'

'My name is Endamon,' said Craw.

Harbard nearly made Craw laugh. He had a showy side to him that was just so un-European, un-English. If you have a talent, the Englishman believes, then you must treat it like a guilty secret. The German – or, worse, the Czech – will somehow contrive to see it as a curse. He will view his gifts like a species of incontinence, to be hidden away and hushed. At the end of his life, he will burn his masterpieces, convinced they are trash.

By comparison, the American, Harbard, advertised his considerable abilities like a fourth of July parade, in which he was his own drum major, cheerleader and colour guard in a thumping, banging, whistling, marching band of intellectual can-do-ism. He flaunted his intelligence, cultivated an idiosyncratic style in his smart mouse-brown Stetson hat pulled down at one side, his full white beard, his cravats and his silver-topped cane.

Craw had once heard a servant use the expression 'Don't put in the window what you haven't got in the shop,' meaning someone shouldn't boast of accomplishments they didn't really possess. Harbard, he knew, had plenty in the shop. In fact his flashiness was, in some ways, inadequate to his intelligence.

Despite his education as a linguist and an anthropologist, Harbard had, as a hobby, designed a more efficient petrol engine carburettor that had been taken up by Oldsmobile. He'd also invented a new drill bit for the mining industry just to turn in a bit of cash for his institute, introduced a well-known burger chain to the idea of a production line, and contributed the 'Harbard Conjecture' to the study of formal symbolic logic. Then there were his four novels, two symphonies, a Broadway musical, and millions made on the stock market – still intact, as he had sold his entire holding at the market's peak on 3 September 1929 and had been in a position to pick and choose when the crash struck six weeks later. Many people of Harbard's acquaintance were heard to thank God he couldn't paint or draw, otherwise they would be forced to strangle him, safe in the knowledge that no jury would convict them. Actually, strangling him would be far from easy. As a young man he had played in the first ever game of American Football for Yale against Tufts, and had also excelled as a wrestler.

The surprising thing about Harbard, Craw thought, was that, in some ways, he was playing his intelligence down. His flashiness made him seem more stupid than he was. He must have known that. He was as far from a fool as it is possible

153

to be. All Craw had to do was convince this searing, questing intellect that it was mistaken.

'Your name is Endamon Craw. Of course it is – your name is what you say it is, though I wonder why you chose anything so unusual. Some trouble at the passport office, I bet.'

Harbard was right, as ever. The name had stuck out at Craw from a register of the dead of the Great War – one Damon Craw. It was similar to his previous identity, which he liked, but different, which he needed. Armed with the original Craw's birthday and place of birth, he had obtained a birth certificate which, for some reason – his own bad handwriting, perhaps – had been returned incorrectly as Endamon Craw. The identity had made him feel better – that he wasn't stealing some dead man's name – and, more practically, provided him with the ability to get a bank account, an electricity supply, a driving licence.

Craw said nothing, just stared at Harbard, willing himself into composure.

Harbard went on, 'What are names, anyway? Little anchors we throw out into the shifting currents of our identity, marking points in the whirl of endlessly contingent meaning. Names are hopes, really, aren't they? Hopes that I am the same person today that I was yesterday, that I am separate from you, that we are different from this,' he tapped the table, 'and, of course, they are mightily convenient if you need to send someone a letter.'

He smiled, his teeth an over-dentised unnatural white. Craw was a stone, unresponsive and blank. He was looking at the tendons on the professor's neck. That was it. He wasn't thinking, wasn't planning. He was just looking at the tendons on the professor's neck.

'Do you know,' said Harbard, 'that every cell in the human body replaces itself every seven years? Or so they seem to think. So the "me" that you knew in Yale isn't even the same person physically as the person who sits here before you today.'

Craw said nothing; he just looked at the professor. Muscle under skin. A prominent carotid artery visible at the thinner edges of the beard. No. Not that. Harbard went on, seduced by his own words.

'The me of ten years ago is not the me of today. So in what sense am I still the Ezekiel Harbard that was dipped wailing into the baptismal font? Also, each of those cells is outnumbered twenty times by the bacteria in my body. Are they me, too? Without them I would die, so they must be. We are several, Crawford, and we are legion – no wonder you changed your name. It seems almost philosophically bankrupt to keep the same one.'

Harbard blew out an eye-watering blast of smoke which shook Craw from his reverie.

'Can I go now?'

'No.'

'What law is keeping me here? Who are you, anyway?'

'Don't be coy, my dear fellow. I am attached to a special division of a special division of the US Military, and have been further attached to a new, very special division of a merely special division of British Military Intelligence until such time as the US enters the war.'

'If the US enters the war.'

'It is inevitable. It is foreseen.'

The words shook Craw, seeming to echo across the centuries from a high, cold place where his destiny had changed forever. Harbard put out the cigar.

'Thank God for that,' said Craw.

'You don't like cigars?'

'I ...' Craw realised he had been trapped.

'Yes, you never did like them, did you?'

Craw felt his heart sink. It wasn't actually an admission of who he was, but Harbard had scored a point against him.

Harbard slid a photo across the table. It was a posed, late nineteenth-century thing, showing Craw with a stiff moustache, next to a young and vigorous-looking Harbard. The two men were in mortarboards and both carried books. Behind them was an American flag, at which Harbard gazed lovingly. How had Craw let himself pose for that? He had avoided being photographed for this very reason: that it might one day come back to trap him.

'The likeness is remarkable, is it not?' said Harbard.

'The years haven't been kind to you,' said Craw, shoving the photo back.

'But they've been very, very kind to you. Let me show you some other things in my file.' He flicked over a series of documents.

'This is interesting indeed,' he said. 'Some records of bank transactions, a legal name change certificate, some fakes of academic qualifications, which I must say are very good and, in fact, are not true fakes, in fact they're fake fakes,' he seemed to find the idea funny, 'because you do have those qualifications but not under that name, a transaction from Coutts involving a banker's draft for four hundred guineas cashed by one Crawford Manden just last year. A Crawford Manden who was killed in a boating accident in 1892, according to the *Yale Daily News*.'

'What has this to do with me?'

'Well, since Professor Crawford Manden gave your address, I thought you might have seen him. I think you would notice it, wouldn't you – another professor living in your house? Particularly one who had been recently resurrected.'

Craw said nothing again. He had been lazy. He was a poor record-keeper and had found the banker's draft at the bottom of a case one day. He should have thrown it away but thought there would be no harm. Crawford Manden had never existed outside America, so how could that come back to haunt him in Britain? One hundred years before, the separation between the US and Europe had been immense. They might as well have been on different planets. Imperceptibly, those worlds had been coming closer together. It had been too big a risk, taking up the same profession he had so enjoyed in America.

He had thought that the Atlantic would protect him. He would only ever talk to colleagues in the US by letter, never see each other face to face. There was no risk, he'd thought. But there had been.

'Where did you get all this stuff?' said Craw.

'We've been watching you for a while. And I had your house searched two days ago. It was one of the reasons we moved you up to the Midlands with Balby. That butler's always there, isn't he? You want to get that painting somewhere safe, it'd be a terrible shame to lose it to the Blitz. I dispatched your man to London to do just that – I hope you don't mind my presumption.'

Craw breathed in. There was only him and Harbard in the room. His first instinct was to kill his old friend where he sat, leave the camp with as little fuss as he could manage, and then just disappear. First, though, he had to find out who Harbard had told. The game, he could see, was up, denial useless any more. He would speak to Harbard openly. It would be a relief to share himself after so long. Then what?

Images flashed in his head: Harbard lying back in the chair with his neck broken; Harbard on the floor, his face blue with strangulation. Craw bowed his head. He had lived over a thousand years with the belief that had been instilled in him as a child – that as a son of the royal line, his life was more important than anyone else's. The old king had been buried with six sacrificial servants, and it had struck no one as odd that these people should give up their lives when their master died.

If Harbard stood in his way or frustrated him, then it was in his upbringing that he should die. He had known other Viking kings kill for as little as a slave failing to keep a fire going. Was it right, though? The democratic age had entered him to a degree and he could no longer think as clearly as he once might have. But what if Harbard found a way to detain him? How many others would die if the transformation began? Did Harbard need to be eliminated so others might live?

'What authorisation did you have to search my home?'

'Have you heard of a ... Hmmm, what is he called? Winston Churchill? Just been made prime minister, you may know the name, I think.'

Craw smiled to himself. If the future is not visible, then what is left but to enjoy the moment?

'If you had remained under my influence for longer, I would have cured you of this vulgar habit of name-dropping.'

Harbard broke into a broad grin. 'You know, the facts of this case for a second, and just for a second, made me think I might be wrong.'

'Then they must be extraordinary indeed.'

'I think they are. What are you, Crawford?'

Craw swallowed. It was a question he'd often asked himself.

'I don't know.' He was speaking the truth.

'How long have you lived?'

'Can anyone hear this?'

He looked around him. It didn't look like the sort of place that had any sort of listening device but, there again, that was what a place that had a listening device would look like. It was a standard barracks, though. There was no interrogation facility and, unless they'd quickly stuck a microphone in the blankets before he arrived, he was safe.

'On my word, no.'

'We will conduct this in the old language,' said Craw, in the Norse of his people.

Harbard started, and replied in the same tongue, 'You never said you could speak Old Norse!'

'You never asked.'

'All the time you could have saved me!' said Harbard.

'You enjoyed the discovery, you wouldn't have wanted it as a gift.'

'Well, where am I going wrong, what can I improve?'

'Not much,' said Craw.

Harbard recovered his considerable wits. 'So you have lived since, when, the Viking age? That's incredible.'

Craw lowered his eyelids in assent.

'So ...' Harbard was beyond excitement. 'What have you done, what have you seen? You're a walking mine of information.'

'I have forgotten.'

'You have forgotten the Somme, the American Civil War, the Industrial Revolution? You have forgotten the sailing of the *Mayflower* and the death of the Red Man, you have forgotten what happened at Guttenberg, and you have forgotten Stamford Bridge and Hastings? Did you, at any point, notice that the management had changed in this little island of yours, around 1066? No, your speech pattern. Western Norwegian? The coming of Christianity, the conquest of the west coast by Harald I? Did you ever get woken up in the night by the odd war on your doorstep?'

'I remember little of use or of sense,' said Craw.

'That is a truly poor memory.'

Craw sipped on his whisky. 'I have moved like a wave horse on the whale roads and have left no trace I can follow.'

This wasn't his usual turn of phrase, but he had been speaking the language of his childhood for a few moments now and it was asserting its hold on him. It was suited to such ways of speaking; it almost demanded them. In a subtle way, he was someone different when speaking the tongue of the Vikings from who he was when speaking English. Myths and fables entered into his speech just as Hollywood films did that of his contemporaries in 1940. Everyone in London was saying things were 'swell' and calling people 'buddy' in an attempt to be Clark Gable or Bette Davis. Even those who weren't trying to be a movie star were picking up the phrases from the lips of their friends. The Vikings, all wanting to be legendary heroes themselves, often spoke as if they were part of those legends.

Harbard raised his eyebrows and sat back in his chair.

'I'd worked out that you had lived a long time.'

Craw focused again on Harbard's throat.

'Who drinks of the cup you have drained so dry?'

'What?'

'Who knows my secret?' Craw's voice was cracked and his face was pale.

Harbard's eyes suddenly widened in alarm. He knew enough physiology to recognise what was happening. Blood was leaving any of the areas unnecessary for fighting, flooding out of the face and the vocal cords and into the limbs.

'Are you thinking of killing me, Crawford?'

'It would seem a trifle impolite after such a splendid hamper.' Craw was still pale.

'That's not a "no",' said Harbard.

'You are an intelligent man, so I will present you with my problem. My secret cannot be known. It will not be known.'

'Why not? You'd be the curiosity to end all curiosities.'

'You have your answer there. I am a prince of the blood, not a zoo animal. You tell me how I ensure your silence.'

'This is classified top secret.'

Craw nodded. That, at least, was a start. There would be no learned papers from Harbard for the foreseeable future.

'So who knows?'

'Me and my immediate superior. He only knows sketchy details, though — that you are an occultist who is known to have achieved results.'

'Does Churchill know?'

'No. Good God, you're not thinking of bumping off the prime minister, are you?'

Craw laughed. 'No. Churchill is a man of my station. I would simply require him to give his word.'

Harbard's eyes widened. 'Of your station?'

'I am a prince. Churchill is descended from a similar, though less elevated, noble warrior line.'

'So you would kill a social inferior to ensure silence, but merely require a nod from a duke to feel your secret was safe?'

'Of course.' Craw thought this self-evident; it was as if Harbard was asking him if the grass was generally green and the sky, on the whole, blue.

'You did a good job of hiding that attitude at Yale.'

'What do you want from me?'

'Oh,' said Harbard, with a sarcastic dip to his voice, 'let's see if you can work it out from this. If we're taking on titles I think you should give me one, Your Majesty. I'd like to be known from now on as the Grand Louvetier!'

Harbard's head hit the door behind him, hard, as Craw leapt over the table and took him by the throat. The door was made of cheap wood and it smashed under the impact, the old man falling limp in the corridor.

A guard on a chair leapt to his feet and levelled his rifle at Craw. *Bang!* The soldier shot, a foot away from Craw's head. He missed. Craw had turned aside and avoided the bullet. He used the momentum of the turn to take the weapon from the guard. The man's face whitened as he saw his gun in the prisoner's hands. He took a step to one side and Craw, carrying the gun, walked past him.

He strode down the corridor towards the outside of the building. The soldier with the Thompson had heard the noise and entered from a side door, standing in front of Craw.

'Stay right where you are, Sonny Jim.'

Craw didn't break stride as he advanced towards the man. The soldier squeezed the trigger. Nothing happened. The gun had jammed.

'Shit,' said the soldier. He was fixated on the weapon, pulling out the magazine and reattaching it. Craw just walked past him out of the building.

'Prisoner escaped, prisoner escaped!'

Other soldiers on the parade square came running towards him. The Thompson man had freed the misfed bullet in double-quick time and reattached the magazine. He pointed it at Craw, but did not fire. It was too dangerous with his colleagues closing in on the academic.

Craw dropped the rifle and broke into a run, dodging one soldier and then another. He was making for the main gates. The soldiers couldn't keep up with him, he was too quick.

In fact, Craw was not running as quickly as he could. If he escaped, he wanted them to account him a talented sprinter, not something stranger.

'Stop or I fire!'

Two soldiers with .303s took aim at Craw's back. He jumped the vehicle barrier at the camp's entrance. He was fifty yards from a T-junction where he would be out of sight and able to run as only he could. A couple of rifles cracked behind him. Craw stumbled. He took a few steps more and then he fell.

'Got the bastard!' said one of the riflemen.

'That was my shot!' said the other one.

But the soldiers were wrong. They hadn't felled Craw at all. Someone else had.

17 Mrs Voller's Recovery

Gertie Voller recovered well from her ordeal. In fact, in the days following her session with Devya she seemed in uncommon good spirits. She played more tennis, walked the hills around the castle, and even started to socialise with some other wives. It seemed to her husband that she had taken well to life at the castle, and that the things that had so disquieted her when she arrived – the failed humanity of the SS, the pyjamaed corpses of the prisoners, the shadows that seemed to lap like a dark lake at the edges of the bed, the ceaseless sawing – all those no longer bothered her.

Max, however, was not faring so well. The appearance of the crocodile had disturbed him and he felt bullied and oppressed by von Knobelsdorff. On top of this, what had he done to that *Kapo*? In an instant, and to save his own skin, he had condemned him. He had acted instinctively and hadn't thought through the consequences, but was that a defence?

Then there was Michal. He had seen a change in the boy. At the start of the month he had noticed he was very, very down, hardly talking, not wanting to play chess, staring into space. Max had flattened out some bread and cheese – meat was getting scarcer in the canteen – and gone to bandage it to the boy's head. He had brushed Max's hand away.

'No friend?' Max asked. 'For friend?'

'Friend dead,' said Michal.

Max had applied the bandage anyway. It wouldn't do for it to suddenly disappear, revealing no mark at all.

So Max hadn't been sleeping. At night the castle works went on late and, when they had stopped, the banging and hammering seemed to continue in his head, as if he himself was undergoing a refit. In the early hours, between sleeping and waking, sometimes he imagined little men running around inside his head with saws and hammers, chipping away inside his skull. Then he'd come back to himself with a jolt. He sat in his room, or stood at the windows looking down at that awful camp and wondering what went on there – knowing what went on there. He couldn't work out a way to bring himself and Gertie out of the castle without either of them coming to harm.

To make things worse, Gertie had started dropping in on him at the lab. She had taken a dim view of the crocodile.

'It's horrible, Max, why do you keep it?' she said.

'Von Knobelsdorff's insistence. I'm trying to work out a way to get it to go back.'

Gertie looked around the lab. 'This won't do, you know, we need to get you something more fitting your station.'

'My station?'

'You are my husband, Max, and that makes you special. We must plan big things for you.'

She kissed him on the lips and put her hand to his face. He closed his eyes and drank in her scent. He found her electrifying. He nuzzled against her hand. The cuff of her blouse had slid down on her arm, revealing a very attractive wristwatch.

'Where did you get that?' he asked.

'Oh, that – I've always had it.'

'You've never worn it before.'

'No, I just dug it out from the bottom of my jewellery box and thought I'd put it on. It's nice, isn't it?'

She showed him her wrist. The watch was an elegant thin band with an octagonal face in platinum. People can still have secrets, Max thought. He'd known her since she was fifteen and she'd never mentioned it. It really was a fine piece; there was a depth to its silver that cheaper metals would never reproduce.

'It's lovely,' he said. 'Is it Art Deco?'

'I expect so,' she said brightly. 'Come home early tonight, I

164

have something for you.' She put his hand to her breast. The door was open and Max felt embarrassed; he feared discovery.

'Go on,' she said unhooking a button, 'go on.' She put his hand underneath the material of her blouse and encouraged his fingers inside.

'Gertie,' said Max, 'I—'

'Crocodile inspection! Stand to!' said a voice. Max's hand snapped back as if scalded.

Behind Gertie were a couple of SS dummies, low rankers, close-shaved blond hair, perfect Nordic types. Max found himself inwardly giggling. Which one of these was going to get the call from the terrible shitty Knights of the Black Sun? Which one would end up with his head on a staff of oak, gazing in blankness while von Knobelsdorff's madmen waited for him to speak? What would he say? 'Give us a gottle of geer!'

He'd seen a ventriloquist do an act with a dummy of Hitler before the war. What had that said? 'You can't put me back in the box, not with my arm like this.' The ventriloquist had made the dummy salute. Yes, that would be funny. 'Now, you lot. Don't lose your heads.' Ha ha ha ha ha. Where was the ventriloquist now? Nowhere good, he supposed. He wondered if they'd shot the dummy, too. He wouldn't have put it past them. A ticklish, sick snigger welled up in him. He swallowed it down.

He was laughing about a death, laughing about murder, and murder for the most ridiculous reasons. He had always found life funny until he came to Wewelsburg, but this laughter was something else. It sounded different in his head; it had a harsh quality to it, reminiscent of a school sneak smirking at a cruel prank. It was a snotty, sawing snigger that recalled, if anyone, Haussmann. He didn't like that laugh and he didn't want it inside him.

'I hope this is worth the interruption,' said Gertie, turning to face the SS men. She did not do up the button on her blouse. Nothing was visible but, Max thought, she had made no attempt to conceal what they had been up to.

The SS men were embarrassed. 'Only a second, *gnädige frau*. We need to wait for— Ah, here she is.'

There, in her turban and silks, was the imposing figure of Heidi Fischer – Devya, to those in the know. She nodded at Gertie, not quite managing to catch her eye, and said *Sieg Heil* to Max.

'Haven't you caused enough trouble?' he said.

'I am concerned about this animal,' said the priestess. 'Please allow me into the room.'

'Gladly.' He and Gertie stepped out while Devya knelt to look at the crocodile in its crate.

'It stinks!' she said.

'That'll be amphibious carnivores for you, then,' said Max.

'You haven't changed its bedding recently.'

Had he? He'd fed it and squirted water in, but he hadn't changed it for a week.

'This creature is ill. It needs to go back to the zoo,' said Devya.

'Exactly what I've been saying. Maybe you can get von Knobby to OK it. I don't want the thing.'

'Send it back, then.'

'He won't let me.' Max said the words slowly and carefully, as if to an idiot.

'There's no need to be aggressive!' said Devya.

Max honestly thought this was the funniest thing he'd heard in years. 'There's no need to be aggressive!' from an SS employee whose rooms were serviced by the starved, beaten, animated corpses of the Bible Students. 'There's no need to be aggressive!' from the woman who was providing Hitler with divine justification for his trampling of Europe. 'There's no need to be aggressive!'

He started to laugh again, that nasal, snuffling laugh he could hear inside him. He tried to stop it but that just seemed to make it worse.

'Just fuck off,' he said, through his giggles.

The brutality of his reply seemed to strike Devya like a

sudden gust, blowing away all lingering hope of a productive relationship with Max. She pointed her finger at him.

'Steps,' she said, 'will need to be taken.'

Max couldn't catch his breath, he was laughing so hard.

'I'm shitting myself, love,' he said.

Shitting himself! That conjured up the image of the knights in that chamber, sitting with their legs crossed for a week. The laughter got harder and harder and harder until it was painful.

'Someone's in a good mood!' said Gertie brightly.

'Let's see how long it lasts.' Devya clicked her fingers and summoned the SS men to follow her up the stairs.

Max controlled himself and kissed his wife. There was a phone call. He answered.

'Nuthouse.'

'It's me. Haussmann.'

Max went slightly cold. The report. For a second he had forgotten about that. He affected calm.

'What can I do for you, boss?'

'Good news – your experiments can proceed, we've got hold of one of the boy's relatives.'

Max felt a tremble go through him, almost as if something had struck the castle and sent a hum through its walls.

'Right.'

'They'll be arriving from Sachsenhausen next week. Don't get excited, they'll have had anything worth having over there.'

'Yes.'

'Oh, and one more thing. I was wondering if you'd seen ... Well, it's almost embarrassing to ask, but have you seen a lady's watch anywhere? My wife was playing tennis with Gertie and she thinks she might have accidentally left it there. It's an Art Deco thing, quite valuable.'

Max looked at Gertie. She smiled back.

'No,' he said, 'but I'll ask my wife.'

18   A Question of the Weight

There are competing visions of the afterlife, thought Craw, in his anthropologist's way. 'Now the truth seems stranger than any of them'. He heard voices around him and from within him.

'We had little to do with the Finns, we found their manners hateful.' Who was saying that? Scenes from a lecture came back to him. 'The *makara*, the dead child being of folklore. Note the linguistic similarity to the Hindu *Makara* – a semi-divine aquatic creature often associated with a crocodile.'

Craw's mind seemed full of the chalk dust of all the lectures he had ever attended or given. He loved lectures – life in theory, flattened and laid out on a board, literally reduced to black and white. It all seemed so graspable in lectures, so capable of being understood. And then there was the sound of rain on high windows, a memory of other days in other rooms where the rain had beaten on the panes, tea had been drunk, things said and misunderstood. Life in practice was more difficult.

Fugitive thoughts ran through his mind like luminous ocean streaks, appearing suddenly before flashing into the depths. How long had he spent chalking things on boards, talking about customs and practice, sympathetic magic, dead and reviving gods, rituals and sacrifice and invocation, as if it all been no more than so much print?

He saw himself in a lecture hall, reading from notes and saying, 'Men mistook the order of their ideas for the order of nature, and hence imagined that the control which they have, or seem to have, over their thoughts, permitted them to exercise a corresponding control over things.'

Yes, they had got it wrong, imagined that the world operated to psychological, not natural laws, that men could shape the world by their thoughts. Craw knew, though, that they could not. That was the preserve of the gods.

There are, however, more mundane rituals that impose themselves upon us.

In the early spring of 1922 he had spent two hours preparing for a lecture, writing his notes onto the blackboards to save time the next day, as was his habit. An over-zealous new cleaner had rubbed them off. A young colleague had been with him when he discovered the error. She'd picked up the board rubber and blown chalk back on to the board.

'Oh well, I tried,' she said, and smiled.

A week later he had kissed her by the fountain in the park, watched rainbows forming in the spray, and vowed to leave her soon. They had parted, but not soon. Every time he stayed late to write his notes onto the board for a morning lecture he would think of her, think of writing some instruction to the cleaner not to remove them, and then write nothing, as some sort of gesture to luck. It was, he knew, irrational.

Then he was at the edge of the black water, by the black shore, the water flat and still, seeming almost solid. Even the path of the moon on the water was smooth; only its tiny glitter showed that you could not walk upon it. He looked down into the water and saw, not his own face looking back at him, but that of a hideous wolf.

He heard a voice beside him.

Cuando llegue la luna llena
iré a Santiago De Cuba
iré a Santiago
en un coche de agua negra
iré a Santiago.

Spanish had always been a struggle for Craw but he understood well enough.

When the full moon rises
I'm going to Santiago De Cuba
Going to Santiago
In a coach of black water
Going to Santiago.

Of course, he recognised it as the work of the Spaniard
Lorca. The poem gave him a shiver. Things that were hidden to him in his everyday consciousness were revealing
themselves now. The poetry, he felt, signified the presence
of something or someone he would do well to avoid, but to
whom he was bound in the most fundamental way.

Poetry, death and battle seemed to be around him in a way
he couldn't quite pin down, as if they were not fully present
but seeping in through a crack in his consciousness.

He could hear music, the pipes and horns of his youth, but
also another, stranger rhythm – a shaking, sliding Rumba
Guaguancó that he had heard played by a Cuban band that
had visited Yale at the turn of the century.

The poem went on, talking of palms that wanted to be
stalks, bananas wishing to be jellyfish. The imagery made
Craw feel faintly nauseous. His nostrils filled with the smell of
burning and he thought that some hermit must have started a
fire on the beach, but he could see no fire.

Another voice said, 'Then I realised I had been murdered.
They looked for me in cafes, cemeteries and churches ... but
they did not find me. They never found me? No. They never
found me.'

Then he was having a conversation with someone.

He said:

'If you are my daughter
Tell me – why won't you look at me?'

A girl's voice replied:

'The eyes with which I looked at you
I gave up to the shadow.'

He said:

'If you are my daughter
Tell me – why don't you kiss me?'
   The girl said:
'The lips with which I kissed you
   I gave up to the clay.'
He said:
'If you are my daughter
Tell me – why won't you embrace me?'
She said:
'The arms that embraced you
   I have covered up with worms.'
And then there, from the corner of his eye, was what he took for the flash of sunlight on glass. The child was at his side. Blonde, and beautiful, long dead.
   'Kari?'
No, it was the girl from the riverbank in Stratford. She had a satchel at her side and, from it, she took out a schoolbook.
   'Hello, Mr Wolf.'
She gave him a self-conscious grin, and began to read.
   'The title of the poem is "Domestic",' she said, 'and really it should be read in a quiet and comfortable air, touched with the smell of warm linen and the soothing sounds of a radio play.'
   She coughed and began:

> *The knives in the knife drawer are all for you.*
> *Bleach and weedkiller, caustic soda too,*
> *Have purposes known beyond purpose meant,*
> *Uses exceeding domestic intent,*
> *Label warnings have been read and re-read,*
> *Potential assessed, if disregarded.*

'What?'

> *When all of mother's household tasks are done,*
> *And the vinegared panes let go the sun,*

When the floor is swept and the grate is black,
The plates are sparkling in the plate rack,
Windows once open to the clean cold air,
Are closed again, odours no longer there.
There is still you, present as the dust on her unreachable
  shelf.

'Kari, why are you saying this to me?' said Craw, though he knew it was not Kari.

'She's here,' said the girl. 'Your friend. Oh, why don't you come? She'll call to you for sure and you can do your old dance.'

'Dance?'

'The one that goes *Grrrrr!*' The little girl mimed the action of a dog ragging at something.

Another snatch of song went through his mind, a music hall refrain.

'Oh, turn his face to the wall, mother, his picture shall hang on black string.'

The girl smiled and put her hand out to comfort him.

'You just took a little turn when she stepped back in, that's all, you and she are so very close you're bound to feel it,' said Kari. 'Oh, why don't you come? She is waiting, see. There will be all the blood you can drink and he will be there. She's speaking to him.'

'Who?'

'The great hater! Odin!'

Far in the distance Craw could see a castle of three sides on a large hill.

'Great evil is done there,' he said.

'Then you'd think you'd feel at home, wouldn't you?'

'I cannot leave this place,' he said, gazing out over the still water. His words seemed almost independent of him, separate from his thoughts, in which he longed to be away.

'I have come to bargain for you,' said the girl, 'to lead you away.'

172

'What do you have to bargain?'

'Only my blood,' said the girl. Her body snapped open like a sugar beet, a fountain of gore spurting over the wolf, stealing his vision and short-circuiting his senses in its sticky heat.

Craw opened his eyes. It was a drawing room in the Victorian style: wood panelling, a heavy Moorish lamp in lattice brass, and paste gems hanging from the ceiling, casting shadows about the room and counterpointing them with blurs of red and blue. He was lying on an improvised bed with a tartan blanket over him. The open fire was lit and, at a small table next to some deep armchairs, brandy sparkled in a decanter.

Into his view came a young woman of around eighteen, pretty, with chestnut curls, a mannish shirt and smart high waisted trousers.

'He's awake, Uncle. I'll fetch him some beef broth,' she said.

'Wait here for a second, my dear, I think your presence will be useful for a moment.' It was Harbard, unharmed, apparently.

He was right, of course, and had correctly conjectured that Craw – who had taken the age of chivalry to heart, who had watched it evolve into the age of the gentleman – could never kill him in the presence of a lady. Craw blinked the dizziness from his head and focused. His mouth tasted of smoke and ashes, and he felt as though he hadn't eaten in days. It was not yet the craving of his wolf hunger, though it bore a trace of that feeling, just an ordinary human appetite honed to keenness by three days without food.

Craw felt alarm rise in him. Had Harbard let this woman in on his secret? If he had, then what?

'Lady, your skirts are on fire,' he said in the old language.

The girl didn't react, but looked to her uncle. Harbard smiled.

'This is my niece, Eleanor,' he said in English. 'She is more concerned with dancing than scholarship.'

'As any young woman should be,' said Eleanor.

Her uncle was teasing her, but she showed no embarrassment

and Craw thought she had inherited the Harbard boldness. The girl sounded vaguely American, he thought, and he was right. She'd been at school in England at the start of the war and her mother – in the style of the upper class – had seen no reason to withdraw her. That would be giving in. She was at a country school, safe from the bombs; the passage home was potentially perilous and, anyway, no woman of breeding wants her daughter under her feet where she might interrupt her social life.

'Where am I?'

'Just to the east of Coventry. At Coombe Abbey, a military intelligence facility.'

'What happened?' said Craw, again in Old Norse.

'We'll come to that,' said Harbard, in the same language. 'First, can I dismiss this poor girl? Can I have your word that you won't attack me or run off? You'll be free to go in a day, I promise you.'

Craw looked at the girl, then at the brandy decanter's amber deepening in the firelight.

'You have my word,' he said.

'Time to go now, Eleanor, I think. He can have his broth later.'

The girl left the room and Craw looked around. Outside the window, in the encroaching dusk, a soldier stood guard. So he was a prisoner, was he?

Harbard caught the meaning in his glance. 'The guards aren't for you,' he said. 'This is a facility of Military Intelligence, and they have been so kind as to make some rooms available to me. Some privacy, I think.' He drew the heavy red curtains.

What had happened to him? It was the same feeling that had knocked him from his chair in his study in London. If anything it was less painful, because he had simply passed out, but it was unmistakably similar to his experience in London. Perhaps, though, there was a simpler explanation. Harbard had given him some food just before the attack. That made him suspect that he might have been drugged in some way.

Poisons and narcotics did affect him in the short term, something he was thankful for in the case of alcohol. He scratched his back. Had a bullet hit him there, leaving that slight tender spot? So long out of combat, Craw was interested to see that he was still largely invulnerable to conventional weapons. He wanted a drink but Harbard showed no signs of offering him one.

'Did you put some sort of tranquilliser in that food you gave me?'

'No.'

'Then what stopped me at the gate?'

'I have no idea. By the time I had recovered from your assault they were bringing you back on a stretcher.'

Craw nodded. In the space of two months he had received two blows, the like of which he couldn't recall for over five hundred years. He had a feeling that whatever had caused them wasn't too far away from Coventry. It might seem a miracle that a man could be struck down at his desk or in the open air by an invisible hand. But was it less of a miracle that a petty criminal had suddenly started speaking in Old Norse?

'You called yourself a name I haven't heard in a long time,' he said.

Harbard laughed a short little laugh, rather like his niece's, Craw thought.

'The Grand Louvetier? The chief wolf hunter of the French kings. A little local difficulty around Gévaudan in about 1764, I think. The hunter was one Monsieur Antoine, I believe, whom for a long time I actually believed to be you. He certainly had your fine tastes. But you were Monsieur Chastel, were you not? A hermit? Not like you, Crawford. Were you trying to lie low for a while? Were you trying something new?'

Craw looked to the wall. He flexed his fingers, tapped the roof of his mouth with his tongue, squeezed a thumb into his waistband. He felt human again, no sign of the stirrings of the days before. It was as if the wolf inside him had taken a blow at the gate, rather than his physical body. He had only known it like this once before: 1764, Gévaudan, where, as Harbard had rightly conjectured, he had been trying something new – namely, a reversal of the curse that had brought him under the wolf's power. Sacrifices had been needed, certain steps taken. It hadn't worked. All he had achieved was a strange quickening of his conversion to a wolf, and a strangely quick remission. Not like in the films, but happening over a period of weeks. The effects had been relatively mild but they had taken three years to stabilise. Three years and a hundred dead.

The Louvetier's was a name that filled him with dread. The pain had been immense. He had actually remembered his transformations, and the memory of his slaughters had kept him from sleep for years.

'How did you discover all this, Ezekiel?'

'I don't exactly know. Like several things I could mention, I could put it down to chance, I could put it down to the reward for ritual and devotion, attuning me to certain tides in the affairs of men. I think a combination, like a gambler. I've had luck, but I've also studied the form book, so to speak. Sorry, I am forgetting my manners.'

He liberated the brandy from its bottle and poured Craw a glass. Craw held it up to the firelight, as if appreciating the drink's colour. In fact he was looking for signs it had been adulterated. He could see none, so he sipped at it, lit a scented cigarette from a proffered box, and watched the smoke make lazy dragons in the lamplight. A gramophone quietly played Schubert. The qualities Craw valued most in life – calm and repose – were restored.

Harbard spoke: 'I had suspected something strange about you, Endamon. I knew you for ten years, between thirty and forty, youth to middle age, and, although you were very careful to adjust your dress, to begin to wear those rather ridiculous half-moon spectacles, it was obvious that you didn't age a day. I could have put that down to your luck. I did put it down to your luck but then, ten years ago, I saw you.'

'Where?'

'I came to Britain for the first time and visited the British Museum, and there you were, in the reading room with your head in a book. I was sixty. You? Still thirty. Naturally I took this for a remarkable similarity. I certainly didn't want to embarrass myself by approaching a stranger, but I was curious to know if the Victorian thinkers were right, if physiognomy influences character. In short, I wondered what you were reading, whether a man who looked so much like you would share your tastes. So when you got up to go for a break I looked.'

'And?'

'I am flattered to say it was one of my own works, though an insubstantial one – *Newton's Alchemy* – you know, the one that assesses his examination and use of the Emerald Tablet, and explains rather brilliantly the influence of magical thinking on generalised binomial theorem.'

'I know it.'

'Well, you see it wasn't so much the coincidence of you looking exactly like you, acting exactly like you and reading one of my books, albeit one I had given you for your birthday and signed accordingly.'

Only Harbard gave his own books as birthday presents. Craw had taken it to the library to make use of its bibliography.

'It wasn't even the handwriting. I recognised it immediately, of course, and helped myself to a sheet from your notebook. When I returned home it was easy to compare it to a letter you'd sent to me thirty years before. No. I had seen you, Crawford. In meditations, in my ... inner investigations, I had seen you. You walked with me in my visions. I heard you speaking. And then you popped up. I had to investigate.'

'Seen me?'

Harbard waved his hand. 'All in good time.'

'Why did you not approach me?'

'I realised there must have been some reason for you

abandoning totally your previous life and taking on a new name – you had left your membership card on the reading desk, you see. I also guessed that, as you had not contacted me, you were not all that keen to see me.'

'So how did you come to your conclusions about who I was?'

'I didn't just proceed by the conventional means. There are, as you know, practices by which the truly dedicated may gain information.'

'What practices?'

'Self-denial, meditation, ritual.'

'Go on.'

'It seemed pure fortune that in 1935 the German Thule Society invited me to travel with them to Tibet. I thought they were a bunch of crackpot occultists' – Harbard dipped out of the Old Norse into the vernacular – 'but they were picking up the bill, so I went. I did wonder at the time why I had accepted to go with such a bunch of halfwits but there was a reason. I believe I had been directed to do so.'

'By whom?'

'I can't quite say. Something I met in my investigations. A distinct consciousness, anyway, whether an annexed part of my own mind or a separate entity entirely I can't be sure but, in the presence of this ...' he shrugged, 'this thing, I felt it important that I accept the invitation.'

'And?'

'I went. The whole trip was a washout. Well, there was one interesting character – an SS man, believe it or not. Middling clever, but what they would have called a "moral imbecile" in the nineteenth century. Theophrastus the Greek would have called his type the "unscrupulous man", but my friend Hervey Cleckley at University Hospital Augusta would call him a psychopath. I had some very interesting conversations with him.'

'What about?'

'The magical uses of ritual transgression of cultural norms.'

'The magical uses of torture, cannibalism, murder, sex, defilement and humiliation, in other words.'

'Well put. He was willing to go further than ... Well, let's put it this way, it makes you realise what we're fighting against. But he had a problem.'

'Which was?'

'Much of the work in the area of transgression relies on the essential morality of the magician. Your sanity can peel back if you practise cannibalism, for instance, and are revolted by it. If you have no sanity to strip away, no morals to offend, then you're just enjoying a tasty snack. He couldn't achieve what I could achieve.'

'Have you practised cannibalism, Ezekiel?'

Harbard smiled. 'Of course not. There's more than one way of skinning a cat. Though I haven't skinned a cat, either – that's more your native occultist, the Great Beast Aleister Crowley's stock in trade, I understand. But then I made a discovery.'

Harbard had the egotist's habit of pausing for a response from his listener, to taste their interest, to make a pretence that they were involved in what was essentially a monologue. He had an equally irritating tick of presenting his information in stories, marshalling his facts to contain punchlines and suspenses. This made him an entertaining dinner guest, but very frustrating if he had anything important to tell you.

Craw sipped at his brandy. The fire crackled and, from down the hall, a clock chimed out seven times. Harbard went on:

'Local traders were always looking to sell you anything they thought you might buy, which was a lot. We had a youth following us for days, trying to sell us things. He began to irritate the SS man – von Knobelsdorff was his name – as we ascended into the mountains. Even so, the boy wouldn't go away. So I bought a worthless shamanic drum from him in order to get him to go away and prevent the SS from murdering the youth, as I was sure they would if the mood took them. It was strange, as soon as I'd bought this thing, the scales fell from my eyes and I terminated my involvement in the mission and went back to Lhasa. This, however, had an extraordinary effect on von Knobelsdorff, one that I could have predicted, had I given it a second's thought, in fact one that I did predict half way down the mountain, which caused me to take precautions.'

Craw tapped at his palate with his tongue to encourage the scent of the brandy to mix with the gloriously sweet cigarette. The capability to enjoy either was a hallmark of humanity, he thought. Beasts naturally shunned smoke and strong alcohol. Harbard leant forward in his chair and said:

'Of course, von Knobelsdorff couldn't conceive that I'd just become bored by him and gone home. He thought I'd got something of worth. Naturally, I had to take precautions and, by luck, met up with a party of British adventurers in Lhasa who were preparing for a mission to look for lost cities on the Tibetan Plateau. I stuck to them like glue, which meant it was more difficult for the SS to just shoot me and take the drum.'

'Why didn't you throw it away?'

'That would have convinced them I'd hidden it, and God knows what they would have done to me then. No, I remembered my James Frazer. You do remember Sir James Frazer, don't you, Crawford?'

'One of the foremost men in my field. Yes, I should say so.' He inwardly smiled at how effortlessly patronising Harbard could be.

Harbard held up his hand and said, with mock seriousness, as if taking an oath of allegiance, 'The holy tenets of the god Frazer: "Imagination acts upon man as really as does gravitation, and may kill him as certainly as a dose of prussic acid." I think it was the Prussian connection that recalled it. Anyway, I thought that, if he thinks I have some important artefact, let him believe it. I knew that he couldn't shoot me in company, and I kept my own revolver near my bed at night, so I decided to see what he would bid for the drum. I was surprised by the results.'

He jumped from his chair and went over to a glass-fronted cabinet full of books.

'He bid this,' he said, opening the cabinet, 'and I'm happy to say it is now kept in slightly better condition than the way von Knobelsdorff was treating it. You wouldn't transport a penny dreadful like that, let alone a work of this importance.'

Harbard took a long, thin tin from the bookcase. Then he went over to the occasional table and, from beneath it, he took out a leather bag, of the sort doctors use. He opened the bag and produced a muslin sheet, which he laid out on the floor. Then he took out two paper bags. He passed one to Craw and took one himself. He opened his bag, shook two cotton gloves into the palm of his hand, and gestured for Craw to do the same. They both put the gloves on. Harbard took out a short penknife from his pocket, wiped the blade on the muslin, and pried open the box.

'This gives me hope for the entire war effort,' he said. 'The Nazis seem incapable of recognising items of importance even when they have been pointed out to them as items of importance. This, I believe, was bartered for bread by an occultist they'd locked up just after the Reichstag fire.'

'They lock up occultists?'

'And anyone else they don't like the look of. There are occultists they favour and those – the majority – they don't, let's put it that way. God is similarly down on the wizards and soothsayers, you will recall your Bible, so anyone setting himself up as God tends to take that view. By the by. The fact he had this book and that I was guided to it is a sign that ... Well. Yes. I'm on the right track, I know.'

Craw had rarely seen Harbard look so alive. His voice cracked with emotion and his eyes seemed to sparkle as he carefully produced a faded blue notebook from the metal box and laid it down on the muslin.

'Von Knobelsdorff had this for light reading, believe it or not. Er ...' Harbard swallowed slightly and put his hand to his throat. 'I have your word there will be no repeat of the business in the barracks.'

'I have given it,' said Craw.

Harbard nodded and gestured to Craw to pick up the book.

'You clearly remember the Louvetier,' said Harbard.

Craw did, sort of. He remembered that he associated the name with great pain, he could see a picture of him, dressed in his blue brocade, the court's idea of how a hunter would look.

He looked down at the title page. It was in English.

> Being a fulle and troythful accownt of the deelinges of the Grand Louvetier to His Majestie Louis XV, M. d'Enneval wyth the wolffe of Gévaudan as relayted to Mr Edmund Keene, vysiting priest of the holy Roman Catholic Church by dyrect appointimente of his holiness Pope Clement XIII.

Harbard seemed hardly able to contain himself and took the book from Craw and began to read.

'This is what d'Enneval said to the priest,' he said:

> My Jesus. Often have I signed the death warrant by my sins; save me by Thy death from that eternal death which I have so often deserved. My Jesus, who by Thine own will didst take on Thee the most heavy cross I made for Thee by my sins, oh, make me feel their heavy weight, and weep for them ever while I live. My Jesus, the heavy burden of my sins is on Thee, and bears Thee down beneath the cross. I loathe them, I detest them; I call on Thee to pardon them; may Thy grace aid me never more to commit them. Jesus most suffering, Mary Mother most sorrowful, if, by my sins, I caused you pain and anguish in the past, by God's assisting grace it shall be so no more; rather be you my love henceforth till death. O Mary, Mother most sorrowful, the sword

of grief pierced thy soul when thou didst see Jesus lying lifeless on thy bosom; obtain for me hatred of sin because sin slew thy Son and wounded thine own heart, and grace to live a Christian life and save my soul.

'Quite a fit of piety,' said Harbard. 'A little too little too late, one might think. We can skip a bit of that, it does go on rather.' He read on:

I know the wolf. I know him in his habitations, his occupations, his outlooks and his many and several moods. From a boy I hunted him in the hills of Normandy and as a man have travelled the land finding and killing the animals others could not find and kill. My father was Grand Louvetier before me and his father before him. My own boy will not continue the tradition. I am finished with wolf hunting now. It has bought me a fortune, but a hollow one, and for that I thank and blame the Dubosc Stone that I came by in my 20th year.

Harbard turned to Craw. 'There is no further mention of that name "Dubosc" but I have established that there was a discovery of Viking treasures by a farmer Dubosc. He turned up five hundred livres' worth of Norse gold while ploughing. It sparked a mania for digging in the area, but all that happened twenty years before d'Enneval is writing. I speculate that he found the stone he is referring to in the field of the hoard, and that no one else had thought it of interest. Either that, or perhaps the farmer kept it because he couldn't sell it and gave it to d'Enneval for some service. They lived close by, so perhaps the farmer knew the boy and wanted to mark his accession to Grand Louvetier in some way. You would have thought that giving him a stone would be a memorable and cheap way of doing so.'

183

'A stone like the one that Yardley had in his hand?' Craw was sure that Harbard would have been given all of the details by Balby.

Harbard shrugged. 'I thought so at first but now I believe not. That was of a hand. This he describes as engraved with *"un loup arraché"*, a wolf erased, which I think is a heraldic term. In this case, I think it just means, raggedly drawn.'

Craw forced his mind back to the time of the Louvetier. It was no good. His wolf state had wrecked his memory. Some things he could remember clearly – a poem, the movement of the sun on the mountain – but other things were gone entirely. All he knew was that there was a disaster associated with the Louvetier. Before him had been a quiet life in mountains. Afterwards, blood enough to wash the peaks away. It was that that made him bolt.

Harbard read on:

> The ways of the wolf had always been clear to me but, after that terrible pebble came into my belonging, there was nothing he could hide from my insight. Who could find a wolf like I, no matter how deceitful and careful he may be? None. My rare and particular understanding increased my fame throughout our France. So the stone, which I accounted a charm, brought me renown and monies, though it bought me no happiness. For in knowing the wolf so well, I came to love him and it was a great pity to me to kill the fellow. In the hills or the mountains, tracking our prey, living under the cold stars, comfortless and alone but for God, who was to call the difference between he and I? We were brothers in the hunt, though I played Cain to his Abel, and at night heard the voice of his blood crying to me from the ground. For pity, for pity.

Harbard shook his head. 'Now you can say this is the voice of a madman or what you like, but ...' He flicked through the book.

Normally, thought Craw, Harbard would have delighted in unfolding the knowledge slowly, savouring it and withholding the revelations he had to list in order to intrigue and delight his listener. Here, though, he seemed gripped by some fever to get to the end as quickly as he could, to share the secrets he had discovered.

'Look, he relates how he was called to Gévaudan in the Margeride mountains of the Languedoc. There had been killings, and gruesome ones, by a beast that was not a wolf and not a man.' He read on:

> It is a supernatural country, where those at church on a Sunday clothed in Christian modesty may be only hours from the naked revels of the witches' sabbat, dancing in shame before the fires and calling forth frightful spirits. Truly it is called the Pagus Gabalum, the land of the Gabali, a heathen tribe who affrighted the lord here in antiquity. Heresy is here too, with the Cathars rejecting his Holiness in his wisdom. It is a benighted country of shale and slate. Is it no wonder God saw fit to curse them with the visitation of the beast.

Harbard continued, detailing the state of the beast's murders when the Louvetier was called in. Madame Merle, who had her eyes sucked out and the beast spat a fountain of her blood at her attempted rescuers; the infant Marguerite Lèbre, torn to pieces in front of six witnesses; a girl who cried to her sister, 'There's a big wolf behind you!' and who ran, only to be overtaken by her sister's head bowling along the floor; another girl whose brother was abducted by the beast. She ran into the wood to rescue him and found him lying on his face. Only when she turned him did she see the mess the beast had made of his belly and chest. The beast, she said, was the size of a cow and of a reddish appearance. By its tracks it was thought it able to leap for five *toises* – over thirty English feet.

> I set out to snare him in the normal way with baited pits and to track him by hounds. But my subtleties were useless against him and I caught nothing but ordinary wolves. It was the collapse of the town-house that led me finally to him. The good folk of the town had convened to discuss the capture of the creature but so many of them did cram into that space that the floor gave way and it was only by God's mercy that not more were killed. The people cried sorcery. I did not believe them, the weight of numbers being the cause of the collapse, but it gave me at least a direction. Perhaps the beast had been sent by a sorcerer. Accordingly I called for the names of suspected wizards, thaumaturgists and other sundry devil workers in the area. It led me to the mountain, the hermit, and my undoing.

'And then,' said Harbard, 'there was Madame Jeanne Jouve, who fought away the beast.'

The name seemed to stir something in Craw. Jeanne Jouve. He tried to picture her but only came back to Adisla, beautiful by the lakeside.

> Madame Jouve who, at Fau de Brion, came upon the wolf to find it had killed her husband. She drove it off with nothing but her hands and rocks picked up from the ground. The beast had picked up her child too but Madame Jouve drove him away, leaving the infant unharmed. I was intrigued to know how this woman had managed to fight away the creature and with what charms. So I set out to question the lady at her house. I had expected some rough peasant

186

cow of a woman but I was astonished by what I found, a lady of fine features and golden hair, truly a queen among women though her rank was humble and her accomplishments few. She showed no fear of me, though I was dressed as the King's man, and answered all my questions boldly. Surely I think that, had she not been so far below my station, I would have asked for her hand without delay. The lady admitted the use of no charm or talisman to repel the wolf, though I assured her it was wolves not witches that I sought. I asked her to describe the creature and she said he was a good sized wolf, though unusual in that he had stood up on his hind legs to take her child and had seemed to examine it, rather than to bite it. 'So what, lady, did you say to the beast?' I enquired and she said only that she had told him have pity. I could not believe that the creature had responded to this entreaty and was about to leave to return to my lodgings when she, bold and without respect to my rank, asked me if I had not one more question for her. I said that I had not and she, impertinent as a child, said that I should have. I asked what that might be and she said 'You should ask what the wolf said to me.'

Harbard looked up from the book to meet Craw's gaze. He could see that the academic was trembling. 'Do you remember, Endamon? Do you?'

Craw swallowed. If it had been her, Adisla, reborn, he would have told her he loved her. He forced his consciousness back to the room. It was as if his thoughts were all filtered and jumbled, as if he was trying to fix his mind to a point of reference, as a man seeking balance fixes his eyes to a spot on the wall.

'Love,' said Craw.

Harbard read on:

And the lady told me that the beast did declare its love for her, drop the child and run.

'Who was she?' said Harbard.

'I do not know,' said Craw. He felt tears trying to come to to his eyes. 'I remember nothing of it.'

'So we have a beast whose heart melts for love. Now see what the Louvetier finds.' He continued:

The qualities of the wolf hunter are many but foremost among them is luck. Without it the most talented tracker may fail. I was an excellent tracker and, as such, a lucky man. My tour of the habitations of the wizards and hermits had not been fruitful. In particular I had not located the hut of one M. Chastel in the high Cévennes for days, though I had been directed to it. I wandered the hills by day, looking for signs of our wolf, but he was always where I was not and I heard tell in hamlets and at huts when I rested of slaughters several in the villages. It was the third week of my wanderings that I came upon what I thought to be a derelict hut. The roof was in bad repair and the shutters were broken. The day, though, was inclement and the mountain weather turning worse so I opted to seek what shelter I could. In the name of Jesus I would not have stayed there but for the rain. The place was dark and had a powerful stink to it that I could scarcely abide and it seemed no living thing had been there for years. And so I would have thought had it not been for the blood. At first, as I sat, I took it for damp but only when I stood did I see the crimson on my hands. Every surface of the hut seemed to drip with it. I recoiled and was about to run, to accept the absolution of the cleansing rain, when I saw a glint of gold. It was the corner of something poking from its wrapping, scarcely seen through the slats of a crate. I pulled some planks from the crate, threw off its shroud and beheld her face – Madame Jouve, but not Madame Jouve, for she was painted most sacrilegiously as the Madonna, our Virgin, queen of Heaven. I was about to smash the thing for its impiety when I felt the air change in the hut. Something was with me and I heard a voice, low and broken, like a choleric gasping for breath at the last. 'Do not turn,' it said, 'for I have no wish to harm you.' Like a good hunter, I had my hand on my gun and it was primed and ready. 'Look to your own harm,' I said and turned. Had I walked away and never looked over my shoulder my immortal soul would not be in peril this day.

Harbard seemed possessed. 'Enough of this! Do you know what happened, Crawford, do you know what you did? You tried to transfer the curse, to have the Louvetier take on your burden and free you to live as a man. The result? You went mad and went on a rampage of slaughter. Or he did. Look at the accounts. Sometimes the beast appears as a wolf, sometimes as a demented man. You engineered some method of control, some way of preventing your transformation, and – more than that – of passing on its powers to others. I think it was to do with the stones, the Dubosc Stone at least. If we could find that, or an imitation be made under the guidance of revelation ... Have you thought of the implications of that, of what that might mean if we could harness what you have and use it against the enemy? You are shot and you are unmarked, you live for centuries and, if half of what I suspect is true, you would be the most formidable weapon ever deployed on a battle field. All I propose—'

Craw shook his head. 'No.'

'Just no?'

'The cost is too great.'

'Greater than allowing the Germans to win the war?'

'The Germans will not win the war,' said Craw, 'not if, as you guess, the US enters it, not unless the Soviets come to their aid, which I don't think they will.'

'I wish I was so certain. Perhaps you are too high to involve yourself in our affairs. Perhaps it is a matter of indifference to you.'

'It is not a matter of indifference. This country is now my home and, as such, I owe it a duty. It is just a question of the possible, and of ... the weight.'

'The weight?'

'How does a hundred-and-fifty pound man become a wolf of ten or more times that weight? From where do the necessary proteins to build that sort of creature derive?'

Harbard looked surprised. 'I hadn't thought about it.'

'Well, I have and I have come to no good conclusions, but, believe me, I care who wins this war. Care for humans is of utmost importance to me. It is a condition of my own humanity.'

Harbard's eyes widened.

'I hadn't seen,' he said, 'that it might be a question of, of *diet*.' He sat forward in his chair, pondering the implications of what Craw was telling him. 'Will animal flesh not do?'

Craw lowered his eyes to indicate that it would not.

'Almost fifteen hundred pounds of meat. People.' The implications of what Craw was telling him sank in.

'I plucked the figure of ten times from the air,' said Craw. 'The reality, I fear, may be much more.'

For once Harbard was stunned into silence.

There was a knock at the door.

'Come,' said Harbard.

'The police are here, Uncle, have your crimes finally caught up with you?'

The girl was at that age where young women discover irony, everything she said teasing or arch. He hated to look on youth and to consider its decay.

'As Crawford, or rather Endamon, here will tell you, my

190

crimes have only been those of vanity and hubris and the police do not yet arrest for those, or the courts would be full indeed.'

Craw's face was impassive but he wondered if they had come for him again. They had no reason to keep him, he had broken no law. On the other hand, the world of war was full of red tape, so perhaps he had.

'Send them through in five minutes,' said Harbard. 'I have something to discuss with the professor.'

The girl left.

Craw breathed in deeply, trying to collect his thoughts. There was a smell of something beneath the odour of the fire and the brandy. Rotting meat from somewhere below stairs. He sipped at the brandy and inhaled its aroma. His mind, he thought, had been disordered by whatever had cut him down at the gate. He could taste it, though, at the back of his palate – a smack of sickness and disease.

'The Nazis may or may be close to a breakthrough in this matter. They may have deduced things from my own conversations, knowledge shared in good faith before we knew truly who they were.'

'What did you tell them, Ezekiel? Can you bear to keep nothing to yourself?'

Harbard actually coloured. Craw had never seen him like that before.

'There are possibilities, I ...' He looked into the fire. 'I need to tell you that ... Look at the back of the book.'

Craw did, to see that about ten pages had been neatly excised. All that was left was the stubs of pages.

'Yes?' he said.

'The front of the book is the history and theory of how you and he set about lifting the wolf curse. The back pages relate to the practice. Rites. They are what I discovered von Knobelsdorff had removed. I was so much congratulating myself on getting something of this worth for the price of the skin drum that I didn't check it properly when he handed it over. He has it in his power to do these things, or to try. The only thing holding him back, ironically enough, is his lack of humanity.'

'And what are these rites?'

'I never saw them, but at a glance.' Harbard shrugged. 'I'm an academic, not a salesman. I was too keen to close the deal.'

Craw turned down the corners of his mouth. It was the first shred of fallibility Harbard had ever acknowledged. He must, Craw thought, take this thing very seriously indeed. Again, the smell of putrid flesh came into his nostrils. He had been, he thought, on the shores of death and now its smell clung to him.

'So the Nazi might realise what?'

'I don't know. There are possibilties.'

Craw shook his head, as much to free it of the stench of rot as in disagreement.

'But he might not realise what he has.' He sensed Harbard's fear.

'I wrote and asked for copies of the pages from von Knobelsdorff. He refused. I fear I may have alerted him to their value.'

'And what is their value?'

Harbard leafed through the Louvetier's book. 'There are pointers here,' he said, 'avenues, that might ... I fear that this might be used to summon you.'

'The only thing that could summon me is the dinner gong.' Craw's voice was harsh, and he reproved himself for speaking in such an imperious way. He softened his attitude and said, 'Talking of which, I could do with something to eat.'

He could as well – he was ravenous, but comfortably so, the sort of hunger that would be satisfied by a roast dinner and pudding, not that sharper thing that dwelled within him.

'The police are waiting to see you. You could see them while you eat.'

Craw's look of alarm was so striking that Harbard laughed.

'Dinner's becoming an informal occasion, Crawford.'

'Then we must resist the tide. The policemen can wait.'

They were functionaries, servants, not men of the blood. But was it right to treat them in such a way? The thought surprised him. Perhaps the feudal period, with its habits and attitudes that had endured in him more solidly than any memory, was finally leaving him.

Harbard shook a bell on the occasional table. There was no reply. He shook it again. Still, no one came. Harbard got up in irritation, went to the study door, and opened it to pus and bone and teeth and blood. He was staring into the jack-o-lantern smile of Mr David Arindon.

19 Encroachment

Gertie was angry when Max confronted her about the watch.

'It's not hers, it's mine,' she said.

'Well, I think we should tell her that you have one very similar in case it causes any confusion.'

'OK, it is hers, but she stole it. She told me she got it as a birthday present this year, which means she got it from the camps. Smelly Haussmann wouldn't have paid full price for that! So it was stolen off someone. Which gives her no more moral right to it than I have. It's mine. That's the end of it.'

'What if she sees it?'

'She won't. I won't wear it when we socialise with them.'

'Gertie, what's happened to you? You've never stolen anything in your life.'

'It's not stealing! Mrs Haussmann is a fright. This watch needs to be worn by someone beautiful. The craftsmen who made it would have wanted it that way. I can't believe you're making such a fuss.'

'Have you thought for a second of all the problems this could cause me? Haussmann's my boss,' said Max.

Everything seemed to be mounting up on him. Sleep would not come, even though he had prescribed himself enough barbiturates to stop a rhino. Sleep? He should have been able to hibernate on the amount he'd taken. Now Gertie seemed to have cracked under the pressure and developed this ... kleptomania.

Even Michal, who had once seemed a point of sanity in all this, had changed. Since the death of his friend he had become harder. The boy hadn't exactly become withdrawn, just that the pleasant aspects of his personality had seemed to wither. He had become rather grasping, always asking for cigarettes or coins. Max sympathised with the child; he knew what horrors he had faced. But Michal was no longer as easy company as he had been. Max had scolded himself.

'All you don't like, Max,' he had said, 'is that he's becoming less of a victim.'

Gertie had her hand on her watch as if to defend it.

'That about sums you up, doesn't it, Max, the problems things cause you? Other husbands would have tried to move things forward at the castle. Other husbands would have grasped this opportunity and be getting me nice things, instead of worrying about the fate of some monkey.'

He'd had enough. He had to tell someone, someone who was still on the sane side of the world, the side with moral content.

'It's not a fucking monkey!' he shouted.

Gertie went quiet. He felt ashamed of the violence of his outburst, and his wife let him feel that shame in a few beats of silence. Eventually she spoke.

'I know, it's a boy. I hear the rumours in the castle, Max.'

'And you still want me to go ahead?'

Gertie cast her eyes to the floor. 'How can you not?'

'Well, as you might imagine, I've given that some thought.' He was curt and bitter.

'And your conclusion?'

'There is no conclusion. I don't know. I've tried stalling them in every way I can. I'm not killing that boy, though, whatever they do.'

'What might they do?'

'I don't know. I will have countermanded an order of Heinrich Himmler. What do you think they'll do? Whatever they fucking like.'

Max looked out of the window of their room, down towards the camp, that new chimney seeping white smoke into the sky. It seemed as if the plume was like a hand stretching towards him, or like a bridge across which he might walk.

He'd avoided acknowledging what it was when he'd first seen it. Steam. The human body is seventy-odd per cent water. 'Seventy-odd? Oh, come on, Max,' he said to himself, 'you know that fraction.' His mind wouldn't work, though, he couldn't even recall that basic fact. His brain had given up, surrendering many of its higher powers under the constant stress that robbed him of sleep. The plume was from a crematorium. How could a camp of that size need a crematorium? There were less than six hundred people in it, mostly the Bible Students. In that population, in a year you'd be unfortunate to get two deaths. And yet the plume, the plume that stretched towards him like a pale snake across the blue, blue sky, could be seen almost daily.

A terrible thought came down on him. All he'd seen at Wewelsburg was ad hoc bullying, beating and cruelty. The overwork and short rations were systematic but the violence, though regular, was off the cuff, depending on the boredom of the guards or if the Jehovah's Witnesses, with suicidal bravery, suddenly announced they would not work on a project out of some moral scruple. How he admired them, how he wished he had that in him to just say 'Put me on the landing craft, take me away from my Gertie, kill me. I will not be part of it.' But he didn't have that species of open courage. He told himself that he couldn't put himself in the firing line, for Gertie's sake.

Still, the terrible thought grew in him. Many of the SS were lazy, corrupt, stupid, inadequate and, in a vast number of cases, simply crap at their jobs. To call Haussmann a second-rate doctor was an insult to second-rate doctors, and he was one of the brighter ones. Like all fanatics and fundamentalists, to Max they seemed fundamentally thick. Even the Witnesses, he thought, were stupid. Why not just make things easy for themselves, say 'You know what, there is no God, open the camp gates, I'm off down the boozer'?

Haussmann had actually asked Max's help in designing some other experiments, ghastly things, and he had been shocked at just what a blunderer the man was. And yet he was in charge of professors, in some cases.

However, he couldn't deny there was a policy, spoken or not, of murder by overwork. The SS wanted to kill their victims, but they didn't seem overly concerned if some survived. They at least offered a chance of survival, or the pretence of a chance of survival. If you had a talent, were a craftsman, or just lucky, you might just manage to keep breathing – little more. And still the plume stretched out over the camp almost daily. This was that terrible thought. How many chimneys would they need if they ever became organised in their murders? What if murder became the sole aim of what they were doing? What if they just dropped the pretence, went for the throat? No work, no beatings – just murder. The plumes would blot out the sky.

Gertie touched his face. 'There are nasty rumours about you, Max,' she said.

'Like what?'

'"Little Michal Wejta's getting rather fat. He has been ordered to be rested. No one can lay a hand on him. What goes on in that little room of your husband's with the gypsy queer?"'

Max laughed. 'Funnily enough, he's not a gypsy. Surely you don't believe that, Gertie.'

'Of course I don't. But lies breed freely in bored garrisons.'

'What do you think I should do?'

'Compromise?'

'What does that mean?'

'Find a way to meet them halfway.'

'Become half a murderer?' he said.

'A lot of those people are going to die anyway, Max. Surely with the sick ones you'd be doing them a favour.'

'Gertie!'

'Sorry, Max. I don't know. I mean, there are no good options here. None. Heroism is all very well but only if there's a point. You can't save anyone. Well, anyone but yourself.'

'I'm not ...' Max wanted to say what he wasn't. A killer? A torturer? The words would not come.

He looked at Gertie and wanted to hold her. The stress was affecting her as much as him. That, he was sure, was what the theft was about. A woman of Gertie's sensitivity couldn't be surrounded by such horrors and emerge unscathed. He would take the watch back to Haussmann and drop it in his office. It would all be all right. All of it. Yes. It had to be.

'Come on, Max,' she said. She came to him, kissed him , he held her and they made love on the bed.

'There is nothing but you,' he said. 'You are all I have.'

'And I you,' said Gertie.

At nine there was a knock on the door.

It was an SS man. In his arms was a crate with the crocodile inside it.

'It has come to the attention of Senior Storm Command Leader von Knobelsdorff that you have not been caring for this creature correctly.'

'Is this a joke?' said Max.

'I assure you, no. The room you are keeping the crocodile in is too small. It is an aquatic reptile and needs a dry/wet environment. Your kitchen area has been deemed suitable. I am to set up the animal's living conditions. Please show me to the correct area.'

'Max, this is horrible!' said Gertie.

'Tell him "no",' said Max.

'He anticipated your response,' said the SS man, 'and states that there is no possibility of refusing this order. Furthermore you are to meet him at your lab at 1.20 sharp tomorrow afternoon.'

'Why at my lab?'

'He wishes to see your experiments. Faster progress is necessary. The Senior Storm Command Leader accepts your experiments with the first subject are ongoing. Therefore a new patient will be sent up in the morning, you will prepare the patient, experiment immediately and the Senior Storm Unit Leader will oversee what you are doing.'

Max glanced at Gertie. She looked pale.

'Leave that thing outside,' he said. 'I will deal with this once and for all.'

'I will not leave it here. I am authorised to use force to install the crocodile if necessary.'

'Use it then, you fucking—'

'Max!' said Gertie.

He was quiet.

'Let them do it,' she said. 'We will work our way around this tomorrow.'

The guard saluted. He clicked his fingers and a group of three Witness workers entered behind him, carrying bags of cement.

'Try not to make a mess,' said Gertie, as they came in.

The workers toiled into the night and by 3 a.m. had finished. Max opened the kitchen door. A pond, made from a cut-down bathtub, had been concreted into the floor – or rather, concrete had been fixed around it to construct a sort of island in the middle of the kitchen, a good eight feet in diameter. There, in the water, was the top of the crocodile's nose. It lifted its neck out of the water and hissed at him. Max had a strong urge to go in there and stamp on it, an urge that he didn't think he would be able to resist for very long. He didn't just want to kill this crocodile – he wanted to hurt it, to watch it suffer. He saw visions of what he might do with boiling water, or with a skewer.

He shook his head. What was he becoming? The tension of clinging to his decency in this terrible castle, like a man caught in a torrent might cling to a branch, was overwhelming him. He was awake, but it seemed that he dreamed. He saw the faces of the prisoners before him, their youth eaten by starvation and work, he heard the sound of beatings echoing in his head, the stain on the wall left by von Knobelsdorff's butchery, that horrid plume of smoke stretching towards him, twelve idiots waiting for a dead man to speak and, right in the deep of his mind, he heard the sawing – day and night, the sawing, the banging, the reconstruction. Now he couldn't even go in to get a cup of acorn coffee without entering the stink of a creature, stepping round that surreal construction, the little hell von Knobelsdorff had made in his home.

Something, Max decided, needed to be done, something drastic. In or out, with all the consequences. He needed to make the decision, and by tomorrow morning. The SS would have to be embraced or defied. There was no middle ground with them, no slipping around them. He looked back at Gertie, sitting on the bed in her slip and examining the stolen watch. The moonlight turned her skin to silver, as if she was a figure from a myth who had become so beautiful that the gods had transformed her into a statue, so that they might enjoy looking at her for ever. She was, he thought, the only thing in his life that made any sense.

20 Moonlight Sonata

'Eleanor!' Harbard shouted, as the ghoulish Arindon shoved past him into the room.

Craw stood facing Arindon for a second, each man frozen in surprise to see the other.

Arindon's face was a swollen mess and Craw found it difficult to believe that an infection had not taken him. The poor man was still in his bloody hospital robes, though barefoot and filthy. To Craw, the madman appeared as a strange double, a reflection of his own inner turmoil.

He forced his mind back to reality. Was it better to detain Arindon here and question him under police custody? No, there was no guarantee he would get the sort of privacy he required. Better to let him go a little way and interview him privately. He felt instinctively that he knew something of value. Coventry spivs don't converse in Old Norse as a habit. But what of the girl, Eleanor? And the staff? Craw felt no sympathy for whatever fate had befallen the cooks and servants at Arindon's hands. As a nobleman, he simply didn't see his inferiors as belonging to the same species as him. What he felt, though, went as deep as sympathy – that he had missed his duty of care towards them. Humans are pack animals, and packs have hierarchies that bind those on the top as much as they do those below. It was natural for Craw to expect tribute of goods and services from farmers and serfs, but equally natural that he should defend the peasants if they were threatened. If anyone had suffered he would take it as a stain on his honour, though he cared little for their actual pain.

Arindon had seized the opportunity allowed him by Craw's indecision to crash through the French doors looking out over the lawn. Balby and Briggs, alerted by the noise, came running into the room along with the girl, Eleanor.

'Eleanor, darling, you're safe,' Harbard hugged her to him and then turned to the policemen. 'Shoot him!' he shouted. 'Shoot him!'

David Arindon, still in his hospital robes, was running away, across the grass of Coombe Abbey, past the ornamental lake and into the trees.

'I haven't got a gun,' said Briggs.

'And he hasn't actually done anything,' said Balby.

They went out through the French doors onto the lawn, peering out into the moonlight, trying to see which way he had gone. The guard came lumbering up with his gun.

'What's all the noise?' said the guard.

'Aren't you meant to tell us that?' said Harbard.

'I'm allowed a leak, aren't I?'

The air steamed around them as they breathed. It was cold; there would be a frost. A moon hung in the clear blue November sky, full and heavy. It was five o'clock, just beyond sunset, a glorious evening.

Only Craw had the eyesight to see Arindon moving off into the trees. He had to speak to him, to question him if possible. *Forad* – monster. The word beat in his mind like a shaman's drum. Did Arindon know something, or had something been shown to him? He had to find out.

'Come on,' he said.

'Don't put yourself at risk, this is a police matter,' said Balby, but Craw was gone off.

Across the lawn, a leap over the ha-ha, and through a small area of pasture. The woods were alive with the smells of birds, rats, and the putrefaction of Arindon's wounds. Craw's vision was sharper too, more attuned to the moonlight that came streaming through the trees. He felt human still, but it was as if his wolf nature had calmed since that visit to the black shore and was now more like a tool at his disposal. The way was clear to Craw, Arindon's smell hanging in hollows between roots, smeared on trees as he passed, caught on ferns, bright and obvious as the trail of a slug in the moonlight.

Craw moved silently and quickly, running through the woods unheard. From ahead of him, fifty yards away, near the road, he could hear repressed breathing. Arindon might have been mad, he thought, but he had enough sanity, or survival instinct, to try to quiet his breath. He saw no need for a rush as he made his way towards his man. He would subdue him and question him in whatever time he had before the police arrived. Whatever was said, and in whatever language, he didn't want Harbard getting involved.

'Don't worry, Professor Craw, we're coming!' It was Balby, with a torch beam raking the trees.

'Leave him to us, we know what we're doing!' shouted Briggs. He was running through the trees, crashing like a wild boar.

'Ssshhh!' Craw hissed, but it was too late. Arindon was up and running, onto the road, which was glittering white in the light of the moon, and towards a parked police car. Arindon jumped in. Craw felt certain that, no matter what his criminal past, he would not be able to start it without tools and, as a gentlemen, he hated to introduce any more kerfuffle into a situation than already existed. Also, the quieter he could be, the less likely the police would get there before he did. The policemen were going off in the wrong direction, so he just walked up to the car. In fact, he thought, Arindon had imprisoned himself. If he wanted to get out the other side it would take time for him to move across the seats, negotiate the gearstick and open the door. Craw would be able to move around the car and wedge him in.

The policemen came crashing to the edge of the wood.

Craw looked into the car. Arindon looked out, his burst smile like a ghoulish exhibit beneath the glass.

'*Vord?*' said Craw in the old language, and then, 'Wife?'

'*Hrafn.*' The word sounded warm and wet through the man's mutilated lips. Was it a word? Had he said 'raven', or was it just some failed attempt at something more mundane?

A torch beam was on Craw. His interview, it seemed, was at an end until he could get Arindon alone.

'I have him gentlemen, if you would be so kind,' he said.

There was a short bark. The car engine started and Arindon drove off.

Craw looked at the policemen. The policemen looked back.

'I left the keys in,' said Briggs. Balby shook his head. 'Well, I didn't think there'd be anyone out here, did I? Why didn't you stop him, Professor?'

But Briggs was talking to the air. Craw was already striding away down the long drive of the abbey, pulled by a scent of oil, rubber, leather, and the sweat of fear, to where David Arindon had gone.

'I shall need to talk to you!' Balby shouted. 'Where are you going?'

'To stretch my legs, officer,' said Craw.

'To stretch ... Oh, what's the point.' Balby turned to Briggs. 'Let's get back to the house and report the car missing,' he said.

Craw broke into a run. He followed Arindon's scent down past the houses of the Brinklow road and into the old centre of the city. It was an easy trail to follow on such a still clear night, with little traffic on the roads and the high, clear moon that seemed to purify the air. There were few people on the streets, as the factories had not yet finished their twelve-hour day shift and those who had business in the city had left before the sun went down.

If the bombers did strike, he thought, they would have an easy time of it under the moon. Not a chink of light shone anywhere on the ground but he could still read the billboards.

Colds spread in crowded shelters. Take Vicks with you.

The Government calls on poultrymen to produce more eggs. Don't trust to luck, insist on the inclusion of Milkiwey in all your poultry mashes.

God, how he hated these capitalists, like rats feeding off the corpses of their heroes. If he had any say in it he'd have had them shot for their opportunism.

A mile out of the city centre, Craw was stopped by a patrolling policeman and asked to present his papers.

'A long way from home, sir.'

'Yes,' said Craw, 'I am here at the invitation of an Inspector Balby.'

'God-botherer,' said the policeman. 'Though a good copper, they say.'

Craw nodded. 'I should say so.'

'You were running. Do you mind if I ask why?'

'To get where I'm going more quickly and to keep warm.'

The policeman looked him up and down. He seemed to Craw a hulking and cumbersome thing, very Anglo-Saxon, heavy boned and shambling. His smell was of pitch and of soil, and Craw guessed that he might be a keen gardener.

'You get into a shelter,' said the policeman, looking up at the moon. 'There's bound to be a raid tonight.'

'London's their target. I doubt you'll see more than a stick of bombs here.'

'Well, let's hope they don't hit another picture house. I still haven't seen *Gone with the Wind*.'

Craw smiled and bid him good night, following the scent of the police car, the distinctive leather of the seat leading him forward for a time then, at another junction, a tendril of the scent of Arindon's decaying flesh pointing the way. The Victorian brick of the outskirts gave way to the Tudor alleys of the centre. Then he was in the wide space of Broadgate, the shops far apart and the tramlines vacant like long slimy eels, the street almost empty.

It was ten to seven and people had left the centre in fear, but not anticipation of a raid. Down to his right was the large medieval church that he took to be the cathedral. There was a huge arched window facing the city centre, though it had been boarded up. In large letters, someone had painted the words *It all depends on us, and we depend on God.*

Behind the arch was the spire, massive against the moon.

Craw paused and looked around him. Coventry was, he thought, a handsome town. He took comfort in the humanity of that thought but, in a bargain with the beast, sniffed the air again. Arindon was in front of him and to his right, inside what he took for the cathedral.

There was the police car, its front stoved in where it had hit a large static water tank that had been put out for firefighting. The car had been moved away from the dented tank and parked neatly.

A car came around the top of Broadgate. Craw could see it was Harbard's Humber Snipe. It pulled up and Balby and Briggs got out.

'What are you doing here?' said Balby.

'Looking for Arindon.'

'You should have told us if you knew where he was going. I've waited an hour and half to get news of the car. How did you know he'd be here? How did you get here?'

'The cathedral is smaller than I imagined it,' said Craw, ignoring the questions.

'That's not the cathedral,' said Briggs. 'It's Holy Trinity, the other mob.'

Craw looked down the side of the building. Yes, there was the outline of an even larger church behind it.

'I think, sir, that you ...' Balby did not continue the sentence. He looked up at the moon. He changed the subject. 'He's not in the car, let's take it out of here and examine it in the morning. I don't have a good feeling about tonight.'

Craw looked across Broadgate. All the trams had stopped, no cars moved.

An air raid warden moved past the sandy brick of the new Owen Owen building and down the hill towards them.

'We'll be OK here, boss, they'll be after the factories anyway,' said Briggs.

'It's still not safe to spend any longer here than we have to. We've done as much as is sensible, we've found the professor and established that Arindon is no longer in the car. Everyone sane has left here, we should do the same.'

The words hit Craw's back. Already he was making his way up the steps towards the massive front of the medieval church. A scent of dried blood and infected flesh lay like a carpet on the church steps.

'What exactly do you intend to do if you find him?' Balby shouted. 'You're a danger to yourself and us.'

The end of his sentence was lost under the keening of the sirens. Craw looked up from the top of the steps. In the distance, against the moon, he could see planes. How many? He did a quick count as they passed. Thirteen. It would, he thought, be a substantial raid.

Craw stepped into the church and looked down the aisle, through a succession of Gothic arches. Above the first was a figure of Christ at the Last Judgement, at his right the saved, at his left the sinners. It was a doom painting, a medieval work to show the faithful their reward and the sinners their terrible fate. At the bottom, on Christ's left, stood the mouth of hell, depicted as the jaws of an animal.

Craw recalled Matthew. 'Then the king will say to those on His right hand, "You have my Father's blessing; come, enter and possess the kingdom that has been ready for you since the world was made ..." Then He will say to those on his left hand, "The curse is upon you; go from my sight to the eternal fire that is ready for the devil and his angels".'

He moved down the aisle, looking into the pools of darkness under arches to his left and right. There was no sign of Arindon, though a flavour of blood hung on the air.

And then it was as if an angel had come into the church. The stained glass of the window at the end had not been boarded up, and it seemed to burst with light. For a second it was as if Jesus had come to life in the windows and was coming down to judge him. A flare from a pathfinder was clearly above them. A pathfinder? Craw went cold. Thirteen aircraft had crossed the moon. He had thought they were the raid.

What if they hadn't been the raid, though? What if they were just dropping markers for the main force of bombers behind? How big might that be? As if in answer, that mumble sprang up low in the distance, clearly a way off but intense, with a deeper note than he had known in previous raids. What was coming?

Balby and Briggs came into the church.

'Professor Craw,' said Balby, 'you need to get to a shelter. The raid's on top of us. Arindon will have to wait.'

Balby had seen the flares descending on their parachutes, two of them near him. They had seemed, he thought, like the angels who had visited Sodom.

Craw, in the church, looked savage and strange to Balby. The stained glass had been designed to dazzle in the sunlight. In the million candlepower of the flares it filled the inside of the church with a shattered rainbow that coloured Craw's skin as if he was some gaudy reptile.

'These are flares,' said Craw. 'There will be at least five minutes before the bombs drop, and they will only be incendiaries to further mark the target. I estimate we have twenty minutes before we are in real danger, gentlemen. The church has a crypt, if the worst comes to the worst.'

He walked off down the aisle towards the great image of Christ on the cross at the end of the church. He breathed in. Beneath the old smell of incense and wine and ancient wood was another odour, more distinct. Blood. Arindon was there, he was sure.

'Get into a shelter, Professor Craw!' shouted Balby.

'You go,' said Craw.

'Get into a ...' Balby's voice was lost as a sound like heavy rain hit the roof.

'Those will be incendiaries,' Craw shouted. 'You might be better employed helping your colleagues fight the fire rather than bothering me. I will join you shortly.'

The quality of the light began to change. Before, under the brilliant flares, the stained glass had marked their skin like a strange dye. Now small fires were starting outside and the light began to undulate and shift.

'Get ...' Balby shook his head and ran out of the church.

Craw began to look around the altar, in between the pews. He could smell Arindon's blood somewhere and he could smell something else, now he was nearer to the source. An undertone, a feeling in the smell, a hint like the taste you can't quite place of something alien and yet very familiar. Could it be wolf?

At the south side of the church was a window, God seated with Jesus at one hand, the Holy Spirit at the other. The Trinity. Three in one, the divine on earth.

He could smell the fires now, that rich scent of phosphorus, like garlic, as if some hideous cook was adding seasoning to the city. He felt a shift in temperature. Where would you go if you were looking to hide? Up. The trail dragged him to the back of the church, into the cool white interior of an office. It led to a thick door. He opened it and was surprised to find himself outside. To his right he saw a flight of narrow stone steps leading up to another door. These, he thought, would take him to the tower.

He moved towards the steps. From the corner of his eye, he caught movement. Two ARP men – air raid wardens – were coming from the direction of the cathedral, their faces obscured by black gas masks. One, he noted, was carrying a Thompson sub-machine gun.

He thought nothing of it and entered the tower, making his way up the tight stone spiral staircase, illuminated through narrow slits by flares and by moonlight. He was halfway up before the incongruity of what he had seen struck him. ARP men did not carry sub-machine guns. Who were they, then? He couldn't think about that, he had to find Arindon and see what he might reveal about these murders and, more importantly, his wife. Up, up and up. Below him was a faint, glow, sporadic like the flash of a far-off lighthouse. A flashlight, he guessed. The men were following him. Were these Harbard's 'dark forces', the people who had sought to summon him? Perhaps they would be able to tell him something of his wife. If there were competent sorcerers about, Craw thought, he would talk to them no matter what side they were on.

The white flashes below him were now answered by red and orange ones from above. He was nearing the end of the climb and the door at the top of the tower had clearly been left open. He stepped out onto a narrow balcony, made treacherous by buttresses protruding across the floor. The battlements were no more than thigh height. He'd have to be careful if he didn't want a quick trip to the roof below. He looked out over the city.

> *The sun turns black, earth sinks in the sea,*
> *The hot stars down from heaven are whirled;*
> *Fierce grows the steam and the life-feeding flame,*
> *Till fire leaps high about heaven itself.*

The prophecy his forefathers had spoken of, the prediction of the end of the world, was coming true, Craw was sure. From the top of the church steeple the city burned, the heat haze making it look like something under water, flickering anemones of flame, reefs of fire streaking through the dark, while above him, like great rays, moved the bombers.

Craw had never seen anything like it. The whole city seemed to be burning and yet, he knew, this wasn't even the beginning. First would come the marker flares, then incendiaries to turn the whole town into a beacon to guide in its real destroyers – the heavy bombers with their high explosives and mines.

The tower was at the centre of the church, and four roofs spread out from it in the shape of a cross. On them, small groups of men worked, throwing down incendiary bombs with spades, smothering fires with sand and extinguishing them with stirrup pumps. They were brave defenders of the faith, of a symbol, of something more important than factories or fuel dumps. Throughout history, Craw thought, humanity had striven to protect things that, to a cynic, mean nothing. He, however, knew the importance of anchors for the mind, of lighthouses of faith and belief that allow a direction through the chaos of existence. He closed the door to the balcony and was disappointed to see that it couldn't be barred. He moved around the tower quietly and there, in the east and wedged into the narrow space of the floor, was the crumpled figure of David Arindon.

Craw went to him.

'Vord,' he said. 'Vord.'

Arindon turned to Craw. He did not look well. His face was ragged, torn, black with soot and dirt.

'Fenrisulfr?' said Arindon, the word hardly distinguishable through his ravaged lips.

The Fenris wolf, slayer of the gods, the slaughter beast, offspring of that tricky fellow, the god Loki. Craw shivered, despite the heat of the burning town below him. In his mind he saw a hillside, a black mountain against a grey sky. And then the hillside had seemed to move and that terrible eye had settled upon him. That was his name. Fenrisulf, he who would fight the Gods on the final day. Was he to do that one day?

'mælir Óðinn
við Míms höfuð.'

Craw could hardly make out the words, but he knew them well enough from his visions at the drowning pool. A sensation of claustrophobia overtook him, his mind felt sealed under a close darkness.

'Once more Odin speaks with Mimir's head.'

Vision failed under a blinding light and the tower shook. A big bomb, and near too.

'Vord,' said Craw, kneeling over Arindon. 'Wife.'

Craw heard a click behind him. He looked round. There

was one of the men in gas masks. He had levelled a Thompson gun at Craw.

'I'm helping this man,' said Craw, 'you'll need to help me get him ...'

Arindon was fumbling in the inside of his jacket, trying to pull something out.

A burst of bullets cut into Craw's back, pushing him forward over Arindon. The pain was excruciating but he had felt worse. He looked up to see the second man, who had come round the other side of the tower. He was levelling a pistol, not at Craw but at Arindon. Behind him the machine-gunner was refitting a magazine.

The pistol fired and Craw saw something extraordinary. The hair on Arindon's head was parted momentarily, but the bullet didn't penetrate. Again the pistol fired. This time a hole appeared in Arindon's prison smock. But no blood. No penetration. Arindon, too, seemed shocked, and just gazed up at his attacker. Craw was stunned and he might have just sat there for in shock, had the man with the pistol not missed on his third shot and hit Craw hard in the chest. Again, the pain was terrible, though the bullet bounced away without breaking the skin.

Craw didn't think. He leapt up from his crouched position, past the seated Arindon, and caught the man with the pistol in a tackle below the arms, driving him up and over the balcony. The machine-gunner had refitted his magazine and fired again at Arindon. In the fraction of a second before Craw closed the distance between himself and the Thompson man, the gun discharged two shots, one of which hit him and one of which struck Arindon under the arm. One more went off as he lifted the machine-gunner off his feet and threw him to the floor. This shot ricocheted off a wall and also struck Arindon. As the Thompson hit the floor it jammed on fire, leaping like a jumping jack and discharging its load of remaining bullets on the balcony of the tower, hitting Craw, hitting Arindon, hitting the man who held it. Blood filled the air, blood and smoke and fire and noise. The impact of a shot pushed Craw back onto Arindon, and then something happened that was not meant to happen. Arindon had located what he was looking for in his jacket pocket.

It was as if the bombs and the fire were in Craw's blood, in his brain, in his mouth and his eyes. The change was on him, and as he had never known it. Craw fell apart.

The wolf stepped out of him. In front of Craw on the balcony was himself as he had never seen himself – as a huge wolf, an extravagant lolling tongue rolling under teeth the size of knives.

The machine-gunner was screaming, holding his side, blood pooling on the narrow floor of the ramparts. The wolf looked at Craw and said:

A lyttle somethinge for myne hungers, sir, if you please.

The voice was speaking in no language Craw understood; it was almost as if he saw what it said written across the inside of his skull in a ripper's scrawl.

Then Arindon was there. He had somehow come past the great wolf as if it didn't exist. Craw's limbs seemed robbed of movement. There was a sudden stillness. The bombs themselves seemed to cease in one of those odd pauses in the progression of things, like they say happens when an angel is passing, an interlude in the Luftwaffe's moonlight sonata, a silence to express the following noise more deeply. Arindon held something above his head.

Myne hungers, sir, do not disregard or disavow them.

Arindon stepped towards Craw. In his hand he held something that Craw could not name, but could understand.

Myne hungers, sir, are as sharp as needles.

There was a rattle beneath them, like a giant rat scuttling over the roof. It broke that frozen moment. An incendiary had struck but failed to ignite on the church roof. It clattered along, like a drunken drum roll to announce the recommencement of the bombardment of sound.

Arindon put his hand towards Craw, and he felt a sharp

pain in his chest. He looked up to see an inch of rusty metal protruding from just below his shoulder blade. He tugged on the end but his hand slipped. He looked down at his fingers. He had cut them. It was generations since he had seen his own blood, and the sight fascinated him.

Bombs burst around him, there was heat and flame and the sound of falling timber and smashing glass. He stood and the city seemed to whirl; the cathedral next to him was in flames and the light was more blinding than a desert day.

He tugged again at the metal in his chest. This time it slid out – a thin piece of rusted steel about eight inches long. He looked at it glisten. The metal had a slight curve to it, he thought.

Indulge myne hungers but this little while.

The wolf spoke again. Craw dropped the metal onto the balcony. It was as if the firestorm was in his head now, huge pressures condensing and crushing his thoughts, blasts ripping through reason and restraint.

The machine-gunner groaned and rolled over.

Craw heard a voice in his head.

Little pig, little pig, do let me come in.

'I will let you in,' Craw heard his own voice replying.

The wolf sprang forward at the groaning man, tearing his throat with his teeth, ripping at his clothing with his claws, pulling away the outer flesh of the torso and driving his muzzle deep into the liver, into the heart. Craw was transfixed by the wolf's attack, fascinated by the beauty of its muscles, the deep lustre of its fur. There was a sound behind him. Something was scrabbling about. It was Arindon. He had picked up the piece of metal but now Craw could see it for what it really was: a beautiful Arab sword, subtly curved, catching the fire of the burning town, itself becoming part of that fire, as if Arindon had caught hold of a bloody crescent moon.

A flash of memory. A sword, a terrible curved sword held by a fierce warrior with bone-white hair. Himself, a wolf, gazing up at it. What was the sword's name? Death. Yes. Death. The Moonsword.

Arindon spoke, clearly and unhampered by his ruined lips.

'I have seen the most, and widely has my mind travelled.' He held up the shard of the moon. 'This sword was poisoned with the dreams of witches.' The voice began to distort and Craw saw again that stabbed-out scrawl on the inside of his his head:

Orl yr possibiliteys wylle collaps. Amme I notte yr brothere?

He saw a man with long white hair standing before him, the strange curved sword at his side. He saw the same sword, too, rising in candlelight, like a curve of flame to cut him and ... what? To kill him? It was an ancient weapon, he thought, his ancient bane.

Then Arindon was gone, away down the stairs and the wolf finished feeding. Craw looked about him. The wolf was gone, too. Craw was covered in a strange slime. An iron taste, odd and delicious, was in his mouth and below him lay the torn corpse of the Thompson gunner.

The world was different to Craw now. The sounds of the burning city were overwhelming, its odours by turns frightening and enticing. He could smell his own thick blood, the fires, the ruptured gas mains and sewers and death, death everywhere, reeking up at him from the streets. Underneath it all, though, he smelled Arindon. The trail had been subtle and elusive only hours earlier. Now it was like a warm current in a river that he could follow to its source. But more than that, he could smell attitudes and emotions on the stones upon which Arindon had sweated: exultation, the end of fears, and something more – a sense of completion. The smeared sweat on the inside of the tower said Arindon was going back to something he considered home and, through the bombs and the fires, Craw only knew that he felt compelled to follow.

21 Limits

Max had spent a sleepless night with his wife at his side, wondering what to do.

As Gertie slept, it seemed that he could almost see her ambitions as physical things in front of him. She didn't want to stay a jobbing doctor's wife for the rest of her life. She wanted a fine house in the country, a motor car, jewellery. The theft, he decided, as he looked at the watch – Gertie had not removed it before getting into bed – was a symptom both of stress and desire. He had not tried hard enough to please her. His life had been one of selfish indulgence, of feet up in the office and drinks down at the beer hall, at least before he came to the castle.

There was no way out, he thought. The grandmother would be someone marked for death anyway and, who knew, perhaps in an even fouler way than dying in that chair. He would make it quick and it would be finished. He would write up his report, conclude that everything von Knobelsdorff was doing was right, and that would be an end to it. It would all be over. Then he would take his place in the SS and worry about the future as it happened. With tiredness and stress, such thoughts can seem reasonable. He had never been someone who did right, nor someone who did wrong. Always he had pursued the path of least resistance. And here it was again. What he really wanted was an end to the turmoil that had gripped his mind.

The next day he was in early. He had no idea what it was that sent him to the lab at six in the morning, but he found himself rehearsing every situation imaginable, from telling von

Knobelsdorff where to stick it to performing the operation. Could he do it? Max was aware he was no hero, but he wasn't a villain either. Could he not do it? He knew that news of his refusal would go straight to Himmler. And then what? His fate would be in the hands of that oily rat. He leaned forward, his head in his hands. What an idiot he had been. His fate was already in Himmler's hands, and had been from the moment he'd sent that stupid paper. Whatever happened now was his fault, for sure, but was it his responsibility? Moral cowardice, Arno had noted, loves fine distinctions.

He waited and waited, smoked and thought, and finally it was 9 a.m. and the subject of his operation was delivered.

He had not counted on them sending him a child. She came up from the camp with Michal and a guard.

The girl was small and dark and familiarly starving, her eyes large in her shrunken face. She wore the violet triangle of a Witness. Max sent the guard away. He went into the room with Michal, and they both sat smoking and looking at her. She couldn't have been more than seven years old. Max started to tremble. This was the person von Knobelsdorff had picked out for him to murder in the most awful way. He looked at the girl's name on the form: Maria Amsel. Suddenly he snapped to his senses. There was no way on earth he was going to butcher a child.

He picked up the phone and called the camp commandant, Haas.

'Dr Voller here. The patient you have sent me is unsuitable.'

'Oh ar, why would that be, doc? The girl's not suitable, eh? Girl not suitable, everyone!'

The commander spoke in a suppressed giggle. Max could hear laughter in the background, too.

'She is not related to anyone in the camp.'

'Yes she is, her old mum's up painting the second floor scullery now. We were going to have her sent down this after, when von K arrives.'

'She is still not suitable, I—'

217

'Still not suitable!'

There was a gale of laughter in the room.

'What's so funny?'

'Well, we had a little bet between us down here that you wouldn't want a girl.'

'Why not?'

'Oh, we reckon they don't quite suit your, er, tastes, let us say.'

Max struggled to control his temper. 'This experiment requires a patient who has not long to live.'

'Well, make her have not long to live,' said Haas. 'You can send her back here and we'll do her over for you if you like, and then she will be suitable, but let me tell you this, Doctor – prisoners are valuable commodities round here, and you ain't getting another one until that one's dead. Fucking queer.' He put down the phone.

So now Max had two children to protect in that tiny room. He looked at his watch. There were a few hours before von Knobelsdorff arrived. First he went to the canteen and fetched some bread and soup. He felt good to be doing something that a doctor should be doing: ministering to the needs of the sick. He returned the tray to the lab and bid the girl eat. She wouldn't – too scared.

'Michal,' he said, 'get her to eat this, she needs it, I'll be back in a second.'

Michal nodded and said 'Cigarette?'

Max gave him a couple, not the pack he normally would have handed over. He had a feeling he'd be wanting the others.

He found the second floor scullery quickly. A party of Witness women were refitting the entire thing, not painting as the commandant had said. Had he got the right place?

'Maria Amsel,' said Max. 'Is anyone here the mother of a Maria Amsel?'

A woman looked up, pale and thin in the typical way.

'I am,' she said.

'You are a Witness.'

'Praise God through Jesus, yes.'

Praise God, what for? he felt like asking. *For the horror of what he's doing to you?*

'Your daughter is also a Witness?'

'Thank Jehovah, yes.'

He took her by the arm, shooting his eye at the *kapo* to keep him from complaint. He led her into the corridor.

'I'm going to say what I have to say quickly and I need your immediate assent. Today I am to kill your daughter.'

The woman welled up with tears, shaking, raising her fists to him but not hitting him, just waving them in the air in impotence.

'We can save her,' he said. 'What I want is for you to tell her to renounce her faith. Then there can be no reason for holding her, still less for killing her, in fact it would be illegal. It won't get her out of the camp straight away, but it'll be a big step in the right direction.'

The woman put down her fists. She looked directly at him, tears still streaming down her face. Then she just shook her head.

'What?'

The woman puckered her chin. 'No. no.'

'It's only words, love. Just words. Just say she renounces her faith and acknowledges the authority of Adolf Hitler and she will live to grow up. She doesn't actually have to believe what she says. Come on, there is very little time. You can go too, you can both do it, come on!'

She shook her head even more vehemently. The shape of her mouth changed again; it was tight and determined. This time when she looked at him it was as if she looked right inside him, like Gertie did, like she knew all his secrets and everything he was. But Gertie looked with love. This was something else. Another sort of complete understanding.

The woman said, 'Hope in Jehovah and keep his way, and he will exalt you to take possession of the earth. When the wicked ones are cut off, you will see.'

'What?'

'I cannot save anyone. Only Jehovah can do that. "The salvation of the righteous ones is from Jehovah; He is their fortress in the time of distress." She will live again when he calls.'

'Don't pass off responsibility on to some dreamt-up god,' he said, 'this is up to you. If you cling to your God, you are going to kill your child.'

The woman's tears had stopped. She looked directly at him.

'No,' she said, 'I think it is you who is going to do that.'

Max cried out in anguish and ran. Now it was he who was weeping, great tears that he'd dammed up inside him ever since he'd come to that place pouring from him in a torrent. He ran all the way back to the lab. He'd had it, he thought, had it with everything. He was going to do what he could, get the kid into a car, drive somewhere – maybe even Salzgitter; Arno would put her up, Arno would help, for sure. They could hide her in one of the spare rooms of the clinic. What would become of him? That didn't matter. They couldn't touch Gertie for it – it would be his crime.

He made the lab and opened the door.

There was Michal, still sitting in the chair smoking, his feet against the wall, but where was the girl? Michal had a large scratch running from his eye to his mouth. How had he got that? Max looked down at his feet. There in the tiny gangway was her body, red-eyed, with marks at her neck.

'Michal,' said Max, kneeling to put his hand on the dead little girl, 'what has happened here?'

Michal looked at Max and said, in the German the doctor had taught him, 'Soup is for me.'

22   Run to Earth

The pressures of the firestorm were all about Craw as he staggered out of Holy Trinity. It was as if he was caught in the lungs of a sleeping god; one minute the air crushed in on him, the next it sucked away, leaving him fighting for breath.

His wound had been more severe than he thought and he felt dizzy from loss of blood. He held his jacket in to his side, applying pressure in the hope of stemming the flow.

Nearly bent double, he made his way out up towards Broadgate, The fires were so intense that he could hardly see for the blinding light. He felt the heat on his face and blisters rising on his forehead.

Fire, Craw knew, was a potential harm to him. He could resist it far better than an ordinary man, but that didn't mean he could disregard its effects.

He peered through the heat haze looking for Arindon. The world around him was unrecognisable. Even the streets had changed, tramlines broken and buckled, reaching up like some odd undergrowth; the streets themselves seemed to sweat with the ichor of burst sewers, and a pall of smoke rose up above the buildings as if their souls were rising to heaven. Up on the roof of the church, firemen worked as if in a silent film, all human sound drowned under the terrible bombardment.

Craw was changing, he could feel it, what he had eaten having its effect, however small at first. His limbs felt thicker and more powerful, his brain more solid, less nimble. He could concentrate on his task – finding Arindon – but the 'why' for that kept slipping from his mind. Arindon might have some information that would lead him to his wife; Arindon might lead him to the perpetrators of those awful crimes; Arindon needed to be found for his own safety – all good reasons, but all jarred slightly sideways in Craw's mind as the digestion of the machine-gunner got underway.

A landmine exploded maybe five hundred yards away and he was dashed to the ground, but still he didn't lose Arindon's trail. There it was, evaporating in the heat, sizzling almost, registering in a sense beyond smell.

A man ran past Craw, his face black and his clothes ripped.

'This shouldn't be happening!' he was shouting, his voice muffled and distorted under by the thick air of a distant bomb blast. 'This shouldn't be happening!'

His words jolted something inside Craw. It shouldn't, he thought. They should be going for the factories, not the city centre, not the cathedral. What was the point of it?

It was wanton destruction but, worse than that, stupid. No military commander targets a ladies' hosiery store; no tactical advantage could be gained by bombing a cathedral or homes. And then he saw the reason – terror. The Nazis were gangsters and this was gangsterism on huge scale, a brick through the window, a punch in the back. It had been done for pure intimidation. The senselessness was part of the rationale.

Craw caught the trail more strongly. Arindon was running east across the wide space of Broadgate, through the burning banks, around the rubble of a collapsed portico, and into the heart of the fires.

Craw ran as hard as he could, trying to forget the pain of his wound, trying to avoid the terrible fires that were raging all around him. The Regency buildings had been set far apart but, once you had crossed Broadgate, you were into the Elizabethan and medieval heart, half-timbered buildings that seemed almost designed to burn.

He ran down the tiny lanes, choking on the smoke but still able to follow his quarry. His senses had awakened to the supernatural aspects of Arindon's presence. The current that seemed to trail behind Arindon now brought insights to him that would not be available even to the most perceptive wolf.

He saw terrible visions of torture, felt the pain of skin pricks on his face, hooks sliding into his biceps, and felt something odder still. Arindon, through his pain and debasement, was coming home, finding something that had been locked within him.

Arindon's presence pulled Craw through the alleys until, at a corner of a small and stinking entry, he turned. Down there, he knew, was his man. It was as if a pool of him collected in the doorway of a disused shop, into which he could thrust his hands and drink in Arindon's stories. 'He is vanquished,' said the trail. 'Now I shall aspire to greatness.'

Craw stepped forward. He was in front of a half-timbered shop which was on one side of an alley that a rat might have found a little narrow. The buildings almost touched on the second storey and were no more than eight feet apart on the bottom. The windows were boarded up but a grimy sign hung on the front: *Miles Taylor, Artist's Materials*. There clearly hadn't been much call for those since the beginning of the war because the shop was shut up. Below his feet, Craw could feel Arindon's presence as a sort of hum, like a wasp trapped in a jar. He was in the basement. The door was closed. Craw felt his side. He was still dizzy, though the bleeding had stopped. He breathed in. Yes, he was getting stronger.

He heard a voice at his shoulder and saw that writing scrawl across his inner vision again.

Sleye theme alle, sir, and thy healthinesse shell be fullie restored.

The wolf inside was speaking to him.

Craw tried the door. It was open.

23 A Little Death

What is the point of doing good? To please God? What if you have no god – then what? You didn't deny God; you didn't howl into the heavens and hear them echoing and empty – none of that. The idea just never really occurred to you. The church, the hymns, the Bible they bought you when you were twelve – you never for a second thought any of what they said was true, and you had a hard time believing that anyone did. Then why be good? For harmonious living? That would make good dependent on the prevailing culture. Is it true to say that murder is always wrong, like you could say dogs bark, as a fact? What of the good that sacrifices one life to preserve and enrich others, or the good that ends a miserable and wretched life? And is preserving life always right, simply as life alone? Is there a moral imperative to ask what sort of life it is that deserves saving? Is that judgement even possible? Can good even be explained by scientific method? In which case, what use is it as a category?

And even if we can agree on a definition of good – which it seems that without the all-too-convenient word of God we cannot – how do good and bad actions impact on the essential human? Is it the act that defines the person, or is there something intrinsic that enables us to say 'He did a bad thing, but he is still a good person'? How many bad things, or to what depth of badness must we sink, before we can say that a good person has become a bad one? And then, are we consistent, unitary things? If I have committed evil when I was twenty, am I still evil at sixty after a life of good? Is there atonement? Is there forgiveness? Oh no, here comes God again.

Max sat in the SS canteen, oblivious to the unpleasant stares elicited by his regular army uniform, smoking his cigarette and drinking sharp acorn coffee. Gertie had acquired more jewellery – a fine silver chain with a single ruby like a drop of blood hanging from it. He had never seen it before. He watched the tip of his cigarette. There was the sound of the sawing of the castle's reconstruction, always there, like an asthmatic laugh pulsing through his mind.

When you have done what Max had done to the old lady in his lab, then there are only dry questions of ethics because you have drained intuition from your moral life. You didn't need to argue things out – you knew. In your bones. And now, because you have turned away from what you knew to be right, all you have left to save yourself are questions, and you ask and you ask and you ask until one day you hope the questions will allow you to be that person who knew right from wrong again. Until then, everything must proceed as if from a manual. If not, then what? Well, then the world is devoid of any moral content at all. You smoke your cigarette, you drink your coffee, or you don't, you make that living person dead, and it all means the same to you.

The light from the window of the canteen caught the cigarette smoke, which rose to the ceiling like a drop of blood unfurling in water. Alive, then dead. A threshold crossed – and now what?

Still the table on which he rested his hands, still the floor beneath his feet. Everything was exactly as it was. Max inhaled the bitter Salem and blew out again.

'If you want it to be so, Max, then the world still turns,' he said to himself.

He noticed grease stains on the windows, dirt at the edges of the tables, a small speck of red beneath his thumbnail. He thought that, in a way, more should have changed, but nothing really had. He noticed the grease more, that was all.

The problem had been identifying a viable alternative course of action. What would cause the greatest good to the greatest number or the least harm to the fewest? No, Max, no, you can't get away with that. His approach to the problem had been entirely more emotional, more physical. He had felt itchy and hot, then cold, had been too aware of where his shirt touched his body, the stiffness of his collar. He had felt that strange chemical flushing through his system, tightening his stomach and loosening his knees, the same one that he had felt when they had told him his father was dead. There were only fragments of thought, disintegrating as he tried to stick them together in his head. The woman had been going to die anyway. If you shoot a man as he is falling off a tall building, is it still murder? It was only afterwards that the arguments, the justifications, the inner rebukes had come.

Max had not slept the night before Michal's grandmother arrived. He was well aware of what was facing him, and was at a loss to come up with a course of action. Gertie had kissed him in the morning, that drop of blood at her throat, that watch on her wrist, and he felt for the first time in his life that he couldn't share something with her. They had moved apart. She had said she had arranged with one of the other ladies to drive into Paderborn and go shopping for clothes.

'Does our ration book allow that?'

'Oh, Max. All right, I'll tell you. One of the ladies in the town is having a sale of clothes that weren't needed at Sachsenhausen.'

'Weren't needed?' said Max.

He looked out of the window. Mid-November, snow on the air. How long had he resisted the SS now? Months. The death of the girl had bought him some time. He had told Michal that he would take responsibility. Did he mean responsibility? No. He meant credit. It had increased his standing with the concentration camp guards; news had reached Haussmann. It had told the SS he was a good egg, one of them. Except he wasn't one of them. Van Knobelsdorff hadn't turned up after all. Busy? Forgotten about Max? Max couldn't be bothered to think why.

Gertie was angry with Max for his attitude to the clothes

sale. 'Well, they're not going to ask for them back, are they? What do you think should be done with them? Throw them on a fire?'

Max had a vision of people like wild animals, cornered, trapped, killed and skinned. Off with their pelts of clothes, off with their jewels and their watches, their glasses, and even their teeth, then discard the bones and the flesh. Bury the morals and concentrate on the practical, problems of process and disposal.

'Paderborn is a big city. It's not safe. They bombed Munich just days ago.'

That had been even more anxiety. His Aunt Christa lived in Munich and didn't have a telephone. It had taken a day to find out she was OK.

'I never had you down as a defeatist, Max Voller,' said Gertie. 'I'll be perfectly all right, we'll be back before dark.'

He was too tired to argue and had gone to his lab.

He arrived at the door to find a spotty, sandy-haired young guard sitting in a camp chair, with an extremely old lady standing shakily on sticks in front of him. Suddenly the tension that Max had been feeling for weeks snapped inside him, and he cuffed the guard on his arm.

'Get off your fat arse and allow this woman to sit down!'

'It's my chair,' said the guard. 'I brought it in case there would be a wait. There was a wait, I'm waiting – what's the problem?'

Max didn't even bother speaking. He just upended the chair, tipping the man down the stairs.

Immediately he felt sorry for what he had done. The old lady was frightened by his violence and staggered forward, trying to run away. With alarm, he noticed her legs were shackled. She needed a bath chair, not chains.

The guard regained his feet and looked at Max.

'You are getting a name for yourself. You think the SS should stand while monkeys sit? Pah!' He spat on the floor. He fixed Max with a stare while readjusting his uniform. 'You disgust me.' Then he gave a quick Heil Hitler and disappeared off, Max cared not where. Max picked the seat and gestured for the old lady to sit on the landing outside his lab.

The woman was old, really old and very malnourished. She could hardly stand and he thought it a miracle she had survived Sachsenhausen. His illusions that what went on in the camps was no more than a little rough-house were long gone. At Wewelsburg he'd seen a woman twenty years younger than the one in front of him kicked to death for the inability to pick up a sack of cement. How had this lady got by? She was the sort of patient that, had he seen her under normal circumstances, he would not have bothered treating. He would have eased whatever pain she was feeling, made sure her living arrangements were clean and comfortable, but he would not have troubled her with medical intervention. She must have been the wrong side of ninety and might die any day.

He tried to examine her but she wouldn't let him, shrinking from him in fear. He couldn't blame her. Whatever he did, he realised, he was just another German uniform to her, a killer tarred with the shame of all those other killers in their black boots and death's head insignia. He was with the SS, even if he wasn't a member, because he wasn't against them. But how could you stand against the tide of history? Haussmann was right; these people's time was up. Was Max going to be the first rat in history to join a sinking ship?

Max opened his lab and phoned down to the camp to arrange to have Michal sent up. Then he put her in the lab and locked it, not because he was afraid she would run away, but because he feared some wandering SS goon might come past and make her his brutal sport. Next he went to the canteen and got the woman bread and soup.

By the time he got back, Michal was there with a guard. Max couldn't feel angry with the boy. He had been brutalised, seen a cared-for friend die, many friends perhaps. He'd kept Michal on. Why? Because he had a soft heart? Or because he needed to believe there was hope of forgiveness in the world?

Violence was all around the child, and it was as inevitable that he would be touched by it in some way as it was that you would get wet if you stood in the rain. So he did not feel angry, he felt something else – an intense, soul-sick disappointment.

'Here's your boyfriend,' mumbled the guard.

'What?'

'Here's your prisoner, sir.'

Max flushed. No one likes the experience of being an outsider and, for a mad second, he wished his SS membership would come through quicker, just so he could have this bastard running round the courtyard until his legs were three centimetres shorter. Did he even want to be a member of that grisly crew? Could he refuse?

He wanted to say something but he couldn't. The other guard had been right; he was getting a name for himself. He should join the SS, he decided. Then at least he would be in more of a position to influence things. Maybe he could even get a job in the *Ahnenerbe*. Haussmann was no one's idea of competition. A little fantasy ran in Max's head where he took over medical research for the Reich and shut everything down.

He dismissed the guard and said to Michal, 'I have a surprise for you.' He opened the door. 'It's your gran.'

The old woman looked at Michal and she at him. He could see no recognition in either of their eyes.

'Grandmother?' said Max.

'Cigarette?' Michal made a smoking motion and smiled at Max a big, pleading, smile like you might see on the face of a child in a sentimental painting.

Max shook his head. It was inevitable that the SS would make yet another mistake. Still, that was the rationale for his experiment out of the window. He didn't have to kill anyone, so he had to regard the error as a happy one. He was irritated to be surrounded by such incompetence, and his relief was mixed with anger at the level of stress he had been made to suffer for absolutely no reason at all.

'Get to the camp,' he said to Michal.

The boy didn't understand.

'Cigarette?' Again, that smile.

Max was getting sick of the boy's constant pleading and, for the second, wanted him out of his sight. In his fantasy Michal was a confidante, someone who would help him think of a way to save this old lady, not a grasping little scrounger.

'Go!' Max pointed back out.

'Cigarette!'

For the second time in five minutes he found himself manhandling someone down the stairs.

The old woman looked at him with alarm. He didn't want to frighten her, but he didn't want to stay standing in the hallway either, with its through traffic, so he stepped inside the tiny lab and closed the door. Then Max nearly jumped out of his skin. The woman spoke to him, in German. They'd said she was Polish, and she didn't look the sort to have attended language school.

'Why am I here?'

Max felt tears coming to his eyes and he brushed them away with his sleeve. He leant to the wall for support. Instead he put his hand on the headrest of the restraint chair.

'You speak German?' he said.

The woman leant forward. She had seen his tears and was puzzled by them.

'We travelled here very much before the Nazis came to power.'

Max nodded. A gypsy, then.

'Why am I here?' Her voice was like someone shaking a tray of sand.

'We thought he was your grandson.'

She looked surprised. 'You are organising reunions now?'

'No. It's something else.'

'You are troubled.' She sounded like she might expire at

any moment. She actually leant forward and took his hand.

'Please, I don't want my fortune read, I've had enough of that stuff.'

'I need no fortune-telling to understand your problem. You are a good man in a bad situation. You have a wife—'

'How did you know that?' said Max, shocked. Was this his psychic, right here in front of him?

'You have a wedding ring,' said the gypsy.

'Oh yes.'

'It is easier to bear consequences when you are alone.'

'Yes,' said Max, 'things may go hard on us if I don't please them.'

'How will you please them?'

'I have to create psychic phenomena.'

'What?'

'Magic,' he said. 'I have to do magic.'

'In here? With this?' said the gypsy, slapping the chair with the back of her hand. 'With this you cannot do magic.'

'I know,' he said, 'but I must try.'

'You must be born to it,' she said.

'Can you do it?' For a mad second he thought he saw a way out. Weren't gypsies meant to be magical? Maybe he could get her to come up with something.

'No,' she said.

Bang went that avenue of escape. However, the woman wasn't the boy's grandmother. That was indisputable. He'd just have her sent straight back. Back to what? The main camp, Sachsenhausen KZ. Maybe his wife would buy her coat, if she'd ever had one.

One way or another, this woman was a goner, he thought. Still, it didn't have to be him that killed her. He picked up the phone to order a truck to take her back. Wrong woman, end of story, but he knew that virtually the only place she was safe, even momentarily, was his lab. She had bread and soup, water. On the truck on the way back, would she become the sport of guards? He was as good as killing her by ordering her returned. She was in a machine that made death, and it seemed almost academic which of its cogs finally did for her.

Still, it wasn't going to be him. He couldn't save her, but he wouldn't kill her. He picked up the phone and began to dial the transport department.

'So glad we caught you, Doctor Voller. A cancelled appointment and I see you are free, please commence.'

The odour of glazed violets filled the room. The door had been opened. It was von Knobelsdorff. Why had he come in early? To catch him, of course, to catch him. There was Haussmann, poking up behind him like the devil on his shoulder. But von Knobelsdorff needed no devil.

'You said you achieved some remarkable brain readings on your machine. I would like to see them. We don't need anyone receiving them to detect them, do we? Do we, Mr Professor Haussmann?'

'Oh no,' said Haussmann, shaking his head like the organ grinder's monkey.

'So commence – indulge me. Hurry up, your patient looks as though she might pop off at any second, and wouldn't that ruin things?'

The woman was trembling, she knew von Knobelsdorff's sort. Max was trembling too. What was the nature of what the SS were asking him to do, when it came down to it? The movement of a hand. He looked inside himself. What did he have to stop him in that movement? An unspoken understanding of decency that he had learned from his parents, a pleasant way of behaving that had never been tested. It all seemed so slight. There was nothing to draw on. He thought of the Witness and her refusal to save her little girl. Where did she get that strength from? He thought of Gertie. No, he could not give her up.

If you looked at it in one light, giving in to von Knobelsdorff was such a little thing – just placing objects in relation to each other. The saw. His arm. He could not, even in his mind, speak the third object. He thought of an El Lissitzky painting he'd seen before the war. Just a relation of lines and circles. So things seemed to Max. What was that painting's name?

Then the woman was in the chair, strapped down. The death's head on von Knobelsdorff's collar had been polished to a high shine. It seemed almost to wink at the doctor. Max felt his arm move. The rest of the details? He could not revisit them.

Von Knobelsdorff had stood so close to her as she suffered that it had hampered Max's movements. He recalled his elbow knocking against von Knobelsdorff's chest as he used the saw. What he did remember was the woman's voice as he'd started doing what he had to do.

'Against thee. What thou do is against thee.'

Max didn't understand the words because they weren't uttered in his language. They weren't uttered in any language the old woman understood either, though she framed the words perfectly. It was an incantation brought back from the Egyptian wilderness by Peseshet, priestess of Set, god of the desert, famine and destruction. A jackal-headed man had taught the words to her in her meditations and starvations, she said. It had been handed down the generations, daughter to daughter, until it had reached the old woman.

The gypsy had said she could do no magic. Who can say, though, what magic is? It hovers at the edge of the day to day like light reflected from water, like something seen from the corner of the eye but vanquished by the full gaze. So she could no more *do* it than she could do a dream, do love, do hate.

'Is that noise normal?' von Knobelsdorff had said. Even he seemed to find the woman's words discomfiting.

'Quite normal, eh, Max?' said Haussmann, with a chummy wink.

Max just went on sawing, blank and distant. From somewhere not too far away in the castle, another saw joined in, in a hellish duet. The EEG machine squealed and scratched. The noise dominated his senses, draining sight, banishing taste and

233

smell. Only feeling, that vibration in his arm, remained clear. He was hoping to work quickly, to kill the woman before her suffering became too great. The point of the experiment, however, was to keep her alive.

Baila Brono Aljenicato – the old woman had a name – looked up at him through her bloodied eyes. All she had said so far was an incantation. The psychologist Jung might have argued that it had the power of an ancient archetype, that it referred to the deep stories and ideas buried in humanity's collective psyche and – though neither the utterer nor the listeners knew its meaning – it had some power on the subconscious of those who heard it, and he might have been right. But it was only a prelude.

She uttered a curse, a proper curse, one that had been marinated in fifty centuries of hatreds and resentments, that had festered beneath ill-treatment, exclusion and pogrom, and that had been allowed crawling into the light of day perhaps ten times in all those years.

Craw, who was the victim of a curse himself, might even have been able to tell the experimenters where it came from, given enough thought on the subject. They, of course, would only have been interested in how to do it, which is a different thing entirely. There is no 'how to' with a curse. In fact, wanting to curse someone normally guarantees that it will fail. The curse comes out only when you're trying to hold it in. To fly out, then, it needs the pressure of restraint. Curses have a habit of exacting a price on those that make them, and no one who didn't hate as deeply as it is possible to hate would ever be willing to pay it. But Baila Brono Aljenicato, whose children and grandchildren had been taken to the camp with her, and who had seen enough horrors for ten of her long lifetimes, was willing to continue suffering long after she was dead, as long as her enemies were suffering with her.

She struggled against herself, though; she tried to bite down what was rising in her throat, but the hate in her was so overwhelming that she feared more to hold it in than to let it go. A loathing, primordial and deep and utterly unstoppable, burst from her like pus from a boil.

To Max, the language of the priestesses of the Typhonic Beast sounded like something being shredded, some grinding machine breaking itself apart on a loose cog. He assumed it was just the effects of the agonies the woman was suffering. Was this the sound of magic? Was there any power in what the woman said? Who knows? The kind of people who inspire others to curse them are very often those whose lives are heading for ruin anyway. So it would never be clear if all that followed was a result of the curse, or if the curse was simply a marker on the path of a man's collapse.

Had he been able to understand what she was saying, Max may actually have taken it for a blessing. In fact, it was the worst curse humanity had managed in all the millennia of trying.

'May you find what you are looking for,' she said.

24 An Artist in Residence

The door opened on to a cramped hallway. The house bore all the signs of disuse – no carpet on the floor, only scraps of newspaper. There was very little light, but Craw's eyes needed hardly any. He breathed in. There were two people inside: Arindon and one other. Then he noticed another note in the smell. No. There were more than two people. There were others, too, encased in a sediment of fear – sweat, blood, piss and shit. They, though, were not alive.

There was a coat in the hall. He touched it, drank in its psychic residue. Longing, despair, frustration and envy seemed to drip from it.

Craw walked down the hallway, not bothering to tread carefully under the noise of the blitz. To his left was a doorway. He looked into a room. Even to his eyes the room was dark. The shutters had been put up with the blackout in mind and the only light came in obliquely from the front door, which he had not closed behind him. Craw suddenly remembered he'd taken the lighter from Jacques. He took it from his pocket and sparked the flame into life. He could see the room was clearly the business part of the former artist's supplies shop. There were shelves stacked with papers and paints and there was a counter. Clearly it hadn't been used as a shop very recently, because a large desk with a drawing board on it had been placed in the public area. Someone was using it as a studio.

An explosion near the house seemed to shake it to its foundations and, for a second, Craw had the sensation of being at sea, like when a boat unexpectedly strikes a sandbank. He went into the room and looked about him.

The room was disordered, with the remains of dinners and

half-drunk cups of tea lying around on the floor, along with papers, discarded bills, an umbrella, cardboard boxes, old paintbrushes in jam jars. Craw shivered, with the revulsion of his centuries of fastidiousness. The emotion came back to him as if muffled. Operating in his conventional human reality was possible but difficult for him, a sensation like listening to music underwater – some aspects quieted, some oddly amplified.

His wolf nature was rising up in him and the smells of the night were livid in his mind. They seemed to unlock a hoard of memories inside him. He saw cities burning in his mind, heard the laughter of girls, recalled Yale and Cambridge in the smell of chalk. Everything in the world now related directly to him. He was the beast, the creature that relates only to himself, and the odours of the night pulled colours from his mind – the bright shields of his kinsmen, gold, nights that blazed with fire and days in the blinding ice. It was as if all that he had done and seen was rising up in him as the final expression of his dying humanity, just as the buildings around him blazed red and green in their own moment of change. Tomorrow, they would be something else.

Craw went to the drawing board. There was nothing on it, but next to it was a sketch pad. In the flickering light of the lighter he could just make out, on the cover, a thumb print. It was difficult to see what colour the print was, but he didn't need to see. He could smell. It was blood, reeking of excitement. He opened the book.

Sketches of the reveelede, read a title page.

Craw gave a start as he leafed through the book. There were ten or fifteen illustrations of the pebble that Balby had showed him, but this time, the area around the hand was not scratched away. He could see clearly now that the hand was torn and bloody at the wrist and around it were the jaws of a wolf.

A word sprang up in his mind, a word Arindon had used. 'Brother.'

Craw let the flame of the lighter die and leant forward on the desk in darkness. His hand touched something cold and metal beneath the drawing board. He pressed the lighter again and looked to see what it was. It was a wood plane. He took it out and held it in front of him. The odour of blood and stress seeped from it, though there was as much stress on the handle as there was on the blade of the plane.

A normal human being might have been able to smell the putrefying Mr Arindon by now. To Craw his presence was enormous, almost tangible, like the gaze of a million bats falling on the back of your neck in a sightless cave. Craw did not turn to face Arindon when he sensed him in the doorway behind him. He instinctively wanted his opponent to commit himself. Arindon did not disappoint, springing across the floor at Craw's back. He was slightly taken aback by the man's speed, but managed to turn quickly enough to surprise Arindon and strike at his weapon arm, breaking the wrist and causing the shard of the Moonsword to go clattering to the floor. Craw deliberately didn't try to stop Arindon's movement, but allowed his charge to continue on to a firm head-butt.

Arindon collapsed to the floor and then Craw was at his throat, Arindon kicking and spitting and turning to throw him off. Craw fought for control of Arindon and of himself. He couldn't afford to kill this man, but he ached to do so. Arindon shoved his desperate fingers into Craw's face to fight him off, but Craw bit at them, taking a ring finger off at the knuckle.

'No, Endamon, no, no, Vali.'

The name Vali seemed to shiver like a cymbal in his mind. His last transformation had jarred so much in his head that he no longer thought of himself by that name. It was as if the shattered pieces of his mind were reassembling. He was seeing things that had been locked away to him for centuries. He saw his own face in front of him, but weathered and aged.

'No, Endamon, no, Vali, no, Jehan, no, Loys!'

These names were his too, he knew.

Arindon writhed underneath him, but to no use. Craw had him by the throat and was choking the life from him. He could not contain himself. This time the wolf spoke as if from within him. It was as if he could feel its muzzle protruding from his own face.

Finyshhe himme, sir, slake mye thyrstss.

Craw was no longer human, not even animal, just a hunger encased in flesh. He sank his teeth into Arindon's arm, tearing away a gob of meat.

Then there was a mild thump below his shoulder blade and a warm, wet feeling began to spread down his back. Craw felt dizzy as one of his lungs filled with blood. He gave a final squeeze on Arindon's neck and then let go, turning to see a completely naked man clasping the metal shard in a cloth he was using as an improvised handle. Craw felt stunned, unable to act. The man stabbed the Moonsword into him again, this time into the solar plexus.

Craw became detached from reality, suddenly fascinated by the appearance of his attacker. The man was smeared in a red and grey pigment that picked out patterns of raised flesh on his body. Why had Craw not realised before? Why hadn't he seen? The colouration made it so obvious. The marks on the body were meant to represent an animal's fur. Those on the man's face, picked out in black, white and red, were monstrous jaws. Craw nearly laughed.

In front of him was a werewolf, or someone trying to become one. His senses swam as he thought of the irony of dying at the hands of such a creature. He waited for unconsciousness, but unconsciousness didn't come, just a sort of paralysis.

The painted man kicked Craw hard in the guts and Craw fell forward onto the floor. Craw looked up into the blackened eyes of the carnival creature above him.

The man spoke:

'When the Gods saw that the Wolf was bound fully, they took the chain that was wed to the fetter, and which is called

"Thin", and passed it through a great rock — it is called "Scream" — and stuck the rock deep down into the earth. Then they took a great stone and drove it yet deeper into the earth and used that stone for a fastening-pin. The Wolf gaped horribly, and thrashed and strove to bite them; they thrust into his mouth a certain sword: the hilt caught in his lower jaw, and the point in the upper; that is his gag. He howls hideously, and drool runs out of his mouth: that is the river called Ván. "Hope"; there he lies till the Twilight of the Gods.'

A stick of bombs fell very close, turning the roof of the house into the skin of a gigantic drum.

'The All-father is here, come to offer his sacrifice to the fates and end this war!' said the man. 'He is here! Bind him!'

Arindon, seemingly oblivious to the pain of his injuries, took a pair of heavy handcuffs from the shelf behind the counter and secured Craw's arms behind his back. Craw felt cut off from his power of movement. All he could focus on was that shard of metal protruding from his chest.

He felt himself pulled to his feet. He was shoved forward into the hall, which flickered with the light of the burning city. Then he was kicked down the stairs into a basement.

He looked up. About the room, hung like deflated balloons, were human faces, stripped from the bone. There were three fleshless corpses on the floor of the room, stinking, discarded like a scholar might discard the notes that had led to some dead end of thought. The walls of the basement were covered with runes smeared out in blood. Craw read them: Transformation, Strength, Hail. Hail, the thing between fire and ice, the rune of betweens. And there too, like an N with a line through it, was the Wolfsangel rune. Placed with its bars horizontally, it meant 'wolf trap'. Upright, as it was, it meant something else: 'Werewolf'.

Craw felt something go over his head. It was a noose. The rope tightened about his neck and he was pulled forward face down. Then he was rolled on to his back. Arindon's ragged smile was above him, tying the rope to some stake in the floor.

His feet were secured and he felt a weight on his chest, but it was no weight, just that shard of sword stuck in him.

Craw let out a gasp and felt something sharp being thrust into his mouth. When he tried to close his mouth again, he couldn't. Something like a nail or a pin had been wedged between his palate and his bottom jaw, keeping his mouth open.

'He is present,' said the painted man. 'In this destruction, he is present. Begin.'

Arindon let out a torn chant in the Norse of Craw's people.

> *I know I hung on a wind-torn tree*
> *nine long nights,*
> *Wounded with a spear, dedicated to Odin,*
> *myself to myself,*
> *on that tree of which no man knows*
> *from where its roots run.*
> *No bread did they give me nor a drink from a horn,*
> *downwards I peered;*
> *I took up the runes, shrieking I took them,*
> *then I fell back from there.*

Craw tried to cough as the noose tightened about his neck. The painted man looked down at him.

'I shall tickle his heart.' He reached forward and took the protruding end of the Moonsword shard and agitated it.

Craw felt as if he was going to vomit. Things were becoming clear to him, illusions peeling away. He could tell that, whatever this strange painted individual had achieved in the past, he was achieving nothing now. He was in the middle of a magical ceremony but no magic was there. The man facing him wasn't a sorcerer but a murderous fool. And yet, something strange was beginning to happen to him. From far away, beneath the bombs, he thought he heard a woman's voice singing.

25 The Well

Mrs Daecher had lost her necklace, she told Max when she met him in a corridor. It was quite a valuable thing – a single ruby set in silver – but it also had sentimental value for her, because her husband had bought it for her to celebrate his induction into the SS. She was mystified as to where it had gone because it had not left her rooms. They were serviced by Witness cleaners who were noted for their honesty. She left the door open during the day because it never occurred to her to lock it. Who in the SS was dishonourable enough to spend time opportunistically checking whose door was open and whose wasn't?

Mrs Cullen, too, had lost some jewellery – a beautiful diamond eternity ring that she thought had cost her husband a year's wages, but had cost him only some bread and water, as he was in the envied position of senior administrator at Sachsenhausen. She had gone to buy dresses in Paderborn with Mrs Voller, and somehow it had become lost while she was trying them on. There had been quite a hunt for it but nothing had been discovered.

Then there was Mrs Braun's Tiffany bracelet. She had left her house in the camp to go to dinner with the Haussmanns in the castle, but when she arrived it was missing. She'd asked Mrs Voller if she had seen it, because she had bumped into her in the courtyard as she got out of the staff car. They'd chatted briefly and arranged to meet to play tennis. Had she dropped it then? Mrs Voller didn't think so.

Max sat eating his dinner opposite his splendidly adorned wife. She had bought a beautiful pale blue evening dress with lace at the shoulders, and she wore her hair tied in a knot at the top. A diamond bracelet sparkled on her right wrist, the wristwatch on her left, and at her throat was the blood ruby, catching the candlelight like a deep wine. She was unearthly beautiful, he thought.

'Was von Knobelsdorff pleased with you?' she asked.

Max bit into a potato. His appetite had been disturbed at lunch but now, at dinner, he was very hungry. He couldn't muster the energy to reply to his wife.

'Was von Knobelsdorff pleased? Can we get rid of this crocodile? It's a grotesque circumstance to have to live like this.'

'Von Knobelsdorff is grotesque. He is a lunatic,' said Max.

'I'm sure you exaggerate.'

Max looked at his wife and, instead of cherishing and loving her beauty and her kindness, for the first time in his life it felt like an affront, a sick joke that it should exist in such a world of barbarity. He wanted to smash it.

'Today, on the Senior Storm Command Leader's instructions, I tortured to death a pleasant old gypsy lady. In the next weeks we will locate family pairs. In some experiments we will not tell, say, a brother that we are killing his sister, in some we will. We will assess the reactions and the sharpness of any psychic phenomena produced. There will be no psychic phenomena, because there are no psychic phenomena. In the meantime, von Knobelsdorff will be in the north tower with eleven other lunatics, meditating around the severed head of an SS colleague in order to put themselves in contact with forces unspecified, unknown and non-existent. Do you want more wine?'

He poured her a glass.

'Well, that is grotesque,' said Gertie. The news hadn't shaken her as he had thought it might.

'Exactly. Makes the crocodile seem not so bad after all.'

'The crocodile is still very inconvenient. Perhaps I should speak to von Knobelsdorff. A woman's touch is sometimes what is required.'

'No!' Max didn't want her anywhere near von Knobelsdorff. Gertie sipped on the wine. 'As you wish.'

Von Knobelsdorff's dreams had been troubling him in a way almost unique to occultists. In the dream, he was a boy, walking in his home town. He approached a sweet shop and went in and bought the largest bar of chocolate anyone had ever seen – it was bigger than he was. And that was it. No demons, no goddesses, no spirits from the flame. Von Knobelsdorff had dedicated his life to the occult arts. He didn't want chocolate in his dreams, he wanted angels and devils.

As Harbard had conjectured, von Knobelsdorff's mind was not structured as ordinary people's are. The normal mind is like an orchestra, its sections blending or not blending, producing a tune or falling into discord; it has levels and interactions, bass parts and treble. The moral imbecile von Knobelsdorff's mind was more like the single note of a violin – taut and unrelenting. He wanted power and influence but he would have been better off as a soldier in the field, where his brutal decisiveness and single-mindedness would have been assets, rather than trying to reach into sensitivities he simply did not have. There's no point studying trumpet music for thirty years if you have no fingers to play.

But Gertie Voller, or whatever strange thing was looking out from behind her eyes, had a level of sensitivity that was catching – contagious, almost – and it recognised no walls or locks.

So, in the north tower chamber of the *Schwarze Sonne*, the twelve thrones in a circle, the light of tall arched windows at their backs, the many-armed swastika inlaid on the floor, among the marble and the gold of the Over Group Leader Hall, where five years of meditation and self-denial had brought one solitary vision of a man thought to be Odin, von Knobelsdorff sat beating the worthless drum he had got from Harbard and waiting for the myths of his ancestors to come true.

*

Max finished his meal, sat blankly at the table, unsmoking, undrinking, unreading. Something in the form of his wife stood behind him, stroked his hair and sang a strange song:

> *One did I see in the wet woods bound*
> *Like to lawless Loki in shape*
> *There sits Sigyn, sad by her man*
> *Would you know yet more?*

> *I saw there wading through rivers wild*
> *Treacherous men and murderers too,*
> *And workers of ill with the wives of men;*
> *There the snake sucked the blood of the slain,*
> *And the wolf tore men; would you know yet more?*

Though the words of the song were disturbing, Max found them soothing. He imagined his wife with a tangle of wool in her hands, pulling and teasing it into a single thread. It would all be all right with Gertie there, he thought. Somehow she would work it out.

'What's happening?' In the hall with the dead men, Gertie stirred in her sleep.

'A wolf needs a trick, dear,' said a voice. 'Remember the wolf? I'm calling him on, spinning him in.'

Behind Max the song continued:

> *The sun turns black, earth sinks in the sea,*
> *The hot stars down from heaven are whirled;*
> *Fierce grows the steam and the life-feeding flame,*
> *Till fire leaps high about heaven itself.*

Von Knobelsdorff, only hours into his meditation, felt something stirring. This wasn't some vision of a god he had willed into being, almost like someone waiting for a bus for too long begins to hear them in the distance even when they're not there, but something more profound, a deep tremor inside him. He looked about him and the tall arched windows of the room were not windows any more, but doorways through which he could walk. He had to restrain himself from crying aloud in pleasure. His faith had been rewarded.

Under the bombs in that bloody basement, tied and pinned to the floor, Craw's vision failed. When it came back he was no longer where he had been. He was sitting on a wide black shore, while behind him a tall hall, equally black, was glossy with writhing snakes. At its front one enormous snake stretched its head up into the sky, hissing out a plume of venom. The painted man, the sorcerer, was nowhere to be seen and neither was Arindon.

Gertie sang on, stroking her husband's hair:

> *There she sits in the old Iron-Wood*
> *And nurtures the brood of Fenrir*
> *One of them in his wolf skin*
> *Shall be the snatcher of the moon.*

'A wolf? Did you say a wolf?' said von Knobelsdorff, from his place in the knights' room. He could hear singing from outside. He turned to his fellow knights, but in their place on the thrones were only skeletons crumbling in the uniforms. Von Knobelsdorff smiled. The import of this vision was clear – he was the chosen one of the knights, perhaps even of his whole people. He stepped out through one of the archways and saw he was on a promontory on a long black shore. Away in the distance smoke seemed to be rising from the horizon. He felt compelled to follow it.

At the snake-wreathed hall Craw cast his eyes to the distance. There, beneath a tall three-sided castle, a lady in a cloak and cowl of deep blue was making her way down the shining black beach. She bore a spool of thread in her hands. Who was she? His mind would not register it; he knew her, he was sure.

Craw wanted to get away from the beach, away from the hall of serpents. Something was in there. He could sense it snuffling and hacking in a teeming darkness. He knew what it was, and had to resist the urge to run to the front of the hall and fling open its doors.

He fought his way up the shore, over the dunes of obsidian, beneath a crescent moon that cast an unnatural chill on the land. At the top of the last dune he looked out over a blank plain, wide as a desert, the ground like coal. The only feature on the whole field of black was just visible in the middle distance. Rising from the glittering floor was a protuberance of some sort. He took it for some volcanic feature, a blow hole from a long dead lava field, but it was too regular for that.

It was a landmark anyway, so Craw decided to head towards it. He lost track of time. It seemed that he walked for days but the moon was constant, the weather unchanging. Eventually he came to the object he had seen in the distance. It was a pool, a perfect circle, three feet high and about ten feet in radius, spilling over with a silvery water. He recognised it as a well. The liquid sparkled silver beneath the moon.

There was something else that Craw could not quite see. In dreams, the eyes will not always obey the commands of the mind, and it was the same here. There was something at the corner of his vision but he could not focus upon it.

He struggled and struggled and, in the end, he managed to turn his gaze to see, next to the well and mounted on a stake, a man's head. It was of an extraordinary beauty but not of the sort that could be captured by artists. It seemed to shift, to be all ages and all races, Celtic, Norse, Phoenician and Saracen, Briton and Eastlander. Beneath the stake was a headless corpse, naked and lying face down. In its hand was a fine drinking horn, inlaid with silver.

From down the dunes the lady in the blue hood was walking

towards him. Who was she? He could place her, given time, he was sure.

Craw knew where he was, and he had no desire to be there any longer. This legend had been drummed into him countless times as a child by the hearth on the long evenings of winter. This was Mimir's well, the oracle waters of the very first god and, on the stake and at his feet, was what was left of Mimir. Craw wanted to leave. But then he could see someone else there. It was a tall bearded figure in a broad-brimmed hat. Harbard!

Craw tried to speak but, again, the pain in his mouth was excruciating. Harbard smiled at him and pointed towards the well.

Something was happening to gravity, or to time, because Harbard's movements seemed unnaturally slow. The moon looked down. The waters shimmered, cold and deep. With effort, he approached the well and touched the waters. He tried to drink but the liquid just ran through his fingers. He shook his hand and a drop, a tiny drop, of water splashed down onto the body of Mimir, transforming it.

The god was no longer naked. Craw looked down at him. He wore the smart black uniform of an SS man with embroidered Gothic writing on the sleeve. *Doktor*. There on his collar was the skull and crossbones, the death's head that seemed almost to mock the vacant space above it.

'The wolf will be yours and then I can go back to Salzgitter,' said the head, in German.

'How do I find it?' said a voice.

Craw was aware of a presence at his side. Another man in SS uniform, hard-faced and commanding, with a long scar from his eye to his chin. Behind him the lady was coming, the tall lady in a cloak and hood of deep blue silk.

'Who are you?' said Craw, to the SS man in front of him.

'Majesty,' said the SS man, sinking to one knee.

Craw felt compelled to turn away but, as he did, he caught a glimpse of himself in the waters. He saw the head of a wolf looking back at him. He didn't want to look there, though, he wanted to look somewhere else.

The SS man had the right idea, he was looking behind him from where he knelt, he'd got his gaze going in the right direction and no mistake, that one, he was a wise one, an insider, he'd been given the wink all right, that crafty old fox, he knew which side his bread was buttered, he knew ... Craw's thoughts were crumbling, he felt his mind sliding out of the picture. Someone else was there. Who was it?

'This beast is on his way, Crawford,' said Harbard. 'He is near you and when he finds you then it will be calamity for you and for the world.'

Craw could say nothing, the sensation of the pin in his mouth preventing even a word.

Craw heard a song.

> Then sought the Gods their assembly-seats,
> The holy ones, and council held;
> Names then gave they to noon and twilight,
> Morning they named, and the waning moon,
> Night and evening, the years to number.

'That's us!' shouted von Knobelsdorff, 'assembly seats, council, that's us.'

> Three times burned, and three times reborn,
> Oft and again, yet ever she lives.
> Bright one they called her who sought their home,
> The wide-seeing witch, Gullveig, wise in magic;
> Minds she moved by her magic,
> To good women a joy she was.

There was something wrong with that poem, Craw thought. He had heard it before, he was sure, but it wasn't good women that Gullveig delighted. What sort of women was it, then? He couldn't remember, his mind numbed by the trance and the magic.

'Where do I find this witch?' the SS man shouted.

He seemed quite crazed and Craw had a strong urge to kill him right there, just to make him be quiet. There had been a witch. Yes, the first time he had transformed. A witch, a crazed, tunnel-dwelling woman whom hallucination and madness followed as the wake follows a ship.

The song went on:

> *I know where Odin's eye is hid,*
> *Deep in the wide-famed well of Mimir;*
> *Necklaces I had and rings from the All-father,*
> *My speech was wise and my magic wisdom;*
> *Widely I saw over all the worlds.*
> *On all sides I saw Valkyries assemble,*
> *Ready to ride to the ranks of the Gods.*

Craw realised it was the lady in the cowl and cloak who was singing. Though the voice seemed more affecting than any he had ever heard. The notes of the song seemed to make his flesh and his bones resonate and hum.

'She's offering us unlimited power!' shouted von Knobelsdorff. 'Unlimited power! Show us who you are, show us your face, Lady seeress! Where is Odin's eye? What do you see? Tell me! Tell me!'

The lady kept walking towards them and Craw was sure he had seen her before. Behind her was the hill and the three-sided castle. Above even that was an enormous black wolf – so big, it seemed it would swallow the moon. The wolf threw back its head and let out a slavering, steaming howl that shook Craw to his bones.

*

250

'There is our weapon,' shouted von Knobelsdorff. 'The Fenris wolf! We can bring him here and harness his power. It is as I thought, the ancient Gods are with us. What do we do, Lady? Reveal yourself to us.'

The lady was standing next to them now. She cast back the hood of her cloak and stood before von Knobelsdorff in her crushing beauty.

'Mrs Voller!' said von Knobelsdorff.

'You will have your wolf when I have my gold!' said the lady.

Craw tried to turn his head, forcing his unwilling neck to turn so he could see her. Why couldn't he turn? Ah, he could, with effort. And then he saw her, just as she had been that last day before the battle. Yes. There had been a battle.

'Hello Vali,' she said

'Adisla,' said Craw. He had no exclamation in him, no exultation. It was just a sudden and solid feeling of being complete, after so long being broken. He stretched out towards her to take her in his arms.

'Enemies have engulfed me,' he said. How had he not noticed that his hands were bound with iron manacles?

'Then what are these shackles?' she said. 'I will not have my love fettered – throw them off, it is easy for you.'

The beautiful lady put her hands onto Craw's hands. He tensed his muscles and the shackles split and fell to the floor.

The wolf on the hill gave a guttering, snuffling cry, screaming into the night. The noise seemed to possess Craw, filling him full of the most incredible energy. He threw back his own head and howled in reply.

'Now,' said Harbard, 'we shall see.'

In the castle, Gertie stopped singing and took her fingers from her husband's hair. Von Knobelsdorff was back in the chamber of the Knights of the Black Sun, collapsed on his throne.

*

Craw was back in the bloody basement. Craw looked at his hand. He had something in it. A shard of bloody metal. He threw it away. The remains of the handcuffs clattered to the floor. What was it? A hand? How can you have a hand in your hand and it not be attached to a person? He dropped it.

The door was open, the heat of the burning city seemed to sear away all thought. Something ran and his instinct took over to catch it. There was a scrabbling he could not recognise. The painted man was trying to get up the stairs, but had slipped in his panic. Craw felt himself move and then there was something of candy colours in his hands, a peeling orb of reds and blues and brilliant whites. The only distraction was the drumming of fists against his shoulders and his head as Mr Endamon Craw ate the painted man's face and the painted man tried in vain to stop him.

The bomb struck and it was dark for a while.

26 Revelation

Balby had forgotten the case he was working on when he'd stepped out of the crypt.

The future usually arrives by increments, sneaks up on us slowly and, only when some seed of memory sprouts in our mind – a face we haven't seen in twenty years, a style of car we had thought obsolete, or even the flash of light on glass – and sends us back into the past, do we ever really compare it to the present.

We walk unseeing into the future, like an uncertain bather feeling his way out in the water down the slope from the beach before the sudden drop, where the feet scrabble and panic for a floor that has fallen into blackness. Only once before had Balby experienced a feeling like he had when the all-clear sounded and he stepped from the church. The death of his wife.

You imagine that it is the moment of loss that will be hardest, the second you realise that what you love has gone but, he knew, that was not the worst of it. His difficulty had come four weeks after his wife's death, when he had sat alone in their living room and thought to himself, 'This is it. It's like this for ever. Everything from now on is aftermath.'

Balby had grown up on those streets, their alleyways. The inconvenient closeness of the buildings, their age, were in his heart. He was a man who liked to feel connected to things – to his job, to his town, to his wife.

He and Briggs had tried to help throughout the night, smothering incendiaries, tending to the wounded, but at 3 a.m. a Royal Engineers colonel had ordered them into the shelter of the Holy Trinity crypt. The bombing was too intense, there was no safe way out of the city and, as the colonel said, the last thing he needed was two more bloody corpses to clear up.

So into the crypt they had gone, and tried to sleep. Balby may even have slept, he couldn't tell, but then the all-clear sounded and he was on his feet.

As he pushed through the small door at the entrance to Holy Trinity and looked out on the burning desolation before him, it was as if some higher power looked down on him and said 'What you are, who you are, where you come from – all these things are as nothing to me. I have seen the valuable and the decent, the precious and the true and, with a gesture of my hand, I have swept them away.'

Balby was under no illusions as he looked out at the twisted tramlines, the burnt-out buses and buildings, as he breathed in the crematorial air, that he was witnessing the work of the Devil. The cathedral was in ruins, the windows of Holy Trinity all blown out. The sky was an utter black, an unnatural light provided by the fires, rather than the sun. What God-hating demon, what desolate spirit had passed this way? Words came into his mind.

'By the time Lot reached Zoar, the sun had risen over the land. Then the Lord rained down burning sulphur on Sodom and Gomorrah—from the Lord out of the heavens. Early the next morning Abraham got up and returned to the place where he had stood before the Lord. He looked down toward Sodom and Gomorrah, toward all the land of the plain, and he saw dense smoke rising from the land, like smoke from a furnace.

'The sun was risen upon the earth when Lot entered into Zoar. Then the Lord rained upon Sodom and upon Gomorrah brimstone and fire from the Lord out of Heaven; And he overthrew those cities, and all the plain, and all the inhabitants of the cities, and that which grew upon the ground. And Abraham got up early in the morning to the place where he stood before the Lord: And he looked toward Sodom and Gomorrah, and toward all the land of the plain, and beheld,

254

and lo, the smoke of the country went up as the smoke of a furnace.'

'No,' thought Balby, this was not the work of God. The people of Coventry could be base and brutish, but nothing they had done could call down a vengeance like this. There was some other hand at work here.

'Fucking hell!' said Briggs at his side.

Balby had been going to say there was no need for profanity but, he realised, he was wrong. If there was ever need for profanity, not as an escape valve for pressure building in a crude brain, nor even as a sort of balancing hand thrust out from the mind in an attempt to keep stable, but as a straightforward description, it was then.

'Hell,' said Briggs. 'This is Hell.'

It had the smell of Hell too, the acrid stench of the high explosive mixing with the mean little stink of domestic gas and the choking wafts of the noxious fires. From inside the rubble he could hear screams, like the damned in torment.

The all-clear had sounded not ten minutes before, but already the streets were filling up. Helpers were coming in to the centre, gawping at the destruction, unable to believe its scale. Troops and firemen scoured the rubble looking for survivors. Two water board vans, unable to go any further through the tangle of tramlines and craters, stopped down the hill towards the Burges, and men got out with surveying equipment. From the same direction Balby heard a loudspeakered voice telling people to report to help the rescue teams. The smell of gas was strong in the air. He realised that the mains must have been hit. From craters water spouted, as if some mocking spirit had thought to ornament this desolation with fountains.

The two men didn't need to discuss what to do. They just found a fire officer, identified themselves, and asked how they could be most useful. They were put to work digging. Though neither man had really slept, neither felt like sleep, working on some reserve of energy they didn't know they had. As policemen, they took the worst job: carrying bodies – or what was left of them – round to the back of Cathedral Lane and laying them out for identification. Someone had to search through the pockets for identification cards and, where they were legible and intact, pin them to clothing so that people might find their friends and relatives.

There were strange scenes everywhere. Down the hill away from a church a fruit shop had been hit; all the fruit sat in the window, burnt and caramelised like a dish gone wrong, and a strange mucus seeped across the pavement. Balby realised, to his surprise, that it was fruit juice, coming from the broken window. Across the road a man sat on the pavement, naked but for an ARP helmet. His clothes had been blown completely off him but his body seemed untouched. He was dead though, Balby knew. A tree was still standing outside the church and in it was a dead dog, blown there by a blast.

Word came in from out of town with the crowds who had come in to help and to see the damage. Radford, where Balby lived, had been hit hard. Never mind. He had lost what he had to lose in 1919. Anything else was just stuff, though he offered a prayer for his neighbours. Briggs, who lived in the Chapelfields area, had less to worry about. The bombs had hit the Alvis tank works, but damage to the houses had been light.

Night was starting to fall and the men took a pause. The fires dimming, the warmth of exercise leaving them, both suddenly realised how cold it was. Another fireman walked past briskly. Balby knew him but, in his tiredness, couldn't recall his name. Hunter, Philips – something short, anyway.

'Ah, coppers,' he said, 'could you do one last thing before you knock off? There's a couple of blokes up there on the roof of the church, on the cathedral side, and we haven't had time to get them down.'

'Very well,' said Balby. Then he remembered Craw. He had forgotten him in all that destruction. What had happened to the academic? There was no profit in thinking about that. He was either alive or he was dead.

The two policemen made the roof via the spire stairs. They

were both exhausted and found the going hard on the narrow spiral. There were two bodies on the roof – one a middle-aged man in a tweed suit, the other an ARP man in a gas mask.

'A long way up,' said Balby.

'I don't fancy making the trip twice,' said Briggs.

'No choice.'

Briggs shrugged. 'We could just pitch 'em over the side.' Balby's eyes widened in horror. 'They're already dead, it's not going to do them any harm, is it? And it saves us a climb.'

'Just get his legs,' said Balby. 'We're going down the stairs.'

The two men struggled down the narrow stairs with the man in the tweed suit and left him in the lane. Twice they dropped him. Briggs, Balby thought, was probably right; the corpse was not going to get any deader with a fall onto the grass. It was a matter for him, though, of making an effort, doing right by the dead. The corpse was a Mr Andrew Ford, according to his papers. Very likely killed from clearing incendiaries from the roof, thought Balby. Then they climbed again.

Balby made his way carefully over the roof to where the figure of the ARP man lay. Even through his tiredness, he immediately saw something was wrong. If you have been a detective for long enough you begin to recognise the familiar postures of death, as if the grim reaper had tastes and preferences in his work for what goes with what. Balby had assumed the man had been killed by shrapnel. But those weren't shrapnel wounds on his chest. And, now that he gave him his attention, he saw that the man must have fallen. The body's twisted attitude gave that away. People who have collapsed tended to look more orderly in repose. This man had been hit by a substantial force. A bomb? Probably.

He looked around the edges of the man's mask. He saw no reason why he shouldn't remove it, so he did. Even Balby, so long inured to horrors, started at what he saw. For a second the pall of smoke seemed to break and the moon came through, picking out the world in black and white. The policeman perhaps wouldn't have seen the pattern in any other light, just have taken it for a random collection of raised scars. But the moon, coming in at such an oblique angle, like a low searchlight, joined the dots for him. Looking back at him, among swirls and confusions of points, was a representation of a pair of animal jaws. In that light they were frighteningly realistic. Balby had little experience of art. Craw or Harbard might have thought that whoever had marked the flesh had managed to capture the spirit of a snarling carnivore without actually being strictly representative. Balby just shivered.

'What's up, boss?' said Briggs.

Balby, as tired as he had ever been, heard only one word of what Briggs said: 'up'.

He turned his eyes to the spire of Holy Trinity, defiant against the smoke-black sky like the word of Christ in a world of sin.

'Up it is,' Briggs said.

The academic had last been seen going up that spire. Balby's duty as a policeman meant he had to at least see if he was up there. Also, he had been the one responsible for bringing Craw to Coventry. He needed to see him, and soon, practically and morally. The marks on the ARP man's face would require Craw's attention.

Up the winding stairs they went. When Balby got to the top he couldn't avoid looking out.

'Woe, woe, O great city, O Babylon city of power, In one hour your doom has come.

'Alas, alas, that great city Babylon, that mighty city! For in one hour is thy judgement come.' The words went through his mind.

'Bloody mess,' said Briggs.

'Yes,' said Balby.

Everywhere he looked there was destruction. Was this the hour? Was the Second Coming at hand?

Balby forced his tired mind to practicalities. He made his way around the balcony. The moon had disappeared again. He looked up to confirm what his ears told him. No sirens, no planes, and no possibility of planes under that pall. He took out his shuttered torch and shone it into the darkness. His foot kicked something. He pointed the torch down. A Thompson gun.

'What in the name of God is that doing up here?' said Briggs.

Balby didn't reply. There was something else. A gas mask, another one. He touched it. It felt funny; the skin of the mask didn't collapse under his fingers as he thought it might. He felt something wet on his hand. He'd guessed what it was even before he smelled it. Blood.

He picked up the mask by its respirator. The weight confirmed what he had already sensed. He turned the mask over in his hand to see a shock of blond hair. He felt his guts clench. It was a severed head.

Balby shone the weak light of the torch down at the mask. Even among the horrors he had seen that day, this one stood out. This was not a bomb victim, Balby instinctively knew. The presence of the gun had unsettled him, as had that of the mask. No one wore them; that method of attack had never been used on cities, and it was likely that it never would be, each side fearing reprisals in kind from the other if it was. Still, he pushed his assumptions from his mind and tried to examine the facts.

Balby turned the head and, through the glass of the mask, saw two eyes looking back at him.

There was, he noted, a tear in the surface of the gas mask. Unmistakably, there in the rubber, was the outline of a human bite. He carefully removed the mask.

The head was marked with those skin lesions, and the bite had penetrated into the flesh of the cheek. Balby breathed in. What was the world coming to? Wasn't there enough madness in it without this added horror? In some ways he felt like a man who had been ordered to put out a candle in a burning house. His task wasn't so much futile as nonsensical. But he had been ordered. The big criminals, the ones who had dropped the bombs the night before, weren't his concern. He had been allocated this macabre corner of a chaotic planet. That was his to straighten out, so straighten it out he would.

The policemen exchanged a glance. Balby exhaled and felt dizzy. He hadn't noticed that, since seeing the gas mask, he had forgotten to breathe.

'Watch that,' he said to Briggs, as if he expected the head to fly off.

He put the head on the floor, inside the mask to prevent it from picking up dirt. Then he moved down the tiny balcony, over the slippery floor towards the body. He saw straight away that it had been mutilated in the most horrible way. It was wearing torn blue overalls. Virtually the whole chest and abdomen had been removed, so much so that, though the man was lying on his back, Balby could see a white nub of a vertebra. He shone the torch on the uniform. He didn't like what he saw and so pulled back the overalls to confirm it. As he had thought. A bullet hole at the shoulder. The man had been shot at some point, very likely by the Thompson. This, he thought, was dark work.

'Come on down and see this,' said Balby.

Briggs stepped over the head and carefully made his way along the balcony.

'Bullet wounds,' said Balby.

'A bullet didn't do that, more like high explosive.'

Balby pulled back a ragged flap of overall at the man's arm. There again was the bite mark. Briggs had seen human bites many times before, most notably on David Arindon after his wife had sunk her teeth into his arm during one of their fights.

'The bomb didn't bite him.'

Briggs knelt to see the wound closer. As he did his hand went forward and touched something in the dark. It was a leather thong and, on it, a pebble. Balby came over to see and they shone the torch onto the stone. It bore an etching. A terrible wolf had its jaws around what was clearly a severed right hand.

'Like Arindon's,' said Briggs.

260

'We need to get Craw and see if he's still in one piece, and Harbard as well,' said Balby, looking up from the body. 'Now.'

Briggs nodded. Despite his tiredness he was glad to have something to do. The raid had been fierce. He was single, his parents dead. He had no wish to go home to his digs because he feared what he might find there. Like many brutal people, Briggs was a sentimentalist. He could bear to dig strangers from the rubble, even to pitch their bodies off church roofs to save him effort, but he wouldn't have wanted to find his landlady among the ruins, or to hear that she was dead.

'How, though?' he said.

'We'll get a car. Do you know if there's a key for the door to this spire?'

'Search me.'

The two men descended to the church. Balby could think of no other course of action but to leave a note on the lower door. There were no bobbies to spare to guard it, and realistically no chance of anyone going up to the balcony for a while.

He stripped a page from his notebook.

'Closed by order of police. Phone Balby 341.' Then a thought struck him. Was the station still standing? No one had said it wasn't, so he presumed it was. He fixed the note to the door with a nail from the floor tapped in by a piece of rock, and they set out into the street.

The policemen didn't get a car, but they did manage to requisition a butcher's van. The butcher was an old man, too frail for heavy labour, and he'd been standing outside where his shop had been all day, waiting for a request to help, waiting to feel useful. He'd helped make tea in the Queen's Messenger van that supplied food to the bomb teams. He'd handed out sandwiches, offered cigarettes, and tried to make sense of it all in his mind, but with no success. It was like life upside down to him. Unsettlingly, he was virtually the only man in the street who was not flecked with blood. He'd been there from first light and was now hovering at the edge of the rescue operation in the bright moonlight. The request for his van finally made him feel he was doing some good, and he gave it willingly.

'We'll bring it back tomorrow morning,' said Balby.

'Do!' said the butcher. 'Business as usual the day after, if I have to sell the meat off a table in the street.' There was something in his jauntiness that Balby found difficult to bear.

Balby and Briggs loaded the ARP man's body into the back of the van and drove off to Coombe Abbey. They negotiated their way out of the ruined city centre with difficulty. Already the Royal Engineers had cleared a path to allow vehicles in and out, but still they had to be careful. Balby felt a surge of pride in the army's quick work. Had Uncle Adolf realised what he'd taken on? If he did, then he wouldn't be sleeping soundly in the Eagle's Nest, or whatever silly name he gave to his house.

The van took them out of the city into the colder air of the countryside. The road seemed to suggest itself to him; it was as if he had no hand in where the van went and was just a passenger, like Briggs, asleep in his loud snores.

Why couldn't Hitler have called his house something normal? The house Balby had shared with his wife had been called 'The Nook'. What was wrong with that, Herr Schicklgruber? Adolf Gitler. Adolf Twitler, Adolf . . .

'What the bloody hell was that?' It was Briggs speaking.

Balby came back to consciousness with a jolt and hit the brakes. Had he swerved in his tiredness? They were at the beginning of the long drive to Coombe Abbey.

'What was what?' he said

'Something ran across the front of us!'

'A deer.'

'No, it was a man. Bloody idiot at this time of night. He came from nowhere.'

Balby rubbed at his eyes. 'Shall we just get to the house?'

'Yeah,' said Briggs. 'Do you think they'll let us have a lie down?'

'I expect so,' said Balby.

He double declutched, and took a last glance into the woods. He could see nothing. It was late and he was tired. The van moved forward and Balby longed for sleep.

27 Mrs Voller Grants an Interview

'Senior Storm Command Leader von Knobelsdorff, do come in,' said Gertie.

Von Knobelsdorff stepped into the chamber. He was conscious of the smell of fish coming from the kitchen.

'Mrs Voller,' he said, bowing, and kissing her proffered hand. 'Thank you for agreeing to see me.'

She looked incredible, he thought, dressed in a black velvet jacket adorned in gold braid with two panels of decorated mirrors covering the breasts. And what jewels! Those exquisite sapphire and diamond earrings, that ring in silver and aquamarine, though the stones were nothing to the beauty of her eyes, which seemed to von Knobelsdorff to be the most lovely he had ever seen in his life, a light violet that made him think of the cool light of mountains, or the metalled skies of a winter dusk. He was not used to such thoughts.

'Not at all – would you like coffee?'

'Yes, I would. Your dress, it is wonderful.'

'Oh, do you think so? It's a Schiaparelli, do you know her?'

'No. She's very talented.'

'Yes, much of her work is inspired by Dalí.'

'The surrealist?' said von Knobelsdorff, trying to mask his discomfort but, finding himself out of practice at masking anything, only succeeding in making it more obvious.

'Oh, I know the party leadership frowns on such things, but that's more for the benefit of the lower orders, is it not? We are sophisticated people and allowed more, shall we say, diverse tastes.'

He stiffened slightly. In theory, he knew, he should have the dress taken and destroyed. Possibly he should even have had Mrs Voller punished. However ... However ...

'You wouldn't be a dear and just pop the coffee on yourself, would you?' said Gertie, 'I'm afraid I'm not very good at all that, smacks of cookery and below stairs stuff to me.'

Von Knobelsdorff had to remind himself that this was a jobbing doctor's wife, not some grand duchess. If she was as he had seen her in his vision, then she was far more even than that. More rational people than von Knobelsdorff might have wondered how, by chance, a goddess had happened to appear at the castle. He, however, had no doubt at all that the goddess, or witch, or whatever she was, was there because of him and the magical practices of the *Schwarze Sonne*. An alternative explanation – that he was simply a bystander in something that had been going on for years before he existed and would continue for years after he was dead – would not have occurred to him. If there was an occult battle taking place, he could only think of himself as one of the warriors, not one of the displaced, the downtrodden, a psychic refugee.

'Where is the kitchen?'

'Just through that door, if you would be so kind.'

Von Knobelsdorff had, in the excitement of his vision, forgotten his little trick on the Vollers. He opened the door to the fearful mess of the kitchen, the concrete pond that Max had struggled, for his wife's sake, to keep clean, the clammy atmosphere from the heat of the always burning stove, the stink of fish, and, there in the water, the crocodile. It was bigger than when he'd seen it, seventy centimetres long maybe.

'Ah.'

'Yes, Senior Storm Command Leader?'

'Does, er, does that bite?'

'Quite frequently, yes,' she said, with the same look of expectation on her face. 'If you make a loud noise it will probably scuttle off. Two sugars for me, please. I managed to get some last week. You'll find it in the jar behind its nest.'

Von Knobelsdorff clapped his hands. The creature didn't move.

'Would you like me to have that removed?' he asked.

Gertie said nothing; she just sat looking at him with a fixed smile.

'I will have it removed,' he said.

'And the concrete on the floor?'

'And the concrete on the floor.'

'In fact,' said Gertie, 'I have been thinking. I don't find these rooms suit me.'

'There are none better, it was only chance that saw you allocated these.'

Gertie's smile was unrelenting.

'Oh, but Senior Storm Command Leader, where do you live? I hear the SS leadership's rooms are quite palatial.'

'They are all taken.'

For the first time, Gertie's smile disappeared. 'I see.' She coughed. 'Excuse me, my throat is quite dry.'

Von Knobelsdorff, a stranger to charm, did not understand what she was asking.

'The coffee?' she said. 'Come, it will be quite an experience for you. "Sigurd versus the Dragon" – I know my husband enjoys his nightly re-enactments of that myth.'

Von Knobelsdorff clicked his heels and turned to the kitchen. He approached the kettle and, by necessity, also the crocodile. The creature hissed at him.

Inside the living quarters, Gertie turned her profile against the window, as if posing for a painting. There was a gunshot from the kitchen. Then another. Then a third. She didn't blink. After a few minutes von Knobelsdorff emerged, the smell of gun smoke accompanying him into the room as he carried in the acorn coffee on a tray.

He smiled. 'Please be careful in there, I have had to leave the pistol on the side to allow it to cool,' he said, in the tone of a slightly nervous undertaker enquiring if madam will be choosing the standard or the de luxe package. Von Knobelsdorff had no talent for civility, and rather overdid things when he attempted it.

266

'Miss Fischer *will* be upset,' said Gertie. 'Now, what can I do for you?'

Von Knobelsdorff looked around him in a shifty way, as if he expected eavesdroppers. He didn't quite know how to approach a woman he strongly suspected to be a sorceress. Did she know she had this power?

'Lady, have you ...'

'Ah!' she said, pointing to the coffee cup that he had placed on the occasional table.

'Lady?'

'Coaster! They're in the kitchen too.'

Von Knobelsdorff didn't know what to say. No one had spoken to him that way since he had been a youth. His normal response would have been to ignore her or to tell her to mind how she spoke to him, but he was on unknown ground here. He had to proceed carefully. Accordingly, he fetched the coasters.

'Will there be anything else, Lady?' he said, as he brought them in.

'For the moment, no, but I'll let you know if I think of anything,' she said. 'Now, sit and tell me what's on your mind.'

Von Knobelsdorff did as he was told and began.

'You have seen me before, Lady?'

'Often, All the ladies speak of you and admire you.'

Von Knobelsdorff smiled. 'I don't mean around the castle. Outside the castle. In a dream, perhaps.'

'Senior Storm Command Leader, I am a married woman.'

He was not adept at reading anything other than fear and weakness in other people. He could detect no teasing in what Gertie said, and was flattered but not too flattered. He expected the love of women but no part of him really wanted it.

'I must ask you to sign some documents,' he said.

'Really? How vulgar.'

'It will enable us to talk freely.'

'Then how can I demur?'

Von Knobelsdorff produced a folder from his briefcase and opened it.

'Official secrets,' he said. 'A formality but very necessary. Everything that is to pass between us is to be top secret.'

'You will disappoint the tennis ladies. Your doings are of great interest to them.'

'Identify the gossips and I will have them spoken to,' he said, again in his undertaker's tone.

'Well, now we are speaking confidentially, I can say Mrs Haussmann, Mrs Cullen, Mrs Braun and Mrs Daecher are the principal group, but I could bring you the names of others. Mrs Daecher in particular seems convinced you are contacting our Aryan forefathers along with eleven other Knights of a "Black Sun" in your little room in the north tower.' Gertie finished signing.

'How could she know? That is classified information.'

'I expect Mrs Haussmann told her. You know – she who has all those lovely jewels. She seems to know everything that goes on around here. I believe her husband keeps her informed.'

'I see,' said von Knobelsdorff, with a tight jaw.

'But you did not come to discuss loose talk in the castle.'

'Indeed not. I am a blunt man so I will speak bluntly.'

Gertie's lips pursed, as if to indicate that she had rather feared that might be the case. Having said that, he seemed to be struggling for the words.

'You are here to ask about my husband's experiments?'

'Indeed not, no.'

'But surely you must be aware of how well they complement your own work?'

'In what way?'

'It was while attending my husband's laboratory that the visions first came upon me.'

'Visions?'

'Yes. You on a high throne, surveying a broad and prosperous land. And then that business by the well.'

Von Knobelsdorff actually licked his lips, a small protrusion of pink going from the left to the right of his mouth, like a dial measuring pleasure.

'When do these visions come?'

'All the time. I see them strongly now, as strongly as I have ever seen them. It is your presence that inspires them, I am sure. You have a psychic sensitivity about you, sir, I can tell that.'

This conversation could not have been going better from von Knobelsdorff's point of view.

'What exactly do you see?'

'Why, you in command of a mighty wolf. But this isn't any wolf. This is an incarnation of the Fenris Wolf, an incarnation of a sort. Have you heard of the Fenris Wolf?'

'Of course. The wolf that will eat the Gods on the final day of judgement. That could be difficult. We feel we had some success in summoning Odin some time ago. Is the wolf not his enemy?'

'You did what, dear?'

'We summoned Odin.'

Gertie dabbed a napkin to her lips in a polite suppression of giggles.

'Oh, dearie me, what an idea.'

'I don't quite see ...'

'No, you don't, do you, Manny? I should leave the seeing to me if I were you.'

'I am your superior in these matters. I took myself to that place with the well and ...'

Von Knobelsdorff was having increasing difficulty finishing his sentences. His throat felt dry and his jaw stiff whenever he said anything that seemed to displease Gertie. It was a very new experience for him, and not one he was at all sure he liked.

'*You* summoned Odin, the All-father, the lord of slaughter, that battle-hungry fellow, king of magic, master of thought and memory, you clicked your grubby little fingers and along he trotted, did he? Do you think he had any say in the matter? Did he salute you when he appeared?'

Von Knobelsdorff was not used to being addressed in this manner, and felt his anger rising inside him.

'The ceremonies have been proven to work. We have encountered the figure of a man who—'

Gertie gently put down her coffee cup with roughly the effect on von Knobelsdorff of someone slamming down their fist and screaming in his face. He actually flinched.

'I know what you've met,' she said.

'What?

'Nothing you should want to. There are others you know, who are much further down the route than you. Do you know who?'

'I thought I recognised one other person at the well. It was a fellow I met in Tibet.'

'Yes. Well, he already has that wolf by the ears and, unless you get cracking, then before long he'll have him dancing to his tune and you will be a very sorry little Manny indeed.'

The SS man nodded. 'I—'

'Ah!' Gertie leant forward and put her finger to his lip.

As she touched him it was as if doors were opening and closing inside him, to reveal rooms that seemed to seethe with snakes, rats and other vermin, or to bang hollow against nothing at all. It was a disconcerting feeling. He had never been aware of the whistling caverns that existed inside him and of the flat unfertile plains of his mind. There were things missing inside von Knobelsdorff, emptinesses that he had always regarded as a source of strength. But, as Gertie touched him, he began to experience them as a lack. It was as if for his whole life he had been looking at the floor, never thinking what was around him. Now he had lifted his head and seen himself alone in a vast desert under a dark and starless sky, and felt the implications of that isolation. It made him shiver but it also thrilled him. This woman, he thought, represented all that he had been looking for. He had no doubt she was a sorceress far more powerful than any he had ever encountered, nor did he doubt that it was his experiments that had brought her to the castle. He needed to control her, though,

270

to ensure that whatever they accomplished together was seen as his achievement, not hers. It wouldn't be too difficult, he thought. After all, she was only a woman, and who in the party would believe that she had achieved anything at all without a man's guidance?

'You need to call the wolf here,' she said. 'I have done some preliminary work, but to carry things forward we will require action of a certain sort.'

'What sort?'

'I will tell you when some of my needs are met. Suffice it to say that there is no point in bringing him here unless we can control him. What rewards have you prepared for me?'

Von Knobelsdorff floundered. 'Er, well, you will have the eternal gratitude of the SS.'

'Oh dear.' Gertie took on an expression like an empress being invited to domino night at the *Bierkeller*. 'I was rather thinking a substantial sum of money might be more in order.'

'You are aware that I could just command you to help me?'

There was a deep silence.

'Although,' said von Knobelsdorff, 'I will see what I can do.'

'You do that,' she said, 'and do take that crocodile with you when you go.'

'I'll send someone up for it.'

'I would prefer you to take it. Now,' she said. 'Oh, and Manny ...'

'Yes?' said von Knobelsdorff.

'Mrs Haussmann has something of mine. It's a pair of lovely tiger's eye earrings. You couldn't retrieve them for me, could you? She might be a little reluctant to give them up.'

'Believe me, she will give them up,' he said.

'I know I can trust you, because if you bring me what I want, then you will get what you want. By next time we meet, I shall have something for you to set you on a path of greatness.'

'Do you know what I want, Lady?'

'What do we all want, darling? The end of your enemies.'

Von Knobelsdorff wet his lips with his tongue. 'Well, it would do for a start.'

28 Last Gasp

In an upstairs bedroom of Coombe Abbey, Craw breathed hard. He had been out of the rubble a day now, his wounds already healing. The transformation was visibly upon him. Already his muscle was thicker, his nails too. His teeth seemed to have shifted in his mouth, to have twisted very slightly, and he could not stop rubbing them with his tongue.

His shoulders felt too big for his body and his voice, when he spoke, was deeper. His fingers seemed not quite to fit together in their normal way, to be wider than he was used to. He made a fist. The fingertips met his palm at a strange angle. The conclusion was clear. They had grown.

He looked at himself in the mirror. No one who did not know him very well would suspect him to be anything other than a well-built man. Anyone who did know him would think he had put on a little weight, that his face was puffier than usual. He himself saw the muscle stiffening at his neck, felt his shirt too tight across his arms and chest and knew, it was a new Endamon Craw looking back from the mirror.

Even more disturbing were the thoughts he was having. The rage which had caused him to consume the painted man had passed but, as his body had absorbed the man's proteins and fats, his mind had absorbed something of him too, along with that of the machine-gunner on the spire. Craw felt displaced in his own consciousness, a feeling akin to that he had in his fingers and teeth. Things did not quite seem as they were and, as he ran over his familiar thoughts – pieces of music he liked, art he admired – he found them subtly changed. Only his thought of his wife, that face by the beach as he prepared for battle, remained constant, like a lantern by which he might set his course. He was beginning to see that his love for Adisla was not as selfish as he had thought. It was the sole thing that kept the wolf at bay, that stopped the slaughter beast entering the world.

He could hear the muffled voices of the policemen from the room below him. He hadn't yet revealed the fact of his survival to them, though they had nearly discovered it when they'd narrowly missed knocking him down on his return to the abbey. When he had told Harbard his story, or at least that which he could tell him, Harbard had thought it important he rest and consider what he was going to tell the policemen before letting them know he was still alive.

Craw's visit to the black shore was a development, Harbard had said, that was important and would require careful thought before action. He had not been able to explain his own presence there beyond saying that it might have been a hallucination.

A couple of hours went by and Craw sipped at his brandy. He was pleased to find that the packet of handmade cigarettes he had left on his last visit were still on a bookcase. He smoked those and thought his thoughts. It was as if the encroachments that the wolf had made on his mind had also awakened a human faculty inside him to fight it. Memories were swarming back to him now, ever more confusing. He saw the black hillside, saw the eyes of the wolf upon him, and began to recall what had happened. He saw Gullveig's face, spitting out her anger, but he couldn't hear what she said. There was another presence too, someone in borrowed clothing, he thought, like he had borrowed the clothing of the wolf. There was a fluttering in his mind, as if a great multitude of birds was present – no, not birds, but feathers, millions of feathers surrounding and engulfing something. But what was it? Then the memory moved and he saw only Adisla again.

There was a knock at the door.

'Come,' said Craw.

The door opened. It was Harbard. He came into the room.

Even in his own disordered state, Craw could see his old friend was fighting down agitation, struggling to put on a calm front.

'I have given the events you related to me some thought,' said Harbard, 'and it seems that things were more advanced here than I had realised.'

Craw swallowed some more brandy. From the corner of his eye there was some movement. He turned to see what it was, but it was gone.

'There has been an attempt, it appears to me, to dip into the same source of power that created you.'

'Power?' said Craw, shaping the word carefully.

Harbard shrugged. 'Whatever that might be. From your own account of your vision there were several presences at the well. Arindon spoke of trying to steal your wolf. The Nazi talked of the wolf as a weapon. And then the perplexing image of the lady.'

'*A lyttle somethynge for myne appetytes, sir.*' The wolf was in the corner of the room again.

Craw forced the words from his lips. 'Whatever is happening, I need to find that lady.'

'Why?'

'Because when I meet her, I know I will have peace.'

'Always yourself, Endamon, always yourself. Continents are on fire and all you think of is you.'

'The curse,' said Craw, grinding out the words, 'affects more than me.'

'*Myne appetytes, sir, I begge thee please.*'

'Are you all right, Crawford?' said Harbard. Craw had paled and was sweating, his eyes not focused on the professor.

'*Myne hungers wylle notte tarry, sir.*'

'Your hungers will wait,' said Craw.

Harbard put his hand out to Craw. 'Crawford, I think it is time you let me play Louvetier.'

Craw put his head into his hands. He could feel the breath of the wolf on the back of his neck, hear its voice imploring him, see that demented scrawl on the inside of his eyelids.

'*Lette me steere you, sir, lette me guide youre hande.*'

'I have a way to control this, I am sure,' said Harbard. 'I have studied the writings, made deductions. I think we can harness what's inside you.'

'How?'

'We need to go back to the bomb site, to the rubble. We need to go back to the black shore, but this time you will be with me and together we will fight the wolf. I think I know what the Louvetier was missing.'

'Yes?'

Craw's body was bursting with energy, not uncontrollable but uncomfortable. It was a magnified version of the feeling you might have after four hours in a waiting room, uncertain of how much longer you might have to endure, every door slam, every creak promising your liberation but never delivering it.

'You were cut by something,' said Harbard.

'Cut, yes.'

'I believe it to be part of a relic, one that is mentioned at various times in connection with your transformations down the centuries. It is a crescent of some sort, perhaps a sword rumoured to be enchanted to kill you.'

Craw gulped, thought of the crescent of fire he had seen on Holy Trinity, thought of his father, the dread Authun's curved weapon that he bought from eastern merchants.

Harbard continued, 'Crawford, I have been a fool. When I said I exchanged a shamanic drum with von Knobelsdorff, it was not quite that. I was covering my own embarrassment. I thought it relatively worthless at the time. Well, not worthless, more an obtuse avenue of exploration, something that I couldn't immediately use. The Louvetier's book was of more obvious importance.'

'What did you give him?'

The wolf lolled its tongue. Its eyes were on Harbard. Craw's eyes were on Harbard. The wolf and Craw, Craw and the wolf – what was the difference between them? Craw fought to understand how he was different, how he was *other*, to this thing before him. What a daft mistake, what a chump, what a silly billy, what a nincompoop and a fuzzy head he had been. Of course he wasn't different from the wolf – they were one and the same. How could he have made an error like that? The wolf was he and he the wolf, to huff and to puff and to blow the house in.

Harbard's voice went on over the chaos of Craw's thoughts like someone playing a melody above the crashings and scrapings of a demented orchestra.

'It was part of a sword. I had traced it to Tibet over many years of research, but my angel had not spoken of it. The book seemed to be the important thing. My new guide, who leads me now, has revealed the mistake I made. I believe the people you found in that house are a Nazi cell, and they have that relic with them. That's what you were stabbed with. It also might explain what happened in your study and at the gate. I think it might have some effect on you, however temporary, at a distance. They summoned you here to Coventry to try it at close range, and they intended to either control you or usurp your power. Arindon is involved, I'm sure, though it can only be as a pawn.'

He saw Craw's glazed expression, heard the deep breaths he sucked in as he fought for control of his mind.

'Crawford,' he said, 'we need to go back to that house, back to the black shore. If we can find the sword then we have a chance to at least control this thing that's in you. To beat it, use it even. I can reveal to you now, that has been my aim ever since I learned of your remarkable existence. You have a gift, Crawford, and we must learn to harness it.'

The pressure in Craw's head was unbearable. No, not unbearable. Craw would endure it. He thought of his wife. She was near, he could sense it, and he felt in his marrow that meeting her would not only bring him peace but make sense of it all – explain what had happened to him and how it might be avoided. He just needed to stay human long enough to find her. He controlled his voice.

'Take me there.'

29 The Wolf Stone

The witch inside Mrs Voller moved Gertie's hands down the smooth rock of the castle's exterior. Gullveig, so rich in magic, knew what she was looking for but, inside the castle of gibbering shadows there had been too many distractions for her to focus correctly. There the dead had screamed at her from the walls, tugged at her clothes as she passed, come imploring from doorways and darknesses, asking her to recognise and remove their agonies. Outside, she could think.

Things had gone as she had planned and von Knobelsdorff had come up with a little gold and, pleasingly, something far more valuable. She shook the beautiful bracelet on her arm with pleasure. Von Knobelsdorff himself had personally stolen it in his time in Warsaw. He had stolen a lot there, and he'd only ever bothered to have the gold valued. He'd given it to her more in hope than expectation, because Mrs Haussmann claimed to have lost the tiger's eye earrings. Gullveig the witch, though, had an appreciation of fine workmanship that was so much more developed than von Knobelsdorff's. She knew it was a thing of great worth, more like an ornamental bracer than a bracelet, extending from the wrist to the forearm and delicately wrought in glass and enamel.

Its inspiration was the speedwell flower, five stylised stems rendered in white and blue. Von Knobelsdorff thought he had fooled her when he gave it to her, but the witch sensed its value. It would have paid for von Knobelsdorff's retirement, had he quit the SS at that moment.

So Gullveig was pleased with the gift and inclined to think well of the Senior Storm Command Leader.

She had not yet seen exactly how she could trap the wolf

but, as an instinctive seer, she knew that some method must exist. And if the wolf could be made, perhaps he could be unmade, his powers transferred to someone more deserving of them, perhaps someone like von Knobelsdorff, whose motivations were simple, which made him easier to control. Then the god who dreamt her might be denied his sacrifice in this world and pass into nothingness. If Ragnarok did not play out on earth, then it must play out in heaven. It could be done, she was sure; she had an almost tangible feeling of the future, as if its possibilities were threads she could tease in her hands, examining which would hold fast and which might break, which might be woven to useful purpose.

Even to Gullveig, the castle was unusual. It was a significant place, she thought, a place that had drawn magic to it down the ages. Or not magic – something like it: slaughter, injustice, the worst of men. These things, though – what the priests called evil – were very like magic. The wilfully wrong, the perverse, the abhorrent were all keys to magic that the witch had turned before and might turn again.

The castle seemed like a rock in a sea of blood. The blood smashed against its sides, forced its way through its courtyards and exploded into plumes in dungeons and cells. Outside things were calmer and she could begin to feel currents, tidal pulls in the deep miseries that surrounded Wewelsburg and which led her to where she needed to go.

She saw at once that it was the hill. It took her an afternoon to hike there but she didn't notice the fatigue. She was happy, after so long in that choking hall, to step outside on the mountain, smell the frost-clean air and feel the grass beneath her hands as she climbed.

The boy, she thought, had died in the forest, halfway up the climb, there in the hollow. Had the wolf been here before? It felt like it, but she could not be sure. She did know, however, that there had been a chase and that the intent of the chase had been to transcend the natural world. The archaeologists who had found the child's body had assumed, from the tattoo on his forehead which the acid soil had preserved, that he had been a sacrifice.

The truth, the witch Gullveig knew, was more complicated. She sat down at the bottom of a recess and watched the trees towering about her. It was a good place, she thought. The visions she wanted would be available there. She began to sing to herself, a wordless tune in a scale that sounded like the music of the wind in the mouth of a cave.

Her mind disconnected from the present reality and she saw the boy face the wolves. She felt the currents of blood swirling around her, felt the boy's mind like a vibration, felt the hopes of the tribe he came from, felt humanity as tributaries of emotion pouring into a scarlet ocean.

He had been running hard, but she felt no fear in him. As she floated into his consciousness, she realised he had not been running away, but towards the wolves. The pack turned to go but the boy stepped forward, limping. He had not been limping when he ran. Gullveig knew he was speaking their language.

'Take me,' he was saying, 'I am weak.'

As the animals closed in, his mind became clearer to her. The bright-plumed legionnaires burning the villages, the retreat to the forest of the tribe and the shaman's decision that it would be the boy who would go to the wolves. Not sacrifice. Transformation. He was not giving himself to the animals, he was taking from them.

In that moment of change, of the mingling of human and animal spirits, was the key to other changes, other places she needed to go. Gullveig felt a heat come into her cheeks as she stepped through the gate of the boy's pain to touch all the other magical transformations that had occurred and ever would occur. She saw them like a twinkling field of frost beneath the moonlight, like little points of light sparkling in the air in front of her. There was a presence there, she could feel it. She heard a sound like the sea, but it was not the sea – rather a clamour of voices raised in anger, pleading, exultation – and, with them, the sound of metal upon metal, cries and groans and even, distantly, gunfire. She heard snatches of crazy poetry, dissonant music and, somewhere, a dry drum beating out an idiot rhythm. A voice in her head began to sing, high and sweet.

> *The moon is gliding*
> *Death is riding*
> *Don't you see a white spot*
> *At the nape of my neck*
> *Garun Garun?*

Long ago, she had lived under the earth among witches like herself. Memories came back of what she had tried to do, along with the voices of her sisters.

> *Ride, let us ride*
> *The hills in darkness hide*
> *Craze him and race him,*
> *The wretch off the way*
> *So he never may*
> *See the light of day*
> *Never see the sun another day.*

So long ago, so long ago. She had mistaken herself for someone else. Such a powerful witch, such a strong sister. She was a god who had forgotten he was a god. He? It. Odin slid between sexes as easily as a human might change a shirt. Gullveig the witch was Odin, tricking himself to his own death, a dream of sacrifice to the fates to forestall the real thing. Well no more. The dream would break free of the dreamer.

The poems were leading her back to where she needed to go. She thought of the lady who had come to her at the hall. Another line of poetry seemed to enter her head.

This is your card, she said, the widow
The Lady Beautiful in Tears.

Gullveig felt her head swim. The personality she had dislodged was a strong one and now she even confused it for a second with herself.

She saw that others, too, had tried to part the wolf from his gift. She saw the Louvetier, that wily hunter, and he had brought something to the wolf. It was a stone with a carving upon it, the head of a wolf. Now she saw its importance – how it had drawn the dream of the wolf, how it bound the wolf.

'A rock called Scream.' Yes, a fragment of the rock onto which the Gods had bound their enemy the Fenris wolf, where he will lie dreaming until he awakes to destroy them.

In her vision, the seeress saw the Louvetier in his brocade and silks lay down his gun. The hated wolf had welcomed him to his hut and they had worked together. What were they trying to do? She saw the Louvetier marking and cutting his own skin. Why? To make him recognisable to Fenrisulfr, the terrible wolf, to become part wolf himself. Gullveig felt angry. That power was not the Louvetier's to take, it was hers.

Her senses jumbled and she felt the presence of the trees and the animals of the wood seething around on her. The forest seemed to have moods within it, all distinct and several but also of one voice, the many identities blending into one like humans in a crowd. Now Gullveig was in another hollow, in another place, another mountain. It was warmer here and she could smell summer, hear a woodpecker's call, and feel the gentle green light of the sun filtered through the leaves of a pine grove.

There was a pool at the bottom of the hollow and, at first, she thought the wolf was drinking from it. But he wasn't; he was scratching and turning and shaking his head, as if trying to free himself from something. In his jaws he bore a scrap of cloth. Then it was moonlight, a huge bright penny moon turning the glade to silver, and the wolf was changing. She saw his legs bend in strange ways, the fur of his head begin to tear and rip and, out of the skin, came, choking and crying, a man. He scratched off the skin against a rock and plunged into the pool.

Gullveig watched him writhing in the water. He climbed out and lay panting on the bank, his skin pale in the moonlight. There was someone else watching too. At first she thought it was the All-father, the man with the eyepatch, but it wasn't, or rather wasn't quite. This man had no patch, but he wore a broad-brimmed hat and was smoking a cigar. She knew that he wasn't really there. Gullveig could see visions, but she could also see all those who had seen the vision before. Time meant nothing. The man wasn't watching at the same moment she was watching, but he had watched before and had left a print of himself there. It was the figure she had seen at the well, the companion of the wolf. What did he want? Nothing that she approved of, she was sure of that. Insidious, troubling her like the odour of burning might steal upon a lady reading in her drawing room, the thought came into her head. That man in the broad-brimmed hat wanted to control the wolf but not for gold, but from want of knowledge. He needed to see what immortality was, to go on voraciously understanding the world until the end of time and, more, he wished her present mortal allies harm. She knew who he was. The All-father, forgotten to himself once more, unknowingly making ready his old dance with the wolf, the dance of teeth and blood. He would need to be stopped before he could complete his sacrifice and forestall the end of the Gods. The gods would end, their dreams outliving them. The dance needed two partners. She could call the wolf and she could take his power to stop the sacrifice from being made.

The events of her vision had shown that the wolf could be parted from his gift, however partially.

She returned her attention to the man who had emerged soaking from the pool. At his throat she saw the pendant, the fragment of the magic cancelling rock was like a piece of the night to her. He couldn't see her, she knew, so she walked nearer. He was weeping and holding the cloth to his face. She smiled as she recognised it. It was a lady's handkerchief, of the sort she'd seen when she'd been to Middle Earth before and entertained the courtiers of Versailles with her spirit summoning, and it was stained deeply with blood.

The imposter tore at the pendant on his neck and threw it into the pool. Then he ran, naked and mad beneath the moon.

Lost in her delight at the wolf man's torment, Gullveig's mind slipped from where it should have been; her concentration wavered.

Gertie Voller had slept for a long time by the fire in that strange hall and she woke feeling quite refreshed. The fire was now low and the hall much less smoky. Through a vent in the roof she could see a bright blue day outside and thought that she might like to go out.

She looked around the hall and saw that the dead were sleeping, lying on benches at the sides of the room with the remains of dinners on golden plates about them, drinking goblets discarded at their sides. She had no fear of these strange men, though she felt curiously vulnerable in another way, almost as if she were undressed. She felt her hand. Her rings, the diamond engagement ring and the wedding band, were both gone. She hadn't removed them since she'd married Max nearly five years before.

She looked around her to see if they were by her side, but they weren't there. Then she remembered. Gullveig, who had said she would help her with the wolf was gone. She had taken the rings.

Gertie felt indignant and cheated. What right had this woman to steal her jewellery? And what was that nonsense about her being her sister? She felt a hot flush come over her, that peculiar feeling unique to the discovery that you are the victim of a theft.

In front of her, fifty metres or so away, was the door that

the witch had gone through. Gertie made her way towards it. But as Gertie walked forward, she was surprised to see that the door got no nearer. Or rather, it did get nearer but then, some lapse of concentration on her part, a deviation of her attention as her eyes wandered to the sleeping ranks of dead on either side of her, and the door would be as far away as ever.

At first she thought that, in some weird way, she was being returned to the same spot but, when she looked to her left and right, the men on the benches were different. She set off opposite a fierce-looking Chinese warrior, complete with a tasselled spear and armour of steel pieces. When she looked, the door was as far away as ever but she was next to a huge Zulu, sleeping next to his assegai and skin shield, a bullet hole clearly visible in the centre of his forehead. When she looked back, the fire she had left was far away. And yet the door in the hall of the dead was no nearer.

Gertie resolved just to walk and to see what happened. She was sure that she must get hungry or thirsty eventually, although she was aware of neither sensation just then.

She walked on and on, past the hoplites and the blue painted Celts, past elaborately dressed dandies with half a head missing, past Mongol warriors and armour-clad knights, scruffy pioneers and immaculately presented redcoats. The variety in the ranks of the battle dead seemed endless, their numbers unimaginable. Gertie seemed to walk for days in the long hall. She lost track of time, never sleeping, never tiring, just walking down the rotting ranks of heroes with that door never any nearer, just fifty metres away. She began to feel helpless and alone, to fear that she would never see her husband again. All the positive feelings about Wewelsburg she had managed to cultivate in herself were now gone. It was the castle, she was sure, that had caused this nightmare. Had she wandered into some room within it? She looked at her finger, to where her engagement and wedding rings should have been, and cursed Gullveig who had taken them. It wasn't for their value but for what they represented – her husband's love.

Gertie was not helpless, however. Her sensitivity, which seemed to emanate from her like a light perfume that could pervade a room for hours after she was gone, had a different quality in that hall. It was as if she felt the emotions of the dead as she passed them – fear, anger, pride, defiance, yearning and trembling washed over her like ocean currents, now hot, now cold, now turbulent, now gentle, as she walked. But there was more. Her progress seemed to trouble the dead themselves, to stir them in their sleep. More than one warrior cried out as she passed, each one a different word but meaning the same thing. Aula, Kema, Zolzaya, Marianne. A girl's name. Words came into her mind, she didn't know from where: 'This is your card. The Lady Beautiful In Tears'.

Then a voice said something that seemed peculiarly familiar to her.

'Signy!'

She looked to see where the voice was coming from and saw, on a bench, a huge man. He was wearing a mail tunic that seemed too small for him, and carrying a spear. His face beneath his blond beard was fat, white and bloated and she realised he must have been drowned. The man turned in his sleep.

'Tell my wife she was as good a woman as ever kept a key. Raise my sons as your own.'

She didn't know what to say to this sleeping giant and might have passed by, but she let her instinct guide her. She reached forward with her hand and touched him on the forehead.

'Wake up,' she said.

The man stirred and opened his salt-swollen eyes.

'Who troubles me here in the hall of heroes?'

Gertie said nothing, but she took the man's hand. It was cold, and in other circumstances it might have made her shiver. She had an unexpected sensation, though, not of his cold transferring to her but of her warmth flooding into him.

The man let go of her hand and picked up his spear.

'To battle,' he said.

Gertie shook her head and spoke, though she didn't know where the words came from.

'This is not the time for battle. See, all your companions are asleep.'

The giant looked about him and seemed puzzled.

'Then I cannot be awake, for every day we fight as one and every evening we feast as one. It is the will of Odin and the goddess who owns these halls,' he said.

Gertie was relieved to see that the man didn't mistake her for the lady. She was sure Gullveig had been lying when she had said that Gertie and she were related. She couldn't be, she thought. Gertie would never steal someone's jewellery and abandon them in a place like this.

'But you are awake,' she said.

The man nodded. 'I think you know my wife.' Gertie said nothing. 'How is she?' he said. 'The company of these heroes is a great honour but I think of my family often.'

'Perhaps,' said Gertie, 'we might go to find her.'

'I would like that,' said the giant.

He stood and Gertie took his hand again. It seemed warmer than when she had touched it the first time. The two walked towards the door, and this time it got closer. In a few paces they were next to it and the giant lifted the wooden beam that secured it. Then he opened the door and stepped through.

In the woods near Wewelsburg, Gullveig fell back through the gate of the wolf boy's pain as if propelled by an explosion. She could no longer feel Mrs Voller sleeping inside her. The warmth of that kind lady had spread through her mind, as comfortable as the purr of a cat dozing on her lap. Now it was gone. This puzzled Gullveig. She thought to return to her halls, but her business in Wewelsburg wasn't finished and she wasn't sure that Mrs Voller's body would be up to a second possession.

There was something in Gullveig's hand, something she

at first took for a ruby. Blood, a drip of blood. She put her hand to her nose and mouth. More blood. She had forgotten what fragile vessels human bodies could be. Mrs Gertie Voller needed to survive if Gullveig was to do her work in this world. That concern for the health of Gertie's body placed a limit on the magic, she thought. A realisation hit her, a cold tingle in her stomach. Wherever Mrs Voller had gone, she was not attempting to oust Gullveig, so there was nothing to worry about immediately. Still, it added a new urgency to her actions. She wanted that stone. Gullveig stood.

The moon had come up, a crescent against a metal sky.

'Gévaudan,' she said to the trees, the name coming unbidden into her mind. 'We must get to Gévaudan.'

She turned back to the castle. There was no time to lose, she knew. The Senior Storm Command Leader's moment had come.

30   Ezekiel Harbard's Sacrifice

The army Austin 10 could only take them to within half a mile of where they needed to go. After that the roads were impassable, blocked by burnt-out vehicles, cratered beyond use, or barred by roadblocks in place because of unexploded bombs. The driver pulled up, Harbard and Craw got out, and the car pulled away.

Harbard led the way, his style of dress toned down to a long overcoat and wide-brimmed hat. Coventry, in late November 1940, was no place for flamboyance. If anything, he could have been mistaken for an undertaker, many of whom still moved among the ruins, or a doctor, carrying his traditional bag.

Harbard and Craw made their way through the collapsed houses and craters. Harbard said nothing. His normal teasing, cleverer-than-thou tone had left him. He had spent the day away from Craw in meditation, trying to contact his angel guide. Craw himself had been in his own dream world – sedated with a good dose of Luminal. It was the one saving grace of his condition – drugs did appear to have a limited effect on him and offered some respite from the storm in his mind.

Harbard had shaken the werewolf awake at four in the afternoon. He had spoken just one word: 'Success.' Craw had smelled blood on the old man, could still smell blood as they walked through the ruins and, by the taste that settled on his lips and rose up within him in subtle degrees of variation unknown to humans, the werewolf knew whose blood it was. It was Harbard's own. Craw tasted great nervousness within the hormonal sediments of the blood, resolve and something else. A sour note of sadness.

Craw was sweating, despite the cold. In brief instances he felt clear-headed again, and then he would hear that hissing, rasping voice at his ear and be plunged back into a battle with the second nature that lurked inside him. He looked up to see a familiar sign on the side of a shop, or rather, on the only side of a shop that remained. *The Government calls on poultrymen to produce more eggs. Don't trust to luck, insist on the inclusion of Milkiwey in all your poultry mashes.* A comfortingly human thought returned to him. How was it, he thought, that these billboards seemed to survive? Still, there was the story of his existence in microcosm. On his way into town he had thought the advertisement despicable. Now, in all that destruction, he found it familiar and comforting.

When he'd fled the slaughterhouse of the painted man, he hadn't taken in what was around him. Now he saw it for the first time.

The city was still smoking in the weak light of the winter dusk. It was devastated, and for a second he couldn't believe that such destruction could be real. It looked like a model, some warning of what might happen if the power of a modern air force was turned against a town. But it wasn't a warning, it was an illustration.

Craw thought it might have resembled a volcanic field, or a forest after a fire, but there was no 'like' here, nothing to compare it to. It was the past in ruins, the charred remains of everything that had gone before, the *tabula rasa*, the wasteland. Odin, the god of his people, had been the lord of battle and of poetry. To Craw, the two things were caught up in each other – beauty and destruction. Lines of verse, of Whitman and Eliot and the Bible went through his head, mingling with the stories he had heard at the fireside as a boy. All that humanity, now gone.

The infinite separate houses, how they all went on, each with its meals and minutiae of daily usages,

And the streets with their throbbings throbb'd, and the
cities pent—lo, then and there,
Falling upon them all and among them all, enveloping me
with the rest,
Appear'd the cloud, appear'd the long black trail,
And I knew death, its thought, and the sacred knowledge
of death.

The black angel had gone over and seen no Passover sign, *Jarð sal rifna ok upphiminn.* The earth shall be rent and heaven above. Asgard in ruins, the plain of Ithavoll burning. So will I stretch out my hand upon them, and make the land desolate, yea, more desolate than the wilderness toward Diblath, in all their habitations: and they shall know that I am the Lord. 'This is your card, she said, *Le Loup arraché.* The broken wall, the burning roof and tower. These fragments ...'

The entire centre of the city had been destroyed, reduced to a prehistoric plain. Stalagmites of timbers were all that was left of houses and yet, even in this destruction, there had been survivors. A house here, half-timbered and white, a whole block there, but next to it, simply a space where houses had been.

The men made their way through the ruins. The moon, still full, was just a smudge in the sky, hardly visible beneath the pall of smoke that hung over the city.

They picked their way to the house, through the surreal and blackened landscape. Next to the step of a smashed building lay six shrouded corpses. They reminded Craw of mice lined up at a back door by the house cat. The image brought him back to himself, the feeling of the warmth of the hearth in his mind, and then it took it away again. There were people there. Compassion and humanity were still within him but it was as if they were no longer fixed to their proper objects but floated inside his head attaching themselves to random thoughts and falling away again.

'Here?' said Harbard.

Craw nodded. He was suddenly very cold indeed.

Craw led the way with a flashlight. The top floor of the house had been blown away but there was a gap through the debris into the cellar, which was still intact. This was how Craw had got out and it was how he now went in. Harbard followed with difficulty, twice stopping to sit down and catch his breath.

Harbard was behind Craw and he too carried a torch. Fingers of light stretched through the darkness into the cellar, throwing a shifting lattice of shadows onto the floor below. The odour of death in all its shades of candy filled Craw's nostrils. Harbard put his handkerchief to his face as if he would retch but, though Craw recognised the smell as that of rot, it registered in a different part of his brain, sparking his hunger.

The house had not been searched and Craw was shocked to see a face looking out at him from the shadows. It was not a face, though, but the empty skin sack of a human head, eyeless and boneless, hanging on a hook like a deflated balloon. Harbard was shaking slightly, he thought, and concern for his friend fought with his wolf nature, to whom weakness in others raised the strange excitement that came with the identification of prey.

Craw went down. In the dark he couldn't see the shard of the Moonsword, though a shiver within him seemed to speak of its presence.

A line from the Apocrypha of the Bible came back to him: 'Through envy of the devil came death into the world.' He thought of Balby. To have that man's solidity, his uncompromising sense of his self, he thought, and then the thought was lost in a tumbling crash of other ideas, words, rhymes and sensations. It was as if he could feel the valves and passageways through which his blood surged, as if they were opening in new ways, admitting new chemicals to his mind.

Harbard clambered down through the dark. He spent no time looking for the metal shard. Instead he lay the torch on the floor and opened his doctor's bag.

'You are a magical creature, Crawford.' Harbard seemed to be having difficulty speaking, and looked very pale in the yellow beam, 'so you will find this easier than I. When I go over, you will follow, I'm sure. The way, however, is hard, the cost of wisdom very great.'

He let out great plumes of steam as his breath hit the cold of the evening and, in the funnel of torchlight, he seemed almost a supernatural creature himself.

'I have paid a price tonight and must pay a still greater one.'

He took out from his bag a small spirit burner of the kind that is used on camping trips.

Sitting on the filthy floor, he lit it, its blue flame sending new shadows out into the cellar and allowing a better view of the room's interior. There was the devastated body of the painted man, no more than bones, next to the rotting corpses of his victims. There was the bloody floor, the runes on the wall, the torture tools that the painted man had used to try to force magic from the screams of the innocent.

Harbard did not comment on the hideous sight. Instead he took out a white cloth and a scalpel. He played the scalpel in the flame for a few minutes, shook it in the air to cool it, and laid it down on the cloth.

'Now,' he said, his voice shaking, 'I said there were ways of magic that do not require one to make a victim of others.' He took off his overcoat and his jacket. His shirt was soaked with blood. He removed that too. In the dancing light of the spirit flame, Craw could see deep lacerations on his chest. 'You make a victim of yourself.'

He sat on the floor and began to sing.

> A heart ate Loki, in the embers it lay
> And then among men came the monsters all
> The sea, storm driven, seeks heaven itself,
> Over the earth it flows, the air grows sterile;
> Then follow the snows and the furious winds,

For the Gods are doomed and the end is death
For the Gods are doomed and the end is death.

Then comes another, a greater than all
Though never I dare his name to speak
Few are they now that farther can see
Than the moment when Odin shall meet with the wolf

For the Gods are doomed and the end is death
For the Gods are doomed and the end is death.

Harbard repeated the words again and again, to hypnotic effect. Craw could see the old man's eyes start to glaze, the spirit burner rendering his face gaunt and pale.

Craw sat looking at the old man, drinking in the smell of the blood of his wounds, that blood calling to the hunger inside him. Then Harbard was in front of him. He took the werewolf's hands and stared into his eyes. Craw lost track of time. He heard Harbard saying words that were familiar as a nursery rhyme.

Hearing I ask from the holy races
Of Odin the old who gave his eye for lore
Nine worlds I know, the nine in the tree
With mighty roots beneath the mould.

Craw saw in his mind the six corpses on the step get up and begin to dance: mother, father and four children, a perfect family of the dead. Then the wolf was standing next to him, whispering out its sweet inducements to murder.

Craw heard music and snatches of poetry and the sound of steel on steel. The air felt dense, almost unbreathable and, from somewhere, a poem started.

Witch
torturer of men

and cliff-dweller
and wolf mother.
   Ulcer
   disease fatal to children
and painful spot
and abode of mortification.
   Hail
   cold grain
and shower of sleet
and sickness of serpents.
   Constraint
   grief of the bond-maid
and state of oppression
and toilsome work.
   Ice
   bark of rivers
and roof of the wave
and destruction of the doomed.
   Týr
   god with one hand
and leavings of the wolf
and prince of temples.

The words were not in Harbard's voice. They made no sense but Craw saw runes tumbling in front of him, ancient symbols whose meaning struck deeper than words.

The rhyme continued.

A ravening wolf, a brother's slayer
A broken sword and a burning flame
All-father, mightiest of poets
All-father, lord of the hanged
Binder of the wolf, terrible ruler
Accept these gifts we offer.

There was a sensation in the room like the fluttering of a million feathers and Craw heard a voice in his head.

'I am with you always.'

His eyes cleared and he was by the well. Harbard was in front of him, a headless corpse at his feet, the head on a stake next to it.

The wolf was nowhere, neither was the three-sided castle. It was not so much a terrain as two stripes, one on top of the other, black for the floor, a sky of silver and petrolled metal. Craw felt more in control of himself in this place. He looked around him. There, thirty feet away, lay a long curved Arab sword, catching the colour of the sky as if the blade were a puddle of mercury. The wounds in his breast ached and he knew the shard that had pierced him had come from that awful weapon.

And then there was the sensation of the rushing feathers, come and gone in a breath. Craw sensed a panic in the air that seemed to spread out into the flat terrain. The ground itself seemed to tremble. One god was leaving, he thought. Something else was replacing it – nothing you could see, nothing you could hear, just a furious and terrifying presence. A poem ignited like a firework in his head, each word streaming colours through his mind.

> Lastlie stode warre in glittering armes yclad
> With visage grim sterne lokes and blacklie hued
> In his right hand a naked sword he had
> That to the hiltes was all with blood imbued.

Craw felt fear rising up in him and he had a strong desire to flee. He didn't run, though. Whatever the presence was, he knew he had some business with it.

Harbard had studied the best way to do what he did next, though no book learning could give you self control to do it. He sat on the floor next to the cloth, the spirit burner and the scalpel. Once more he played the scalpel in the flame. Then he put it down and lifted the eyelid on his right eye with his left hand. He jabbed in his thumb and levered out his eyeball. The old man didn't scream, but his whole body shook. His hand reached for the scalpel and he picked it up. Then he severed the pink strands of the optic nerve. There was a spurt of blood. He vomited.

Harbard cast the eye into the well.

'Down,' said a voice that seemed to shake Craw's soul.

Craw wasn't sure what happened next. Did Harbard over-balance and fall into the well? Did he dive in? Or did the waters of the well rise up like a mighty hand and pull the old man in?

The waters splashed across the floor in puddles and, in them, Craw saw visions. He saw Harbard with the hooded lady, taking the lady's hand; he heard the lady speak:

'We'll work out a way to get that silly old wolf together, shan't we? Maybe we'll even make another wolf. I've got just the fellow for that.'

He heard Harbard reply, 'I'd like that.'

'Then come,' said the lady, 'spend a while with me. We will talk and you will tell me all your secrets.'

'I'd like that.'

Harbard was walking away to the castle with the three sides, ahead of the lady, along a long promontory over a sea of blood.

From the silver puddle the lady turned to Craw and took down her hood.

'I am waiting for you, Endamon. You who were called Vali. Only in my arms will your wanderings cease.'

He tried to grasp at the puddle but the water just slipped through his fingers. In the water on his wet hands he saw the Louvetier, in his silks and carrying his arquebus. The Louvetier took up the curved sword from where it lay and struck at the wolf, but the wolf pawed him down, knocking him to the floor, sending the sword spinning from his hand.

When the Louvetier stood he was no longer a man but half a wolf, a thing between species, ravenous and afraid. The Louvetier stretched out his distorted arm to point at Craw as he retreated.

What did that mean? Craw was on his hands and knees; he scooped up the well's water in his hands and peered into it. The torn face of David Arindon looked back at him.

'Kin,' said Arindon, from the water, 'they have cut me from you with the Moonsword and I would have what you took from me.'

In the water he saw a vision. The curved sword was there – yes, the Moonsword! – and so was the painted man. Arindon was suspended from his biceps and back by hooks. The water seemed to speak to him, telling him that this had been some sort of experiment. The painted man and another presence beside him were trying something. The Moonsword moved and he felt that stabbing pain he had felt in the house in Crooms Hill, the same one he had felt at the gate of the army base when he had tried to run away. He saw himself slumped forward in his London study, and he was aware that something had stepped away from inside him. Then Arindon had taken the chains from which he was hanging and used them to climb off the hooks. The painted man seemed elated.

'We have cut the wolf from him!' he said.

But the other presence had said 'no'. Something else had walked into David Arindon and it wasn't the wolf, though it seemed very like it. A name from centuries before came to him: Feileg. His brother, his wild brother who ... what? They had become one. How? Oh no. Oh no. Craw saw a face, so like his own, in front of him, heard the crack of bones, the tearing of flesh. The knowledge flashed before him like a fish in the dark, there and gone in a moment.

Craw saw the terror on Arindon's face as the painted man and the other dark presence tried to restrain him. They were trying to fit something about his neck, a pendant of some sort, like the one that had been found on Yardley.

'The wolf needs a collar,' said the unseen man. 'This will make him do what we want.'

But the collar hadn't worked. Craw saw Arindon's escape and his flight from the house. Arindon had sneaked on to a train at Coventry station and jumped off as it slowed for a signal in Crackley Woods.

Craw could hear something behind him, a huge snuffling and a grunting. At first he thought it was a steam train but the breath was too irregular. He couldn't allow himself to be distracted, couldn't afford to turn. He needed to know what Arindon had seen, what was terrifying him. He looked into the water and the answer appeared. The experiment on David Arindon had been too successful. He had been to the black shore, visited that well, and knew all Craw's secrets. He was afraid of the wolf.

There was an enormous snarl from behind him. Craw turned to see the red jaws of the beast closing in on him. All breath left his body as he pushed the wolf away, the water of the well splashing in visions from his fingers. Then something strange happened. He was no longer under the animal's teeth, fighting for his life. He was looking out through the eyes of the wolf at the struggling man in front of him. The shock of this dislocation seemed to send a lightning bolt through his mind.

'No!' he tried to shout. 'Not this!'

And then his eyes cleared and he was back in the basement.

Harbard was in front of him, unconscious and bleeding from the eye. Craw's mind felt assaulted from every angle; clinging to the human was now like trying to play piano while someone demolished it with an axe.

He could do it – just, just. He put Harbard over his shoulder – the weight was nothing to him – and carried him up the broken stairs into the dark street. He needed to find his wife. She was at that three-sided castle, he knew; she had said as much. Harbard would recover and then authorise his journey.

His long search would soon be over, if only he could remain human for long enough.

The evening streets sizzled with the savour of meat. Harbard's bloody body tantalised him with its spectrum of odours. His hunger was becoming ever more powerful. The wolf had recognised him, had put its teeth upon him and it wouldn't be long now – he felt it in his marrow.

An ARP man was walking through the rubble.

'Help, here, help!' Craw shouted, and the man came towards him.

Craw put Harbard at his feet. He had blood on his hands, blood in his mind. His senses were red and he needed to eat.

'Have you dug him out?' said the ARP man. 'Wait, hang on, you don't look so hot yourself, mate. Wait for a doctor.'

Craw leapt at the man, taking him down to the floor in one movement, his hands at his throat. The man gave a short cry as Craw began to squeeze the life from him. Hormones seeped from the man's skin and Craw breathed them in – fear and shock registered in his nostrils, but something else impinged on that other sense, the one that had allowed him to track Arindon through a firestorm. The man was thinking of his children.

Craw willed his fingers away from his victim's throat. He sat on the man's chest for a second, looking at his own hands. And then he ran, as hard as he could.

His condition had taken him. The change was irreversible, he could feel it. It would only be a matter of days before the hunger became uncontrollable. His humanity was like something glimpsed across a busy road, now visible, now obscured. Soon it would be gone entirely. He had one course of action available to him, one hope that he might be saved: find that castle and find his wife.

31 Findings

The black of the uniform, the red at the cuff. The hair neatly brushed, the nails clipped. It was night and Max looked at his reflection in the *boulangerie* window. He touched the armband on his right arm, admiring the detail of the Gothic lettering. He read it: '*Doktor*', reversed in the glass. Then he touched the patch on his right collar. The death's head. It was him all right, though it didn't really look like him.

'Very becoming,' Gertie had said, as he'd shown her the uniform. 'You see, we're on our way to the top!'

The whole canteen had stood to applaud when he went in, and he'd been asked to sit with his comrades in the officers' section. He had been fast-tracked into the SS; not for him the formality of the torchlight procession in Berlin and the ringing oath of loyalty in front of thousands of his comrades, although that would come. For some, said von Knobelsdorff, exceptions can be made. He'd been sworn in personally by Himmler, giving him great kudos among his new colleagues. Himmler had, he thought, looked like a weedy runt – a terrifying, weedy runt.

Now he was in the square of a medieval French town; he wasn't allowed to know which one. They'd flown there from Paderborn but he hadn't been told where they were going. Max would have liked to have known where it was, though. He loved France, and this was just the kind of place he would have liked to visit with Gertie under different circumstances, with its half-timbered houses supported on pillars to form a wonderful arcade around a central square. The place dripped with history. It had a beautiful church with carvings of heads on the end of buttresses, even one of a tortoise. He would have loved to have known by what accident that sculpture had come to be there. It was a lovely light, too, the soft amber of ornate lanterns deepening the wet flagstones. History was great, he thought, when it stayed in the past. Living it was a different matter.

He watched von Knobelsdorff addressing a gang of locals who had been assembled by the local army.

'You are on a mission for the Reich and you will be honoured to perform it. You all have experience of swamp draining?'

Alongside him a policeman translated and the locals nodded.

'Good,' said von Knobelsdorff. 'Get in the trucks.'

There were two trucks. Twenty men climbed up into them, ten in each, and into the back went the same number of armed SS men. Max waited to see which truck von Knobelsdorff would take – he climbed up into the cab of the leading one – and he took the other. He couldn't sit any longer in the smell of those glazed violets. Max noticed that, as the first truck pulled away, the SS men pulled down the canvas at the back to obscure where they were going. Craw had a feeling this was for the benefit of the soldiers, not the prisoners. He knew the SS well enough now to doubt the workers would ever be coming back.

They drove for hours up into mountains, and Max gave up trying to see where they were from road signs. Many of them had been removed by the resistance or during the invasion, and Max was tired anyway so he slept. He was awoken by the sound of sawing. It was dawn, and a couple of the labourers were felling trees to build a fire for the SS.

Bivouacs were being put up low to the ground. Clearly the SS might be there a while and clearly that made them vulnerable. The tents were placed near trees, to take advantage of the sparse natural camouflage.

They were near a large pond and already it was being drained, a pipe running out of it and pumping its water away down the hill. Von Knobelsdorff recommenced his speech, translated by the policeman.

'You are honoured to be asked to work for the Reich. From the shit at the bottom you will collect all stones. All stones. You will put the stones out on the canvases for inspection by us. Any unusual stones must be brought to my attention immediately. You will work quickly and you will work well. There are plenty of you fuckers, so I don't mind shooting a few of you if I find you slacking.'

Max got out of the truck and lit a Salem. It was cold, though the view was pleasant. They were in a valley in some rolling, high countryside of pale grass and pine trees. In the distance were some flat black mountains. Around the pond were three or four large oval granite rocks. He would have taken them for some sort of standing stones but, when he looked out over the landscape, he could see others. They were clearly a natural phenomenon, though a strange one.

An SS trooper was setting up a light machine gun on a patch of high ground. Max was pleased it wasn't pointed at the workers but out into the hills. Other troopers scanned the countryside with binoculars. Obviously the resistance was around these parts, he thought.

'Trust me to get shot for the wrong reason,' he said to himself, a touch of his old flippancy returning.

Then he realised, he wouldn't be shot for the wrong reason. He was no longer Max Voller, wag and appreciator of fine wines, nice countryside and pretty French girls. He was one of *them*. He was a German soldier working for the Nazis and, worse than that, an SS man. Worse than that, he was one of the death's head crew. He imagined Arno there, joking, 'And worse than that?' There was no worse than that. Perhaps there was. A death's head man, a *totenkopf*, who knew what he was doing was wrong. Did that make him better than the enthusiastic bastards? In no way, he decided. To hold on to his scruples now seemed like such a lie to him. He'd made his choice when he'd accepted von Knobelsdorff's offer to join the SS. He'd actually felt flattered that they'd made him a Storm Command Leader, one down from Senior Storm Command

Leader von Knobelsdorff himself. Gertie had been proud of him. Oddly.

'Stop whining, Max,' he told himself. 'This is how it is, this is how it's going to be. Get used to it. It's reality.'

It was nearly noon by the time the pond was pumped dry. Then the really painstaking work began. The mud was dredged up and filtered through wire sieves. 'Christ,' Max thought, 'I'm going to be here a while.'

He wasn't at all sure why he was there. Officially, it was to 'give guidance' to von Knobelsdorff. He couldn't have imagined that arrogant fucker wanting guidance for himself. So who had insisted upon it? Himmler? He hoped so, just for the protection that would bring him. But why did he need to go? Best not to ask, he concluded, and just be glad he was out of the lab for a day or two.

Max had never considered the variety of rocks there might be at the bottom of a pond before. Here there seemed a great many, large, small and every size in between, down to stuff that was no more than shingle really. Was von Knobelsdorff going to look at every one of them? He was. Noon became afternoon, became early evening. Max began to think they would be sorting out stones in the dark. He sat in front of a canvas by the fire, looking at pebbles the workers brought him. He didn't even know what they were supposed to be looking for.

Max had been working four days in the stink and the mud when he found it.

The work was unrelenting from dawn until dusk with no lunch break, so that every hour of daylight could be used. However, even von Knobelsdorff, the superman of the SS, had to go to the lavatory occasionally. Soldiers in the field piss freely in front of each other but, for some reason, von Knobelsdorff was bashful in this way and went to the back of a truck to wet its wheel out of view of the others. It was on the fourth day, when he was so engaged, that Max saw the stone.

A labourer brought a bag of pebbles to him and carefully spread them out on the canvas. Max had to stop himself thanking him. He'd done that the first time the man had brought them over and, without thinking, accompanied it with a smile. The terrified eyes that looked back at him had told him to keep a professional distance from these men in future. Smiles and thank yous wasn't what it was about.

He'd been about to sweep yet another load of pebbles into the discard pile. He wasn't even really looking, so crazy did he consider the idea of having to pick out 'unusual stones'. What were they looking for – a diamond? The labourer whose job it was to remove the examined stones and throw them down the hillside started to spade them into a sack. Then something caught his eye and he passed it to Max.

Max examined it. It was a small triangular grey pebble, covered in pondweed. The shape of the stone was unusual and, on impulse, he scraped the pondweed away with his thumb. It was then he saw the wolf motif. He would never account for what he did next. He shook his head and tossed the pebble to the floor next to him. The labourer went back to shovelling stones.

But then Max stood up, levering himself off his hands. As he did so, he picked up the stone and hid it in his hand. Then he went to the back of the truck, from where von Knobelsdorff was emerging, and went as if to piss himself. He looked at the rock. It bore the clear image of a wolf scratched in to the pebble in a design that couldn't have been current for a thousand years or more. The wolf was simple, yet stylised, and reminded him of the dragons he'd seen on Viking ships. He considered showing the stone to von Knobelsdorff straight away. At least then they might get to go into a town for a little dinner and warmth. But he didn't. He put the stone into the top pocket of his tunic. Then he went back to his task. He wasn't going to say that he'd found it. The longer it took them, he thought, the longer the labourers would live.

32 Departures

Craw opened the thick top secret file, his fingers shaking. He needed to get away imminently. The wolf in the vision with Harbard had taken him by the throat but, in that terrible moment, he had switched sides and seen his own body struggling to be free of him and felt the exultation of the kill.

The wolf was coming free of its fetters and, soon, he would no longer be able to control his actions and his thoughts. With amylobarbitone and alcohol he suppressed the feelings inside him. He was clinging to humanity by a thread, just, just, finding the itchy, energetic, bursting feeling within him unpleasant. Once he started to like it, hope was gone.

Military Intelligence had been quick getting the file sent over once he'd arrived at Coombe Abbey and told them Harbard was in hospital. It seemed almost as though they'd been expecting him. A thousand photos of castles were in front of him, a mixture of reconnaissance, clippings from guidebooks and history books, and even postcards. The file had been assembled to help its operations behind enemy lines. Here, and more strangely, it was being used to identify a castle a man had seen in a dream. It would have been a relatively easy task for someone in a stable frame of mind to look through them all, the work of maybe a couple of hours skimming. Craw's patience was stretched taut, though, his concentration wandering. So it was fortunate that the fiftieth photograph he looked at was a reconnaissance shot of a three-sided castle rising from a thick forest of pine. The castle was under heavy reconstruction. The photo bore the legend *Wewelsburg Nr Paderborn. SS? See file TS9343.*

There it was, exactly as in his vision.

He heard the door to Harbard's study open and two men came in, one in an army colonel's uniform and the other in a plain grey suit. What the colonel said next shocked Craw, even through the disorder of his mind.

'So you're the bally werewolf, are you?'

Craw focused on the man. He was short, sandy-haired, with a drinker's red face. The other man was taller, dark and thin. They both stared at Craw as unselfconsciously as doctors inspecting a cadaver.

The taller man whispered under his breath in the half-concealed way of a condescending public school sixth-former, 'I had been told to expect a gentleman.'

Craw's appearance was currently anything other than that of a gentleman. The languor of the British upper classes was nowhere to be seen. He was agitated and restless, pacing and running his hands through his hair, even in front of guests. There was enough of Endamon Craw left in the werewolf to feel the slight, but not enough to marshal a reply. What would have been his reply in normal circumstances? A witty retort? No. He would have been impassive and silent and just allowed the fellow to feel the crassness of his own remark.

He was aware, though, that he had changed. The thick feeling he'd had in his body had intensified and spread to his face. There was a sensation of lengthening, too, a tension in his limbs that no amount of stretching and shaking would stop. His face itself looked thicker, his forehead muscular, his bottom jaw pushing forward, as if waiting for the one on top to catch up. His muscles had been changing fastest of all. They had become pronounced to the point of caricature. His shirt wouldn't fit him and he'd had to come down to the drawing room in a robe. His brain was feeling the transformation, too; it felt like some broken dodgem car that wouldn't quite steer straight.

The colonel was better bred than his colleague and kept his thoughts to himself. The sentence 'This chap'd have been some use to Darwin' went through his head, but he didn't voice it.

'Don't worry,' he said, 'only three people in the world have seen this file, and one of them is currently unconscious at the hospital.'

'Do werewolves smoke?' The taller man seemed to find the whole thing rather amusing. He offered a cigarette. Craw extended his hand and took it.

'May we sit?' said the colonel. Craw gestured to the sofa. The colonel, however, took Harbard's chair.

'I am Colonel Martin Cheyne of Military Intelligence Special Division. This gentleman is MI5 top brass, no names, no pack drill. In the light of what has happened to Professor Harbard we are reviewing this case.'

'By which we mean "you",' said the MI5 man.

Craw swallowed. If he concentrated on his own hands, the blue tunnels of veins under the skin, he could hold it together. If he looked at the men – well ... He didn't know. He looked at the cigarette. What do you do with that? Right, you light it. He struck a match, put his shaking hand up to the cigarette, inhaled the smoke and concentrated then on the next task– listening to these men.

'Professor Harbard was given the time and the resources to develop several theories and possibilities. You were the most promising avenue. He felt that you had a condition, ly-canthropy, from the Latin *lukanthropos*, *lukos* wolf, *anthropos* man.'

'From the Greek, surely to God,' said the MI5 man. 'Where did you go to school?'

'I said Greek, didn't I?' said Cheyne. 'And Shrewsbury, as I'm sure someone in your position must know, along with what I had for dinner each night, if you're doing your job right.'

Craw was beginning to shake and rock back and forth.

'Are you OK, old chum?' said Cheyne.

'I need to proceed,' said Craw, forcing out the words.

'To where?'

Craw held up the photo of the castle.

'OTQ, I'm afraid,' said the MI5 man, 'under any circumstances, but particularly in your state. Why do you want to go there?'

Cheyne took up a file. 'It was of interest to Professor Harbard.'

'Have I seen that file?' said the MI5 man.

'No,' said Cheyne, 'it has no bearing on internal security.'

The MI5 man snorted.

Cheyne peered closer at Craw. He noted the sheer muscularity of the man, the strange sensual, snarling mouth, and those hands, the fingers too long, the nails too thick.

'This lycanthropy is a mental condition, I take it?' said the MI5 man, who was also peering at Craw.

'It has physical effects too, according to Harbard, not least longevity and a heightened constitution,' said Cheyne. 'Furthermore, it ...'

Craw could wait no longer. He forced the words out of himself:

'Time is short.'

'Short for what, old man?' said Cheyne.

'I am changing. The wolf is coming.'

'What happens if "the wolf" arrives?' said the MI5 man.

Craw sucked on the cigarette.

'Everyone dies,' he said.

Cheyne looked at the MI5 man and then to Craw.

'How are you proposing to go – I mean, what as? A spy?'

'Yes.'

'Like that, hacking and coughing and shaking? A fine spy you'd make.'

'Let me go,' said Craw.

Cheyne flicked through the file. Then he shut it abruptly.

'No,' he said, 'you are too valuable here and require further study.'

Craw was gasping now, struggling for every word.

'Further study has done for Harbard.'

Cheyne raised his eyebrows and turned back to the file.

He leafed through several sheets and removed one piece of foolscap. He passed it to Craw.

'What do you know about this?' he said.

It was a superbly rendered sketch of a three-sided pebble. On it, in a stylised but simple early Viking style, was the head of a wolf. The legend read *E Harbard vision of 11/13/40. Gévaudan/Lozère region. Investigate poss locations.*

Craw went flashing back in his mind to the vision at the well, and those pebble pendants that the painted man had placed so much faith in. They had seen the wolf stone, or at least its idea had been suggested to them, and were trying to make a copy. So far they had got it wrong. But what would happen if they, or their accomplices, were successful? Could it be reproduced? Craw was not certain it could not.

'The professor seemed to think this could be both the key and the cure to your condition,' said Cheyne.

Then Craw remembered: that awful night, the women dead in the field, and his struggle to tear the pendant from his neck. He had thrown it into that pond near the Viaduc de l'Enfer. The stone had brought him control, but at too high a price. He had been able to witness his crimes, to remember them. And yet, it might now buy him time to find his way to Wewelsburg, to face whatever had inspired Harbard's magical journey there, and to find his wife. The very thought of her seemed to quiet his bestial nature. Would her touch offer some longer cure?

'I can find it,' he said. 'Get me to Gévaudan.'

'Well, half time Sonny Jim,' said Cheyne. 'First you want to go to a castle in Germany, now you want to be dropped off in the French countryside. We're not a travel agent, you know.'

'If I find that,' said Craw, holding up the picture of the stone, 'then Harbard may come back. There is a war. He is captured. He can come back.'

'He's not gone anywhere, he's in hospital,' said Cheyne.

'He has gone,' said Craw. 'Though his body remains.'

The two secret service men looked at each other.

'I don't believe a word of it,' said the MI5 man.

Cheyne held up his hand. He had come again to a passage in Harbard's file that gave him pause for thought. 'If I am incapacitated or killed, dispose of E Craw immediately. Incarceration unlikely to work. Act immediately. Immediately.'

It was clearly a rushed note, with a lot of *immediately*s, he thought. It was an instruction to kill Craw, by the most straightforward reading. Cheyne, however, was a moral man, and considered that summary execution of innocent people was exactly the sort of thing he was fighting against. He couldn't believe that was what Harbard had meant. Then what? Had he known the man would ask to be transported?

'Neither do I believe it, necessarily. However, we have financed this project up to now and Professor Harbard has proved a great asset to us. We are in nonsense stepp'd in so far, that, should we wade no more, returning were as tedious as go o'er, so to speak. And, of course there is another very good reason for considering this man's wish. He frightens me. We have enough lunatics in England already. Dropping one of them off over France quite appeals to me. Let the local Boche worry about him. My problem becomes Jerry's problem, I like the sound of that.'

'He could compromise everything,' said the MI5 man. 'He knows your name, he knows the nature of this special defence project rubbish. Even knowledge of its existence would be a propaganda victory for the Nazis. They'd accuse us of devil worship.'

'And they might be right, from what I've read,' said Cheyne, holding up the file. 'Look, I don't like this project. Harbard's flat out in the hospital, unlikely to recover. This fellow's plainly doolally, and I doubt he will impress the Nazis as a spy. They'll probably shoot him of course, which might tie things up nicely. I say we send him over there and get back to some honest soldiering, sabotage and ambush. A clean book.'

'The honest soldiering idea's attractive,' said the MI5 man. 'You know I regard this whole thing as hogwash.'

'You have stated that opinion with tiresome regularity, and I am not inclined to completely disagree with you,' said Cheyne. 'But, but, butty but. Craw, are you confident you can locate this stone?'

Craw nodded. 'Get me near Gévaudan, the Lozère, the Val de l'Enfer near the Viaduc de l'Enfer. I will know it when I find it.'

'You can't expect me to risk an agent on a man in your state by giving you contact details,' he said. 'Although, if you can make it to a town, I may give them your description and have them look for you.'

'If I have the stone,' said Craw, 'then I will return.'

Cheyne looked him up and down. Every sinew on the man's body seemed to be stretched to bursting. He looked at his watch.

'Have you ever used a parachute?'

Craw had – in 1815, in Covent Garden, as a guest of the ballooning Garnerins. That descent, he didn't think to point out, had been from a gondola beneath the canopy. He just nodded.

'Right,' Cheyne said, 'gather your traps. You leave in half an hour.'

The MI5 man's eyes widened in surprise.

'If it were done, when 'tis done, then 'twere well it were done quickly,' said Cheyne, holding up the file. 'Immediately and all that.'

Craw swallowed. Soon, one way or another, he would have his release.

33 Help for Dr Voller

Max had been searching through stones for two weeks. In that time the dig had needed to be reinforced because the resistance had discovered their presence, and they had come under brief and inaccurate mortar fire. Ten more SS had been assigned to the dig from the local area, though there had been no attack since the first one – thanks, Max thought, to von Knobelsdorff's swift action.

He had simply stood in full view of the mortar and started executing labourers with his pistol until the fire stopped. He shot three that way, which slowed the work and made the other prisoners fearful. Two escaped that night. The next day at dawn, Von Knobelsdorff shot his fourth man of the week as an example of what would happen if further escapes occurred. With only four prisoners left, more needed to be sent for.

Max watched the executions impassively. For the first time, he could see the method in von Knobelsdorff's brutality. Yes he'd shot four men, but what was the alternative? Give the mortar time to home in on them and then lose four of their own men? And how was he going to stop the prisoners trying to escape? What was he meant to do – ask nicely? He felt a flush come over him in shame at those thoughts, but it passed. This was war, and you would be an idiot to try to change the rules of the prevailing reality.

The prisoner had been brought over in manacles and kicked to the floor by a guard. Von Knobelsdorff didn't even extinguish his cigarette; he just stood over the man and dispatched him with a single shot to the head. Nothing showy, no delight in it. Quick and functional, Max thought.

He had actually developed taste in death, though not yet

for it. So the pistol shot to the side of the head struck him as a nice way to go. Hey, the machine gun wasn't bad either. It wasn't being starved or worked into the ground, although the men were being both starved and worked into the ground. It was quick, that was the main thing, and it wasn't grisly or terrifying like a guillotine or, worse, his chair. It was the sort of death he would have chosen himself.

Something terrible had happened to him, though. Sorting the stones was wet work, and he had hung his tunic on a stake in the ground to dry it in front of the fire when von Knobelsdorff shot the man *pour encourager les autres.* The brain spray had marked his jacket.

'Do you mind?' he'd said. 'That's new.'

Von Knobelsdorff smiled and said, 'Blame the Frenchmen, their brains are like mush. If I'd shot a German you'd be lucky to see the bullet come out the other side.'

Max thought it was terrible enough that he had been able to say something so flippant as a man was shot in front of him but, worse, he had shared a joke with von Knobelsdorff. He shivered when he considered what that meant. 'What are you becoming?' he asked himself, and then he realised that the question was now irrelevant. It was more a matter of what he had become.

It was obvious to him that von Knobelsdorff didn't really know what he was looking for. A stone in the pond. How far were they going to keep digging? It almost occurred to him to produce the pebble he'd found, just so he could get back to Gertie. But although Max had come a long way since Salzgitter, he was not yet at the point where he would sentence fifteen men to death just so he could get some rest and recreation.

The stink of the pondweed got to him, though, and the constant wetness of camp life. He had a fire built near where he was working but even that was irritating in its way, the smoke blowing over him in the eddying mountain wind. He wanted a bath, a bed, and his wife's embrace, preferably in that order.

He was just thinking of Gertie when he saw, scrabbling down a hillside, the figure of a French peasant. He stood and tugged at the arm of an SS Storm Man, a junior NCO.

'Maquis?' he said.

The man put binoculars up to his eyes.

'Not armed,' he said, and picked up his rifle.

'What are you doing?' said Max.

The Storm Man shrugged. 'Shooting him.'

Max shook his head. 'How are we going to rule this place if there's no one to rule? You can't just go shooting people for being there.'

'He could see.'

'See what?'

The Storm Man shrugged again, like Max had a point. He put down his rifle and went back to sorting stones.

When Max looked back to the mountain the peasant had gone.

Endamon Craw had been lucky and unlucky on his descent. His parachute training had consisted of some screamed sentences from the aircraftman who had hooked him up to the rail.

'Legs together, fingers crossed, arsehole shut,' he'd said.

On the way over, the man, unnerved by Craw's appearance, had talked non-stop. The one thing that had penetrated Craw's fermenting brain was this: no amount of jumps prepares you for landing on a mountainside at night. His safe landing – anyone's safe landing – was a matter of luck.

The night was dark, the moon trapped behind clouds. Craw was shoved through the door of the small plane and he had fallen into the blackness. Then it was as if some angel of the air snatched at him and he began to float down. He could see nothing in the night – no lights of farmhouses, no reflections of water. And then, away to his right, he'd caught sight of something. A fire. He knew instinctively that was where he needed to go.

He had been lucky in his landing, at least. A clump of pine trees had caught his fall. He was undamaged and left dangling not four feet from the floor. It was easy to unclasp the chute. On the down side, he couldn't get the parachute off the tree. It was there to announce to anyone that someone had come in from the air that night. Military Intelligence had counted on that difficulty arising for its operatives before. The parachute was a German one. It would raise suspicion, but less than its British equivalent would have.

Craw had stood and breathed the air of Gévaudan for the first time in nearly three hundred years. A rush of images tumbled through his mind, the first nights when the Louvetier and he had worked their magic. He had, he was sure, reversed or defeated the curse. And then the change had come racing upon him, in a matter of weeks. How many had they killed between them, he and the hunter who wanted to become a wolf? One hundred over three years. It had felt like restraint.

On the ground and in the woods, the night came alive for Craw, full of sounds and smells. He felt like an animal, though the purpose of why he was there was still clear in his mind. He sniffed at the cool breeze. From the north was the smell of fire, and of men. He needed to go towards that. He was hungry.

He made his way towards the fire, from drystone wall to drystone wall, keeping low from animal instinct rather than to disguise his progress. When the walls gave out he kept below the line of the top of the hills as wolves do, unwilling to risk his profile showing against even that black sky.

The fire that warmed von Knobelsdorff and Max was only visible from the air. They had secreted it in a hollow, more out of good practice than anything. The Maquis knew where they were and, if they fancied their luck, they could attack. Still, no point in making it easy for them. Throughout the night sentries watched and a man sat at the machine gun.

Craw lay flat at the top of the slope, his animal senses taking over. He could scent the boredom of the men on sentry duty, the fear of the manacled labourers; he could hear the uneasy sleep of the men in the bivouacs, smell sweat, canvas, the latrine pit.

His eyes were attuned to the dark and he could see much more than any human. Shapes moved across the night – men with guns – and the mass on the floor was the prisoners, huddling together for warmth in the cold air. There was a stirring and, from the body of prisoners, a man rolled away. It was clear to these men what their fate was and, working at their bonds in the dark, they had agreed that whoever could escape should escape, never mind the rest. One man had spent nights working with a piece of wire to unpick the lock on his manacles. Finally he had succeeded, and Craw saw him slip away down the hill. He followed, skirting the camp low to the floor.

Craw saw the prisoner's slow and careful movements as he backed away from the camp. Silently he tried to move around to the man's rear. All the excitement of the hunt was on him, his flesh bristling and seemingly alive, his senses keen as he saw the man move down the hill. He thought, though, without words, that he could track him for a mile or so. He'd take him at a safe distance from the camp, so not to cause alarm. Then he would eat. No, not that.

'Stay where you are. Who's there?' The command was in German but Craw understood it perfectly.

Max had been unable to sleep and had got up to go down to the latrine. However, he had found the bank back up to the camp slippery, and had gone round to get back in by a lesser gradient. That was when he'd seen the movement. It had occurred to him that it was a prisoner escaping. That wouldn't have worried him, he'd have bid him goodbye with a merry wave. But he couldn't take the risk in Maquis country that it was the resistance. Max was a practical man and no hero.

Craw's instinct was to disappear, but two strange feelings overtook him. One was that of being displaced from his mind.

He wasn't exactly looking at his body, but his rational self seemed to separate within him. It was as if he was observing himself, without any power to influence what he did. He had, however, undeniably regained a portion of his humanity, and felt as dislocated as an accident victim waking up in hospital when the last thing he can remember is stepping into the road.

The second feeling was even more bizarre. He simply couldn't move. Other voices joined the one that had issued the command. Then another voice, from a dry and corrosive presence, spoke.

'Don't stand right next to each other, it's what they want, you fools, maintain your position. Look for muzzle flash and then get the MG 42 on them straight away.'

Max, peering into the dark, shivered. Even though he hated von Knobelsdorff, he had to respect his ability in the field. He radiated not calm, exactly, but a light excitement, as if the dark night full of murderous Frenchmen was just the sort of challenge he'd been waiting for all his life. He had the impression that von Knobelsdorff thought more clearly under the stress of battle than he did at his office desk.

The Senior Storm Command Leader was brave, he thought; brave but vacant. Max wasn't brave. He turned on his flashlight and swept the night. Then he had the intruder in his beam. He levelled the torch at Craw, shining it into his puffy, brutish face. He drew his pistol.

'I have him!'

'Deal with him, then. No one else approach, you'll be sitting ducks. And put that fucking flashlight on the ground, Voller, unless you want a bullet up your arse.'

Max threw the torch to Craw's feet.

'Pick it up,' he said. '*Prenez-le lampe-torche. Maintenant.*'

His schoolboy French wasn't up to much. Craw, however, understood both the German and the French instruction. He picked up the torch while Max continued to level the pistol at him.

'*Placez les mains ou je les voir.* Hands, where I can see them.

Allumez le torche dans la visage. Shine the torch at your face, I don't want you seeing me.'

Craw did so, and Max was surprised by what he saw. He'd always thought the Nazis' claims of subhumans were rubbish. As a doctor he had seen enough wonky, idiotic, ill-formed Germans to know that they were far from the master race. Jesse Owens' performance in 1936 had also left him smirking at the Nazis' pretence of racial superiority. But the man in the torchlight really did look like a subhuman. His face was strong but misshapen, his forehead thick with muscle. He looked, Max thought, like a Neanderthal. Even the hand that held the torch was thick and gnarled, as if the muscles had grown too big for the bone. Max had never seen anything like him.

'Don't fuck about, shoot the fucker,' shouted von Knobelsdorff. The Senior Storm Command Leader had become much more boysie after a week in the field.

'He could have information,' said Max.

The idea of torturing someone rather appealed to von Knobelsdorff after such a frustrating time at the pond. It might, he thought, help him unwind.

'Bring him in then, towards the fire.'

'*Allons-y*,' said Max. 'Let's go, over there. *Pres de la feu.*'

Craw walked forward towards the fire, feeling more like an observer than a participant in the scene. Why did he feel compelled to obey this man's commands?

The fire hollow was a pronounced dip in the earth, like a huge saucer but at an angle on the hillside. The SS had increased the protection around the exposed bottom edge by piling up rocks. The fire was well hidden on dark nights and there was no way a sniper could get a clear shot at it, even if they had wanted to sentence one or more of the prisoners to a reprisal killing.

'Right,' said von Knobelsdorff, 'can someone get one of the tyre irons? I need to heat it up. Let's have a look at our midnight caller, shall we? Fucking hell!'

He looked at Craw in the firelight. He too was shocked by the man's appearance, but not as shocked as Max. Von Knobelsdorff believed in subhumans and thought he saw them everywhere. He'd never quite seen as bad a case as this, though. The man's face gave him the creeps. It was quite savage, and he looked at you as if he wanted to tear your liver out. Von Knobelsdorff put his initial fright behind him. All the French looked at you like that.

'Hmm,' he said. Something about the man gave him pause for thought. 'Let's play this one by the book. Take his clothes off.'

An SS trooper strode towards Craw but, as he did, Craw let out a growl, low and chilling. The man stopped dead.

'Can we not tie him up first?'

'Get on with it,' said von Knobelsdorff.

He too had been taken aback by the growl. He'd seen a tiger at Berlin Zoo, stood not five feet from the animal's mouth at the front of the cage. That creature had roared at him, a roar that in the memory seemed hard enough to knock him flat. He'd felt a sudden connection to the past, as if down the centuries a little part of his ancestors had stayed within him and spoken to him then. The look of the creature, its teeth, its smell, but above all that roar – they all said one thing: 'run'. Max was right; von Knobelsdorff was a brave man – or rather, he was regardless of his own personal safety, which is not quite the same thing – but the presence of that beast said something to him on a deeper level than bravery or cowardice, short-circuiting his mind into panic. He had reminded himself of the presence of the cage and had flicked a cigarette end at the creature, to the amusement of some children.

'He might be dangerous, he's built like a brick shithouse,' said the trooper.

Von Knobelsdorff produced his pistol and walked within three feet of Craw, levelling it at his head.

'If you move I will kill you,' he said. 'Keep still. Voller, translate.'

'Si vous budgez, il vous tuer, reste la, n'attaque, er, gardez *toujours et permettez lui d'enlever vos vetements,'* said Max.

Craw felt strangely calm as Max spoke to him, the raging feeling of change he'd experienced in England still. The trooper stripped Craw down.

'Standard torture technique,' said von Knobelsdorff to Max. 'Makes him feel vulnerable without flipping him out too much. Thing about torture is, it's an art. You can't just go straight in with the heavy stuff or they go nuts, and you have to calm them down before you can get any sense out of them.'

The men looked at Craw in the firelight. Max, in all his years of medical practice, had never seen anyone with such advanced musculature. The muscles were virtually tearing through the man's skin.

'That's what a life of labour does for you,' said von Knobelsdorff. 'Ask him where his comrades are.'

'Ou sont votre amis?' said Max.

Craw felt compelled to reply truthfully. *'Mort.'* His voice was low and cracked.

'He says they're dead, sir.'

A trooper was searching Craw's clothes.

'No weapons, no nothing, sir.'

'No papers?' said von Knobelsdorff.

'No.'

'Ou sont votre papiers?' said Max.

'Je ne les ai pas,' said Craw.

'He says he hasn't got any, sir,' said Max.

'There's one of two explanations, then, isn't there?' said von Knobelsdorff. 'Either he's an escaped POW or he's the village idiot.'

'Could be both,' said Max. The SS men laughed.

'Ask him what his name is,' said von Knobelsdorff.

'Comment vous vous appellé?' said Max, who couldn't remember if that was right or wrong.

Craw looked at Max. He was straining to connect with his body, to make himself give a convincing reply to the man's questions.

'*Ce qui peuplent l'appel vous*? What do people call you?'

Craw heard himself reply. '*Monstre.*'

Von Knobelsdorff laughed. 'Well, looking at you, I should say they got that right, son. Voller, what do you think? I'm inclining towards village idiot, aren't you?'

'I can't believe he's with the Maquis, sir, or at least not to-night – he's unarmed, and I think he'd have to be the world's worst scout. He doesn't look exactly capable of detailed reconnaissance.'

'Indeed not,' said von Knobelsdorff, 'but let's just be absolutely sure.' He turned to a trooper, 'Daecher, you're a big bastard, give this man your tunic and helmet. Give him back his trousers, too.'

The trooper did as he was told.

'Right,' said von Knobelsdorff, 'tell him to sit up on that wall, Voller.'

Max did as he was told and Craw, having put on the German uniform, climbed up on to the lip of the bowl, onto the pile of stones surrounding it.

'You sit there until morning,' said von Knobelsdorff. 'We'll see if your friends are out there. If they don't shoot you, come dawn, I will.'

'What would be the justification for shooting him, sir?' said Max.

'He's a spy. Look, he's wearing SS uniform.'

Each men held the other's gaze for a second and then Max began to laugh.

'Very good,' he said, as von Knobelsdorff began to chuckle too.

Somehow Max's growing complicity with von Knobelsdorff was beginning to disturb him more than the brutality that surrounded him.

The doctor couldn't sleep and so he agreed to watch the new prisoner. He was struck, not only by the man's physicality but by the docility of his nature. He just sat on the wall, saying nothing, staring into the distance. He didn't even shiver. What it would be, Max thought, to be really thick – to be excused life's complications and pressures and just spend your time digging ditches, sleeping and drinking. To live as the animals lived – what would that be like? No sense of tomorrow, no past weighing you down, as happy as a pig in shit. Did this man even understand what von Knobelsdorff planned for him at dawn and, if he did, would it have improved his lot?

Craw looked out over the valley into the teeming night. Flocks of sheep moved in the distance; the scent of the breath of the escaped man, heavy with stress, came drifting in on the breeze. He felt paralysed, unable to do anything without Max's command.

Max felt the little pebble in his tunic pocket. He had damped down most compassionate feelings in him since starting his terrible work at the castle. But looking at this beastly man on the wall, he felt them stir inside him. This was his chance to redeem himself a little. He would, he decided, try to save him. Why him, why not one of the other workmen? Max had given up on questions like that. Someone has to be saved, someone has to die. Why had his aunt's neighbour been killed in the Munich air raid and his aunt had survived? What difference does it make how we decide? Perhaps it's all decided for us, he thought; perhaps one of von Knobelsdorff's gods sat spinning out our fate for us and we have no say in what we do. Max hoped so.

He couldn't let the man walk away – that would be a dereliction of duty – but he could use his influence with von Knobelsdorff.

A cold dawn seeped up from behind the hills and Max heard von Knobelsdorff stirring, the Knight of the *Schwarze Sonne* shouting orders at his batman. He didn't sound in a very good mood. No wonder – two weeks on a freezing hill in France and nothing to show for it. They were shipping out, their time up. Then Max had an idea. Von Knobelsdorff had proceeded on a 'better safe than sorry' policy with the rocks. He'd taken everything from grit up to boulders from in and around the pond. He also wanted three of the very large boulders from the pond's edge moved. They'd broken the planks they'd used when they tried to put them onto the truck, and neither the starving labourers nor the better-fed SS had been able to lift them.

Von Knobelsdorff had sent down into the town for further planks, but they'd broken too. It was impossible that this man could lift them where a team of three had failed, surely. However, it might be worth a go.

'You,' said Max in French, 'follow me.'

Craw got down from the wall. Max walked him up to the trucks and pointed to the smallest boulder, one that you could only just get your arms around.

'Lift that in there,' he said, pointing to the nearest truck. Craw bent and put his arms around the rock. 'Wait, I'll help you.'

Before he could move, the rock had been lifted and was in the truck. It didn't even particularly seem to strain the man.

'My God,' said Max.

'What's happening?' Von Knobelsdorff was still in his vest. It was one of his conceits to shave half-naked and freezing cold in order to impress his men.

'Look,' said Max. 'You – put that other rock next to it.'

The man bent again, using depressions in the stone to gain a grip and lever it up on to his knees. Then he leant back, hoisted it above his head, and lifted it in to the truck.

'He's like Hercules,' said Max. 'My God, I could use a man like that back at the castle.'

'If he can put the third in, you can have him,' said von Knobelsdorff, 'otherwise, bang bang, bye-bye.'

The third rock was two metres tall, and Max doubted the man could even get his arms around it. He instructed him to move the others further inside the truck.

'Now put that in,' he said.

By this point the other SS had gathered around.

'Hang on!' shouted a Sturmmann. 'We need to have a bet on this. A packet of Salem he can't do it.'

'I'll have that,' said someone else. 'A packet he can't.'

Seven men bet that he couldn't, none that he could.

'Make it two packs each and I'll take the bet,' said Max.

'Make it three if you like,' said someone.

'Well, I hate to rob you, but if you're insistent on throwing perfectly good cigarettes away then I'm here to take them.' Max turned to Craw. 'Pick that up and put it in there. It will cost your life if you don't, and worse, twenty-one packs of cigarettes for me.'

The SS laughed. Max was becoming a popular man.

Craw stretched out his arms. Other tests of strength came back to his mind. The Gods forged a fetter of iron called Loedingr and asked the wolf to try his strength against it. The wolf burst it with ease. Then a second called Dromi, of twice the strength. That, too, he shattered.

Von Knobelsdorff had his pistol out, smiling at Max.

Craw pushed his palms into the boulder at the extent of his grip, rocked the stone backwards, and lifted it above his head. The SS gasped as he stepped forward and pushed it into the truck.

Von Knobelsdorff nodded appreciatively.

'You've got yourself a little servant, Baron Frankenstein,' he said, 'along with a lifetime's supply of smokes. The paperwork is up to you. Sort him out with a triangle smartish when we get back. Now let's get ready to pull out.'

Max felt relieved. And then he noticed von Knobelsdorff had not put away his pistol, but was walking down to where the prisoners were manacled.

34 Instinct

Harbard's disappearance was deeply frustrating to Balby. The case he had begun months before had become more and more obscure, and was turning up more and more bodies. The facts known to the inspector were only these: David Arindon was on the loose, severely injured by his own hand, possibly dead from infection by now. Professor Harbard had been severely injured, too, suffering lacerations to the chest and an awful injury to his eye. His wounds had been drawn to the attention of an ambulance crew by an ARP man and someone who, by his description, was Mr Endamon Craw. The ARP man had received quite a fright at Craw's hands. Though the account didn't make sense to Balby – he couldn't imagine Craw attacking anyone – enough strange things had been happening for him not to dismiss the idea that the government's head of antiquities had left an air raid warden with a broken collarbone and a bruised neck.

Beyond this he was in possession of two partial corpses, both of whom appeared to have animal markings on them. Both, it had been confirmed by the pathologist, bore marks of a human bite. The pathologist was sure that the tooth marks of the same assailant were on both corpses.

Add to the mix the fact that Harbard had just got up and walked out of the hospital where he was staying and you had a very murky picture indeed.

Balby sat down in Little Park Street Police Station with Briggs to look over what they knew. They had visited Harbard when Craw was presumed dead under the blitz. He was a very clever man, but not an accomplished liar. He'd kept them waiting for nearly an hour before joining them in the study.

To Balby he had seemed unusually nervous, not just with the news that Craw was missing. Something was happening that the professor did not wish to reveal, the policeman was sure.

Another detail had not escaped Balby's eyes. The brandy decanter, which normally sat on an occasional table to the side of the fire, was gone.

Balby had taken the professor to the butcher's van to examine the body of the ARP man and the head in the gas mask and he had noticed that, underneath the window of an upper bedroom, lay three cigarette butts of an unusual pale blue colour. Craw, he had noticed, smoked pale blue cigarettes. Balby, when on a case, had a generally suspicious and enquiring nature and, almost by habit, he'd bent to look at them. They were handmade jobs, by Lewis of St James's, the crest visible on the paper. He knew Craw smoked handmade cigarettes because he'd discussed how he found the mass-produced items unpalatable. The butts couldn't have been there for long because Coombe Abbey was being run as a military installation and, though it was an irregular unit, it wasn't irregular enough to allow conspicuous cigarettes on the gravel. It led him to the conclusion that Craw must be there. But Craw wasn't there because the professor, an honorary colonel in the British military, said so. Balby, a past master at avoiding jumping to conclusions, simply let the facts rest in his head until he could make more of them.

Then there had been the reaction of the professor when he'd seen the corpses. He'd started crying. Balby knew Americans were more expressive than British people, but the outburst had taken him off guard.

'What do you make of those?' Balby had said.

'I'm sorry,' Harbard had said, 'it just reminds me of some-one I knew.' He'd then looked closer and examined the bite marks for a long, long time.

'I wasn't thinking of the bite, the pathologist can look at that. I wondered about the marks.'

'Same as the others.'

'It occurred to me,' Balby had said, 'that they might be designed to look like animal jaws.'

Harbard's eyes had widened and he'd looked with incredulity, not at the head but at the policeman. Suddenly he was his old self again.

'Why, Inspector, you surprise me,' he'd said. 'Of course that's very likely what they are.'

'And from that we can deduce?'

'The initiation marks of some sect, probably. That's the best I can do, I'm afraid. I really can't go any further than that. It's not my area of expertise, really. I could read up on it if you like.'

Balby had given the professor an evaluating look. The professor was over-justifying himself, though Balby would not have put it like that. He would have just said he could smell bull. Furthermore, Harbard hadn't come up with the sect explanation when he'd seen the photos of the other corpses.

'It can't have made it very easy for him to get a dance on a Saturday night,' Briggs had said. Balby thought he had a point. If the person had allowed the marks to be placed on his face, he wasn't planning to have much commerce with civil society.

Balby had produced the pendant – the wolf's head with the severed hand in its mouth.

'Does this mean anything to you?' he'd asked.

Harbard had taken the pendant and looked at it. He'd tossed it in his hand for a second, barely seeming to consider it.

'Nothing at all, I'm afraid.' It was the most shocking thing the professor had said in his acquaintance with Balby. The policeman was a good student of people, and he was sure that there was very little in Heaven or earth upon which Harbard did not have an opinion. The thought was very strong in his mind that the professor was hiding something. But what? And why?

Balby had been dog-tired and recognised that he was at the end of his capacity for fine thought that night.

'Do you think it would be all right for us to bed down in

the laundry room for the night?' he'd said. 'We've been on our feet for over twenty-four hours now.'

Harbard had just shaken his head. 'Out of the question.'

Balby had almost taken a step back.

'This is war, sir, and there is no guarantee we can make our homes tonight, or if our homes still exist.'

'I said that it was out of the question. This is a Military Intelligence facility, not a flophouse. Now if you gentleman have finished with me, I'd bid you goodnight.' He'd turned to a sentry. 'Ansell, see these men to their vehicle and watch that they leave the property.'

'Well, thank you for your kindness, sir,' Balby had said. 'If we need you again then we'll be back. I hope we find you in better temper.'

In the van on the way back into the mess of Coventry, he had regretted his words. He normally disapproved of sarcasm. Harbard had lost a friend in Craw, he reminded himself, and it was no wonder he was touchy.

That was the last time he'd seen Harbard before he'd been called to the Coventry and Warwick by the professor's niece, Eleanor. The professor had been unconscious in the middle of a ward packed with casualties. He had a patch over his left eye and a swathe of bandages around his chest. The doctor had no idea how he came by his injuries. The eye, he'd said, had been removed cleanly, and the lacerations were quite unlike anything caused by a bomb. More worryingly, there were signs of older wounds, large holes in the flesh of the chest, now partly healed. They seemed, said the doctor, to have been made by some sort of lance.

'It's not unlike what you might see in a butcher's shop pig,' said the doctor.

Eleanor had been distraught, and it had hurt even the hardened Balby to see her fretting by her uncle's bedside. Of course, he'd interviewed the ambulanceman about what had happened, and he said the man had been helped by an ARP man who had needed treatment himself.

330

Balby and Briggs sought to systematise their investigation. First, they had to decide if what had happened to the professor was connected to what had happened to the victims of the original murders and the dismembered bodies of the scarred men at Holy Trinity. In a way he would be relieved if it wasn't – he could pass the case on to another detective team. But the instinct of thirty years of police work had been fired in him. He sensed the cases were linked, and he wanted to get to the bottom of things.

He got the name of the ARP controller from the station and established who had been on in that area that night. He visited the man at his work, fitting armoured cars at the Rootes works. Despite the broken collarbone, the man – a greying old fellow by the name of Nash – had turned up and was doing what he could. That, to Balby, marked him as a good egg. The foreman had been loath to let him go, but Balby had been insistent. Nash went with the police to where he had found Harbard.

'This it?' said Balby.

'They'd just got out of a cellar down there.'

'Bit rum, a couple of days after the raid, isn't it?' said Briggs.

'You'd be surprised,' said Nash. 'There'll be people alive even now under all this – we just can't find the poor bastards.'

Balby nodded. 'Did you see down into the cellar?'

'He brought him up. Do you think there are more people down there?'

Balby shook his head.

'Let's take a butcher's, shall we?' said Briggs.

'Well, be careful,' said Nash. 'You never know, it's rained and that lot could come down at any minute.'

'It was only drizzle,' said Briggs.

'You'd be surprised at how much water that can bring down – it could double the weight of that rubble.'

The men climbed carefully down through the wreckage of the house. They could just see into the cellar through the ruined ground floor, but had to clamber around a mess of rubble to make the stairs down.

It was a clear day, the smoke from the blitz having finally lifted, and the light came down through the collapsed beams and broken floorboards rather like sun through the canopy of a wood. They stood in the cellar and looked around. There was nothing unusual about it, Balby thought, nothing to really indicate that it had been used for anything for a while. It was wet and pools of water had collected on the floor.

The only thing was that the floor was unusually clear. It had the appearance of having been swept and mopped, the puddles of water aside. Balby dismissed it as one of those strange juxtapositions that air-raids bring: a man blown into the middle of the street, still in his bath, the plug and water still in; another lady dead in a shop window, like a collapsed mannequin among other collapsed mannequins; one house unscathed, its neighbours flattened. The destruction had to stop somewhere and, it seemed to Balby, it had stopped at that floor. And then he saw what he had been missing. The sweeping had occurred after the air raid. Most of the ceiling had held under the bomb, leaving the space they were standing in untouched by debris. It had, however, shaken down a mighty amount of dust. The place had been cleaned up since the dust came down; the lino floor had relatively little on it, and the marks of a brush were visible towards the edges in the drying muck. Someone had swept up. Why would they do that, unless they were trying to cover something up?

On one of the walls there were some strange patterns, but they just looked like someone had wiped a brush down the wall after painting something. There was a reasonable amount of paper, some still on the ground floor and some that had blown down below. Briggs was picking up and examining sheets of paper that had survived the rain.

'What do you think of this?' He passed Balby a damp piece of foolscap.

There was an illustration, skilfully done, of a hanging corpse and, below it, a rhyme.

When I see aloft upon a tree
A corpse swinging from a rope,
Then I cut and paint runes
So that the man walks
And speaks with me.

Balby pursed his lips with distaste. Nevertheless, he held the drawing up. Behind the hanging man was a wall and on it a symbol, like a jagged sideways *N* with a line through it. Balby looked to the wall. There was the same symbol drawn out in that red-brown paint. He looked up. Above the symbol was a beam and, sunk into it, a ring. It was the same as the one in the picture to which the rope was fixed. This, concluded Balby, might not be some lurid fantasy but a record of events.

'Bag that and check missing persons for anyone who looks like that,' he said.

He felt a shiver go through him. The hook unsettled him and, when he came to look harder at the picture, there were other hooks too, three big enough to take the weight of a man, others more suitable for a coat or a hat.

'Search around,' he said.

'What are we looking for?'

Balby swallowed and looked at Briggs. 'Meat-hooks.'

35 Mrs Voller Takes to her Room

The fact that Mrs Voller did not emerge from her room during the two weeks her husband was absent was viewed more favourably in some quarters than in others.

Michal, left to tend the lab on his own, for instance, regretted that he could not turn to the lady as an alternative source of cigarettes. However, he had diversions of his own. He had been responsible for taking down the forms for Max to requisition patients. It had been easy work to slip a couple of extra ones under the doctor's nose.

Now he had the opportunity to settle a few scores of his own and bring up a number of people he didn't like to the chair. He was, he said, to continue basic work for the doctor while he was away. So the boy had a diversion and a method of leverage against his fellows in the camp. One way or another, he got his cigarettes.

Mrs Meer and Mrs Haussmann, however, who had had pieces of jewellery removed by the SS while their disputed ownership was cleared up, were less sad at Mrs Voller's sudden disappearance.

And the SS themselves missed her. No one could fail to see what an adornment she was to the castle, so finely dressed and so beautiful. It was rumoured that Max had used the experiments to give his wife psychic powers and that he, von Knobelsdorff and the lady were now engaged in some project of utmost importance.

The corridors seemed drabber without Gertie's electric presence.

Gullveig had given von Knobelsdorff no clear description of the exact stone she was looking for, and she had insisted

Dr Voller be allowed to join the search. And then she had trusted to luck. Max was quite sensitive, in his way, though he had buried that sensitivity beneath layers of cynicism. Von Knobelsdorff, when it came to things like that, was a plank. Therefore, she thought, Max would recognise the stone before von Knobelsdorff did. She felt sure that Max hated the *Schwarze Sonne* man enough to try to frustrate him in his quest. It was not quite a plan as you and I might have one – a wing and a prayer based on deduction and hope. Mrs Voller, or the witch inside her, felt the currents of the future powerfully. The likely outcome, she knew, was that her Max would claim the stone.

Had she been less busy she would have been able to look more carefully, to have made as sure as her magic would allow. She could have moved from sensing likelihoods to seeing near certainties. But Gullveig did not have that luxury of time.

If the wolf became the pawn of her enemies, or even just ran free of her influence, then she would be in trouble.

But the clear problem was that she could not handle the stone. It was a fragment of the magic-draining rock Scream, and she could not speculate on its effect if she were to pick it up. So Max Voller, the lady in the hall's husband, would be the medium through which she would work.

Handling the stone, of course, wasn't the only risk for her. Moving the wolf's attention was very dangerous in itself. The Fenris Wolf would account for the Gods on the final day. It could destroy an occultist, or even an immortal witch, without even waking up.

On top of these concerns was the figure of the old man – the incarnation of Odin, she was sure – who kept appearing in her visions. He was hiding something from her, she could see – something that was fundamental to her. There had been intimations, she thought, that he might have continuing the Louvetier's work. That would explain why she had seen him at the pond where the wolf had thrown the stone. If he could part the wolf from the imposter, then perhaps she could intervene to direct the creature's attention where she wanted it. Again, these were more than conjectures. She ran futures, possibilities and outcomes through her mind like an experienced buyer might run cloths through her fingers, examining the quality of each.

She had begun her trance within seconds of her husband leaving her, and had immediately gone to the well where she had seen the wolf. Even after all that time, he still frightened her with his power, and she knew that she would never be strong enough to face him directly.

No matter. She had seen the old man, too, and he had something she wanted. The Moonsword. That could – if anything could – cut the imposter from the wolf's dream. She'd looked into the man's mind and seen what he had done, or part of it. If the old man could be controlled, if he could be made to finish his work, then he would take on the most dangerous part, leaving her just to call to the wolf in its dream and direct its imaginings where she wanted them.

So she had seen what he wanted – knowledge – and used it to lure him away. He was a trickier customer than she had bargained for.

At first he had seemed enraptured, walking to the castle and entering its courtyard as if in total wonder. The dead were everywhere within it, coming forward to implore her help, begging for an end to pain, to consciousness, to incarceration in the castle. Gullveig was unmoved. If these spectres had wanted their freedom, they should have fought for it in life. Then there would have been a place in her halls for them. Even the children, the sad little ghosts with the lost eyes, induced no sympathy from her. Their fate had been woven as victims and there was no more to think about it.

She led the old man back through the shadow castle of their shared vision, the living inhabitants appearing only as blurs of movement, warps of the light.

*

Harbard himself had found something terrible in the well. At first he thought he would drown as he tumbled through the silvery waters. He had fallen into darkness, but then the light had grown and he was aware of another presence. He opened his eyes to see his own face looking back at him, or rather, a face very like his. It was an old man, grey-haired and with a patch across his eye. It was different from the spirit that had directed him into the well. That had looked the same, but the way he held himself was different. The spirit at the top of the well had seemed a light and mocking presence.

The face in front of him now wore a strange sort of leer. Harbard had seen it before and, in truth, had recognised it in himself. It was like that of someone enjoying a boxing match a little too much, like that worn by spectators when they see a hated fighter trapped on the ropes. This, he felt sure, really was the All-father, Odin the Furious, the war-hungry.

He seemed to be gripping this old man as he fell, and suddenly they weren't falling through water any more. Or rather, what he had taken for bubbles or impurities in the well revealed themselves as pieces of writing and, in particular, runes.

The twisted characters seemed to rise up from an unseen source and disappear above him in the silvery light of the well's waters.

He heard a voice.

'Put me on earth again, for I should rather be a serf in the house of some landless man than a king of all these dead that have done with life.'

It was his own voice; it was him who was speaking, but it was the other man too. They were talking at the same time. He recognised, of course, that the words were from the *Odyssey*, but then he, and the old man, spoke again.

Fed by the blood beneath the chute
The gallows-tree had taken root.

Harbard didn't recognise those words at all, but he said them, in chorus with the old man, as they descended in the waters of the well. He didn't see a gallows-tree, though; he saw the wolf, and the wolf was tearing at something, a man in a German uniform. Harbard thrilled at the sight. It was, he was sure, a prophecy of the success of his endeavours. As they descended, the rhyme changed and Harbard and the man said together:

> *I know that I hung on the wind-racked tree,*
> *Hung there for nights full nine;*
> *With the spear I was wounded, and offered I was*
> *To Odin, myself to myself.*

Harbard spoke the words again and understanding broke over him like a wave.

The god had sacrificed himself to himself. For God so loved the world, that he gave his only begotten Son, that whosoever believeth in him should not perish, but have everlasting life.

Harbard had hung too, and worse, for knowledge. Now his true nature was revealed to him. He was a god, or part of a god, just as the poetry that seemed ready to burst his head was part of god, like the sound of battle was a god, like magic and memory and lies were gods.

> *I took up the runes, shrieking I took them,*
> *And forthwith back I fell.*

Suddenly they were at the bottom of the well, some runes hooked into a sandy floor, some rising like bubbles, others gently falling.

The men touched each other's shoulders and said:

> *You are myself and my sacrifice.*
> *This is the greatest wisdom*
> *And it is the end of songs.*

338

There was the sound of battle, and the poetry came to a screaming crescendo, and Harbard was back by the well and full of cold, clear certainty. To control the wolf, he knew he had to go with that lady. He was afraid of her, and he knew she held the key to a knowledge that would dissolve the difference between him and that terrible old man in the well. He would no longer pursue magic; he would be magic, united once again with the All-father, of whom he was an aspect and a part. He had taken his visions as a sign of the success of his rituals. Now he saw that successful rituals weren't a cause of the god's presence, but a symptom of it. The rituals were how human beings responded to getting near to the presence of a god, more of a bow than a beckoning. There was no calling the Gods; they called you and set you dancing to their tunes, or rather made you the dance, an expression of themselves. The god had spoken to him now, allowed him to drink of his wisdom at the well. But first, he knew he had to go with that lady.

'What is your name?' he asked her.

'My name is Gullveig,' she said. 'I am wise in magic.'

'Are you here to help me?'

'Oh yes,' she said.

Gullveig went into her chamber and sat down on a small three-legged stool. Harbard could see nowhere to sit, but looked around him at the web of shadows. The shadows moved across themselves. It was almost as if the castle was travelling in the dark down some invisible track, and vast unseen structures were blocking the light at changing angles. It reminded Harbard of travelling by sleeper train at night.

'I like to start with a weakness,' said Gullveig. 'What have you given to be in this space?'

Harbard didn't need to reply. Gullveig saw it all.

Harbard had been a good man, moral and thoughtful, but with a terrible hunger for knowledge. She saw him in a library in a huge town. His encounter with Craw flickered before her eyes. Then she saw the research, the dead ends and the fruitless rituals by which he had sought to discover the nature of the wolf. He had travelled widely, to the Red Men of the plains, to the people of the Arctic Circle, and wider, to India, Tibet, China. And then he had stopped travelling and begun his journey inside. She saw the mortification of the flesh, the weeks hanging from those terrible hooks where he went to the shores of death. He had been where others had been before him, through the gates of pain, stripping away illusion. And someone had come to him to guide him. The god in the feather cloak. Loki, that mocker of the Gods. A tall, red-haired gentleman, pale, handsome and terrible.

Gullveig shivered. Seekers after power never did well out of that fellow. His interests were the poor and the inadequate, the faithless and the mild. It was more interesting to him to take a family man who loved nothing more than his children and his hearth down the paths of magic, than it was to reward some knowledge-hungry occultist. She wanted as little to do with him as possible, and it pained her to even see him appear in a vision.

She felt the space of the mountains in her mind, saw the enormous dry plateau with its twisted rock formations stretching up to the sky as if imploring it to take them to join it; she saw von Knobelsdorff, that handsome and murderous oaf, walking the Tibetan paths, saw the exchange at Lhasa, a goatskin drum for the Louvetier's notes. She had one mind with Harbard. It was like a garden through which they both could pass, choosing what to examine, what to ignore.

She saw Harbard in New Orleans working over the book, weighing morality against his desire for knowledge, buying the body from the poor family who lived under the levee, and saw how he had forced himself to eat its flesh. Then she saw the stranger rituals and the visit of the madman. The Voodoo man said he'd been sent to help him by the spirit of Black Hawk that had possessed him at his church.

The pale chief with the dyed red hair had shown Harbard to the Voodoo man and said 'Do as he bids'. Gullveig, that wide-seeing lady, saw how Harbard had gone again into his rituals and had been instructed what to do. He must use this willing sacrifice to step further through the gates of magic. The killing had been slow, but the effects spectacular. The Voodoo man, Jean Lacaze, had died slowly but been reborn in Harbard's dreams, guiding him to new areas of knowledge, pointing out new areas of research. Only when he met Gertie Voller on the black shore did his presence fade.

Then she saw the conversation with the god: Loki in his dyes and paints sitting by the fire, sometimes indistinguishable from the fire. Harbard was weeping, telling the god he could not go on, that knowledge was not enough for him to abandon the principles of his humanity.

The god had thrown powder onto the fire, and Harbard had seen the rise of the Austrian corporal, seen Himmler's scrabblings with the ancient lore, and known that it was only a matter of time before some henchman of theirs made the same connections he did.

'If you don't wish my patronage, then perhaps I should find someone who would,' said the god.

Harbard had seen the way. More knowledge was needed, to drink from the headless god's well. How, though? He was no fool. He'd seen clearly what the price was – his sanity, destroyed through pushing himself to ever greater crimes of torture. The god had come up with the idea of starting with someone whom Harbard felt deserved to die. It was chance that he got the call from England. Spies had indicated that the Nazis were making efforts in the direction of the occult. The generals had thought nothing of it but, in war, every avenue deserves exploration. That was how Harbard had got his honorary colonelship in Military Intelligence. It had made it easy for him to organise the kidnap of Hamstry. Those soldiers knew their work, but he'd realised he couldn't rely on them for long. There was a line beyond which they couldn't be asked to go. The god had advised him to seek help. He had sent him Lucas Taylor, the painted man, an occultist who had moved to Coventry from Manchester a few years before. Some problem with a child meant he was, like the prophet, not welcome on his own turf, he said.

Taylor had spent his life in ritual but, like von Knobelsdorff, he was a psychopath, a moral imbecile. He had achieved nothing, other than the capacity for deluding other fools. Still, fools had been useful to Harbard.

Taylor gave him the people to contact, young men who were already making their own forays into the occult. And crucially, for the next stage of the revealing knowledge of the wolf, Taylor could draw. It was shown that they would need to construct a wolf stone, but the image of the stone was always maddeningly inexact.

And then at the well had come the revelation of what was needed to make a werewolf – the tormenting of the flesh into those patterns, the further outrages against decency and kindness. It was worth it, he thought. Harbard was a patriot who hated the Nazis. If he could provide the Allies with a decisive weapon, then it would be the achievement of a lifetime. So he worked with Hamstry, with the branding iron and the wood plane, and the work repulsed him, shook him, left him sweating away his nights in the dark.

But Harbard became accustomed to what he was doing, was able to tell himself that a man like Hamstry deserved his suffering. Another way of shocking his consciousness needed to be found, so less worthy subjects for torture than Hamstry needed to be sought to fuel his visions. To reach his goal, Harbard needed to shatter through his compassion and his morals, or so the god said. Gullveig saw Loki watching Harbard work, laughing at the tortures he performed, congratulating himself on making Taylor and his silly boy disciples endure the useless pricking of their flesh. Still, he gave up some knowledge, enough for Harbard to try to make the connection between man and beast. The god smiled as he took the old man to the black hillside, feeling his terror. How much more terror would he feel if he knew that hill's true nature? Gullveig felt Harbard's mistake, the mistake the would-be sorcerers had made down the centuries. He assumed he was summoning the god. He didn't see that it was Loki who had taken an interest in him. The god could have given his knowledge in an instant, but he wanted to see how far Harbard would go. Would he destroy himself for the sake of revelation? Did Loki even know he was dealing with an incarnation of Odin? Was his magic strong enough to see it?

Harbard had felt ready to make his first forays into creating a wolf. He had known it would be an experiment, so they had started with someone they could afford to lose. And they had lost the first two, the torture too severe, but the sacrifice had not been in vain. As he burned away his sanity things had become clear to him. They needed two classes of victims: those to be stripped of their flesh, scalped and mutilated in order to propel the sorcerer's mind into places it could never normally reach; and those to be pricked and marked – prototype wolfmen.

David Arindon was the fifth of the prototypes and, with him, the problems had really begun. Things had worked too well. Harbard had been shocked when, under his tortures, Arindon had entered the dreamworld himself. He had revealed to Harbard the presence of the Moonsword, in the collection of an amateur archaeologist in County Durham. Arindon begged him to requisition it, which he had done.

This weapon could kill the wolf or even cut him free from the man who bore his curse, Arindon had said. That was when he had decided to call Craw to him, to examine the wolf more closely, persuade him to surrender his secrets. And although the Moonsword had stopped the wolf running away, it could not bend him to Harbard's will.

In fact, the appearance of Craw had driven away Loki. But something more terrible had taken an interest in Harbard – a force that came smelling of gold and blood and flame, and which sought death upon death upon death. Odin.

Gullveig sat facing the old man in the castle of shadows.

She suddenly felt very cold. She felt the All-father dreaming and, when he dreamt, she knew he dreamt of Harbard. It was then that she knew she was in trouble.

Harbard, who had seemed entranced by his surroundings, suddenly looked at her directly and said, 'Tell me, witch, why should I let you go?'

Gullveig swallowed. Did this manifestation of Odin realise he was the god?

'Because,' she said, 'I can kill the wolf and save your life.'

Harbard didn't understand. 'I will control the wolf,' he said.

'He cannot be controlled for long. Little by little, in his dreaming, he loosens his bonds, seeks to escape his chains. In each of the nine worlds he stretches and writhes. Here he is nearly free and, when he is free, he will bring only slaughter – death to you and to me.'

'I will control him. I will harness his power to good.'

'You cannot. You are his enemy. You are Odin.'

'Yes,' said Harbard. 'I know that now. My mind is clearing.'

Gullveig felt the shadows of which the castle was made tighten around her. So the god had done to him what he had done to her so long before: disguised his true nature from him. The dream that did not know there was a dreamer.

No mortal could have kept the facts of her plan out of her consciousness. She concentrated only on the truth. She wanted to save Harbard's life, even if it meant damning to destruction the god who had dreamed him into reality. Even Odin himself, let alone a weak incarnation of the god, would have had difficulty pulling the details of what she intended from her mind.

Harbard said nothing. In his normal life he danced through his thoughts, picking up ideas, studying them, and discarding them like a girl picking flowers in a meadow. No more. Now, closer to the god who had dreamt him, his thoughts felt like terrible weighty things, huge boulders that, once set in motion, would crush everything in their wake and never stop.

He could not free himself of the idea that this woman was trying to trick him. Did she want control of the wolf? Yes. Her desires seeped from her. He could smell them.

Magic had brought him this far, he thought, and there was no need to deviate from that path now. Ever since his first excursions into the occult he had been coming closer to realising what he was. In the well, he had seen it. No wonder his mind worked so much better than those of ordinary mortals. He was a god, or part of a god. All he had to do was take one further step on the road he was already on. Besides that, a new feeling had entered his head since his time in the well: malice. He thought of Odin and another cascade of names fell through his head: Ginnar, deceiver, Bolverk, evil-doer, Glapsvid, madness maker, Skollvaldr, the treacherous, Ygg, terrible one, Njotr, user, Hrami, ripper. The god had been called those too. Harbard realised he had taken on more than knowledge when he had moved nearer to the god. It was a price he was willing to pay.

'You wait here, witch,' he said. 'You will not interfere with my work.' Around her the shadows tightened, a lattice, a cage.

'Without me the wolf can be freed but not controlled,' she said.

'There is a way,' he said, 'and that way is the same as it has been since the beginning. Greater sacrifice.'

As he stood, he realised – his will was enough to keep the witch locked in that room. The sensation was intoxicating and he wanted more of it. With this sort of ability, he thought, he could deal the Third Reich a terrible blow. Ezekiel Harbard the man was appalled by the Nazis' brutality. The god Odin, who was pulling him in like a star snags a meteorite, had a simpler view, if such a thing can be said to have views. Warriors gain renown only by killing warriors in battle. The murder and processing of men, women and children like farm animals brought only shame.

For now, Harbard had to return to the place he had come from. He turned away from Gullveig, walked out of the shifting walls and weeping shadows, and back to the body of Ezekiel Harbard on the hospital bed, where its eyes opened for the first time in a fortnight.

36 Application

Devya, Miss Heidi Fischer, was puzzled by Mrs Voller's disappearance, and dearly wished to know what it might signify. The fact that Voller had left the castle, along with von Knobelsdorff, gave her time to act. If only she could think what to do. But Devya believed in karma and the power of fate. So was it by chance that she met the boy? He was outside the castle, just by the guardhouse, searching for discarded cigarettes.

She recognised him because she'd seen him enough times with that hated doctor, a man who thought you could dig the gods from someone's mind with a scalpel. It was then that the usefulness of having a spy struck her.

She approached the boy. Even she, who had to move through the castle of the beaten and the starved daily, was shocked by his appearance. He was covered from head to foot in blood, so much so that his whole top half appeared crimson. On his pyjama sleeve she saw an armband in Gothic writing. *Kapo*, it said. The boy saw her coming and smiled his big pleading smile.

'Cigarette?' he said. 'Food, *Mrs*?'

Devya took out a pack of cigarettes and passed one to him.

'Fire?' he flicked his fingers in illustration.

Devya lit the cigarette. He took a deep draw on it and smacked his lips in exaggerated satisfaction.

'That is very good!'

'There are plenty more where that came from,' she said, 'if you get me what I want.'

'Ah, you want doctor information,' said Michal.

'Had it been that obvious?' she thought. She nodded.

'Great risk to me, *Mrs*.'

'What would you want for it?'

'I be your servant when doctor die.'

Devya looked him up and down. 'Is he ill?'

Michael smiled his big smile. 'Can be for right price.'

'A regular little devil, aren't you?' said Devya.

'I sad,' said Michal. 'Room horrible. *Mrs*, you no want to see.'

'Actually, you're wrong there. Yes, I would.'

He shrugged and put out his hand. She gave him another cigarette. He smiled.

'Follow,' he said.

He took her to Max's lab. The interior, Devya thought, resembled something from Aztec Mexico. The floor was filthy with blood, the walls too.

Anyone living at Wewelsburg for long enough, though, became inured to horrors.

So Devya had ignored the girl in the chair, the shallow breath and the shaking hands, and just concentrated on what was in the room. It was tiny, claustrophobic and hot. It also smelled very strongly of cigarettes, the remains of which spilled from a large ashtray on the desk. Along with the type-writer, there were three upright files, of the open sort, on the desk, but only one actual document in them. She took it out. It was a report which gave huge evidence of success, and also detailed prophecies about the gains that were to begin as a result of the meditative occult work of the Knights of the *Schwarze Sonne*. Ice giants would be unearthed and they would fight for the Reich.

Devya snorted and felt her jealousy rise. So Voller was on to something, was he?

She leafed through, wishing she had something with which to take notes. The report seemed a rambling thing, organised by date rather than subject matter. About two thirds of the way through, it began to mention a wolf.

'The subjects have begun to see a wolf, '[wolf spirit]'

The text had been amended in red pen. The handwriting did not match Voller's, which was scribbled onto a pad of notes on the desk.

'Who wrote this?' Devya asked.

Michal came over to see. 'Lady,' he said. 'The dam. His bitch.'

Devya nodded and continued reading.

'This, again, ties in with Senior Storm Command Leader von Knobelsdorff's work with the *Schwarze Sonne*, which has already yielded startling successes. The calling of this wolf spirit, its attraction and binding, is obviously an area best left to the expertise of the Knights. Recommend further action to be taken under direct control of *Schwarze Sonne*.' The female hand had added, 'in consultation with this office.'

Devya read the document with incredulity. Was Voller trying to get himself into the *Schwarze Sonne*, the inner sanctum? That man was some upstart, with his scholarship-boy vowels that stank of trade, labour, and the breath of the pigs who had bred him.

And if the nature of the Knights' work was meditation, why hadn't they consulted her? She had forgotten more about meditation than von Knobelsdorff and his cronies would ever know. Why had she been brought there simply to mark time?

She leafed through the desk. Nothing of note. And then she saw the file, the ivory white paper of much higher quality than anything used for the castle's normal communications, the many-armed Swastika on the front. She opened it and read, only that shallow breath and the clicking of the EEG machine for company. Devya couldn't believe her eyes. She didn't know whether to be exulted by von Knobelsdorff's failures or angered by them. All the funds he had been given – a troop of twenty men for a month, fine rooms, the chamber of the *Schwarze Sonne*, which sounded unbelievably opulent and large from the description in the file. On what basis? 'Limited but promising'. It was clear, comparing the two files, that one of them was a lie. She could guess which one.

She felt the rage building inside her. She thought of Voller's wife lording it over her — a doctor's wife looking down on a priestess. It was intolerable.

If she had known it then, she had the means to destroy Max in her hands. Evidence of the theft from Haussmann's office would be enough to have him shot as a spy. Devya did not know this, though. She turned to Michal.

'If Dr Voller died, I think you could well become my servant,' she said.

Michal smiled and breathed out his smoke.

'You have many cigarettes?' he said.

'Very many.'

'That is very good.'

37 Remains

'Sir, a body.'

Briggs had been searching under some beams.

Balby recognised David Arindon immediately. He was in a small pocket of space underneath the collapsed back part of the house — what remained of the cellar. Bizarrely, he was sitting in an armchair, head back and facing the ceiling, his huge smile giving him an appearance of grotesque satisfaction. Around his neck were several of the pendants that Balby had found with the corpses on the spire. The policeman also saw that all the fingers of Arindon's right hand, down to the bottom knuckle, were missing.

Balby crawled into the space after Briggs.

'Jesus,' said Briggs. 'Do you think he's been in here since the raid?'

'Taking the Lord's name in vain is hardly likely to improve matters,' said Balby, 'but no, I don't think he has.'

'Why not?' The ARP man, Nash, leant in. 'And what in the name of Christmas happened to his face?'

Balby didn't answer. He examined Arindon's filthy hand. There was no evidence to his untrained eye of what had removed the fingers. Shrapnel was the most likely explanation. It was a ragged wound, though. The pathologist, he thought, should have a close look at that.

Arindon was a mystery. His clothes were covered in blood but there was no obvious wound on him. Had the infection of his facial wounds finally taken him? They were ugly and swollen, but not obviously gangrenous or infected.

Balby needed to get Arindon out, to examine him further, but this was beyond his capabilities on his own. He'd need to send for uniform. The sunlight shot dust beams through the lattice of the rubble. It was almost a peaceful scene, he thought.

'This whole lot could go in a minute,' said Nash. 'I think we should get out of here.'

Balby disregarded him. If the place was going to be searched, it was going to be searched properly. He crawled further into the narrowing space of the collapsed ceiling. There was a sour, rotten smell back there. It was dark and he struggled to see. Then his hand touched something that it instinctively recognised as important. He peered into the darkness to see a pair of eyes looking back at him.

'Briggs, get me that torch in here,' he said.

The torch was passed over.

The beam confirmed his worst suspicions. It was definitely a head. Balby was inured to most horrors, but he felt his stomach skip as he saw it. It belonged to a man, clearly, but it was bizarrely decorated, stained with some sort of blue dye. Well, half of it was. The nose and much of the right cheek had been eaten away. And there, in the outline of the ear was, clear as anything, the outline of a human bite. Then other things became clear at the edges of the torch beam. Though Balby could hardly bring himself to turn the light on to them, he did. At first he thought he was looking at something reptilian, like a fossil. Then he realised it was the ribcage and spinal column of a human being. Had it not been for the presence of the head he would have thought he was looking at a piece of archaeology.

Balby was nearly sick. 'No time for that, Jack,' he told himself, 'not helpful.'

He steeled himself and tried to take in the details of the scene. There was more than one body, he was sure. Someone had put them back there in a rough attempt to conceal them; there were marks in the dust where the whole mess of it had been pushed in, a large red smear.

Then he saw something else behind the ribcage – a piece of

cloth, folded over. It looked as if it contained something. Balby used a piece of a beam to fish it out, lying on his stomach. He pulled the cloth to him, put the torch on the floor for light, and opened it. Now he was sick into his mouth. He turned aside and spat it onto the floor.

There were three objects: a spirit burner, a scalpel and, encased in a yellowy fat, a human eye. The inspector never jumped to conclusions, but the implication was inescapable. That was Harbard's eye and someone, however hurriedly, had attempted to conceal it.

Balby breathed in deeply. What was happening? Back to basics. There'd have to be a detailed search of this place using a good many officers. Then take it wider – call on what locals were left, see if anyone recognised this man, if anyone had seen anyone with Arindon. It wasn't out of the question that Arindon had killed him.

Briggs had crawled back out into the main cellar. Balby went to join him.

'Unbelievable,' said Balby.

'What?'

'A head, and other things.'

Briggs puckered his chin. He really didn't want to look.

'Bomb deaths?'

'Not bombs. Have you found anything?'

'Only this,' said Briggs, 'and I've no idea what it is.'

Briggs passed him the item, taking care not to touch its handle, holding it by the fabric. It was about eight inches long, and constructed mainly of silk folded over something solid. There was a short strap around the main body of the item, which seemed to hold the silk to whatever was underneath it. The handle was a small tortoiseshell globe mounted on a chromium-plated pole.

'It's not a weapon, is it?' said Briggs.

'I don't think so.' Balby undid the strap and the silk fell away from the pole in twelve bat wings. 'If I didn't know better ...'

There was a slide on the pole, and he pushed it up to transform it into a small but functional umbrella.

'You don't see many of these in Coventry. Have you seen one before, Briggs?'

Briggs shook his head. 'Marvellous how they make them so small!'

'That's bad luck, opening it indoors,' said Nash.

'Worse than we've been having?' said Balby.

'Probably not.'

Balby inverted the canopy of the umbrella. There was a label attached to one of the struts.

'All new Harco collapsible umbrella,' he said, 'pat. pending. Exclusive to Macy's.'

Briggs and Balby exchanged a glance.

'There are other Americans in Coventry,' said Briggs.

'Was it raining the night you found them here?' Balby asked Nash.

'Fine,' he said.

Balby tried to think straight. If Harbard was, as he suspected, mentally disordered, why had he taken this umbrella with him? More to the point, how had he got the umbrella at the hospital? It would, he supposed, have made a convenient disguise for his eye wound. However, an eye wound wouldn't have marked him out in wartime Coventry. The umbrella might, of course, simply have enabled him to leave the hospital grounds without being recognised, to move across the town without having his identity revealed to the police. And, crucially, if the police had discovered the ruined shop before he did, then he would be able to approach without anyone being able to take his description.

'Where was this found?' said Balby.

Briggs knew what his boss was thinking.

'In the corner, sir. On the swept part of the floor.'

Balby took in the information stoically, like it was bad medicine. The balance of probabilities was clear: Harbard had been back.

They climbed from the rubble. There was no point trying to find a telephone; the police station was only a walk away. Balby left Briggs on guard while he went to request some uniform help. He wasn't sure he'd get it, with the clear-up operation still underway, but he thought he might ask.

It was a clear November dusk as he walked back down the streets. The burned smell of the city took him back to his youth, bonfire night, spuds and bangers. The sky was a beautiful eggshell blue fading into orange in the west. 'Why does man have to ruin God's creation?' he thought. 'This dusk should be enough. Who could want more?' He felt sick to his core with what he had seen.

Once in the station, he sat at his desk and picked up his phone.

'Coombe Abbey.'

It was a housemaid.

'Could you get me Professor Harbard?' said Balby.

'Professor Harbard isn't here, sir.'

'No,' Balby thought, 'I bet he isn't.'

'This is the police. Would you get me the maid who cleans his room?'

'She's not here, sir, you've just missed her.'

'This is a strange request but, can you tell me, does Professor Harbard possess an umbrella?'

'I expect so.'

'Would you ask the other staff to confirm that he doesn't just take one belonging to the abbey?'

The maid left and, when the phone was picked up again, it was a man's voice.

'It's Mr Morris here, I'm the house manager, the butler as was. Can I help?'

Balby repeated his question.

'Yes, sir, an odd little fold-up one. He helped design it, he's a very clever gentleman. Would you mind if I asked a question?'

'Go on.' Balby was hardly listening.

'I'm aware this is an intrusion but what happened to his poor eye? They say he's lost it.'

'He has.'

How did the house manager know about the eye? Balby realised he'd forgotten to ask a pertinent question.

'When did you last see Professor Harbard?'

'This afternoon, sir, he came to pick Miss Eleanor up. They went for a drive couple of hours ago. We expect them back shortly.'

'Did it not strike you as bizarre that a man just discharged from hospital after suffering life-threatening injuries might want to go pleasure motoring?'

'That's what Miss Eleanor said, sir, but the professor was very insistent. He said he needed her help.'

Balby had one more question. He hadn't worked out how Balby had got the umbrella to the hospital and wanted to rule out accomplices.

'How did Professor Harbard arrive at the house?'

'In a staff car, sir, he called the driver from the hospital.'

'And you sent one?'

'He's a colonel, sir. Why wouldn't we?'

So the military had picked him up. How many people were involved in this scabrous affair?

'Has he been out before?'

'Yes, sir.'

'When?'

'He first came back last week.'

'Why wasn't I informed?'

'I don't know, sir.'

Balby set his jaw. He wanted some answers.

'Very well. Would you have Professor Harbard call me on 341 the second that he returns.'

'Yes, sir.'

Balby put down the phone. Harbard had been in the cellar at some point but he knew that already. The umbrella was unique, the coincidence too great that someone else should have left it there. So had he been there before and after the death of Arindon, and whatever terrible fate had happened to the others in that place? Was it stretching it to put him there during the terrible murders too? They were murders, he was sure. The bite, the attempt to conceal – it all added up.

The search of the house would have to start at first light and Balby made the necessary calls, thinking all the time. So why had Harbard been there? Had Craw done something to him and then tried to cover the evidence? Why had Harbard been concealing Craw's presence at Coombe Abbey, then? It seemed ludicrous to suspect his professional advisers of having some role in all this, but then, Harbard had seemed to be hiding something from him the last time he'd seen him. What if he'd decided to investigate something under his own steam? What if he and Craw had known more than they had let on, and gone to look into the matter without the interference of the police? Craw had certainly charged ahead into the city centre to chase Arindon.

He dispatched two bobbies to find and relieve Briggs.

Then he sat by the telephone. When no one had called by 9 p.m., he called the abbey himself. There was no sign of Eleanor and Harbard, said Morris. He said the same when the policeman called at eleven.

It occurred to Balby to ask to come to the house to wait for them, but something stopped him. Instead, he decided he would turn up unannounced. He was unsure who in the military knew anything about this affair, and had a curiosity to discover what he might find if he appeared without notice.

He set off in his car, the wiper blades beating away a light mizzle. It had occurred to him to pick Briggs up, but he thought that he owed the constable some sleep. Had he been down to the ruined shop, he would have found neither Briggs nor the two policemen there. Briggs had suggested that, since it was a foul night, there was little chance of anyone coming past the ruins at all, and so it wouldn't be at all wrong of the policeman to take advantage of his friendship with the landlord of the Silver Sword pub – miraculously untouched by the bombs – to have a couple of pints in the back room.

Balby also missed seeing a stirring in the ruins. With nightfall, the seeming corpse of David Arindon got to its feet and scented the air. The night was alive with smells but he knew the one he wanted – the man who had struck at him with the Moonsword, the man who had put the wolf inside him and then attacked him. Arindon would find him, he knew; he had time. And when he did find him, he wouldn't allow him to trick him again, to stab him when his back was turned. He had thought he was going to die, but then the cellar had seemed to fill with the beating of a million tiny wings and Harbard had left him there for dead. Now though, he felt restored – healthy, even. He had eaten of forbidden meats in that cellar and their goodness had renewed him. He put his scarf around his face, and made his way out into the rain.

38   Dr Voller's New Priorities

When Max couldn't get in to his room, he was immediately concerned for his wife. The door was clearly bolted, or he would have been able to open it with his key. When a couple of quick enquiries revealed that she had not been seen for two weeks, he was beside himself. He ran into the courtyard and ordered three men to take tools from the workers and come and break in the door.

He'd thought of using Monster to break it in. Something had made him hold back, though, and he'd left the man where he was, unloading the stones from the trucks. He instinctively didn't want the brute anywhere near his wife.

A burly Storm Man smashed the door from its hinges with a hammer and chisel while Max stood distraught in the hallway. Something was terribly wrong, he knew.

'Hit it harder, you fucking dolt, hit it harder,' he kept saying. 'I swear to God, if you don't get in there in a minute I'm going to put a fucking bullet in your lazy arse.'

The two other young SS men were looking at the doctor with wide eyes. Had he been in a better state of mind Max might have been able to identify the emotion they were expressing. It was fear. To them, the doctor – an officer – seemed unstable and they wondered what he might do.

The Storm Man finally splintered his way into the room and Max pushed past him to get in.

Gertie was in a high-backed chair facing the room's large Gothic window. As you entered you might just have assumed she was gazing out to the west, taking in the sunset.

He'd feared her dead. Who can sit unbothered while someone demolishes a door not five metres behind them? He checked her airways, then her vital signs. She was breathing, in short little bursts, and had a fast pulse.

'Gertie, Gertie, oh, my Gertie,' he said, 'what's happened to you? Why wasn't the alarm raised? Get the cleaner – send for the fucking cleaner. Why did no one notice? There's been some slack work here, by God.'

He was babbling, he could tell, and he fought to control himself.

The Storm Man stood there gawping.

'Well, go on, man, get the cleaner, I want answers.'

The soldier gave a quick Heil Hitler and ran back downstairs to find a phone.

'Help me get her on to the bed,' said Max to the other two.

The SS men gently lifted Gertie up. She was far from lifeless. Her body, if anything, seemed taut. He could see the signs of dehydration about her, though; she had a temperature for a start, he needed no thermometer to tell that. Most remarkably, her eyes were open.

'Can you close her eyes?' said a trooper. 'I don't like her looking at me like that.'

'Toughen up then. Make yourself useful and go down to the infirmary and get me 400 ml of – no, you fucking clot.' Max scribbled something down on a piece of paper. '*That* immediately – shift your fucking arse. Tell them it's an emergency, and get Dr Lange up here too.'

The trooper Heil Hitlered and ran off down the stairs. Max looked into his wife's eyes. No signs of liver failure, no yellowing. Then she blinked.

'You're with us, Gertie, I know you're with us.'

Until the drip came there was nothing he could do, so he just loosened her clothes, removed her jewellery, and sat holding her hand, hoping she would recover.

All this, he thought, was down to the terrible castle, down to him in his stupidity for sending off that joke of a study. Things had snowballed. How had his wife become involved? How did the sweet girl he'd loved from the day he'd seen her end up there in that room, ridiculously covered in stolen jewels and at the middle of the SS occult madness?

Devya? Had this been Devya's fault? That irritating upper-class mystic with her ridiculous Indian pronunciations. She'd been to blame last time. He clung to that memory – that his wife had awoken and been happy. Perhaps this was some epilepsy or other condition.

'The cleaner, sir.'

Max looked up. The guard propelled a man into the room with the sole of his boot. It was a Witness of about twenty-five years old, but appearing, as they all did, so much older. The man was shaking. A cold feeling grew in Max. He approached the man and examined him an inch away from his face. The trooper moved from behind the Witness. He had an idea of what was coming.

'Why didn't you notice my wife was in this condition?' Max asked.

'There was a "do not disturb sign".' The man's voice was cracked with fear.

'And where is it now?'

'I don't know, sir.'

'No. Perhaps it has flown away,' said Max.

The Witness began to weep. The man's fear was having a strange effect on Max. All his life, his first instinct would have been to reassure him. Now the gulping, the shaking, those terrified eyes, just made him angry. What a useless fucking wimp.

He stepped back from the Witness and looked at the three SS men. They were all lower ranked than him, one still a spotty adolescent. Their eyes were expectant; they were waiting for him to behave as an SS man was meant to behave. Then he realised he recognised one of them. He was the one who had brought the old lady to his office, the one he had tipped down the stairs. 'You're getting a name for yourself,' he'd said.

Max felt himself tremble – not a tremble of the flesh but an inner shaking, a sick tickle that affected him from his knees to the back of the throat. He thought of the war and the hideous camp at the bottom of the hill, getting bigger every day. What the fuck? Swim with the tide or get carried away anyway. He took out his pistol and shot the Witness straight through the middle of the forehead at close range. The prisoner didn't even put up his hands to try to stop him. It was as if he feared some sort of punishment for trying to save his own life.

The recoil on the pistol felt heavy and the tremble inside Max stopped. It was as if that awful vibration, the shaking, had been something rare and valuable inside him teetering on the edge of a shelf. Now it had fallen, irredeemably shattered.

The faces of the SS men were trying to look impassive. They showed, with different degrees of convincingness, that this was normal. The young trooper pulled his lips back from his teeth but then relaxed his face. Later, in the canteen, he would relate to his friends how Voller had looked for revenge before he saw to his wife's medication. Even to the SS, that was slightly shocking.

There was a fine mist of red in the room, along with the haze of the gun smoke. The smell of glazed violets entered the room.

'Page one, rule one, Voller – don't shoot the fuckers on your own carpet,' said von Knobelsdorff. 'Still, don't worry, it's an easy mistake to make, I know I have. Is Mrs Voller ill?'

'Not well,' said Max.

'Hardly likely to be improved by discharging firearms in her proximity.'

There was a noise on the stairs. Dr Lange came in, bearing the large glass bottle and orange piping of the drip feed. Behind him came a nurse. There was activity all around his wife. They dismissed the soldiers so they could strip her and get her into bed.

'You can go too,' said Max to von Knobelsdorff.

Von Knobelsdorff shrugged and retreated. He had been carefully disguising his mounting panic at hearing that Gertie had fallen into a coma. Pressure was coming down on him from on top. Himmler wanted results.

On the other hand, though Mrs Voller's condition put his success on hold, it also deferred his failure. She, he thought, would know if he had succeeded in getting the right stone or not. And if not, what an idiot he would appear. Perhaps, for this stage of the experiment, it was better to go on without her.

Another ceremony, this time using the most likely stones, was required, he thought. It would mean killing another colleague. He looked at Max – handsome, blond – yes, the perfect Aryan type. Was now the time to act?

The days after the discovery of his wife's condition crawled for Max. He was terrified for Gertie, and he knew where he apportioned blame: Devya. Gertie had never been the same since that night of 'meditation' with the mystic. That silly woman in her silks strutted around congratulating herself on her sensitivity, he thought, but when she encountered genuine sensitivity such as Gertie's, she crushed it. Gertie had, he felt sure, suffered some terrible shock at her hands. What else could account for her sudden and ridiculous love of jewellery, the visions she claimed to see?

A feeling of cold spite towards Devya grew in Max, though, as the mystic still enjoyed Himmler's patronage, there was little he could do to move against her.

He saw how Monster unnerved her, and so he did his best to make sure she bumped into the freak as often as possible. If he saw her walking the grounds, he'd send Monster out to go and stand next to her, and he found a range of essential items that needed collecting from her floor. Requests for advice were a good way to go. He'd fill out some note about visions that had been seen by his subjects, and send Monster up with a note to ask Devya to clarify them.

All the time, though, he fretted. What if Gertie didn't recover this time? Then he was nothing, no different from the stones of the castle walls.

Von Knobelsdorff saw what Gertie's state had done to Max. The man was clearly hardly sleeping, not eating even. He was pale and drawn within a week of their return from France. After two weeks the weight was falling off him. This was pleasing to von Knobelsdorff. He still regarded Max as a rival, professionally and personally. There was always the danger that any progress he made might be attributed to Max, even vicariously through his wife. And Max did not deserve such a fine woman. That sleeping beauty would be a better adornment to him. Then her achievements would surely be his.

He had discounted the idea of using Max as the next sacrifice. His hand would be too obvious in that. The answer, once he saw it, almost made him laugh. It had been all around him, had he looked. In fact, it was a method the SS used every day. Death by overwork.

So, through Haussmann, he let it be known that the results Dr Voller was producing were of such importance that he was to work night and day in his lab. At least five subjects a week needed to be examined and reports presented.

When the order came down, it occurred to Max to tell Haussmann where to stick it. With Gertie in such a state, was he not allowed some compassionate leave? But he couldn't just sit there staring at her all day and willing her to come back; he had to do something, just to take his mind away from her. Working harder was not the direction he would have chosen, but it was at least *a* direction.

He found Monster a comfort. For a start, Monster's prodigious strength made it much easier to get subjects into the chair and also his calm demeanour, his docile nature, was soothing. With Monster, himself and a subject in the tiny room, there was little room for Michal, who stood smoking on the landing, the door open for anyone to see what was going on.

His excursions around the castle had been met by hard stares when he had been in the regular army, then friendly attention upon his SS commission. Now people were wary of

Max as he stalked the corridors in that bloody lab coat, with his freakishly muscled defective of a servant and that pale, cold boy trailing after him.

It was noted, however, that his intensity and his dedication to duty in the face of what had happened to his wife, were very SS indeed. Still, it didn't make him liked. As one officer had remarked, 'He gives me the creeps.' He'd nodded towards a Witness labourer. 'He makes me feel how we make them feel.'

No matter, Himmler had said that the SS did not expect to be loved. In that, Max was coming up to type. The organisation was an elite and had no place for softies. The word in the canteen was that Voller was destined for the top.

Max was suffering. It was the volume of reports required by Haussmann that was causing him difficulty. Max himself had set the standard for reporting protocols, and had made them exhaustive in an effort to cut down the number of prisoners on whom he had to operate. Now the throughput was one a day. It was hardly possible to write fast enough to get the information down. Allied to this was the sheer creative effort. Every word that went on to the report was made up. Max saw no psychic phenomena at all. In fact, he hardly saw anything. He had become oblivious to the blood, to the terror in the eyes of the people in the chair, to their screams and the clicking of the needle. All he noticed was the sawing of the castle's endless reconstruction. That never stopped. Even when he went outside into the air, he could hear it drifting up from the camp at the bottom of the hill. The camp had a name now – Niederhagen – and was getting bigger, the watchtowers and huts more numerous, the lorries disgorging the cargo from Sachsenhausen, the men, women and children who were going to build Himmler's dream world, the city of the SS.

'Cigarette?'

Michal had appeared next to him as he stood watching the camp. Max gave him a Salem.

'There are some very good herbs being grown in the camp garden now,' said Michal. 'You should try some. Perhaps I could bring you some comfrey. They say it is very good for female disorders.'

He smiled his overlarge smile and took a puff on the cigarette. Max watched him. The boy looked back at him and his smile faded. He saw something different in the doctor's eyes. Before there had been weakness. Now that was gone and something else had replaced it. For the first time in Max's company, the boy felt scared.

'You look ill, Max. Let me fetch you something from the canteen.'

Max said nothing. Michal's smile did not fade, but inside he was taking a big decision. He had been displaced, he thought. The doctor now depended more on the beast man than he did on him.

Michal went back through the door in the tower and up to the lab. Monster was sitting, as Max had instructed, on the office chair. If the boy hadn't known better he would have sworn the imbecile had grown since he first saw him. Still, he did not resent the creature. He had decided that Max's ship was sinking long ago. It was a pity, in some ways that he couldn't use Max's influence to control this brute but nothing could be perfect. Devya was where his future lay, he thought. Perhaps she might even have the influence to get him out of the camp.

The brass case of the cyanide capsule resembled a shotgun cartridge. Obtaining it had been straightforward. A French spy had been sent to the camp and Michal had guessed he might be his best source. The man hadn't had the courage to use the vial himself but had secreted it in his behind, wary that he might need it if he was tortured very badly.

Michel had come up with the ideal bargaining chip – the date of the man's execution. Since he had become a *Kapo*, the boy had become very friendly with some of the SS. He kept them informed on talk in the camp and, what's more, he was a talented physical clown. He amused them with his funny faces and his impressions of the different sorts of prisoners. He got the information he needed from one of the Storm Unit Leaders. Once the spy knew he was for the chop the next day by the guillotine – a little SS joke on the Frenchman – he had known that he would not be tortured again. He gave over the capsule for a packet of cigarettes.

'Move,' Michal told Monster as he tried to get into the tiny chamber.

Monster looked back at him with expressionless eyes.

'Move!' Still no reaction.

Michal needed to get to the typewriter to write out a requisition for food from the canteen. Monster only seemed to obey Max's commands. He'd been told to sit there, so sit there he did. In the end, in exasperation, Michal reached around the hulking creature and picked the typewriter up.

He balanced it on the restraint chair and typed out a requisition for one smoked cheese bun – Max's favourite – and some acorn coffee. In his time under Max's service he had carefully studied how Max wrote his notes, and had often obtained food in this way. Twenty minutes later, he was back in the room.

Would Monster be able to tell Max what he was doing? He doubted it. Would he even work out what he was up to? No. How to administer this stuff, though?

He unscrewed the container and took out the glass ampoule. If he just spread it on the bun, would it poison him too? Michal knew by rumour that spies put these things in their mouths whole and bit them. He couldn't take the risk that he might get some of the substance on his hands or breathe it in. He put the ampoule in the bun whole. If Max didn't bite it, then he was in trouble. However, he'd cross that bridge when he came to it. Ideally, of course, he would have liked to have put the capsule between Max's teeth when he was sleeping. The trouble was that the doctor never slept, at least while Michal was there. If discovered, he would find an excuse, make up some story about one of the workers in the canteen looking at him oddly as he gave him the bun. Perhaps Max would think it was von Knobelsdorff. Despite his admittance to the SS, Max was not safe from that man. He didn't see what an enemy he had there. Michal did, very clearly.

A month or two before Michal would have made the attempt without worrying. Max, he had been sure, wouldn't do anything even if he did discover the capsule. He'd make some excuse for Michal, allow his weakness to cloud his vision. But Michal had seen a change in Max. The doctor had a new focus on his work. It was as if he was beginning to believe that it might not be useless after all and that, if he increased his efforts, the vile complications of his life would unfold.

Still, the boy was sweating as he put the capsule into the bread. Monster watched him impassively. Craw himself, paralysed behind the beast's eyes, was unconcerned. He had watched Max's experiments in horror, unable to speak, unable to move. He dearly wanted to strike that coward down. The cruelties he had witnessed in his many lives all had a point. Even Mehmet II, the Turk who had taken Constantinople, had only used barbarity as a military weapon, an example to those who sought to resist him. The doctor seemed to have no purpose at all for his tortures, not even his own delight.

What man, he thought, makes enemies of the old and the frail and subjects them to such horrors? No man worth the name, but a snivelling coward. And Max did snivel. As he worked he had a disturbing habit, Craw noted, of talking to his patients, unburdening himself.

'I don't want to do this to you but, you see, I have no option at all, because my own life is in grave danger if I don't and, more than that, the life of my wife. Well, it isn't that she'll die, but to lose me would be unbearable for her and lose me she will, you know, if I don't give them what they want. Do you have relatives here in the camp? I don't ask for any purpose other than to make you understand my situation. Imagine if you were faced with the dilemma of doing something like this, which you know to be awful, or placing them in the gravest distress. And you are to die anyway, you know. This is a lucky way to go, you are fortunate to be here. Yes, the suffering is intense but it is short, short. Very short. I doubt you will be conscious for much of it, though I do regret that you must suffer at all. Believe in what you have to, God if you must. Here, hold my hand, I am here for you. Yes, I am.'

It was almost more unbearable to listen to the man's self-justifying drivel than it was to watch him work. Still, it was remarkable that the wolf was silent under the provocation of that bloody room. Craw knew he must be under some strong enchantment. It wasn't even that he felt compelled to obey. He simply had no control over his body at all. Whatever the mad doctor had stumbled upon had removed control from his body entirely. It must, he thought, be the stone.

His memories of Gévaudan were stronger now: himself with that stone in his hand, facing the wolf on the black shore, beating him down with his hands, the peace obtained. And then the wolf had worked through the Louvetier, coming to him in his dreams to whisper promises of immortality if only the Louvetier would steal back his stone. Craw could see no stone, though. If he could have it, if it would come into his grasp, he felt sure he could face the wolf and win this time. Perhaps he would be free, perhaps he would control the condition, or perhaps the wolf would close with him again, casting his life into misery. The stone, though, was the key to everything, if only he could find it.

Michal put the roll on the table. He looked at Monster. He hadn't seen the creature eat since he had arrived. Why should he bother now? It was, he thought, safe. Michal went outside to find Max.

The doctor was exactly where he had left him, still smoking. He looked a grey and washed-out thing, as if a little bit of the castle's gloom had come outside into the bright day. Max was looking down the valley, noticing that he hadn't seen that plume from the camp chimney for a couple of days.

'You should work, Max,' said Michal. 'Reports not write themselves.'

'I can't concentrate,' said Max.

Michal took the packet of cigarettes from Max's bloody pocket. He flicked one up to his lips.

'Come eat. I bring nice roll. Smoked cheese, Max favourite.'

'I'm not hungry.'

'Then eat it for me. You feed me once, let me feed you now. For your wife. You so thin she think you Bible Student if she wake up now.'

Max's blow, backhanded and hard, caught Michal across the cheek.

'Never say that!' he said, 'I'm not like them. Not like them at all!'

Michal held his cheek, looking at Max with cowed hatred. Still, he forced out the kind words.

'You need to eat for your wife. For Gertie.'

Max snorted and turned back into the tower. Michal went to follow him but Max closed the door on him. The boy looked out over the hills. Oh well, better not to be around whatever happened to Max, he thought. He walked around the courtyard, up to the south tower. Devya was his best hope of protection now.

Max opened the lab door. He saw the typewriter was balanced on the restraint chair. He inwardly cursed Michal. If there was blood on the roller it could be very difficult to get off, and he didn't want his communications smeared in blood; it would create a bad impression. There again, he thought, it might create a better impression. He had noticed that, since his experiments had begun in earnest and since the appearance of Monster, he received a degree of respect that made life much easier.

'Out of the way, Monster, *budgez vous, venez sous la porte.*'

He watched the beastly man move. For some reason it was as if all the compassion he used to have had been condensed inside him and now only really operated for this odd halfwit.

Maybe, he thought, I see some of myself in him, his lumber-
ings and his idiocies. Perhaps this man was actually highly
intelligent, and his retreat into the comfortable mind of a
brute was just a response to the times.

Monster got up and stepped outside the room until Max
replaced the machine at the desk. He saw the untouched
roll. His mouth felt dry, not hungry at all. When had he last
eaten? Two days before. The boy was right – he needed the
nourishment whether he was hungry or not. Food would clear
his head, perhaps, allow him to concentrate more fully. He
picked up the roll and bit it. He clacked his teeth together.

'I always loved these, Monster,' he said, 'but now, no taste
at all.' He was going to say something such as 'Where will it
end?' or 'What's going to happen to us?' Instead he put down
the roll and turned to the desk, head in his hands.

Craw, a passenger in that vehicle of flesh, had a strong urge
to kill Max where he sat. His self-pity alone was enough to
make Craw will him to eat the cyanide capsule. He had more
practical reasons for hoping for the doctor's death. If he died,
then Craw might be released. The doctor took another bite of
the roll, chewing as if it was something new to him, or as if it
was cotton wool, not bread he was eating.

'Die,' Craw thought. But then a thought struck him. What
if he still couldn't move? What if someone else – say, that
smirking boy – took control of him?

'What's on your mind, Monster? You can tell me.' Max
asked. 'You look perplexed.'

Craw saw what he needed to do. His instinct for self-
preservation was acute. He had always found suicide impossible before but, perhaps, with the stone in Max's possession,
there was a way. If the doctor told him to kill himself, then
maybe he could. Would that mean no Adisla? Perhaps, but
better that than to live as this man's puppet

And Craw knew that death, for a werewolf, is a curious
thing. His only other experiences of it had been traumatic, but
not final. Would he wake in forty years, as he had done after

Constantinople, to find his previous life returning to him only as nightmares? Would he be forced again to piece together who he was through dreams and fleeting memories? Perhaps. Or perhaps he would just die and be as nothing. He would, as his philosopher friends had noted, never experience non-being, so how could he be afraid of it? It was contemptible hubris to think that your life was so special it in some way deserved preserving forever. No, any risk was worth it to be away from this torturer, this stasis.

'Tell me!' said Max. 'What do you want?'

'Eat!' Craw's German word caught Max by surprise.

'You're brighter than you look, Monster. You want this?' He held up the roll. 'Say if you do.'

'Eat,' said Craw again. It was as if Max's questions allowed him a fleeting control of the body he was inhabiting. He saw his hand raise to point at the roll.

'Here, take it. Eat it.'

He passed Craw the remaining half of the roll. Craw held it. To Max it appeared that he didn't quite know what to do with it.

'Eat it,' said Max.

Craw watched as his hand raised the roll to his lips. Then it was in his mouth, the many-coloured flavours of the cheese percolating through his wolf senses, the texture of the bread seeming strange and unpalatable. There was the crunch of something hard. He was somewhere else, in a rose garden of the most beautiful city in history, a sickle moon rising over the dome of Hagia Sophia in the merchants' quarters of Constantinople. What had sent his mind back there? In front of him he saw a girl, blonde and beautiful, her skin dark from the sun. She took a fig from a tree, peeled it, and popped a piece into his mouth. He bit on it. The scent of almonds filled his mind and Endamon Craw was dead.

39   The Library of Ezekiel Harbard

Balby got to Coombe Abbey at midnight. He had no actual plan as to what he was going to do, but thought he would just see what he could see before he was stopped. There was a guard on the gate, but he'd seen him regularly on his visits there and he was simply waved through.

Harbard's car wasn't there. There were, however, three stout Ford staff cars that he hadn't seen before. He pulled up next to them. There were no guards at the front of the house and no sign that anyone had noticed him arrive. He got out of his car, not bothering to close the door in order to avoid making a noise. He approached the staff cars. By the light of the moon he could see on the dashboard of the nearest a copy of *The London Evening Standard*. Something important was going on to drag people all the way from London, he thought. Was it because of Harbard? Very possibly. He wanted to look at Harbard's room, but he knew enough about the military to realise that the regulation answer to any request was 'no'.

He'd have to work quick, he decided. He tried the French doors. They were open. It was time, he thought, for a look around the house.

Balby moved over the rug of the drawing room to the interior door. He opened it. In front of him was a short wood-panelled corridor, unlit apart from the light leaking from underneath a door on the right wall.

He crept past, down to the bottom of a set of stairs. He looked up. No light from the next floor either. This was good because it said no one was up there, bad because he'd have to feel his way once he got into the rest of the house.

He heard voices from inside the room with the light. It

wasn't the servants speaking for sure – too cultured. The stairs were quiet as he ascended and, once on the landing, he was faced with another corridor going left and right. He tried to work out where he thought Craw had been. Right, he thought. He felt his way through the dark to a door. He turned the knob. He could just make out in the light from the window a lavatory. He closed that door and tried another. This was very dark indeed. He'd just have to take his chances. He stepped inside, closed the door and felt for the light switch. Then he turned on the light. He was relieved to see blackout curtains in place. No one would notice he was in the room from outside the house.

There was a double bed, neatly made, a large chestnut wardrobe and, by its side, a travel trunk in pale seagrass and brown leather. The initials on the lid, E.H. in neat brass, told Balby he had found what he was looking for. The only note of disorder in the room was at the side of the bed. About twenty books lay on a bedside table and on the floor next to it.

Balby knew he would have to work quickly. First he opened the wardrobe. Within it were Harbard's garish suits, some in a loud check, others in bold and very un-English colours. He knew that at any second he might be discovered, so he went as fast as he could, searching through the pockets. He found next to nothing – a small cigar cutter, a couple of American coins, and a library card for Coventry Central Library.

Balby pocketed them anyway. Anything was better than nothing to bring him closer to Harbard.

Next he addressed the case. It was empty. Then the books. Balby had known that Harbard was an academic with an interest in idolatrous practices, but he was unprepared for what he saw there. Some of the books seemed very old indeed, bound in calfskin with yellowing pages or barely held together by thin cloth covers.

He read the titles: *Daemonologie* by King James I (1597) *and Newes From Scotland* (1591) *declaring the damnable life and death of Doctor FIAN, a notable sorcerer who was burned at*

Edenbrough in January last; *The Black Pullet* or *Treasure of the Old Man of the Pyramids*; *Dogme et Rituel de la Haute Magie*. There was a book called the *Picatrix*, the cover of which bore an embroidered symbol of a stylised wolf's head under a crescent moon. Each book seemed to refer to some strange pagan practice.

He picked up one with a strange cover, the texture of a light pigskin. There was no title on the cover, but Balby felt compelled to open it. The pages were of some very old paper material that had been cut the old fashioned way – by the purchaser. They all bore ragged edges. The title page read *Cultes Des Ghoules* by Francois-Honore Balfour, Comte d'Erlette. 1702.

It was a handwritten thing in French, and at the corner of that first page was a thumbprint in blood. Balby turned through the rest of the book. More bloody prints. Who reads a book when their hands are covered in blood? When Balby reached the illustrated section in the middle of the book, his questions were answered. Madmen. The drawings were grotesque – every kind of torture and devil worship rendered in fine lines. Some of the pages were loose.

He took one out. It appeared to be from a different book and in a different hand.

Callynge and Bynding of the Wolffe. Gévaudan, Yeare of Grace 1776. it said.

These had clearly been cut out of something and bore the most terrible illustrations of all. Balby couldn't bear to look at them. One of the pages, however, stood out. In fact, he realised, it wasn't a page at all, but a sheet within the book – a copy of the obscenities within, rendered with something more than an exactness. The copies were faithful, but the artist had a better eye than the original; the proportion was better, the rendering of light and dark more sophisticated.

A chill went through Balby. He was no art critic, but even he could recognise it was the same hand that had completed the illustrations at the collapsed house. He folded the piece of paper and put it into his shirt pocket.

'What are you doing?'

Balby looked up. A tall man in military uniform was looking down at him. He had a pistol at his belt and the flap of the holster was unclipped.

'My job,' said Balby, standing. 'What are you doing?'

'Pretty much the same. You must be Inspector Balby.' Balby nodded. 'Well, your time here is up, I'm afraid, I'm going to have to insist you leave now.'

'And I'm going to have to insist that you stay, now. I've got some questions for you, sir. What is your connection with Professor Harbard?'

'I'm his boss,' said the soldier.

'Well, in that case, I'd say you had some explaining to do.'

The man gave him a small smile.

'Afraid not,' he said. 'If you come downstairs we have the authorisation. This is now a military matter.'

'Can I ask, sir,' said Balby, doing his best to remain polite, 'if you had anything to do with these murders?'

'What murders?'

'The murders that I was investigating. The murders that are now a military matter.'

'No, I did not.'

Balby remained impassive. 'Do you think Professor Harbard did?'

The soldier looked at the floor before replying. 'I would remind you that you are bound by the Official Secrets Act. It seems possible.'

'And do you know where he is now?'

'If I did I wouldn't be standing here,' said the soldier. 'Harbard has exceeded his authority. He and anyone who has helped him will be brought to book. That is more than you need to know, and the extent of what I will say.'

'You have no right to remove me from this case.'

'We're not removing you from the case, Inspector, nothing

so melodramatic. Hardly the British way, I think. You should just be aware that we have completed our own investigation, the details of which are secret. If you and your chief constable wish you to continue to waste your time, then feel free. Whatever you discover will be covered by a D-Notice and the Official Secrets Act and every other type of top secret protection. Remember, too, that there is no prospect of anyone ever facing trial for this. I wish there was.'

'So he walks away?'

The soldier said nothing; he just held Balby's gaze. Balby had been a policeman long enough to read the message in the man's eyes. Harbard was not going to be walking anywhere if Military Intelligence got hold of him.

Balby was only just holding on to his manners.

'Do you expect to find the girl alive?'

Again the man said nothing.

'A shame. She was a lovely girl. Would you like me to describe exactly what is likely to happen to her?'

'I believe it is your car outside.' The soldier gestured to the door.

At first Balby didn't move. And then, feeling ridiculous, he did.

As he came level with the man at the door he turned to him. He wanted to say that he wasn't going to walk away from the case, that he would try to find Eleanor and that he would arrest Harbard for murder and kidnapping, come what may. He wanted to say that the intelligence services did not have the expertise for the case, that they were not experienced policemen. But he said none of those things. Instead, he said:

'Clothe you with the armour of God, that ye be able to stand against the ambushings of the devil. For striving is not to us against flesh and blood but against the princes and potentates, against governors of the world of these darknesses, against spiritual things of wickedness, in heavenly things.

'Put on the armour of God, that ye be able to stand against the wiles of the devil. For we wrestle not against flesh and blood, but against principalities, against powers, against the rules of the darkness of this world, against spiritual wickedness in high places.'

The soldier made no reply; he just held open the door, Balby moved off down the stairs, certain in his mind that he would not abandon Eleanor.

40 Witness

It took Max several seconds to register the collapse of the monster. When he did, he sprang forward. A doctor's first instinct in such cases is to clear the airway. He pushed his fingers into Craw's mouth, to pull out the remains of the sandwich and to ensure he didn't swallow his tongue. It was as he removed the bread that his finger caught on something solid. Glass. Max instinctively sniffed at his fingers. Almonds. He panicked and ran to the lavatory on the floor above, washing his hands under the tap. He tried to think clearly. Cyanide, blue acid, salts of blue acid. No, it couldn't pass through the skin and it evaporated almost instantly in the mouth. He calmed down. He'd be all right.

He returned down the stairs to see the corpse in the doorway. Monster had gone straight down – no choking, no nothing. He'd just collapsed. He'd bitten into a cyanide capsule that was clearly intended for Max.

For the first time in a month, he thought clearly. It was obvious Michal had administered the thing but who had he been working for? Von Knobelsdorff, doubtless.

He'd seen how the man looked at his wife, even in her invalid condition. Something needed to be done about him. Michal he could handle. The boy was a mercenary and would clearly give his allegiance to whoever could do him the most good. That made him von Knobelsdorff's weak link, at least in the very short term. He could use the boy.

Max looked down at the massive shape of the corpse. He felt curiously free, akin to the feeling someone might get when a loved but very old relative dies. It was as if that was his connection to good lying there on the floor, his last attempt to stem the tide of madness that was engulfing him. He'd known his efforts would be useless, and there was the proof. He might as well have let von Knobelsdorff shoot the man in France. At least he'd have died on home soil.

Max went into the lab and picked up the phone. As he did so he kicked something and sent it clattering. It was an ashtray that had, until he collided with it, been full to over-flowing. The butts spread across the floor in a long yellow tongue. Again he felt that cold rage rise in him, the same one he'd felt when he'd shot the cleaner. In some mad way the fact that Michal had not bothered to clean out the ashtray annoyed him more than the attempt on his life.

He had two phone calls to make. The first was to the concen-tration camp commander. There were no sniggers now Max was a ranking SS officer. He explained that, for the purposes of his experiment, he needed to determine the boy Michal Wejta's racial extraction exactly. Any documents that could be found must be found and delivered from the relevant office in Poland, if necessary. The commander said he would see what he would do.

Would he recommend Michal for the SS ceremony? Impractical – they wouldn't take him. But the chair seemed like a nice idea. Or was it too quick? Should he think of something special for Michal? He was veering between an icy anger and a sort of worn-out boredom. Maybe he'd do noth-ing to the kid; maybe Max deserved him.

The second call was to the disposal section of the camp. He needed a party sent up to take down a body.

'You sound in a good mood, boss,' said the trooper. 'Did the bastard deserve it?'

'They all deserve it, don't they?' said Max.

'Yeah, but some really deserve it.'

'Just send up a party to take him to the oven. Four disposal workers. He's a big lad.'

Max bent to touch the beast. He patted him on the head.

'Well, son, I gave it my best shot,' he said.

Why Max decided to follow the party down to the camp, he didn't really know. Death had come to mean nothing to him. He was SS now. But, he thought, in an un-SS-like way, that he would see his beast off. Part of him was curious to see if they could fit the bulk of his shoulders into the oven, but part of him wanted death to mean something again, to be something that was attended by ceremony. Also, he had never been down to the camp. The idea had revolted him before. Now, though, he was curious.

He followed the party out of the tower and across the courtyard. The Witness bearers could hardly manage the beast's weight, and halfway down the hill to the camp they dropped him, exhausted. Max couldn't even be bothered to put his boot behind them. He just sat smoking a cigarette and looking over the valley while they recovered, shivering in the cold.

The snow was almost painful to look at under the bright winter sun. The forest stretched out down the valley, the river cutting through it like a road of diamonds. How long, he thought, would it take someone to die in there if they didn't have the correct clothing? Would a woman last longer than a man? From how far away could you reasonably expect to bring down an escaping prisoner with a rifle? Was the visibility better or worse in summer? Would your chances be better in July or January? Did the air convection affect how you would have to adjust your sights? They were interesting questions.

The Witnesses recovered and they made their way down to the camp. There was a barbed wire fence running around the outside of it, and Max was interested to see it was in the process of being electrified. Long rows of huts were away to his left, the more solid, brick built accommodation of the SS to his right. In between was a parade ground. The camp was relatively deserted, as all the inmates were up at the castle, working, or starting on the foundations for its expansion into a city, which Himmler had just announced as his plan.

There were a couple of Witnesses and a scrawny-looking

Jew on punishment detail, standing out in the snow of the parade ground in their thin pyjamas, but it was too cold for anyone who had a choice to stay outdoors.

Max followed the bearers down to a squat brick building with a long steel chimney emerging from the top. No smoke or steam was emerging. The top of the chimney had a sort of V-shape cut into it. To Max it looked like a large snake extending its mouth to the heavens, or even the mouth of a baby bird waiting for its mother to feed it.

The Witnesses waited and he realised they were expecting him to open the door.

He did so and looked inside. It was an austere whitewashed room with a stone floor. Opposite the door was the black mouth of the oven, built into an arch of brick. Two rails like parallel bars extended from it, clearly designed to take a coffin. It hadn't occurred to Max that the inmates would get a coffin. No, he thought, too wasteful. They'd be slid in on a tray, or poked in, or something. He was intrigued to know exactly how they'd be delivered to the oven. Questions of detail concerned him now. Over the bars were draped a pair of purple triangle pyjamas. No point burning those, he thought.

In front of the oven were two SS guards, stamping in the cold. The building had no heating and the oven was broken.

'Oven's fucked,' said a guard.

Max said nothing, just let the man's over-familiarity blow in the wind for a while.

'It's always breaking down, sir,' said the guard, recovering his formality.

'How shall I dispose of the body?'

'There's nothing I can do for you,' said a voice.

Max started. It almost seemed to be in his head, a kind of muted tone that you might expect to hear through a door.

Then a pair of white legs appeared from the mouth of the oven, followed by a naked white torso streaked in soot. A man was emerging – an extraordinary fellow, pale and muscular, naked save for a pair of ragged underpants, and sporting the most incredible crop of red hair, shorn short but shockingly vivid. Max felt that internal shaking beginning. It seemed to him that the Devil had come out of that furnace.

The man levered himself upright on the rails and began putting on the pyjamas.

'It's the same problem as last week,' he said. 'The compressed air blower's gone again, only this time you've let it get too hot and cracked the insulation. The whole thing's unsafe. The insulation needs repair and the blower needs replacing. I can't bodge it again, you'll have to send for a new one.'

Max tried to regain control of himself. The reason this man was in such good shape was clear: he was a trustee prisoner and had valuable skills. His own tiredness, not the man's appearance, had spooked him, he thought. Still, he found the man very unsettling and yet he couldn't look away from him.

'So what do I do with the body?' said Max.

'Use the pit,' said the trooper. 'We always did before we had the oven.'

'You are wondering, Doctor Voller, what you need to do with your corpse.' The prisoner technician suddenly addressed Max.

'How do you know my name?'

'The guard called you by it when you came in.'

Was that true? Max couldn't remember.

'Would you like me to show you to the pit? It might be instructive for you.'

'I would like that.'

Max was fascinated by this strange prisoner. He had heard of other concentration camps where prisoners had come to positions of considerable power. Was he one of those, a charismatic? The Witnesses, in his experience, always seemed slightly dysfunctional, as if they couldn't make it in normal society, so they'd created one of their own. This chap seemed totally unlike that. He had a magnetic personality. You could imagine him as master of ceremonies at a Weimar republic nightclub, he thought. God, those were the days.

The technician walked out of the hut and led the disposal party to the back of the camp. He was barefoot, though Max was amazed to see that he appeared not to feel the cold. He began to speak.

'Hitler says that his world is divided into Gods and monsters, did you know that?'

'I did not,' said Max.

'Oh yes, he does. Congratulations, Max, you're one of the gods in your fine black boots. Look at the heaven you have made! See how the earth trembles in the shadow of the heroes!'

He spread his arms out wide to the camp. Max had the strange sensation that the man was enjoying himself.

Suddenly he was close at Max's ear.

'Makes you wonder how the monsters might have made a worse fucking mess of it, doesn't it?'

'I am in the SS, and we obey the orders of Adolf Hitler.' In the presence of this strange Witness, Max replied as if watching himself in a play.

'And in the spirit, not just the letter!' said the technician. 'You have exceeded yourself, my faithless man!'

They were approaching the edge of the pit. How long had they been there? It was dusk and a clear new moon hung in the sky, Venus alongside her. It was eerily beautiful, Max thought.

'The earth is like iron,' said the technician, 'no need to cover these corpses now. Only in the spring will they sprout. It makes me want to quote T.S. Eliot, but that is a sad predilection that is best resisted by men of good taste. Wasn't it him who said that it's better to do evil than to do nothing? Isn't he a silly sausage to say such a thing?'

'Yes, he is a very silly sausage indeed. I don't exist any more, anyone can see that.' Reality seemed changed for Max, like he had stepped out of time. He felt he could really confide in this man.

'And you've done enough evil to exist quite a lot, by Eliot's reckoning – at least as much as an elephant, or even a big house. They *really* exist.'

'I should exist that much,' said Max, 'but I exist like a fly.'

'Make your mind up – a minute ago you said you don't exist at all.'

'I was wrong, I do exist, at least as much as a fly.'

'And, like a fly, you live on the corpses.'

'I had no choice.'

'That is all you had,' said the man. 'You had no faith, no guidance, no scruples when it really came to it. But you did have a choice.'

'No,' said Max, 'there I must disagree. Other roads were closed to me.' He grasped the man's sleeve. 'What would they have done to my wife?'

'What did you do to these wives?' said the man, nodding into the pit. 'These husbands and sons and daughters?'

'I never touched the children. I saved the boy and I showed that good was useless. Misdirected, harmful even. Good is just an intervention, a movement in time, and its outcome is no more certain than any other intervention, including evil. Who knows what future tyrants have died in this camp?'

The man put his arm around Max.

'You would have made a good hero, Max Voller. They were always concerned with outcomes, what history would say of them. Good and evil may have outcomes, but they are things whole and entire to themselves. There is no need to argue with you, you know this. You would not have brought me here otherwise.'

'You brought me.'

The man shook his head. 'Devils do not lead, we only follow, despite what the literature would have you believe.'

'So you are the Devil?'

The technician laughed. 'I think if anyone deserves that title here, Max, it's you. Look to your Bible. Who knows good better than Satan? Lucifer, son of the morning, oh how you have fallen from Heaven, you shining one, child of the dawn! How you have been cut down to the earth. Down to Sheol you will be brought, to the remotest parts of the pit.'

'I need ...' said Max, pointing at Monster's corpse. 'I need to get rid of him.'

'I think that might prove rather difficult.'

The pit was long – about fifteen metres – and deep, at least the height of two men down. It was not full, which in some ways made it more terrible. There was spare capacity there. Max looked down.

'Say hello to your friends, Max. That oven never does seem to work on the days you're throwing away.'

Max looked down. They were in there. His corpses. A twisted hand here, a shock of hair there. His brain refused to put the pictures together, to make them human again, but he knew who they were: the old lady, the Viennese professor, the little girl. He was trembling. The technician put his arm around his shoulders.

'They would have died eventually,' he said. 'It's just a matter of timing.'

'I knew that. It was in some ways a kindness to them.'

No one had called the disposal party but they moved forward, dragging Monster's massive corpse.

'Time to put him in the pit, I think,' said Max. 'Let him be away from me properly.'

The red-haired man turned to Monster and ruffled his hair.

'He is not dead, only sleeping,' he said.

'Is that what your god tells you?'

'It's what your god tells you.'

'I have no god.'

'Sometimes it's a question of your god having you.'

The sun had finally gone down, the burnt orange of the sky giving way to a deep blue. All the stars had come out above the camp and the night sparkled with their beauty. There was a noise from behind him. One of the prisoners on punishment detail, standing to attention on the parade ground, had collapsed.

The other one, delirious with cold, began to tremble out the broken verses of a prayer. 'Our Father in the heavens, let your name be sanctified. Let your kingdom come. Let your will take place, as in heaven, also upon earth. Give us today our bread for this day; and forgive us our debts, as we also have forgiven our debtors. And do not bring us into temptation, but deliver us from the wicked one.'

Monster's body was brought to the edge of the pit. The Witnesses, frozen and hungry, had finally run out of energy, though they caught the words of the prayer, echoing it in a rhythmic mumble, too scared to say it out loud, too full of duty to remain silent.

'As in heaven, also upon earth ...'

'You have never prayed, have you, Max?' said the technician.

'No.'

'I should learn if I were you.'

'And do not bring us into temptation ...'

The moon turned the technician's flesh a ghostly white, the smears of grease and soot stark against his skin. He reminded Max of an angel. Something inside him made him think he could trust this man; something almost made him want his approval.

'Who shall I pray to?'

The technician smiled. 'Pray to what you have. Pray to yourself. Pray to Max Voller!'

'Deliver us from the wicked one ...'

The Witnesses' prayers were driving Max mad. He was taken by a sudden flash of anger and, with all his strength, he heaved Monster's corpse into the pit. The massive body flopped down the slope and disappeared into the gloom at the bottom of it.

The dark of that pit seemed to pull his eyes down into it. He could see nothing now the sun had gone, and it was comforting to him. He couldn't look at it but he couldn't look away, like a child peeking from under bedclothes to see if the monster by the wardrobe is still there. When he finally managed to look up the technician was gone.

He thought of Gertie, alone in her bed. The nurse would have ended her shift now, the doctor finished his round. She would just be lying pale and beautiful in the moonlight, insensible to it all in the darkness. He looked back up the hill to the castle. But there was no darkness at the window of his room in the north tower. He counted again to make sure he'd identified the correct room. No doubt about it. The curtains were open and the light in his room was on.

41   The Grey Ship

Gertie held the hand of the giant and looked around her. The hall seemed much smaller from the outside than it had from within. It was quite an unremarkable wooden building with a thatched roof. It was at the centre of a large and desolate plain. Everything on it had been burned or cut down; no tree grew above a stump. The ground beneath her feet was beaten down by footsteps, almost black, but, into the distance and onto the wider plain, the soil was red. The weak light of the predawn seeped over the plain. On the horizon she could see the smoke of fires rising.

'The armies of the giants,' said the warrior. 'We must move quickly. The host of the hall will be stirring. Which way, Lady?'

Gertie had no idea which way they should go, but she thought it sensible to move away from those fires.

'Down here,' she said.

They descended a gentle hill and began to walk through a valley of beaten earth, away from the rising sun. Behind them they could already hear a clamour of voices and boots as the warriors came out of the hall. Gertie didn't turn back. She just gripped the giant's hand and led him away from the noise.

The valley was long and arid, every shrub cut, every blade of grass trampled, but Gertie felt good just to be outside. She was surprised that she didn't feel hungry, nor did she want to drink.

She said nothing to the huge man at her side, because she could sense how tightly inside himself he had locked his sadness. She couldn't presume to help him with it; all she could do, she thought, was take him away from that awful hall where he had been unhappy.

The sun came up and went down again and strange constellations of stars came out, deeper than she had ever seen them. The moon was a bright sickle. Still they walked, unceasing. In Gertie's mind the rocks became flowers in the silver light, the dust like a road of diamonds leading her to where she wanted to be.

'Do you know what's beyond this place?' she asked the warrior.

'For me, nothing, I fear,' he said. 'I can take you as far as the sea. Beyond that I cannot travel.'

'Why not?'

'You will see.'

The valley gave way to a broad black expanse which glittered in the moonlight. It began to descend and, Gertie realised, the plants and the rocks had gone. Now there were only dunes of that sparkling black sand. Then she saw the sea, its waters a deep silver black. And on the shore, anchored only twenty or thirty metres out, was the last thing she had expected to see: a U-boat.

Gertie had only ever seen one in pictures before. It was smaller than she had imagined and its skin, which she had thought a smooth black, was rather more irregular, with a grey tinge to it. It gave the impression of scales.

The giant warrior sank to his knees when he saw the ship.

'Naglfar,' he said, 'the ship of the dead. This is as far as I can take you.'

'Why?' said Gertie.

'They will not take a warrior that way. They say the wind will not blow west nor the oarsmen row while a warrior is on board.'

'The ship I see has neither sails nor oars.'

The giant shook his head. 'It is plain, Lady – see the crew of the dead sleeping at their benches. See the swan of blood on the wind cloak. The raven spreads his wings.'

By 'wind cloak', Gertie presumed he meant the sail. As to 'swan of blood' – what was that? The same as the raven?

Gertie saw nothing but the silent hull of the U-boat.

'Let's go and see,' she said.

They made their way down towards the still water. As she approached, Gertie could see that the ship did have a very irregular construction. It wasn't even smooth, but tiny bristles protruded from its hull.

'What is this thing?' she asked.

'Naglfar, the ship that will bring in the enemies of the Gods on the final day,' said the giant.

'And can this travel to where your wife is?'

'I believe so, but it has no other purpose than to spite and plague the Gods. It will bring in their end one day.'

'But it will not take a warrior?'

'None has ever gone out this way. None has ever gone out.'

Gertie squeezed the giant's hand.

'Put down your spear and shield,' she said.

'I cannot.'

'Why not?'

'I live by them. They are how I keep my place in the hall, how I survive at all.'

'Throw them down,' she said. 'You are not a warrior. You are a brave man who has fought many battles, but your heart is somewhere else.'

'In the fields, with my plough, at the hearth with my wife.'

'Then put down these things. Take off your armour. Come with me.'

'That ship is made from the nails of dead men,' said the giant. 'It is a bad thing.'

'I am a woman and I don't fear it,' said Gertie. 'Come on. What is your name?'

'Varrin.'

'Have you had enough of death and glory, Varrin?'

'I would see my wife, my sons and my daughters.'

'Then throw away your weapons. Come to the ship as a father.'

The giant's hands were shaking. Gently, Gertie peeled his

fingers from his spear and set it down on the floor. Then she untied his shield from his arm, took off his helmet, unstrapped his hauberk. The giant stood in front of her in only a rough shirt and breeches.

'You are a farmer,' she said.

'I would keep pigs and geese and cut the soil for seed,' said Varrin.

There was a noise, metal on metal, like a scraping. The hatch of the submarine had opened.

'They are unmounting the shields, ready to set forth,' he said

'Then let's go to them.'

Gertie set out into the water, towards the ship, swimming with difficulty because of her skirt. After thirty metres, though, she made its side and clung to a rope ladder.

The giant was treading water besides her. Gertie summoned her strength and pulled herself up onto the U-boat's deck, shivering as she touched the pale bristles of the nails. Then she climbed the conning tower and went within. It was dark, momentarily, inside. When she regained her sight, Varrin was sitting next to her.

'These are strong dead men at the oars,' he said.

Gertie was glad she couldn't see whatever he could. She was sitting on a tiny bed, separated from a cramped interior of pipes and dials by only a half-drawn curtain. She could see no crew on the ship. From behind her she heard an engine start. The hatch above her sealed and the ship begin to move forwards and to sink.

She thought of Max and of home, but other thoughts were coming into her mind. She saw herself standing at another shore, battle all around her. She was saying goodbye to some-one – someone not Max – and she was crying. A man was wiping away her tears. She knew she was bound to him in some fundamental way, and she knew that she loved him. And yet there was another feeling.

'What have you become?' she said out loud. 'You killed

so many, over so many lives, Vali, and though I love you, I cannot forgive you for that.'

She couldn't make sense of what she was saying. Instead she just lay down on the bed and went to sleep.

42 The Uses of Old Maps

The search of the ruined house was ready to start. However, Balby was concerned that with the rain of the night before the structure may have been weakened, and so the Royal Engineers were investigating to see if it was safe. Five good coppers, including Briggs, stood ready to go.

Balby decided to take advantage of the delay and make his way to the city library. It had been hit in the raid and he had despaired of finding anyone there. However, he was amazed to see that, next to the burnt remains, a stall had been set up. A man in a tweed jacket was sitting at a trestle table. Next to him was a sign marked *Returns*.

Balby approached the desk and identified himself.

'You are the librarian?'

'Interesting question. What do you call a librarian who doesn't have a library? I'm a burnt-husk-arian. Mr Shepherd will have to do, I suppose.'

The man's light manner would have irritated Balby under normal circumstances. In that wreckage, though, it made him admire him. Shepherd was thumbing his nose at Hitler, refusing to be cowed. An exemplary attitude, Balby thought.

'I don't hold out much hope, but I was wondering if you could tell me what books have been taken out on this ticket.'

He passed Shepherd Harbard's ticket. The librarian looked at the ticket and stood up.

'Come on in,' he said. 'It's a little messy, I'm afraid, but Adolf didn't respect the "Quiet please" sign.'

The library was largely burnt out. However, a section of the front desk area had escaped the fire. There were tarpaulins covering some sort of large block. Shepherd pulled back the one nearest him to reveal the pale wood of the filing system beneath.

'Weird, isn't it?' he said. 'The whole town catches fire, and the library too, but this box of cards survives. The Lord moves in mysterious ways. Or maybe the Devil just wants us to know what we've lost.'

After some lifting of the tarpaulin and attempts to find the right file, he finally opened a drawer of tightly packed cards and flicked through it.

'There you go,' he said. 'Has someone stolen some valuable rock strata, officer?'

Balby ignored the man's pally overtures and just took the card.

Inter-library loan (Birmingham Central). British Geological Society Survey section 24 Midlands. Year 1835.

'There's another one,' Shepherd said. He passed that over too.

British Geological Society Survey section 24 Midlands. Year 1938.

'Are you sure these relate to this card?' said Balby.

'Certain. Why, what were you expecting?'

'Never mind. Can I keep these?'

'Anything to help the police,' said the librarian.

'Where would I get a copy of these books if I wanted one?'

'They're maps, not books. And ours are with your Mr Harbard. If you can't find him, try one of the pits, I expect they'd have them.'

Balby pocketed the cards and set off back towards the wreckage. Work still hadn't started, and the engineers were lowering down metal props. A haze hung over the city, though it was clearing. What had Harbard wanted with books on geology?

He thought as logically as he could. Why had Harbard wanted two books, nearly a century apart? What changes in rock formations? Nothing at all, not in just one hundred years. So why order two versions? If Harbard was on the verge of madness, as Balby felt sure that he was, what would inspire him to read these two works? He couldn't believe the professor was suddenly interested in different map-making conventions.

Balby couldn't bear to stand idle and wait for the engineers, so he walked through the broken streets trying to make sense of it all. The spire of the cathedral, he noted, had become visible through the haze of the bombing. Ironically, the pall that had hung over the city had made it more difficult for the Germans to come back and finish their dirty work, and so the city hadn't suffered much in the way of raids in recent weeks.

'What changes in the ground?' he thought. The search could go on without him, he decided. He'd drive out to Keresley pit and see if they had a copy of the survey.

He was actually in sight of the winding wheels when he realised the answer was literally in front of him. Mines change. They are dug and they fall into disuse.

The pit supervisor confirmed it. He'd had a copy only of the 1938 survey. It showed, he said, only working mines. For the first time in his police career, Balby sat down with shock. A comparison between the 1835 and 1938 surveys would reveal which mines were no longer in use. Harbard had something to do with the mining industry in the USA, he knew – drill design or something. The conclusion was inescapable.

'Tell me,' said Balby, 'would it be possible to gain access to any of these disused mines?'

'Some of them,' said the supervisor, 'but you'd need two qualifications. Knowledge of mining's one.'

'Yes.'

'And you'd have to be stark raving yampi. It's dangerous down there even if you know what you're doing.'

'Are there many disused pits around here?'

'Hundreds,' said the supervisor. 'It's been mining country since the year dot.'

Balby nodded. As soon as he got a copy of the 1835 survey he could begin his search. It would, he thought, be a long one.

43 Gifts

Max returned to his room to find it a hub of activity. His wife was at the window, looking out at a glorious crescent moon that hung above the snow. The electric light of the room was not turned on. Instead four candelabras burned. In their glow Gertie seemed to shimmer in a long gown made all of golden sequins. All around her functionaries busied themselves. There were cooks and cleaners, two doctors and three nurses, an SS secretary, and von Knobelsdorff himself, the Senior Storm Command Leader bristling with excitement. There even appeared to be a dressmaker in there, measuring out swathes of cloth while an assistant pinned a pattern to a mannequin.

A feast was laid out on a temporary table: meats, cheeses, apples, vegetables on silver plates.

'Gertie!' said Max. 'You're better! My God, thank God, good God.'

Gertie turned to face him and smiled, but not as she had ever smiled before. It was a look of love, but not the love they had known. Max was reminded of the smile on the face of his old boss, 'Fatty' Meer, when he'd discovered he was entitled to a staff car.

'Max!' said Gertie. 'Oh, Max, how I've missed you.'

She threw open her arms and Max came towards her. He could see she was very pale. In her hand was a small handkerchief. He noticed it was dotted with blood.

'Gertie, sit down, please, take it easy. Oh, come here. I love you so much, so much.'

Her smell was changed. Gertie had never been one for perfumes, but now she seemed almost embalmed in a heavy,

clinging scent. Where had she got perfume from, he wondered. It was very difficult to come by. In fact, he'd heard one
woman joke that no more Chanel had come on to the market
since the victory over France, which made one wonder if
the battle had been worth it at all. The army, she had noted,
seemed ludicrously obsessed with plundering items that were
good to no one, such as food.

'And I love you, Max Voller, because you love me so. We
shall be together forever,' she whispered in his ear. Max
kissed her. 'Do you like the dress?'

He did. Gertie still took his breath away. She was wearing
a long flowing evening gown of sequins. Her earrings were
deep blue sapphires, and at her neck was a large necklace
of silver and burnt umber glass. Her beauty was becoming
almost embarrassing to look at; he felt inadequate to it. She
looked like a Klimt come to life.

'It's Lucien Lelong of Paris, secured for me by dear Rudi
here,' she said, 'and the necklace is 1898 Etruscan-style,
Tiffany, I believe. "They froze the fire that burned Troy" –
well, that was what the card in the box said. It was a gift from
the officers of the SS.'

'Lovely,' he said. 'How long have you been awake?'

'An hour.'

Max looked around him. He couldn't believe his wife had
caused such a fuss in just sixty minutes.

'We are to proceed within weeks to the wolf summoning,'
said von Knobelsdorff.

'Knobby's to become a god, aren't you, Knobby?' said
Gertie.

Gullveig, inside Gertie Voller, was in high spirits. Something, she could feel, had taken the attention of the old man
who had imprisoned her, and thus allowed her to escape. She
could guess what it was. His energies were devoted to the
wolf ceremony. The sooner hers began, the better. She was
excited; she could feel destinies entwining all around her,
almost like a tangle of thread in her hands. She needed to do

her work at the same time as the old man was doing his. There was no need to plan, though. Higher forces than both of them were at work. The two rituals would coincide, she was sure of that. She would feel when the time was right. She was sure of one other thing, too. Her long time in the room of shadows had given her the chance to concentrate more fully on the exact outcome of summoning the wolf.

Events involving the presence of gods were difficult to foresee exactly, but she was fairly certain that there was potential for error in her ceremony. Accordingly, she thought she would need a backup for von Knobelsdorff as her chosen person to enter the wolf's dream. Max would do fine. In some ways he would make a better wolf than von Knobelsdorff; he loved her, and so would be easier to control in the short term. But Max was complicated and unpredictable. Von Knobelsdorff was a more basic creature, and easily manipulated if you knew the strings to pull.

'A god,' said Max. 'That'll be nice for you.'

Von Knobelsdorff shrugged his shoulders and looked around the room at the servants. Max recognised that look – something between fear and murder. The Senior Storm Command Leader was afraid his secret had been compromised. He sipped on a glass of schnapps.

'I shall become a more powerful servant to Adolf Hitler,' he said.

Gertie gave him a tight smile.

'We shall require your chair, Max darling,' she said. 'Do get it sent up to the chamber of the *Schwarze Sonne*. You know, the Over Group Leader's Room?'

'Why?' said Max.

'It will make a perfect thirteenth throne,' said Gertie. 'The ceremony will be demanding on one participant in particular. The chair will be a great help to him. Make sure you get a prisoner to bolt it down properly, too.'

Max nodded. 'Exactly what is going to happen here, Gertie?'

Von Knobelsdorff put up his hand. 'Not in public, please. And not for him.' He turned to the others in the room. 'Leave! There is important business to discuss.'

The dressmaker, medics and servants quickly made for the door, glad to be released from such company. When they were gone, von Knobelsdorff continued.

'There is no way a stranger can be admitted to the chamber of the Knights of the *Schwarze Sonne*.'

'Why not? I have been involved in this project from the start,' said Max.

Why did he want to go in there? No good reason — just because von Knobelsdorff didn't want him to, it seemed.

'Because,' von Knobelsdorff glanced at Gertie, 'I am not sure you are to be trusted.'

Gertie looked shocked. 'If you can't trust Max then you can't trust me.'

Von Knobelsdorff stiffened. 'Lady, I have to tell you that disturbing information has come to me regarding your husband.'

'Like what?'

'He has associated with undesirable types. There are rumours against him.'

For some reason Max thought of that strange Witness by the pit.

'If there are rumours then prove them or dismiss them as such,' she said.

'We have no evidence,' said von Knobelsdorff, 'but it is unwise—'

'Show him your devotion, Max, show him your efficiency,' said Gertie.

He didn't know what she meant. He couldn't think of anything. Maybe they had been compromised. Perhaps his association with Arno and those fucking jazz records had come back to haunt him. Listening to jazz wasn't a hanging offence, unless someone like von Knobelsdorff decided to make it one. The time for bravery was over, he thought. Arno and his jokes were history, ready to be swept away by the forces of progress. What did it matter who held the broom? Life, death, friends, enemies – Max couldn't give a shit.

'You are talking about Arno Rabe,' said Max. 'Doctor at the Salzgitter clinic. I had long suspected him of Bolshevik tendencies and took it as my personal brief to keep an eye on him. Only yesterday I received the evidence that I needed to convict him. He listens to foreign radio, and that is the least of his crimes. Search his rooms. What you find there will disgust you.'

Von Knobelsdorff nodded. He had simply been trying to exclude Max from the ceremony. Gertie's evident love for her husband disturbed him. He wanted her under his patronage, beholden to him. Max threatened that. Still, a name was a name. He took out a notebook from his breast pocket.

'Dr Arno Rabe, Salzgitter,' he said. 'We will make sure he receives a visit. But vigilance against Bolsheviks is the duty of every citizen of the Reich. It is not enough to allow you into such an important part of the Knights' work.'

Gertie dabbed at her nose with the handkerchief. More blood, Max noticed.

'I was not referring to Bolsheviks,' said Gertie. 'What have you got for the Senior Storm Command Leader? Something he was too busy to discover for himself, and that his men were too unobservant to see? The thing you just whispered to me about.'

Gertie looked directly at Max, and it felt as if his mind were a house and she was running through all its rooms, some doors opening and closing, others bolted fast.

He reached into his top pocket.

'The stone.' He pulled it from his pocket.

'Max went back to the storage rooms for one last look this morning and found this. His diligence is exemplary – you should wish you had more men like him.'

Max passed von Knobelsdorff the stone.

'Amazing how it was overlooked, really,' he said.

Von Knobelsdorff realised the truth — that this had been hidden from him. However, he was loath to upset Mrs Voller and risk halting the progress his work had made since her appearance. He took it between his index finger and thumb and examined it.

'It doesn't look like much.'

'Well,' said Gertie, 'it might not. But very soon it is going to make you an immortal.'

44 The Fetters Break

Death came to him as a vision of ocean depths. It seemed to Craw that he was at one with the waters, an expression of the unseen movements of cold currents that pushed and sucked at him, taking him ever down beyond the limit of the light.

Time, too, was washed away. Only sound remained, the music of the tides in which he seemed just like a note in the grand symphony of the sea. The beach jarred him awake.

Craw opened his eyes. He was at the edge of a large, still body of water. A sliver of moon looked down from a deep blue sky that seemed impossibly bright with stars. The wet sand beneath his fingers was tightly packed, a deep brown.

Identity begins with the awareness that you are an observer, an old professor of his had said.

Craw sat upright. He was naked, half in the water. Something was lapping against his side. He stretched out a hand and pulled it to him. It was a large and bloody wolf pelt, almost entirely intact.

He had no instinct to move and no doubt that he was dead. The fuzziness that had affected his thinking since the change had begun, the separation from his body that had occurred since landing in France – that was all gone.

He lay at the water's edge for hours trying to come to terms with what had happened. In that place he had utterly failed. He had not found his wife, nor had he even helped Harbard in his just cause against the Nazis. He hoped to be taken out to the sea again, to lose himself in the deep cold currents, to be nothing and no more.

He lost track of time and couldn't say how long he had been there when he noticed the quality of the light change.

He caught a smell on the breeze. Somewhere a fire had started.

He sat up. Still the wolf pelt was bobbing at his side. He was suddenly repulsed by it, and kicked it away. The pelt, though, seemed to be caught around his foot like a nagging piece of seaweed. He couldn't free himself of it. Eventually he gave up. He stood and looked up the beach. Yes, there was a fire, behind a group of plane trees, just visible.

Craw had no inclination to find out who had built it, but he had no inclination to stay on the beach either. He stood immobile for a little longer. He was becoming cold. It was not uncomfortable, but it had the benefit of providing him with a purpose. He picked up the pelt and made his way up the beach.

The fire was only a small one but it was well made, surrounded by a hearth of pebbles and burning brightly. No one was nearby, so Craw sat by it and began to dry himself. He became lost in the flames and the warmth, a pleasant emptiness descending on his thinking.

'Do you mind if I sit here awhile, Brother Wolf?' A voice addressed him in German.

Craw came out of his reverie. In front of him stood a girl, no more than eight or nine. She was wearing sodden striped pyjamas with a purple triangle at the breast. She was terribly thin, and at her neck were livid bruises.

'Please,' said Craw.

The little girl sat and said nothing, joining him in contemplation of the fire. It was a lovely night. The scent of cedars filled the air and cicadas chirped in the grass. After a time, the girl did speak.

'I have been so cold, Brother Wolf. I have been in the sea.'

'You will be warm now,' he said.

'I hope so. You are kind to share your fire.'

'It is not my fire.'

'Then whose is it?'

'I don't know.'

'May I sit, Brother Wolf?' Another voice was behind him, a man's. It was distinctly Viennese, thought Craw.

A figure moved in front of him. It was an old man. Craw saw there was a sharp line of blood running around the top of his head, as if someone had opened it like a teapot and then replaced the lid.

Craw gestured for the man to sit and he did.

'Is it your fire?' asked the little girl.

'No,' said the man. He then became silent, watching the flames. He too, Craw noted, wore those striped pyjamas that the camp prisoners wore.

Presently they were joined by others, dressed the same. There were women and men, young and old. After a couple of hours there were a dozen people sitting by the fire, of all ages and sexes. Death is a democrat, Craw thought.

The little girl sat between the legs of a thin woman who combed out her hair with her fingers. Everyone who came to the fire seemed wounded in some way, but not the wounds of battle. These were surgical cuts to the head and to the face, though replaced, not gaping, as if the flesh had been pushed back into position by some unseen hand. Craw could guess where they had received such wounds.

The fire, the people agreed, was a good one and showed no signs of diminishing, nor needing more wood, though it had been burning for hours.

'Who do you think built this?' asked a blood-soaked man.

'I don't know,' said Craw.

'I built the fire,' said a voice from the darkness. It was old, and the words came out as if forced through an inadequate apparatus. To Craw it sounded like a pebble scraped upon a rock, the words dry and cracked.

A shape moved at the edges of Craw's vision. Only when the woman stood next to him, resting her hand on his shoulder, did he look up. It was a traveller woman, one of the Sinti of the east, he thought. She was impossibly old, it seemed, though her grip on his shoulder was firm. All she had on was a loose robe, no more than a sheet, and on her bare arm he noted the tattoo of a number like Voller's victims bore. What

405

a strange thing. Most noticeable, though, was her eye. One side of her face seemed terribly wounded and bruised, and her right eye had swollen to be no more than a slit. Craw gulped. He felt pity rising inside him.

'Who are you?' said the little girl.

The old woman didn't answer; she just sat down near the fire. Craw noted that, of the assembled people, she was the only one with dry clothes.

'This is a strange place,' said a pale, thin man. 'I cannot be dead, because the dead are conscious of nothing. Has the Lord called us again?'

'You are all dead,' said the old woman. 'Dead, and wrong-fully so. You are unquiet spirits, that is why you are drawn to my fire.'

'Who are you?' someone else said.

'A traveller, and I had thought myself only that until I came here and saw my true nature. I have had a hundred names, child, but here my name is Leikn, and I am guardian of this place.'

'What is this place?' said the Viennese professor.

'It is one of the islands of the dead,' said the old woman.

'Of the murdered,' said another man.

The woman nodded. 'I have been born a hundred times, and I have been murdered a hundred times in a hundred ways. The only thing that unites these deaths is their pain and my revenge. If I cannot rest, than neither can my enemies.'

'I was choked,' said the child.

'And I cruelly cut,' said a man.

'The scraping was the worst,' said the Viennese professor.

'I was too weak, he restrained me easily,' said a woman.

'The doctor has many enemies in the ranks of the dead,' said the old woman. 'It is time to send him what he seeks.'

She threw some dust onto the fire and it flickered red and green. The fire seemed to expand. Now it seemed to surround the group, to be all around them, but Craw felt no heat.

'This is Nágrind, the corpse gate,' said the old woman. 'It is a gate of fire and transformation.'

'I am cold,' said the little girl.

'I too,' said a woman.

'Then ask Brother Wolf to share his clothes,' said Leikn. 'Our pain is a starving wolf. Let us send it where it can feed.'

Craw saw what was being asked of him. He took up the pelt and put it over his shoulders, the head sitting on his own head, his eyes looking out through the wolf's eyes. The little girl came and clung to him, and the others did too. All twelve of Dr Voller's victims hugged together and the pelt seemed to expand to cover them.

Craw felt warm and comforted by their presence; he hugged them to him and seemed to understand everything they could have been, all the stymied possibilities. He felt himself fusing with the others, their flesh becoming his flesh, their minds and sensations tipping into him like burning metal into a mould. The pain rose in him, a searing agony, short-circuiting his personality, whiting out anything other than itself, pain like a charge building in his body, bursting to spark to another point of connection.

In Niederhagen, the first thaw had come and the stench of the pit had become unbearable. For an hour prisoners had thrown wood on top of the bodies. Then a trooper poured petrol down into the pit. He couldn't quite reach out far enough to douse the corpses properly, so he took to throwing the fuel from the can. Five cans went into the pit, and then a prisoner did the dangerous work of throwing in a piece of burning wood.

The smoke began to rise, at first white, then thick and black. From the castle Max looked at the plume spreading out into the cold dusk. It was time for the ceremony and in the castle, the knights were preparing.

Arno had been taken, he'd heard. It was probably for the best. The world had no place for someone like that any more and everyone – everyone – had to look out for themselves nowadays. If he hadn't informed on Arno and his association had come to light later, what would it have meant for him – for Gertie? Gertie! His wife had been gone for days, locked in that chamber doing God knows what. Her transformation no longer struck him as strange but, there again, so little struck him as strange now.

Ever since his meeting at the pit his old certainties had been challenged. He had, he was sure, suffered some sort of hallucination but, what had the Jew Freud said? 'Dreams are the royal road to the unconscious'. He'd felt nearer to the truth of his life when talking to that strange Witness than he had at any other point. He couldn't put into words what that truth was, but its presence was a tumour in his mind. Still, Max was happy in a way. He had seen the chair taken from his room to the chamber of the Knights. Whether there was any power to the ceremony or not, he felt sure of one thing. Von Knobelsdorff was in for a shock.

45 The Land Left Behind

Gertie was woken by the sensation of cold and the sound of the sea. She got out of her bed in the submarine and moved down the passageway of pipes and dials. At the ladder she looked up. She could see the stars. The hatch on the tower was open. She climbed and looked out.

The shore on which the submarine surfaced was strangely familiar to her. They were travelling along a deep fjord where the air was clean and still. It was deep night, but the stars were bright and the moon was high. The water was a perfect reflection of the sky, so it seemed to Gertie that the submarine floated through a lattice of stars.

Gertie noticed the U-boat slowing. She looked behind her. Sheer mountains rose out of the water. In front, however, the land became flatter and she realised that the submarine was preparing to pull up on a narrow bank of silvery sand.

When it stopped she climbed onto the deck and let herself down the rope ladder. Varrin followed. The land they were in was truly beautiful, she thought. There was a bank of heather stretching away beyond the beach, tiny flowers like stars among it, and heading up the side of the valley, a deep forest of spruce.

She and the giant said nothing, but just walked up from the beach. A path of sorts wound through the heather and it seemed natural to follow it. Gertie lost herself in the lovely moonlight, the scent of night flowers and the rhythm of her steps.

The path led away from the fjord, around the base of a mountain and out onto a broad and grassy plain. First they saw the smoke of the fire and then, after a while, the farm itself. It was a low-walled construction with a thatched roof. From a vent at the top of the roof came the smoke. There were outbuildings, too – a barn and a lean-to, some sort of animal shelter.

'It is my home,' said Varrin.

Gertie looked and she could see tears in his eyes.

The two of them walked more quickly towards the building. Two hundred metres away from the farm, they came to a stone, a jagged rock about the height of a man. Gertie thought it looked as though it had fallen from a great height to stick there. There were scratches on it, some sort of writing, though she did not recognise it.

Varrin read, 'Káta raised this stone in memory of her husband Varrin. He fell against the serpent in the service of his lord.'

He was now beginning to weep openly. He ran towards the farm. From under the lean-to a dog burst, a husky-like thing, snarling and barking. Gertie thought it would tear into them both but, as it drew level with Varrin, it threw itself sideways and ran around him in circles, howling madly. He put out his arms and the dog leapt up at him to lick his face.

'Gamr, you idiot!' said Varrin, bending to hug the animal.

Then at the door there was a woman. She was thirty-five, stout, and wearing a long pleated skirt. She said nothing when she saw the giant; she just ran towards him and threw herself into his arms. She called inside and children came running to greet their father.

Gertie watched and she knew the giant's journey was over.

'I must go,' she said. 'I need to go back to my husband, where I came from.'

Varrin hugged his wife.

'How will you do that, Goddess?' said the woman.

'I am not a goddess,' said Gertie.

'You are the Lady Beautiful in Tears,' said Varrin's wife.

'I am not a goddess.'

'Then go and see the other god who is not a god, perhaps

he can help you,' said the woman. 'Look for the hermit who lives on Ryukan at the Gausta peak. Go and see Lord Authun.'

She pointed to the distance and Gertie could see the sharp point of a summit rising from a broad hill.

'Authun is here?' said Varrin. 'Not in the halls of the slain?'

'He renounced arms at the end of his life and now he lives alone on that hill,' said his wife.

Varrin nodded. Gertie could see that the news made him happy.

'He asked me for my life and I gave it,' he said.

'For what?'

'For magic. Now I am dead I can tell the secret. The witches told Authun the heirless to seek a son in the west. A magical son. He found him and his brother there, brought them back to Hordaland.'

'He only had one son, the prince Vali, who went to the drowning pool for wisdom and set off for the east, never seen again,' said Káta.

This meant nothing to Gertie and she left them to their reunion, heading out towards the hill.

Still she felt no need of food or drink and she never seemed to tire. She just kept moving forwards, up and up to the peak. The night was everlasting and, were it not for the warmth, she would have thought that she was in the Arctic Circle. There was grass beneath her feet, though, and only the tops of the mountains bore any snow. It was useless to guess how many days she had travelled, though it seemed like a long time.

She thought of the lady at the hall, and she thought of Max and how she wanted to hold him again. She needed to get back to Wewelsburg – but how?

The grass gave way to a rough track of boulders heading up the mountainside. This was no mountain of the imagination, a perfect peak of glistening snows, but a broad hump of rock like the back of a bear extending up into the base of the clouds. Gertie climbed and climbed, needing no rest. Presently she reached the cloud base and she could hardly see. And yet there was still a track, so she followed it. After a while she knew that someone was beside her. She didn't hear them or see them, but she felt their gaze. Still she walked on through the fog, the presence at her side.

And then someone was in front of her. The woman had called him Lord Authun, but this wasn't a lord, she was sure. It was an old man with long white hair and a white beard. He wore only the clothes of a farmer, a woollen tunic and cloth trousers.

'Let me past.' Gertie was not afraid, which was unlike her in such a desolate place, faced by such a figure, his face gaunt and scarred, his body wiry, more like a twisted tree than that of a man.

The man stood to one side and she walked by him. She was going to hurry away but decided, as she passed him, to turn and speak.

'I'm looking for a Lord Authun,' she said.

'Authun is a lord no longer,' said the man.

'Do you know where he is?'

'Who is it that asks?'

'Just a woman,' she said. 'Someone who needs his help to go home.'

The man seemed to think for a second.

'I am Authun,' said the man.

'I was told to expect a lord.'

'I am lord of myself, which is the extent of my ambitions,' he said.

'Can you help me return home?'

'Where is your home?'

'Germany,' said Gertie. 'Wewelsburg Castle, though I wish that it weren't.'

The names clearly meant nothing to Authun. 'You want to return to a home that you hate, and that is a strange aim.'

'There's someone I love there,' she said.

'Accept your death,' he said. 'It is the best course in the end. If they love you, they will be here, if neither the Allfather nor the Goddess claim them to fight in their halls.'

'I am not dead,' said Gertie.

'You couldn't be here if you weren't.'

'I met a lady at the hall of dead soldiers and she asked me to sleep by the fire. When I awoke she was gone.'

Authun shook his head. 'If that were the case then you could not have left the hall.'

'A warrior showed me the way out. Varrin. He is here now.'

He shook his head. 'Varrin. I killed him as sure as any foe I ever had in battle.'

'He bears you no ill will.'

'It is not his ill will that concerns me,' said Authun, 'it is my own.'

He sat and thought for a while. Gertie thought that, with his white hair and beard, he looked like a child's idea of God, or Father Christmas, or even one of the winds, a white old man in a cloud.

'You are the Goddess,' he said.

'No,' said Gertie.

'Yes, and you do not know it. The Gods are several, and take many forms. Some they celebrate and some they almost forget and, in turn, the Gods are forgotten by themselves. The lady you saw at the hall was just such another, perhaps closer to the original Goddess than you, but only an aspect of that lady, nevertheless. You could not have taken a warrior from the hall if you were not.'

'He took me.'

'Or so it appeared to you.'

'He was lonely,' said Gertie, 'as I think all those warriors must be.'

'You must return to the hall,' said Authun, 'and wait for the lady to come back. When she does, you will return to wherever she has left your mortal form.'

'I will not go back there. I fear she means me no good.'

'How did you get here?' said Authun.

'On a ship,' she said, 'a strange and horrible ship. It was made of dead men's nails.'

Authun received the news as he would a communication in the field. Victory or defeat, his demeanour was always impassive.

'Then it may be time. Come, let us walk down the mountain.'

'What time?' said Gertie.

'The end of the world,' he said, 'or an end. It is, at least, time to confront the Gods, if not defeat them.'

'How will I do that?' Gertie felt rather pathetic. 'I am a housewife.'

'You will know when you get there, for you are the aspect of the Goddess she has cut furthest from herself, the one she most fears. You are, I see it now, the Lady Beautiful in Tears. You are the one the warriors leave behind.'

'I had a vision,' said Gertie, 'that a terrible wolf set upon me. The lady said she would go to trap it for me.'

'You are the wolf trap, Lady,' said Authun. 'Come, let us walk to the shore.'

And Authun led her from the mountain top, down onto the plain. As he walked, others began to join them: dark black women from Africa; pale English ladies in floral frocks; the poor in their rags; others in high wigs and extravagant dresses. With them they brought a host of children tripping behind them. More and more followed Authun and Gertie across the plain, until it seemed they had a multitude following.

Then the mountains approached and Gertie weaved back through the path she had taken to the beach to where the submarine, couched still against the sandbank, waited.

'One ship can't take so many,' she said.

'It can take them all,' said Authun, 'but I fear that it will not. Only those who die peacefully may travel from the lady's shore to here, and only warriors may travel back the way you came.'

'I brought a warrior with me.'

Authun nodded. 'Then you must try to take one of them the other way. If one can travel they all can.'

Gertie beckoned a little boy to her. He was about three years old and very poor, she could see. He wore only rags and had nothing on his feet. He could, she thought, have come from almost any period of history at all. She took the boy in her arms and waded out to the ship, the waters cool about her legs. She told him to cling to her back, and climbed the rope to the top of the deck. The hatch on the conning tower was shut.

She bent to try to open it but it was stuck fast.

'Only warriors,' said Authun.

Gertie felt utterly defeated. She looked up from the deck of the U-boat towards the hills, out over the heather and the little star flowers, up to the pine forest.

'We have warriors here,' she said.

She helped the little boy down off the side of the boat and returned with him to the shore.

'Go to the trees,' she shouted. 'Cut yourselves spears and clubs. Everyone must have a weapon!'

The crowds turned and took to the trees, stripping off branches and hacking out whatever rough weapons they could. It must have been a day before the work was done, though the moon did not set nor the sun come up, and then each woman and child carried a staff, a club or a spear.

Gertie turned to Authun. 'You, I think, need no weapon.'

'I think not,' said Authun.

This time he took a child under his arm and waded out into the waters. Gertie was amazed to see how easily he scaled the rope ladder with the child clinging to his back. In action he appeared not like an old man at all, more like some acrobat impressing a crowd.

Authun made the deck of the ship and put the child down, its makeshift spear in its hand.

'I am Authun the Pitiless!' he shouted. 'White Wolf of the frozen wastes, pillager of the five towns, he who brought the children that the witch used to make the wolf. I had a son, Vali, adopted and he grew to have teeth to eat the moon. I have stocked the All-father's halls with a thousand brave warriors, and thus I demand passage for my army!'

There was a hideous clang and the hatch on the tower flew open. The army of the abandoned was on its way to the hall of dead heroes.

46 Ceremony

Balby had spent a month searching the disused mines to the north of Coventry, or at least examining them. Many of them could not be found, for the shafts had been capped and other entrances filled over with rubble. Of those that could be found, many of the entrances just led in a short way before a flood or a rockfall blocked them. If they were open then they fell away into darkness, impassable shafts reaching down to unseeable depths, the winding gear long gone to scrap.

Like many people who encounter unwanted problems, Balby had learned a great deal about a subject of which he would have been happy to have remained totally ignorant. So he came to know his adits from his shafts and his slope mines from his drift mines.

He knew, anyway, what he was looking for. A policeman pressed for time needs to work on only the most promising leads. First, he wanted an adit. This is a horizontal access to a mine leading to the coal face, as opposed to a shaft that tunnels straight down. He reasoned that even the professor would not have the resources to get the old winding gear going to descend a shaft and that, if he did, it would excite some comment in the local area.

So he was searching for a horizontal or sloping access. He also wanted to see some signs of human disturbance. The existing adits he'd seen were so overgrown that they warranted no further investigation. He had become excited on his second week of exploration when he'd discovered a small entrance to a cave that had been cleared by hand. In there, though, he'd found only the evidence of a lovers' trysting place.

It was the end of week four when he examined the Langley pit.

The map said the pit was sunk into a hill about five miles north of Coventry. Balby had taken his car and was pleasantly surprised to find that the old dirt road to the pit was still intact, enabling him to drive right up to the mouth of the adit. The tunnel was very plain and near the road. Balby could almost have driven into it, had it not been for a sharp step just before the entrance. He nearly didn't get out of his car because he could see the mine had been sealed with a portcullis-style gate. It was the fourth mine he'd visited that afternoon, though, and the last one on his list. Copper's instinct told him to go and take a look.

He climbed to the entrance and immediately noticed something he'd never seen on any other mine before. The entrance wasn't sealed irretrievably. It was hinged and had a padlock. This was a working gate. He looked at the lock. It was new, or at least too new to have been there much more than one winter. He scrambled down the side of the mine next to some bushes. It took him no time at all to find what he was looking for. There were short offcuts of metal that had clearly come from the bars of the gate. They bore the marks of a saw. Someone had modified this gate to turn it from a barricade into an entrance.

Balby's strong instinct was to drive to the nearest factory he could and requisition a pair of bolt cutters. Instead he restrained himself. There was a telephone box in Langley village. He had to proceed carefully but he thought that, if he was right, what he was about to do would be borne out in the long term. He drove down to the village and phoned Briggs. He didn't tell the younger man what he was doing, although Briggs asked.

'Just bring a pair of bolt cutters, a torch and ...'

He was going to say Briggs should see the firearms officer and sign out a gun. He thought better of it. It would excite too much attention.

'Bring a couple of truncheons,' he said. 'I'll be waiting by the phone box in Langley village.'

Briggs was there half an hour later.

'What's the score, chief?' he said. Balby noted, with regret, that he had been watching American films again.

'The "score" is that I think I may have found the girl,' he said.

Briggs's eyes widened. 'Well, tip top. I thought we were winding that one down.'

'You thought wrong. Now let's get those bolt cutters up to the pit.'

The padlock on the gate was not substantial and it snapped easily. There was a long tunnel into the mine, with the remains of a narrow gauge railway track leading into the dark. Briggs turned on his torch. The passage sloped gently down. The rock was limestone and damp, so that stalactites hung down from the roof, and the floor was rough and uneven with deposits of stone.

'They look like teeth,' said Briggs.

'Thank you for that, Constable.'

Balby had prepared himself for any shock, but even he gasped as Briggs's torch caught a glimpse of something reflective about eighty yards into the tunnel. It was a number plate. There was a car down there.

Both men carried on down the tunnel until they were level with the car. A Humber Snipe. This was Harbard's car. It clearly hadn't been moved for a while, because it was covered in dust and limestone splashes spattered the roof. Next to it were four large planks. Briggs shone his torch on them. Car tyre marks. So that was how Harbard had got the car across the floor.

'We've got to get uniform,' said Briggs.

Balby nodded. 'We have to play this by the book. Come on, let's get to the phone and call the troops.'

He was about to step forward when a shadow seemed to move.

'I'm afraid, gentlemen, that won't be happening,' said Harbard.

He emerged into the torchlight. He was gaunt, a shadow of the man Balby had seen at Coombe Abbey; his face was streaked with blood and his vacant eye socket was weeping down his cheek. More materially, in his hand was a Colt .45 pistol.

'I have always found it quaint that the British police do not carry guns,' said Harbard, 'but—'

He never finished his sentence, Balby turned and, with a tight right hook, caught him full in the jaw. The pistol flashed in the darkness and Balby felt as though he had been kicked in the leg. The torch went crashing to the floor and went out. Briggs gave a shout and ran for it, down the tunnel back towards the light.

Balby tried to stand, but his leg had gone numb and he stumbled. He heard a cry from down the passageway. Briggs had fallen too, and was cursing in agony. Balby felt someone brush past him and heard the pistol cock again.

He heard Briggs utter one word: 'Don't!'

The pistol fired, its noise unbearable in the passageway.

Balby felt the tyre of the car on his hand and tried to crawl for cover behind it.

'Stay where you are,' said Harbard. A torch beam cut through the dark.

Balby flattened himself to the floor, though the torch beam had picked him out.

'Good Lord,' said Harbard, spitting and holding his jaw, 'you would break my dentist's heart. Have you any idea what these teeth cost me? That was a very expensive punch, officer.'

'You won't need dentists where you're going,' said Balby. He had been shot, he knew. He was surprised his leg wasn't more painful. It was just intensely numb. Harbard kept the light in his face.

Balby could hear a tremble in the academic's voice. He was

trying to preserve his familiar detached manner, but he was struggling with it. It was something more than what you'd expect from someone who had taken a good blow in the teeth. Balby was convinced he was dealing with a madman.

'Where I am going is down,' said Harbard, 'and you will please lead the way.'

'My leg's done for,' said Balby.

'That is unfortunate.' Harbard seemed to ruminate for a while. 'Your friend was a coward.'

'He was a copper, and he knew the odds. Don't you worry, there'll be a few more like him along in a minute.'

'You are unconvincing, Inspector, though it hardly matters if you're telling the truth. We are nearly where we need to be. When I become what I need to become, you will see the reasons. Believe me, Inspector, the war needs men like me.'

'Men who kidnap young women, men who murder others?'

'I think the war has a great deal of need of men who murder others. Armies wouldn't function quite as well without them.'

'And kidnap young girls?'

'I am a patriot and a democrat,' said Harbard. 'And I will do what it takes to oppose the evil of Hitler. I have seen what he is doing. I have pulled knowledge screaming from forbidden places and I know what we are facing. How many parents, how many uncles, have sacrificed their children in armies, in aircraft and at sea for the freedom of their country? Tell me, how is my sacrifice of my niece any different?'

'Most people leave it to the Boche to shoot their nearest and dearest. What are you doing – cutting out the middleman?'

Harbard gave a short laugh. 'I'm cutting out the man, that's for sure.'

He drew closer to Balby, though not close enough to take another punch. He shone the torch into the policeman's face.

'Our friend Craw has a terrible gift, though he accounts it a curse. He is a werewolf. Do you know what that means?'

'I don't believe in such things.'

'Oh, but you do, Inspector. You believe in God and in

angels and in witches, because the Bible says all those things exist. You believe in a man who can heal the sick by touch, so you very much do believe in such things.'

'This is blasphemy,' said Balby.

'No, you're not listening, it's the reverse of blasphemy. The Bible says that witches and familiar spirits and necromancers and sorcerers exist. I agree with it. If witches, why not werewolves?'

Balby said nothing. He was trying to assess if his leg would be up to rushing Harbard. He had to conclude it would not.

'Craw has a weakness, though, an inability to do what needs to be done. He allows his own concerns to outweigh those of his duty to humanity. I will not make that mistake.'

Balby couldn't bear to listen to any more of this rubbish.

'Your duty to humanity? How about your duty to that girl? Take me to her. Let me speak to her.'

Harbard weighed the request in his mind.

'Can you make it to the lower mine?'

'No, I can't stand.' Balby was beginning to feel faint.

'A pity. I would have liked a witness to what I am about to do.'

He aimed the gun at Balby's head and pulled the trigger. Nothing happened. Balby was too slow to react. He heard a click and thump.

'A misfire,' said Harbard. 'It's clear now, Inspector, so rushing me will only hasten your death.' He cocked the pistol again and pointed it at Balby.

'Let me comfort her.'

Balby was desperate. He did not fear to die; he was certain of his heavenly reward. He feared what Harbard might do to his niece in the name of madness, though.

'What?'

'I am a lay preacher at my church. Let me pray with her, to bring her comfort.'

'You know she is still alive?'

'You wouldn't still be here otherwise,' said Balby.

'You are cleverer than you look.'

'Thank you.'

'It's not a compliment, you don't look very clever.' Harbard giggled a little giggle. His mind was gone, Balby was sure. He had to hope he could reach him, though – persuade him.

'Have some compassion for the girl,' said Balby. The pain was now becoming very bad.

'I have compassion for her. That is what makes her useful to me. That compassion is an ingredient in a spell. Sacrifices must be painful or they are not sacrifices, just offerings.'

Balby shivered at the madness of Harbard's words.

'Then cling to your compassion. "Even in darkness light dawns for the upright, for the gracious and compassionate and righteous man. Unto the upright there ariseth light in the darkness: he is gracious, and full of compassion, and righteous."'

From behind the white light of the torch, Harbard groaned, a deep groan of anguish.

'Do you have handcuffs?' said Harbard.

'Yes.'

'Then put them on.'

Balby did as he was bid. Harbard made him throw the keys to him and then lie face down. Balby heard the sound of tearing cloth and felt a blindfold tied over his eyes. He knew that any attempt to attack would be useless.

'I will lift you, but you must use your good leg to stand,' said Harbard. 'I cannot lever you with both hands, because the other one will be holding the gun I will use to kill you if you attempt to overpower me. Give me your word, in the name of Jesus Christ, that you will not try to escape if I let you go to the girl.'

'You have my word. In the name of Jesus Christ.'

Harbard put his hand in between Balby's manacled wrists and placed his shoulder under his shoulder. In this way, a version of a wrestler's shoulder hold, he pulled him upright.

The going was terribly difficult down the uneven floor of the mine. Balby thought he was going to faint with the pain but he prayed to God and gritted his teeth and got through it.

'You are lucky,' said Harbard. 'It was my original plan to site this operation at the bottom of a shaft. Unfortunately my advancing years prevented it. Still, we must go down a long way.'

And it was a long way. Balby could hardly bear the pain as he leant as best he could on Harbard. Still, he had to keep going. He knew they had gone deep from the sensation of cold and the pressure in his ears. Twice he banged his head and, after that, he kept in a half crouch.

Finally he heard a voice. A girl's cry of anguish. He felt Harbard's grip tighten on his arm.

'Be a man and let her go,' said Balby.

'A bad inducement, I'm afraid,' said Harbard. 'I've told you before, not being a man is the entire point of my work here. Go.'

Harbard snatched the blindfold from Balby and kicked him forward in the same move. Balby fainted for a second with the agony. When he recovered his senses he looked around him. He was in a large chamber lit by a hurricane lamp. The room contained, to his surprise, a workman's hut; the floor was strewn with debris – nails, wire, pieces of wood. There was also a pair of huge water tanks, fifteen feet high by as much round, open at the top and resting on a brick base. It was clearly the remains of the mining operation. The tanks had been decorated in broad paint strokes with that strange rune Balby had seen in the house of the painted man, the one like a clipped swastika. The heads, though, were what really took his attention. There were two of them on stakes, beaten and scarcely recognisable as human. At first he didn't see Eleanor. Then there was a movement at the side of his vision, a flash of a pale dress from inside the workman's hut.

'Who's there?' she cried out.

'Miss Eleanor, it's Inspector Balby of the police. I am a prisoner too, but don't worry, I am going to get you out of here.'

The girl let out a yelp.

Harbard said nothing. He just moved up to the plinth on which the water tanks were resting and sat down. From a cloth he took out a piece of rusted metal.

'You will be missed soon, and so this must begin sooner than I would have wished,' he said. 'Be aware, Eleanor, that I love you. You will die a heroine, saving the world from the scourge of Nazism.'

Eleanor began to sob.

'I wish it did not have to be so, but it is required,' said Harbard. Balby heard a catch in his voice. Harbard too was beginning to weep.

The policeman crawled his way over to the hut. The girl was in a terrible state, half-starved and filthy, awfully cut on her hands with wounds that were swollen with infection. She was manacled to a metal ring on the wall. Balby shivered as he saw there were two more beside it.

'What happened to you?' said Balby.

'I tried to run and I fell.'

'You'll be all right.'

He felt terribly angry towards Harbard for his stupidity and his madness. The girl needed to be in hospital, immediately. He looked out of the hut at the old man. He was replacing the piece of metal in the cloth. It was as if he was checking it was still there. In the better light of the hurricane lamp, Balby could see Harbard himself looked a terrible mess. His face was swollen from where Balby had hit him, and the wound on his eye was seeping liquid. Then he came towards them, taking out his gun.

In front of the hut he dropped a sack onto the floor. The sack was not full but it was heavy; Balby could tell by the way it fell. Then he levelled the pistol at the policeman with one hand and threw down the handcuff keys with the other.

'You will manacle yourself to the wall,' he said.

There were, Balby knew, ways and ways of securing someone with handcuffs. He clicked the cuff onto his right hand

and put the other cuff through the iron ring. This meant at least his left hand was free. He would have preferred it the other way around, but he wanted to keep an eye on where Harbard was. Was his madness enough of a distraction to him to stop him realising what Balby was doing? It was.

'I must prepare,' said Harbard. 'This will be your last night on earth, both of you.'

Eleanor began to cry and Harbard ruffled her hair.

'I am truly sorry. If there was another way ...'

Balby wanted to tell him to save his cant. He didn't want to antagonise Harbard, though. The policeman had carved out a tiny advantage and didn't want to lose it through stupid pride.

'It is time,' said Harbard, 'for the ceremony to begin. The fasting and meditation are at an end. I am ready.'

He threw off his coat and Balby was shocked to see the deep wound in his side – like some blasphemous parody of Christ, he thought. Harbard saw what he was thinking.

'Jesus wasn't the only one who hung on the tree, Inspector. Odin too sought knowledge that way. My quest is nearly done. I am half in that world already. By the end of the evening you, Eleanor and I will be the same person, consumed by the wolf and made into a force that will shake the Nazis to their core.'

'You are mad,' said Balby.

Harbard shrugged. 'Such terms are meaningless. This reality is fading for me, another one is awakening. I shall claim many heroes for Odin's halls. I am the All-father and the servant of the All-father. I sacrifice myself to myself and become three in one, father, son and wolf. I honour him in my killings and become nearer to him.'

'Why did you offer help with the investigation? Why did you call Craw in?'

Harbard said nothing. Balby could see the explanation. How better to make sure the investigation failed than to append yourself to it? How better to identify targets than through the files of the police? And Craw? The old man had seen him as an ally, but he had been disappointed.

426

Still with the gun in his hand, Harbard came forward and unlocked Eleanor from the wall. The girl was trembling, and too weak to resist. He manacled her again with her hands behind her back. Then he picked up the sack and emptied it. Inside was a noose. Eleanor's sobs became desperate and she started to shake her head.

'No, Uncle, no.'

'You have a demon inside you, Harbard,' said Balby. 'Cast it out in the name of the Lord.'

'There is nothing inside me yet,' said Harbard, as he placed the noose over Eleanor's head. 'I go to a glorious fight with the wolf, and to steal his hide for my own.'

Balby was furious, as angry as he had ever been in his life. A girl dying for nonsense. He began to shout out: '"They sacrificed their sons and their daughters to demons. They shed innocent blood, the blood of their sons and daughters, whom they sacrificed to the idols of Canaan, and the land was desecrated by their blood!"'

Harbard shoved Eleanor forward. Balby realised to his horror that he was moving her towards the open-topped water tank. He saw immediately what Harbard intended to do. There was no time for delay.

Ever since he had got into the hut Balby had been scanning the floor for pieces of wire. He saw one at the limit of his reach and leant forward for it. Straining against the cuffs, he managed to trap it in between his index and middle fingers and pull it back. As he worked, he tried to reach out to Harbard with the power of holy scripture.

'You will fail, Harbard, you can only fail. "They defiled themselves by what they did; by their deeds they prostituted themselves. Therefore the Lord was angry with his people and abhorred his inheritance. He handed them over to the nations, and their foes ruled over them. Their enemies oppressed them and subjected them to their power! Thus were they defiled with their own works, and went a whoring with their own inventions. Therefore was the wrath of the Lord kindled against his people, insomuch that he abhorred his own own inheritance. And he gave them into the hand of the heathen; and they that hated them ruled over them."'

Harbard marched Eleanor to the steps at the top of the plinth and stood her facing the tank. In Harbard's hand was that jagged piece of metal. Then Balby saw something even more frightening. Another noose had been suspended from the ceiling. Harbard placed it around his own neck and began to intone:

> *Lord of the hanged*
> *Who gave his eye for wisdom*
> *Odin*
> *Master of magic*
> *Lord of the shrieking runes*
> *He who hung from the tree for nine days and nine nights*
> *Who died and was reborn*
> *He who the spear pierced*
> *Lord of the Gallows*
> *Be here with me now.*

Desperately Balby tried to fashion the piece of metal into an angle. The man who had shown him how to escape had described the correct shape as like the arm of a swastika. Regulation cuffs were, it was well known, easy to pick. But under such stress and with shaking hands, Balby found it hard to force his fingers to do as he bid.

The room to him seemed to go cold. The pressure he had felt in the passageway built.

Balby began to utter the Lord's Prayer to himself.

'Our Father ...'

'*All-father,*'

'which art in Heaven, hallowed be Thy name ...'

'*Holy thief,*'

'Thy kingdom come,'

'*Deceiver,*'

'Thy will be done.'

'Master of thought and memory, Lord of battle ...'

'On earth as it is in Heaven,'

Balby's fingers worked frantically at the lock. Nothing – no click. The policeman took a deep breath. In his mind he heard the voice of his wife: 'More haste, less speed, Jack.'

He calmed himself and addressed the task again, this time slowly.

'Accept this true sacrifice and grant me the power to face the wolf. Slayer of Ymir, who fashioned the world from the giant's flesh, fashion my flesh now and let me stock your halls with heroes.'

The room was getting very cold indeed now. Balby still worked at the keyhole, trying to find the ratchet with the wire.

'Give us this day our daily bread,'

'Strife bringer,'

'And forgive us our trespasses as we forgive them that trespass against us. And forgive us our debts, as we forgive our debtors.'

'Victory bringer,'

'And lead us not into temptation ...'

'Take me now.'

'... but deliver us from evil,'

Harbard jumped into the water with Eleanor, pulling the noose tight about her neck. Balby could hear them thrashing and kicking in the tank. He thought he must be imagining it, but the entire inside of the chamber now seemed to have a thin patina of frost on it. It was as if all the heat in the room had been sucked away.

'For thine is the kingdom, the power and the glory, for ever and ever, amen.'

At last the claw of the cuff sprang free.

Balby leapt to his feet by instinct and nearly fainted with the pain. He fell forward, crawling on his front towards the steps and to the tank, every movement agony.

And then he saw him, at his side – the archangel Saint Michael, the scourge of devils.

Balby thought he must be dying as he looked up at the angel. It was tall and pale, with the most brilliant red hair, and on his back lay long feathered wings.

'Lord help me, Lord help me save her.'

Balby couldn't budge. He had lost blood and the pain was far too much. He drove his head into the floor of the cavern trying to block out the agony.

'I will help you,' said the angel.

There was a scrabbling next to him, a noise like a giant rat running, he thought. He felt his head pushed back with force. He opened his eyes to find himself staring into a ruptured grin. David Arindon had found his trail at last.

47   Gods and Monsters

Von Knobelsdorff had spent the days in the chamber in a state of high excitement. Frustratingly, Mrs Voller – or, as she was now insisting on being known, 'the Lady' – had no role for him. He had expected meditations, privations, some sort of preparation. She told him to concentrate on getting some decent coffee; she was sick of the acorn stuff.

This was a great trouble to von Knobelsdorff, and it did occur to him that one of the other knights had managed to usurp his role. He couldn't really believe that had happened. They all seemed very suspicious of the Lady, until they met her. Then their objections melted. Von Knobelsdorff would have liked to believe their change of heart was down to the male weakness for a pretty face. It was more than that, though, he was sure. The Lady was a powerful force. Shouldn't he take more credit for bringing her to the castle, though? It couldn't be coincidence that her true nature had been revealed after his experiences at the black well. She had been summoned – and by him. Shouldn't he have received more gratitude?

Perhaps Max had some control over her. The doctor was always around, trailing his fat gypsy queer catamite from the camp behind him. There was more than met the eye to those two, for sure.

Gullveig herself was nervous, but not because of the ceremony. The long time in the coma, in that room of shadows, had attuned her mind better than even her months under the waterfall, or on the freezing hillsides, when she had prepared her great magics in years before. When she had been first on the earth she had not known who she was. Now, sure that she was a fragment of the All-father Odin's mind, magic seemed more easily got. And then there was Wewelsburg itself.

Lifetimes before, in the commune of witches, in the caves of the Troll Wall in the frozen north, she had used the screams of her dying sisters to focus her trance. She'd drawn power from rocks into which the anguish of the dead had seeped. In the castle, though, there was no need for additional sacrifice. It had seen more death than even the witches' caves. The wide-seeing lady heard the shadows of the castle mutter and moan, saw faces of anguish in the patterns of the stones, and felt the tide of blood that had lapped through its corridors for centuries.

She was nervous because the presence that had trapped her in the lattice of shadows wasn't too far away. Gullveig knew that it was even nearer the All-father than she was. The being from the well was too much for her to control. However, he had the Moonsword. That would be necessary to separate the old murderer, the man who bore the wolf curse, from the wolf nature. So the being needed to be called.

Once the murderer was dead, the wolf's attention would need to be caught. That was the tricky part. Gullveig was sure of one thing – if the being at the well was an aspect of the All-father, then he could not enter the dream of the wolf; the wolf was an enemy of the Gods and would not have him. She was certain she herself wouldn't enter the dream either, for the same reason. The murderer, she knew, was not quite human and yet not an aspect of a god. She found it difficult to see him clearly, to grasp his nature. Safest, she thought, was an ordinary mortal, and one she could command.

It did trouble Gullveig that she couldn't see the outcome of the wolf summoning. This was because she needed to direct her energies to summoning the wolf, she thought. However, there was a fog around the future. Sometimes when she went looking for the wolf she had a vision of him dead on a shore, water and seaweed around him. And at other times she was

432

convinced he was already in the castle. Never mind – she needed her energies for what was to come.

Von Knobelsdorff was, of course, first into the chamber, immaculate in his black uniform, boots like dark mirrors, the death's head polished to such a shine that it seemed to wink from his collar and from the hat under his arm.

He looked at the restraint chair.

'In the centre of the room?' he said. 'Is that correct? It would imply the sacrifice is more important than the celebrants.'

'It's not for a sacrifice,' said Gullveig.

'Then who is it for?'

'You,' she said.

Von Knobelsdorff took the news without a blink.

'Very good,' he said.

Gullveig had to hand it to von Knobelsdorff; he was a brave man. Tonight he would see how far his bravery would carry him.

Von Knobelsdorff paced the room as the other Knights came in. They were all keen to see the Lady, but less enthusiastic at the prospect of another lengthy period of meditation. Still, it was the price of access to Himmler's inner sanctum, so it had to be paid.

Von Knobelsdorff was always nervous in the Knights' company. His occult investigations had placed him high in Himmler's favour. But Himmler knew the value of keeping a man on his toes, so von Knobelsdorff's promotions had not come as quickly as they might. He was a relatively low-ranking member of the Knights, and he felt his inferior status keenly. He had enemies there, he had bred resentments. Through him the Knights had been forced to sit for days in that chamber; he was the one who had persuaded Himmler of the worth of such experiments. He could feel their malice like a breath on his shoulder.

To be placed into the chair was potentially demeaning, and he saw the sneers and the raised brows as he allowed Voller's monkey to restrain him. They would see, though, they would see.

Max was last to arrive. He had received a letter from Arno asking him to vouch for his character. He had read it. The tone was desperate and it was written in a very shaky hand. 'You seem to have run out of jokes, Arno,' he had said to himself, and then thrown it away.

Gertie smiled at him and gestured to a stool she had placed at the side of the chamber. *What had happened to her? Why had she changed?* he asked himself.

It was as if the violent history they inhabited had gone coursing into every aspect of their lives. There was nothing that wasn't touched by the institutional cruelty that was all around them – not even their love. Did he love her? Yes. Or, he realised, he loved the *idea* of her, as she had been when he had clung to her as they both floundered in a sea of madness. But she had gone down, and he had gone too. It was unimportant to consider who had dragged whom. Was she there any more? Was he there any more? What did he mean by 'she'? You can't touch her personality, you can't play it like a song or read it from a sheet of paper. It was more like a flame than something you could hold. And if you transfer a fire from a match to a cigarette, is it the same flame? Arno would have enjoyed that one, he thought. Except Arno wasn't going to be enjoying anything any more for quite a while because, as he had once observed, everything was fucked.

The Knights were on their thrones in their sharp black uniforms, von Knobelsdorff was in the chair, Max was seated on a stool, and Michal was at his feet. How had he got there, Max wondered. Was Michal now so much part of him that people had ceased to see the boy? Why hadn't he had him killed? Why hadn't he used him as a spy? In the end, he had concluded, he couldn't be bothered. It was as if the unpleasantness of the boy's company was so slight compared to the horrors he was creating himself that it was almost unnoticeable.

Von Knobelsdorff looked very smart, he thought. He

wondered how he managed to get his silver to sparkle like that. What they were doing to Arno? He only had himself to blame for keeping those jazz records. Actually, the bastard still owed him a night on the beer because he'd bet him he wouldn't get into the SS. Had he bet him that? Probably. Yes, he thought so. So who would Max have to call to get Arno released? He didn't want to miss his night on the beer but, on the other hand, he didn't want a dangerous jazz listener walking the streets.

Gertie looked lovely, he thought, though he had hardly spoken to her since she had recovered from her coma. She didn't even come back to bed, but spent her nights pacing the outside of the castle. He longed just to touch her. If he could touch her, he thought, the spell might be broken, and they would all go back to Salzgitter where they would dance in silence to their jazz again. Could you be arrested for imagining jazz? Max had to laugh – of course you could. You could be arrested for anything. Everything was fucked. His thoughts included. None of this was making sense.

As his wife began her incantation, Max's mind began to make connections – brilliant connections, he thought. Clarity had descended on him. After the war he would make his money in silent jazz, hosting dances where everyone imagined the music. If the hall was raided, they could all claim to be imagining Wagner. Or why not play Wagner, but imagine jazz? There were ways of dealing with the Nazis, if only you saw them. Something struck him as wrong about the words 'the Nazis'. You could say it shorter, he thought. Oh yes, that was it. 'Us'. That covered the same idea. Would they let him cut up von Knobelsdorff in the chair? He hoped so, although he imagined his brain would be black – yes, a black mirror, two hemispheres like the toes of his boots.

Gertie was singing, a low and tuneless drone. It seemed to go on for a long time, for hours. He couldn't focus on its words at first, but then they came to him.

He who is sated with the last breath of dying men,
He who defiles the seat of the Gods with blood
The sun turns black and the storm howls
I call you from the iron wood
Devourer, from the shores of death.

Max began to itch. This mumbo-jumbo made him intensely uncomfortable – more than uncomfortable. It was all he could do to stop himself writhing on the stool.

The witch's body went rigid on the throne and she let out a cry, not of alarm but of exultation. A spell is not like a recipe, as some imagine, but more like a puzzle. It had cost her enormous energy, but Gullveig suddenly had what she wanted. Her posture changed, her face softened. For a second, Max thought, she looked like the Gertie of old, but not quite like her, subtly changed.

'Come to me, Vali,' she said. 'You promised to return and I have been waiting so long.'

Then, from somewhere inside the chamber, Max heard the howl. It seemed to resonate in his bones, to shake the walls of the castle and rattle the tormented ghosts inside it. He realised the terrible cry was emanating from his wife, her whole body seeming to hum like a tuning fork. He felt the howl reverberating in his guts, and it was as if everything of him that had been smashed since he had come to the castle was shaking inside him. He imagined his stomach as a bag of broken dinner plates, jangling and twisting inside his body.

From down the valley, the wolf's voice cut through the still air of the night in reply. Max felt his flesh go cold.

The witch smiled. 'He is coming. We will have him here before long. Von Knobelsdorff, you remember your instructions?'

The man in the restraint chair nodded, his mouth tight with determination.

From outside the castle came the sound of gunshots, the tight burst of an MP 42 machine pistol, then another and then, again, the howl. It was a howl that seemed to draw all strength from those who heard it, to send the flesh in a cold creep down the back. Von Knobelsdorff remembered the tiger, the voice of the beast that speaks directly to the limbs and says 'run'.

A knight fled from the hall and ran down the stairs to a window. When he returned his face was ashen.

'We have to let him in,' he said. 'He's killing people.'

'Calm yourself. There is no letting him anywhere,' said Gullveig. 'He is new to the earth now and must eat to sustain himself. When he is done he will come and we will control him – the All-father is stirring. He will help us in this, though that will not be his purpose. Oh. Oh. What has she done? What has she done?'

She put her hand to her nose. A bright ribbon of blood trickled across her fingers.

Gertie stepped down from the ladder at the side of the submarine. It was dusk outside the Lady's hall and the warriors were returning from battle. All along the shore the women and children were disembarking, dropping their wooden weapons and running to greet the warriors. Some of the warriors stood still in amazement; others threw down their guns, their axes and their swords, and came running towards their lovers, their wives and their families.

In the hall of the Knights of the *Schwarze Sonne*, Max watched as his wife fainted to the floor.

Gertie walked with Authun up to the hall as the night fell. They looked back down the shore to see the unimaginable numbers embracing on the beach. The piles of armour and weapons were huge, and already some of the men were getting back into the ship. The moon was up, big and full in the sky.

'They have fought their last battle,' said Authun.

'Yes,' said Gertie, 'although I fear I have one to come.'

'I think so.'

The king gave a knock on the hall's doors and they opened. The hall was empty, save for the gold-heavy lady who had stolen Gertie's rings.

'What have you done?' said Gullveig.

'I have stopped the fighting,' she said.

'You have left this place undefended,' said Gullveig. 'If it falls, I fall, you fall. I must stay to defend it. I . . .'

'One death does not seem so much to save so many and bring such happiness,' said Gertie.

'Here!' Gullveig flung Gertie's rings back at her. 'Get back to what's left of your husband, and die by the teeth of the wolf as you have always died.'

Gertie picked the ring off the floor.

'I have never lived before,' she said, 'so I could not have died.'

Gullveig gave a brief snort.

'Here,' she said, taking a gem from her necklace. 'A jewel for a lady.'

Gullveig pressed it into Gertie's hand. Gertie looked down at it. It was a ruby like a drop of blood. And then she saw: the days on the mountainside, the children running in the sunlight, always the feeling of something missing, always only half a person. And then he returned, again and again, taking her children, taking her lovers, never touching her but leaving her bereft and broken.

She saw other times too: a vision of minarets; a white tower rising by a river; sailing ships and steamers; an old man in a circle of symbols; but throughout, and finally, the hateful eyes of the wolf upon her.

'Your lover is waiting for you,' said Gullveig. 'Enjoy his kiss.'

Gertie put on her rings. Her mind was reeling. Everything had been torn up; everything was different from how she imagined. This life was just a flicker among other lives, and the love she bore her husband was just a faint echo of what she had once felt for someone else. And, for the first time in that lifetime, Gertie Voller knew what it was to hate someone – to hate the wolf and the man who had become the wolf, her lover, her betrayer.

She had the strong urge to get away, to get back to her own life and clear her head of these troubling thoughts.

She walked towards the door and Authun went to follow her.

'Not you, my lord of the white wastes,' said Gullveig. 'You will make good my loss. You took up arms again to come here and you cannot cast them down so freely. You will be my champion and choose my new warriors from the ranks of the battle dead.'

Authun tried to step forward, but found he couldn't move. Gertie put out her hand to him, to try to pull him from the hall, but he was frozen to the spot.

'Go,' he said. 'My destiny was fated long ago. I will serve the Lady here.'

Gertie nodded. 'Thank you,' she said.

She stepped through the door and her vision seemed to fade for a second.

When it came back she was in a very strange place indeed.

An SS general in full dress uniform was bending over her, shaking her by her shoulders.

'Wake up, wake up! The wolf is here – what are we to do? What are we to do?'

Gertie sat up. She wiped her nose. Blood was all over her fingers. She was in a large chamber, surrounded by thrones. Max was next to the general, too but something had happened to him. He was smiling, almost like he was waking her in bed with a cup of coffee.

There was a terrible noise from outside the castle – gunfire and screams, along with an awful grunting and tearing sound.

'What are we to do, witch, how do we control him?'

'What are you talking about?' said Gertie.

48   The Wolf

The trouble had begun when SS Storm Man Andreas Schneider had gone to see if the pit would require any more petrol. The weather was undoubtedly getting warmer, and the bigwigs at the camp didn't want the corpses rotting up and causing a stink. In a masterpiece of bad planning, the SS barracks had been placed in the path of the prevailing south-westerly wind. The fire had been lit to take advantage of an easterly breeze.

At first he had taken the movement to be that of a rat. But then it had occurred to him that any rat would have been killed by the still-smouldering fire. The smell was not pleasant, and he didn't want to hang around too much by the pit. Better safe than sorry, he thought, and decided to get someone to pour on more petrol. He was just looking around for a prisoner to do the dangerous work when he heard someone speak his name.

'Schneider.'

He turned but he could see no one. Schneider shrugged his shoulders. He turned again, heading back into the main camp.

'Sch ... Scch ... Scccchh ... Schneider!'

The voice, he had to conclude, was coming from the pit. Schneider went to unshoulder his machine pistol. Why had he thought to do that, he wondered? He had an uneasy feeling, but he told himself he was overreacting. Long enough in the camps could drive you nuts, it was said.

He walked to the pit and peered in.

He was surprised to see a face looking back at him. He recognised it. It was the old professor, the commie Jew. They'd had a bit of fun with him, for sure. He'd gone up to old Doctor Death at the castle, hadn't he? He knelt down and leant forward to see more clearly. The face was swollen and sickly, but recognisable.

'Schneider!' it said.

Schneider stood up and back in one movement. Not even life in a concentration camp prepares you for a dead man speaking to you. Nor does it prepare you for what came next.

Before he could move again, the wolf rose from the pit – or, rather, not a wolf but a sticky amalgamation of pink flesh in the shape of a wolf, glistening like sweated meat and still smoking from the effects of the fire. The full size of the beast was terrifying. It was three metres high, with a huge head that seemed more like some primordial god's sketches for a wolf. Schneider was frozen to the spot.

'Schneider!'

It was not the wolf that spoke, but a head that seemed buried into the flesh at its neck. The creature had no fur there. Instead it wore a mane of heads, all of which now began to scream out German names.

'Schneider! Fleischer! Krause! Drescher! Gerber!'

Each head shrieked the name of a guard. It was no roll call that Schneider wanted to be part of, so he started to run. The creature moved forward with terrible speed, the heads howling their dissonant chorus.

To Under Company Leader Nussbaum, who had just returned from a trip to the latrines, the creature seemed half formed. Its head was that of a massive wolf, with huge teeth and a lolling tongue. The back legs were like a wolf's, though the flesh was more human in colour, but the forearms were like those of a giant man, and one was shorter than the other. It loped on all fours, but rather lolled to one side as it moved. It was as if some demonic artist had taken the clay models of a dozen humans and begun moulding them into the shape of a wolf, but had left the job half finished. From the beast's chest, a withered arm protruded, grasping at the air.

The creature was too quick for Schneider, catching him by the back of the head with one of its claw-like hands and pulling him struggling towards it. The wolf ate his arm with a snap.

'No,' said Schneider, 'no, Father forgive ...' He never finished the sentence as the massive jaws bit off his head.

Nussbaum ran for it, into the guardhouse to fetch support and weapons. The threat posed by the wolf had removed all shock that he might have felt. When he reached the guardhouse, though, he didn't try to explain.

'Emergency, get your guns, now!' he said.

The observation towers, of course, had already seen the wolf. Soldiers are better off than civilians in such situations; they have something to do, a programmed response to anything attacking one of their company – shoot it. Rifle shots smacked into the body of the wolf and, though the heads on its neck and those on its chest and belly screamed, the bullets didn't stop it from raging at Schneider's flesh. After the guard on the tower had emptied his third rifle magazine into the beast, he began to realise that some heavier firepower was required. The trouble was, there was no heavier firepower. It was a concentration camp, not a military base.

Drawn by the noise, Witnesses and other prisoners had come from the workshops to see what was going on. Confronted by such an awful sight, some fell praying to their knees, others just stared in shock. One party who had been on punishment detail in the courtyard were virtually beneath the wolf as it gobbled at Schneider's body, but they were too frightened, or too surprised, to move. They were standing no more than ten feet from the animal but made no effort to run, even as the bullets from the observation towers zipped above them on their way to smack into the creature's flanks.

Nussbaum had managed to form a unit of five guards armed with rifles, while he himself had a machine pistol. Three others who had been in the guardhouse at the time had simply run for it. The wolf was still bent low over the remains of Schneider when the first volley struck it. Flesh flew off it but there was no sign of blood, or even that it was particularly discomfited by the shots. The only reaction was from the heads, who began to call the names of the guards who were shooting at them.

'Kuester, Ziegler, Weber, Gerste,
Fatty Nussbaum was the worst-ah!'

Nussbaum clicked off the safety catch of his weapon and walked up to within five feet of the wolf, through the Witnesses, who were scattering. He gave it a full clip at point-blank range, reloaded and gave it another.

For the first time the wolf seemed to notice it was being attacked. It turned its eyes to Nussbaum, whose last words, it was attested by at least one witness, were 'Heil Hitler'. In fact, Nussbaum only had one last word.

'Shit!' he said, as the wolf picked him from the floor and snapped his neck. Then it drove its jaws into his body, splitting through the spinal column and internal organs to slice it in two.

The heads screamed in delight as the wolf ate the SS man's flesh. The guards in the rifle party broke and fled. Only Storm Man Schütze Weber remained firing, right into the jaws of the wolf as it approached him. One of the observation tower men had come down and got onto a motorbike. He swept from the camp gates up towards the castle as Weber burst like a pimple under the wolf's hands.

Finally the camp commander, Haas, had been alerted and had seen what needed to be done. If they couldn't kill the beast, they could at least sate it. He came onto the assembly ground with a machine pistol and, with the help of a few men and a willing couple of *Kapos*, started corralling Witnesses towards the wolf.

The beast stood high on its back legs as it swallowed the last of Weber. Had anyone been in a calm enough state to pay attention, they might have seen that, with each body it consumed, it was becoming, by small degrees, bigger.

Other guards saw what their commander intended and began to surround the assembly ground, forcing back the prisoners with rifle butts and pistol shots.

'Stay where you are or you will be shot!' shouted Haas to the prisoners.

'Haas!' shrieked two of the heads. The wolf leapt over the Witnesses to get to him and tore him from the floor with his arms, lifting him up to the level of the mane of heads.

He was left looking into the melted face of a girl. The face said:

'I was a little child playing wild and free,

Tell them all, Mr Haas, what you did to me.'

Haas's instinct for brutality did not desert him at the last, and he tried to swing a fist towards the face. The wolf crushed his body in its hands as if it were not a thing of bone and muscle at all, but something more akin to a sausage. The crunch of gristle made the other SS panic, to run and hide. Prisoners too, ducked down behind huts, cramming in next to guards, finally equal in their fear of the wolf.

The wolf snapped into Haas's body, devouring it in seconds, the heads screaming the commander's name as it fed. The wolf looked up as the heads began to jabber out more names. But then the night itself seemed to scream. The howl came from the castle and the wolf threw back its head in reply.

Then there was silence. After a couple of minutes an SS man pressed a pistol into the side of a prisoner.

'Go out and see if it's gone,' he said.

The prisoner crawled from behind the barracks to a position where he could see the assembly ground.

'It's gone,' he said.

From the sound of gunfire coming from the castle, it was easy to guess where.

49 Dr Voller's Last Experiment

Faith is a strange thing. It defies logic, argument, evidence and contradiction. Sometimes it sustains. The life expectancy of a Jehovah's Witness in the camps, for instance, was much longer than that of an atheist. Sometimes, however, it condemns.

After the wolf had broken through the castle gates it had received a powerful volley of small arms fire and one stick grenade, to no effect. Faith in violence, however, is strong, and the commander of the castle garrison had ordered his men to keep firing long after it became evident that it would do no good whatsoever.

So the list of the dead in the courtyard was a long one. Storm Man Vogt, the motorcyclist who had alerted the castle to the wolf's attack, was not on it.

He had made for an inner room as soon as he had entered the castle, and had watched the unfolding battle from there. One thing was evident to him – the creature was getting bigger. When he had first seen it at the camp, it had been three metres high on its hind legs. Now, only half an hour later, it was nearly four.

This actually pleased Vogt. The doorways to the castle were not that large. The wolf would not be able to get in. The inside of the castle was alive with movement as SS men looked for vantage points from which to fire at the wolf. There were many of them, because that was the way the castle had been designed. The courtyard was meant as a killing ground, in which any invader would have to take fire from all sides.

Bullets smacked into the wolf as it killed the guards who had been too slow to flee. No good. It hardly seemed to notice.

From behind him Vogt could hear an officer screaming into the phone.

'Air support, now, we need Stukas at Wewelsburg Castle. Don't ask me what for, you fucking grease monkey, just get them in the air!'

The courtyard was empty, except for the bodies of the five or six guards that the wolf had taken. The beast didn't pause to eat now; it just looked up at the north tower. The only sound was the crack of rifles and the gabbling heads.

From a window, Max watched with an increasing sense of dislocation. His mind just couldn't take in what was happening. The wolf put its muzzle into the air and sniffed deeply. The heads stopped speaking. A rifle cracked. The wolf fixed its gaze on the tower.

For the first time, all the heads spoke as one. 'Voller!'

The wolf loped towards the bottom of the tower. Its head alone was now too big to go through the tiny door at the bottom.

'We're safe,' said Michal, in the tower. 'It can't get in. Oh, by the hairs on his chinny chin chin!'

The boy had lost his mind, Max thought. It occurred to him to shoot him, but he couldn't summon the energy. He went back up the stairs to the chamber of the *Schwarze Sonne*. His wife was sitting on the floor, looking at her hands. They were covered with the blood that had come from her nose and mouth. Max had an image of her in his chair, under the saw and the knife. It did not disturb him. Whatever he had felt for Gertie, he realised, had been cut away. He had cut it away in that room of his. He was in free fall.

'You need to get out of here, von Knobelsdorff,' said a knight, 'come on.'

Von Knobelsdorff was the only man in the building who seemed calm.

'Let the wolf come,' he said. 'I have my instructions.'

He had a tight grip on the wolf stone the witch had given him.

'Voller! Voller!' The voices were closer now.

Max sat down on the floor of the chamber. Doing things, taking decisions, he thought, had always caused such trouble. His first instinct – inaction – would have been better. What would have happened if he hadn't studied for medical exams, if he'd just stayed in bed? What would have happened if he hadn't sent that letter? Better to do nothing. He lay down, looking up at the ceiling above him.

'It's on the outside of the building!' said a knight.

'Well, I'm going out down the stairs, then,' said another.

The eleven knights ran for it, their studied SS coldness and detachment nowhere as they vied to be the first through the door.

Only Max, von Knobelsdorff, Gertie and Michal remained in the chamber.

'He can't get in, he can't get in!' Michal was almost dancing.

There was a thump at the top of the tower.

'What's that?' said Michal.

'I believe,' said Max, looking up at the ceiling, 'that he's trying to come through the roof. That's what I'd do, were I a supernatural being.' He began to laugh. 'Hey, Knobby, this is a rare success, ain't it? You must be fucking delighted.'

'You will see,' said von Knobelsdorff.

There was another thump and a crash. The wolf had scaled the tower and smashed through the slate of the roof. In recent years the castle had not been designed to resist attack, so lighter materials had been used to rebuild the roof than would have been the case if a bombardment had been anticipated.

The wolf tore away the slates with its arms, sending them crashing down the tower. Then it was into the attic space. The beams of the ceiling were no obstacle. It tore them up, splintering its way down into the top floor of the tower.

Michal went running for the stairs, but only got as far as the doorway. The gigantic head was thrust up against it, straining to get through, a gaggle of heads peering in from the stairway.

'Wejta! Wejta! Wejta!' screamed the faces on the creature's mane.

Michal stood in shock facing it. It shifted itself, pressing its body up against the doorway. The thin arm protruding from its chest shot out, grabbing for Michal's top, but only succeeding in shoving him.

The boy fell backwards down the stairs. Then he ran for it.

Max went up to his wife and put his arms around her.

'Do you remember, darling, when we met, I . . .'

He couldn't continue. All that they had done between them had been obliterated by what had gone on at that awful castle. No, Max, he thought, say it right, it has been obliterated by what you have done.

Gertie was just staring at her hands. A drop of blood fell from her nose into her palm. She seemed fascinated by it.

'There can be no forgiveness,' she said, 'for what you have done.'

'I know, darling,' he said.

'Vali, you should have died forever.'

The words were lost on Max. He just stared up at the ceiling. Already it was cracking, plaster falling onto von Knobelsdorff. Actually, there was an idea.

Max stood and moved over to the man in the chair.

'Since we're about to snuff it, old Knobby, I wondered if I could interest you in participating in a little experiment of mine. I haven't got a saw, but I do have a penknife, which might suffice under the circumstances. I know how you are on me keeping up my quotas. Unfortunately you're the only available subject at the moment, so I'm sure you'll understand I really don't have any choice in this.'

He took out his penknife.

'It's awfully blunt,' he said, 'but with a bit of effort I reckon I can get the top off your skull. This one's for taking the stones out of horses' hooves. I wonder if I can scalp you.'

There was a colossal thump from the floor above and a shower of plaster and small pieces of wood covered them both.

'You have a minute at the most, so do what you think you need to do,' said von Knobelsdorff.

'A minute? Eyes it is, then – with a bit of a burrow I reckon I can get into your brain from there.' He jabbed the blade of the knife into von Knobelsdorff's eye. The Senior Storm Command Leader repressed a scream. 'I'll just push it in and see if I can work this blade up into the old prefrontal cortex. It's the bit that controls aggression, you know, so I'd say you could well do without it. I wonder—'

There was an enormous thump. A hole appeared in the ceiling and a gigantic arm stretched through, feeling into the room, grabbing at the air above Max's head.

'Voller! Voller! Voller!'

Max staggered backwards, away from the chair, leaving the penknife still embedded in von Knobelsdorff's eye. Von Knobelsdorff was fighting down his screams, trying to concentrate on what Gullveig had told him to do.

The huge arm retracted. Now two hands came through, enormous, filthy and clawed. They pulled at the edge of the hole, ripping up boards, joists and laths. When the wolf came in, it was head first, the jaws snapping into the air as it tried to lean in to tear off von Knobelsdorff's head.

Von Knobelsdorff's one admirable quality was his fearlessness. Even he, though, fought against the straps. Gullveig had been right. He needed to be forced to face the beast. The pain in his eye was enormous. He grasped the wolf stone. The beast couldn't reach him. It ran around the top of the floor, scrabbling like some enormous rat, peering in through the hole and hissing.

Max saw his chance. He jumped up onto the chair and pulled the penknife from von Knobelsdorff's eye. Von Knobelsdorff screamed as the blade popped out.

'You know, Knobby, I would never have had the stomach for this without you,' he said. 'As it is, I can do what I want to you without blinking.'

'The All-father is coming,' said von Knobelsdorff. 'I made a sacrifice, myself to myself.'

Max looked around him.

'Can't see the All-father right now, old chap. Just a large wolf that is about to do for the lot of us. Well, not you.' He pulled back the eyelid on von Knobelsdorff's good eye. 'You want a good view of this.'

He drove the penknife in to the white orbit. Von Knobelsdorff blacked out. There was more tearing at the ceiling above, more shrieking of Max's name.

'Spoilsport,' Max said to the bloodied figure in front of him. 'I would have liked to spend some time on you.' With the heel of his hand he drove the rest of the penknife into von Knobelsdorff's skull.

Finally, the wolf tore away enough of the floor to get through. Max sensed it coming and leapt back from the chair. It swung its way through the hole and landed on top of von Knobelsdorff, its massive head level with his bloody face.

The wolf gave a snarl and clamped his jaws over von Knobelsdorff's head. It pulled off the face in a couple of twists, like a dog ripping the felt from a tennis ball. The wolf stone clattered to the floor. The beast threw its head from side to side and von Knobelsdorff's head came off.

Gullveig's plan had been that von Knobelsdorff would confront the wolf, after it had been parted from the human who bore its curse, thereby to take on its curse himself. But Harbard, with the Moonsword, had not yet come. So von Knobelsdorff died at Max's hand, without ever getting near to the destiny she had planned for him.

Harbard's unforeseen delay had occurred because he had become lost on the black shore. He was wandering under the metal sky over sparkling black dunes. There was no indication at all of where he needed to go, and he did not recognise anything from his previous visit.

He took to the water's edge, following it along in search of anything that would give him an idea of where he might go. He seemed to walk for days without any feature at all appearing on the landscape – no well, no hall, no castle.

He was beginning to panic. He had assumed that the murder of his niece would be his final step into a magical consciousness that would propel him to find the wolf and steal its power for the help of democracy.

He gripped the Moonsword, not a shard but long and slim and beautiful under the moonlight. That would see him through, he was sure.

Eventually, more through boredom than tiredness, he sat down and closed his eyes. He was sure he hadn't slept, but someone had managed to approach him without him hearing them.

'Harbard.'

He opened his eyes and sat up. There was no one around.

'Harbard.'

The voice was coming from the sea.

There, forty yards out from the shore, was a U-boat, a grey thing of some strange irregular bristling construction. Harbard thought that it might be some sort of coral life that had attached itself to the ship, or perhaps a special skin for countering sonar.

'Harbard.'

Up on the top of the conning tower was a man he recognised. It was the spirit he had taken for his angel guide when he had first begun his investigations, the tall pale fellow with the burning red hair.

'Hail, spirit.'

'There's no need for the heroic sentence construction. A simple "hello" will do.'

'I am lost,' said Harbard.

'Buddy, are you ever.'

'I'm looking for the wolf.'

'Then let the fool's death be your guide,' said the spirit. 'Look.'

In the distance, something seemed to glint and shine.

'What is it?' said Harbard.

'Another warrior goes to the eternal halls, Father, a brave idiot to fight and fight until he grows sick of it and longs for the fighting to end. But the fighting will never end for him. He has no one to rescue him. That light is the spark that will ignite his damnation fire. I lit it to guide you to him. There you will find the wolf.'

'I will go to him,' said Harbard. 'Where is my horse?'

'Your horse is not here, Father.'

'Then give me your cloak, lie smith, lest I tear it from you back.'

Harbard felt sick. Why was he talking about horses? Did he have a horse? And 'lie smith'? Where had that come from?

The spirit smiled.

'Anything to oblige,' he said, with a laugh, 'even though you are starting to talk rough, Professor.'

He took off the cloak and threw it from the boat. It floated up into the air. Harbard put out his hand and it came to it, settling, he thought, like a hawk.

'Take it,' said the spirit,' I won't need it for a while now.'

Harbard wrapped the cloak around his shoulders and looked towards the distant, glinting light. Millions of feathers seemed to fill the air and he heard the shrieking of a huge host of birds. And then he was in that broken tower, facing the wolf.

50 The Ghost Tower

Endamon Craw had watched the wolf as it made its way out of the pit. He had walked behind it as it made its way up the hill and, as it had entered the tower by the roof, he had entered by the door.

He saw no soldiers or battle, though, and the landscape through which he moved was very different from that of the green valley of the Alme. To him the castle seemed constructed of a lattice of shadows, perched on a black hillside, overlooking a river that hissed and spat as it coursed its way over burning ash. The wolf, too, was different. It was no hideous amalgamation of corpses, but a huge and beautiful creature whose fur was the same rich black as the mountainside. It seemed to move across the landscape like a warp in the light.

He had heard his wife calling from the bottom of the slope. He felt sick to his stomach with nerves. After all these centuries he had found her – found her properly, not just in a glimpse, or at the edge of a dream, or as a face in a painting, but in her flesh.

Craw climbed the tower, the shadows of which it was made seeming to shift as he climbed, allowing glimpses of the dark valley below. The venomous river led out into a broad bay. All along it, it seemed, bodies were piled in heaps, as far as the eye could see.

Craw kept climbing.

The top of the tower was completely open to the sky. In three directions the black plain spread out, its litter of dead stretching to the horizon. The wolf was nowhere to be seen; it had vanished completely. Behind him, though, was a hillside, huge and wide, like the waste from a pit, except no pit was ever built so big.

There was one chair there, a tall thing with straps at the arms and the head. A radiant corpse sat in it, shining like a beacon, but torn and eviscerated. A German officer sat on the floor, seemingly oblivious to his presence. He was looking at something in his hand. It was a pebble like a piece of the night.

And there was Adisla, dressed as he remembered her, in her long white smock with the flowers in her hair. Craw stood just watching her for a second. She returned his gaze.

'I said I would return,' he said.

She didn't smile. 'You have returned already.'

'When?'

'When you took my children. In so many lives.'

Craw felt panic rising up in him. Now he recalled it: the weapons on his skin, the tearing and the ripping; his wife's face, twisted in agony, spitting out a curse. That was the kiss he had promised her. His teeth at her throat.

He sank to his knees.

'I did not choose this destiny,' he said. 'Adisla. The gods themselves demanded this thing. It was fated.'

'Then so is my rejection,' said Adisla. 'I curse you now as I have cursed you before, and the curse falls on me too. There will be no death for you. Generation after generation I will be reborn, you will hunt me down and, when you find me, you will kill me again. You are the beast that consumes its own heart.'

'No,' said the werewolf, 'I will not do it. I would rather die.'

'You cannot die, wolf, only move on,' said Adisla.

'I will not kill you.'

'But you will. It is fated.'

'I did not harm you at Gévaudan.'

'Because I did not remember my curse, so many times have I lived and died. But I recall it now.'

There was a rushing noise, and Craw's vision seemed to fail for a second as the top of the tower seemed engulfed in the beating wings of millions of birds.

Then the noise stopped. Between Adisla and Craw stood Harbard, gaunt and thin, his eye socket red and raw. The old man carried in his hand the slender crescent of the Moonsword.

'You have come to kill me,' said the werewolf.

'Yes,' said Harbard.

'Good, let it be done.' Craw knelt in front of Harbard to offer his neck to the sword.

'I must kill both the others first,' said Harbard, 'for when you die, then the eye of the wolf will fall on the nearest living thing to you. It cannot be this woman or this man.'

Craw saw he was talking about Voller, still in the room.

'What about me, Uncle, will you kill me too?'

Another woman was there. Craw recognised her as Eleanor.

'I have already killed you, Eleanor,' said Harbard.

'No,' said Eleanor. 'I am dying, as you may be, but you have the choice to let me live.'

Harbard shook his head. So that was why he had found it so hard to discover the wolf's whereabouts. He had not gone through with the end of the spell.

'There is no choice,' he said. 'Others have made the sacrifice, others have given.'

'Though not to receive, Uncle. I am dying because you need to know. You would eat up the world with your mind if you could.'

'It is not for me, my dear, I ...' Harbard was starting to break down.

Craw tugged at his arm. 'Come on, you must kill me, I can't do it myself. Kill me. End this.'

Behind the roofless tower the hillside seemed to blink.

'It is ready,' said Harbard. 'The wolf is ready to take me into its dream.'

*

From the chamber floor Max looked around him. Gertie was still sitting staring into the drop of blood in her palm. The terrible wolf was tearing into von Knobelsdorff's corpse. The thing was too big for the room, and was forced to crouch over the body as it ate.

There was a clatter at the stairs. A group of SS men had come in, led by Haussmann, pink and sweating. Obviously help had arrived because they had a Panzerfaust bazooka with them.

Max went to stand. He had something in his hand. That stone. There was an ear-splitting bang and he was thrown to the floor again. The SS had discharged the Panzerfaust. The explosion ripped into the wolf, sending pieces of its flesh scattering across the room. For a second it seemed stunned and the SS men reloaded.

'Voller! Voller! Voller!' shrieked the heads again. The wolf had only been fazed. It cast its gaze around the room and now descended on Max, pulling him off the floor with its hands. Max gripped on to the pebble.

'Stop!' he shouted. 'Don't hurt me!'

The wolf paused without releasing him.

Haussmann signalled for the Panzerfaust man to hold its fire.

'Put me down!'

Max was shaking with fear, only an inch from the beast's jaws. He had given up caring if he lived or died but, staring into that stinking mouth, a primitive instinct for survival kicked in.

The wolf lowered him to the floor.

'It's obeying you, sir,' said an SS man. 'It's following your orders.'

Unseen by Max, in the ghost tower, Craw faced Harbard.

'You will kill me before you kill any of these,' he said.

'No,' said Harbard.

There was a flutter of feathers and Harbard was at Eleanor's side. He pulled back the Moonsword, but hesitated as he looked at the girl. Craw saw his chance. He sprang across the floor and sent the old man sprawling.

Harbard slid back to the edge of the tower and appeared for a second to slide over the side, but again came the fluttering sound and he appeared behind Eleanor. Craw had anticipated this, though, and was already on his way when Harbard reappeared. This time he pulled the old man over by his cloak and, as he did so, tore it from his back. Craw was on top of him, punching his face, trying to force him to use the sword.

'Kill me,' said Craw. 'Kill me and release me.'

Harbard tried to wriggle free, but Craw was strong. The only way he could get him away was to hit him with the sword. He caught Craw a sharp blow on the temple that sent him reeling. Then he was up on his feet, and sprang for Eleanor with the Moonsword.

In the mine outside Coventry, David Arindon plunged into the tank where Harbard and his niece were dying. The old man had the fragment of the Moonsword in his hands. Arindon struggled to pull it away.

'See me,' he said through his useless lips. 'See me! Give me what I am owed.'

Balby swallowed down his pain. It was, he decided, an irrelevance. He stumbled his way up the scaffold to the top of the water tank. There was no time for niceties; he pulled up Eleanor by her hair and slumped her onto the platform. He was sick with the agony of the effort but he forced his fingers to her throat, pulling away the noose. The girl coughed, spluttered. Balby hugged her. She was alive!

In the water tank, Harbard's arms reached out around Arindon, began to pull him down and drown him. Arindon started to lose consciousness.

And then, in the ghost tower, there were two Endamon Craws, or at least one Endamon Craw and one person who looked very like him. The other man was virtually identical but much more heavily muscled, savage in appearance, his body marked with scars, his cheeks roughly tattooed to resemble the jaws of a wolf.

The unmarked Craw reached out his hand towards his twin and touched him. The twin turned and took his hand. The hillside outside the tower seemed to stir. Harbard smiled and lifted the Moonsword.

'What was made will be unmade,' said Harbard. 'Both of you will die under the eye of the wolf.'

Max was still facing the wolf. The head of Baila Brono Aljenicato, the gypsy woman, his first victim, protruded from the underside of the wolf's neck. One side of her face had been burned by the petrol fire. It seemed to make her right eye protrude from her head as if it were looking right into him.

'It's obeying you, tell it to back away,' said Haussmann.

Max turned his head to the left to look at Gertie. She was gone, driven mad by the horrors of the castle. He thought of the future and could see none. All he had was a picture of himself, picking along a long black shore that was littered with a million corpses.

He heard a voice in his head. It was Gertie's, but not Gertie's – altered, foreign.

'There is no forgiveness,' it said.

'Make it move back, sir, I don't want to have to risk the Panzerfaust again,' said a soldier.

Max looked up again at the gypsy's head. A sense of what he had done and what he had lost came crashing in on him like a mighty wave that would sweep him away.

He slid back from under the wolf. Its huge eyes were fixed on him. It really did appear that it was waiting for a command.

'I have made so many corpses,' he thought, 'perhaps it's time I made my last.'

The animal's breath seemed to stifle him, the noise of it sawing into his mind.

'Kill us all,' said Max, and the wolf went wild.

In the ghost tower, Harbard strode towards the two Craws, but the savage Craw, the painted and pricked Craw, ran in to meet him. They fell in a terrible struggle, the Moonsword striking the wolfman again and again, stabbing into him and disgorging fountains of blood. But the hands of Feileg – who had entered the body of David Arindon when Harbard first used that sword to try cut his spirit from that of his devouring brother – were at the old man's neck, and they were not letting go.

From the back of the tower the wolf shook itself in its sleep. All along the mountainside fine ropes creaked and groaned. The wolf was restrained! Tied down! Craw looked up. The wolf seemed to blink, and for a second its eye was upon him.

Craw staggered, the scent of blood flooding his mind.

He heard a voice. It was Adisla's.

'See, tearer, see you do what you always do. You will never escape my curse.'

Then he was upon them – the old man, the twin, and the woman too, ripping into flesh and sinew with his teeth, tearing into muscle and organs with his hands. It was done, and the slaughter was about him. Craw thought nothing. The part of him that did the thinking had been washed away in a tide of blood. He staggered to the edge of the tower and looked up. The Moonsword was thrust through him. The wolf that was the hill was sleeping, though its eye was open. Craw looked into it and his consciousness split. He was on the tower, looking at the wolf, and he was the wolf, looking at the man on the tower looking at the wolf that was the hill. He was the wolf and would never be parted from that destiny, he knew.

The wolf's eye closed; darkness came in on him for a second, and Craw fell from the tower. He saw himself falling as a wolf but, as he tumbled, his fur seemed to come away in pieces and with it, memories, ideas, his personality. Endamon Craw was disintegrating.

In the mine, Balby tried to pull Arindon and Harbard from the water but his strength was spent, though it did not stop him trying to haul the men out.

After ten minutes, he gave up and turned to Eleanor. His concern was now the living, not the dead.

51 Full Moon

The forests of Sauerland are large and dense. Klaus Eberhart would not have ventured so far in, nor gone to the caves, were it not for dire necessity. A wolf pack was in the area and he was determined, no matter what state law said on such matters, to protect his sheep at any cost.

The caves were far in the forest but he knew they were used by wolves. It was a long way for the animals to travel to his flock, but he had had no luck locating them elsewhere, so he thought he'd at least look there. He knew the tunnels to be deep and long. Still, the wolves wouldn't be that far in, he thought. He had two guns – a shotgun and a hunter's rifle – so he felt secure as he approached the hill.

The trees had thinned and he could see the moon up above him, huge and full in the late afternoon sky. He wondered if he would be able to read by it when he made his camp. He had with him a book he shouldn't have had, one you could only get hold of if you had the right friends. 1957 wasn't the year to be seen with relics of the Nazi era.

The book was by Heidi Fischer, the Nazi mystic, about how the Gods endlessly rehearse their battles on earth. Based on a close reading of early Norse texts, she said these battles had occurred throughout history. She was also predicting that all the signs were in place for the end of the world in 1972. Or later. The fates, she said, had grown weary of the earthly sacrifice of the Gods. Next time it would happen for real.

Eberhart took these things seriously and loved to discuss them. Not that he met many people to discuss them with. He'd had a fascinating conversation just the week before, though. He'd been out looking for wolves and had met up with another hunter, a tall red-haired chap, pale as the moon itself.

It was he who had given him the book. He never did get the man's name, but he longed to meet him again to discuss it with him. He half thought he might meet him at the big cave on the south of the hill. The man had recommended he try there because he had seen wolf droppings in the area.

Eberhart approached the cave with caution, his shotgun broken for safety. He was ready to click it shut in a second if he had to fire, though. Wolves are not normally dangerous to men, but any animal needs to be treated with care if you corner it in its lair.

He climbed the short rise to the mouth of the cave. Now he did close his gun. He threw a stone into the mouth of the cave. There was movement within. He was inclined to give it a couple of blasts just for safety's sake but, on the off chance it was some napping hunter or tramp – there were such people in the forests – he unclipped a torch from his belt. Still holding the gun in one hand, he shone it in.

Movement again, but not of fur. Was it a pig?

He shone the torch further in and was astounded to see it was a man, dark-skinned and pale, entirely naked, crouching away from the torch beam. His hair was grey and his beard was long and filthy.

'It's OK,' said the hunter. 'Really, it's OK.'

The man was in an awful state. His hair was matted and he was terribly thin, scarred on the face to the point of revulsion.

The hunter put down the gun and took an apple from his haversack.

'Here,' he said, 'for you.' The man shrank back from him. 'I'll have it then.'

Eberhart took a bite. Then he offered it again. No more luck that time.

Eberhart, who was a simple but not insensitive man, could see that winning the man's trust was no five minute job. He decided to treat the man as he would an animal. So for the next week he hunted the area, cooked woodcock and rabbits, and brought them to the cave mouth, along with a cup of water.

But it was no good; the man would not come from the cave and the food was left untouched.

The day before he was due to leave, Eberhart visited the cave for the last time. The man was sitting on the rock outside the cave, looking up at the pale crescent moon hanging in the still blue sky.

He was naked – not even a cloth about his waist – though around his neck he had some sort of medallion.

The hunter offered the man some dried meat from his pack. No response, but this time he did not shy away. Eberhart approached and sat next to him, nonchalantly, as if he were simply joining him at a bus stop.

What was the medallion? Closer to him, he saw, it was some sort of military dog tag.

Once again Eberhart offered the meat, but the man ignored him. He rocked a little and muttered under his breath. Eberhart strained to hear. The man repeated the phrase again and again. It appeared to be some sort of poem.

> *Satan went to make a man,*
> *But made a skinless wolf instead*
> *St Peter lent a helping hand*
> *A hide to dress the quadruped.*

Eberhart gave a little shiver. That gave him the spooks, but he was curious to find out who this odd fellow was.

He said, 'Do you mind?' The man gave no reply.

Eberhart thought it would be too much to touch the dog tag so he simply leant nearer. The tag was the wrong way round, and could not be easily seen. Could he touch it?

He gingerly extended a hand and turned the tag. It had a perforation down the middle, the same information above and below it. Numbers, No name, just the two jagged *S*s of the SS. One word was on both top and bottom. *Doktor.*

A doctor. SS, too. Eberhart felt no revulsion, only a mild curiosity. He had been ten when the war ended, with little understanding of what had gone on. No one really talked about those days either, and he was sure that half of what was said was made up. But here was someone straight out of the raw past, a living relic.

'You're a doctor?' said the hunter, letting the medallion drop.

The man seemed to notice him for the first time, stopped his muttering.

'I am a wolf,' he said. His voice was gravelly with disuse.

'Then I should hunt you.'

'The wolf is the hunter,' said the man. 'Set a crucifix at your door to keep him away.'

'That is an old superstition.'

'Yes. But it works. I have seen it. Belief has a power that is greater than truth.'

'I believe in my gun,' said Eberhart, tapping his rifle.

'No good,' said the man. 'He ate my love. They shot him many times.'

'This is a real wolf you're talking about?'

'I think so.'

'You are mad.' Eberhart felt no compunction in saying this. The man was skinny enough to make you think he was a camp victim himself, and no danger.

'If I am, it brings me no comfort,' he said. 'I am a wolf. I did things that many men would have done. You might have done them. But some did not. Some did not do these things and would not have done them. The skin split, you see. The skin split and the wolf beneath came out.'

The hunter guessed what this was about. Another guilty conscience. The war generation never spoke about such things but you saw it in their eyes, in their controlled manners, in their conversation. People who only ever spoke of today and tomorrow, never yesterday.

'It was a long time ago,' said Eberhart. 'People did what

they had to do to survive. For every willing killer there were a thousand men just covering their arses.'

The man said nothing, looked out into the trees.

'Do you want me to help you? I could get you a doctor.'

'I am a doctor.'

'So why not go back? Eat. Bathe. Forget the past, find a life again? I could help you.'

To Eberhart, this was a little drama, potentially a big drama, something distinctly missing from his rural life. Perhaps he would be in the newspapers.

'There is no path back,' said the man.

'So what is there?'

'There is nothing. I do not see my love's ghost in the dusk, walking among these trees. I had hoped to see Gertie wandering. There are no ghosts here. No monsters. I do not hear the screams of my victims above the birdsong. I have nothing and expect nothing.'

Eberhart was suddenly angry, not with what this man might or might not have done, but with his self-pity.

'Say I exposed you. Say I went to the Jews and told them an old tormentor is licking his wounds out here? What then? There would be something then.'

Max Voller picked up the gun and shot Eberhart in the head. The trees deadened the sound and the report did not go on for long.

He dragged the body to a lower cave and pushed it in. The hunter's corpse tumbled down the slope and was taken by the dark.

'I am a wolf,' said Max Voller, into nothing.